BLOOMING FUN

BY JANET EVANOVICH

BLOOMING FUN

TWO NOVELS IN ONE

FULL BLOOM

&

FULL BLAST

JANET EVANOVICH

and

CHARLOTTE HUGHES

St. Martin's Paperbacks

This is a work of fiction. All of the characters, organizations, and events portrayed in this book are either products of the authors' imagination or are used fictitiously.

Published in the United States by St. Martin's Paperbacks, an imprint of St. Martin's Publishing Group

BLOOMING FUN: FULL BLOOM copyright © 2005 by Evanovich, Inc. and FULL BLAST copyright © 2004 by Evanovich, Inc.

All rights reserved.

For information, address St. Martin's Publishing Group, 120 Broadway, New York, NY 10271.

www.stmartins.com

ISBN: 978-1-250-78338-7

Our books may be purchased in bulk for promotional, educational, or business use. Please contact your local bookseller or the Macmillan Corporate and Premium Sales Department at 1-800-221-7945, ext. 5442, or by email at MacmillanSpecialMarkets@macmillan.com.

Printed in the United States of America

St. Martin's Paperbacks edition 2021

10 9 8 7 6 5 4 3 2 1

FULL
BLOOM

Chapter
ONE

Destiny Moultrie's long black hair hung like a silk curtain on either side of her face as she gazed down at the dainty palm she held, studying each line and crease carefully. "You're going to meet a tall, dark, and handsome man—"

Annie Fortenberry snatched her hand away. "Oh no, you don't. You're not saddling me with a . . . a man!"

Destiny arched one brow. "You don't like men? They come in handy on cold winter mornings."

The petite woman sitting across the antique Pennsylvania farm table, which seated twelve, nodded, and a thick strand of copper hair fell across her forehead. She raked it back, and it disappeared into the tousled mop that barely grazed her shoulders and gave her a girlish look, even at thirty. "You're right," she said. "On cold winter mornings when you don't want to leave your warm bed and haul the trash to the street. That's the only thing a man is good for."

"Then I probably shouldn't tell you the rest. The really *good* stuff."

"Good stuff?" Annie's green eyes registered interest. She could use some really good stuff in her life. She offered her hand once again.

"It says the sex will be dy-nuh-mite!"

Annie reclaimed her palm and looked at it. "Where does it say that? You made that up."

"The Divine Love Goddess never makes up stuff."

Annie glanced up and noted the serious expression on Destiny's face. Despite the early hour, the woman's makeup had been artfully applied, emphasizing deep-set indigo eyes and high cheekbones. Annie wondered how long it took Destiny to achieve that look. Her own makeup regimen took all of three minutes, beginning with a light foundation to tone down her freckles and ending with a quick swipe of her mascara wand. "Hmm," she said, taking care to hide the doubt in her voice, even though her friend Jamie Swift had claimed Destiny was the real thing. "Very interesting."

Destiny suddenly sneezed. "Uh-oh. I can tell I'm close. I always start sneezing when I'm on to something."

"Good sex, huh?" Annie said. "Jeez, I might have to reconsider. As long as I'm not stuck with him for the rest of my life," she added, wishing she were really more sophisticated and open to casual sex. Instead she followed Dear Abby's advice that couples should be in love before crawling between the sheets together. Abby obviously didn't have this hormonal thing going on that made Annie think about sex a lot.

Destiny sneezed again. "Wow, that was a big one. Either I'm right on-target or I've got a cold. There was a draft in my bedroom last night."

Annie stood and hurried to the kitchen counter, where she kept a box of tissues. She plucked several and handed them to Destiny, who dabbed her nose. "I'm sorry you became chilled last night," Annie said. "It has been so warm this winter that I haven't bothered to turn on the heat."

Which was true. Beaumont was experiencing record-high temperatures for February, and it wouldn't be long before everything was in full bloom. New shoots had already begun pushing their way up through the dirt, and Annie had spied teeny buds on the large peach tree out front. But the old antebellum mansion–turned–bed and breakfast nestled between massive, centuries-old live oaks permitted little sunlight. That, combined with the West Indian coral stones from which the house had been built, kept it a good ten degrees cooler inside than out.

Destiny propped her elbows on the table. In the next chair, an aging overweight tabby cat named Peaches uncurled and stretched before dropping to the floor with a thud. She walked over to her empty food dish, stared for a moment, and then turned to Annie as if to say, *What's with* it?

"The, um, draft in my room last night had nothing to do with the temperature," Destiny said. "There's a spirit in this house."

"Oh yeah?" Annie cocked one eyebrow.

"A ghost," Destiny said. "A dead person, in this case a woman, who for some reason is still hanging around."

Annie didn't know how to respond, so she said nothing.

Destiny shrugged. "It happens to me all the time. Dead people latch on to me like flies to molasses."

Peaches made a guttural sound deep in her throat and gave Annie what she referred to as the evil eye. The cat raised her paw and whacked the plastic dish hard. It skidded across the floor and hit the wall.

"Your cat is hungry," Destiny said.

"She has already eaten," Annie replied. "Just ignore her."

"You've never seen the spirit?" Destiny asked.

"I don't believe in ghosts."

"I'll bet you've felt her presence. A sudden drop in temperature or a feeling of being watched?"

Annie's look was noncommittal, but she remembered instances, a brush of cool air against her arms or the back of her neck, guests complaining of missing items that usually showed up in unexpected places at a later date, plus sounds in the night. "I think you have to be open to that sort of thing," she said. "I'm not."

Destiny didn't look convinced, but she didn't push. "So, do you want me to finish your reading? Find out if you're going to enjoy the Big O anytime soon? Or multiples thereof," she added.

"Multiples?"

"I don't like to brag, but my own personal record is five."

"Holy crap!"

"He was young and good-looking, and we had this chemical thing going. Not to mention the fact he was slow handed, and pushed all the right buttons, if you get my drift."

"Sounds like a keeper to me." Annie hadn't had her buttons pushed in a long time.

"Which is why I married him." Destiny sighed. "It didn't work out."

Annie knew Destiny had been married five times but was currently single. Until a couple of months ago, the woman had enjoyed a hot-and-heavy romance with a hunk named Sam, but she'd pulled back when he began using the *M* word. Destiny had no desire to marry anytime soon.

"So why did you divorce this guy if he was so good in the sack?"

"You still have to be able to talk to a man at the breakfast table, and he wasn't very bright. As time went on, my passion dwindled."

Annie hadn't felt passionate about anything since Jiffy Peanut Butter came out with a reduced-fat variety. "That's too bad," she said.

Peaches began swatting the cabinet door where her food was stored. "That's it," Annie said, getting up from the table. She picked up the cat and lugged all twenty-two pounds of feline and fur to the back door. Peaches hissed. "Go catch a mouse," Annie said, and put her out. "That cat has one goal in her life, and it's to drive me crazy."

"She's uneasy because of the spirit. Cats sense these things."

Annie shook her head. "She's always been snooty and difficult, but my grandmother adored her. Unfortunately, the cat has never liked me."

"She needs to meet a nice tomcat."

"Too late. She's been spayed."

"That explains her sour moods. A good roll in the hay works wonders."

"Well, the only male I'm looking for at the moment is my worthless handyman, Erdle Thomey," Annie said, "but I don't have to be psychic to know that he's laid up drunk somewhere. Wait till I get my hands on him. I'm going to hog-tie him and kick butt."

"Some people like being tied up," Destiny said, studying her nails, "or so I've heard."

Annie grinned. "I don't think we're talking about the same thing." She couldn't help but like the quick-witted, free-spirited woman who had become something of a celebrity since starting her column in the *Beaumont Gazette* less than a year ago. Destiny used her psychic powers to give people, mostly the lonely-hearted, guidance and direction. She stood out in a crowd in her outrageous clothes, which included leather, fake fur in an assortment of colors, and plunging necklines that emphasized perfect oversize breasts. Annie would have given her grandmother's sterling silver to know if they were the product of good genes or a boob job.

"If this Erdle person isn't doing his work, why do you keep him?"

"I sort of inherited him, as well as that crazy cat, after my grandmother died. He lives upstairs in the carriage house out back. He's supposed to do the yard work and repairs around here in exchange for free room and board. I hate to fire him, because he's worked here since I was a kid. He knows there is going to be a big wedding here in two weeks, and that I want everything to be perfect."

"I wouldn't worry about it," Destiny said. "Jamie says your parties and weddings are beautiful. I think it's amazing you're able to provide all that *and* run a bed-and-breakfast."

Annie smiled at the compliment. "I do a lot of juggling, but I enjoy it. This wedding will be special to me since I've known Jamie for so long. We met shortly after she took over the *Gazette*. After her father died," Annie added, remembering how Jamie had struggled for years to keep it afloat before taking on a silent partner. That partner had been none other than multimillionaire investor, technological genius, and philanthropist Max Holt. In less than a year they had turned the *Beaumont Gazette* into a top-notch newspaper and watched subscriptions triple.

In their spare time they had cleaned up town corruption, avoided being killed by hit men and a crazed swamp dweller, and brought down two top Mafiosi.

Despite it all, Max and Jamie had fallen in love and had chosen Annie's home in which to be married. Max and Jamie preferred small and simple to the pomp and fuss of a celebrity wedding that would create a media circus. Which was why the wedding was so hush-hush; even the guests had been sworn to secrecy. Annie hoped they were able to pull it off. She was determined to give Max and Jamie a wedding they would remember for the rest of their lives.

Only . . .

A storm had passed through several nights before, littering the yard with leaves and branches, and Erdle was AWOL.

The rain had seeped through the ballroom windows where Max and Jamie's wedding dinner was to be held, damaging the wood floors and drawing attention to the fact that the floors desperately needed sanding.

And Annie had little spare time on her hands, what with cleaning and cooking three meals a day for her full-time tenants and preparing for a luncheon, a baby shower, and a dinner party all scheduled for that week. Not that she was complaining; that's what kept her bills paid.

Annie's tenant, Theenie Gaither, came down the back stairs. She wore a simple blue housedress, ankle socks, and white sneakers. Her short blue-gray hair, which she had washed and styled once a week at Susie Q's Cut and Curl, had been sprayed so heavily that tornado winds would have snatched her head off her shoulders before mussing her hairdo. "Good morning," she said in a light, fruity-textured voice. She glanced at Destiny, and Theenie's smile faltered briefly as she took in her breasts. "Do we have a new guest?"

Annie introduced the women. "Destiny will be staying with us for a while," she said. "There was a fire in her apartment building late last night, and the residents were forced to evacuate until a building inspector checks it out."

"They think it was faulty wiring," Destiny said. "My landlord is so cheap he won't do anything to the building unless he's forced."

"Oh my," Theenie said, looking at Annie. "Is the wiring okay here?"

"Yes, Theenie," Annie said, knowing the woman tended to fret over every little thing. "Guess what?" she said, hoping to redirect Theenie's thoughts before she found something else to worry about. "Destiny works for the *Beaumont Gazette*. She's the Divine Love Goddess Adviser."

Theenie looked impressed. "I thought I recognized your name. I read your column every day." She headed toward the automatic coffeemaker, where Annie had already set out her favorite mug. "I assume Destiny knows about you-know-what," she said, glancing at Annie, who nodded in response.

"I think it's very romantic that Max and Jamie are going to be married on Valentine's Day," Destiny said.

Theenie gave a shiver of delight. "We're all so excited! I can't wait until I'm allowed to tell my friends at the beauty parlor. They will be so envious. And Jamie is going to be a beautiful bride."

"Jamie's the one who told me about this place," Destiny said, "and I'm glad she did. It's so . . ." Destiny paused as if trying to come up with the right word. "Unique," she finally said.

Annie laughed. "*Outlandish* would better describe it," she said, "but it was my grandmother's dying wish that I not sell it or make cosmetic changes." She gave an eye roll.

"I wouldn't change it, either," Destiny said. "I think it's quaint."

"It grows on you after a while," Theenie said. She carried her mug to the table and sat next to Destiny. "No offense, but are you really psychic? I mean, there are a lot of phonies out there."

"I'm the real enchilada," Destiny proudly stated.

"Oh my! Wait until Lovelle finds out. She lives here, too, but she's in New York City visiting her daughter." Theenie leaned closer. "But then you probably already know that," she said in a hushed voice. "I'll bet you even know what street her daughter lives on." She didn't give Destiny a chance to reply. "Tell me, do you sense anything strange going on in this house?"

Destiny opened her mouth to respond but was cut off when Annie bolted from her chair. "I just heard a car

pull into the driveway," she said. "I'll bet it's Erdle."
She raced to the window. "Yep! Boy, is he in trouble!"
She opened a drawer and pulled out a large rolling pin.

"Uh-oh," Theenie said.

Annie threw open the door. "Wait till I get my hands
on that man!"

Theenie jumped from her chair with the agility of a
woman half her age. "Now, hold on, Annie," she said.
"Let's not do anything rash."

But Annie was already gone.

Wes Bridges parked his Harley in front of the massive
three-story antebellum mansion and stared at it for a
full minute before he thought to cut his engine. "Damn!"
he said, climbing from his bike. "Now that's something
you don't see every day."

He took in the four-column portico, each fluted column adorned with plump gold cherubs. Lavishly carved
dentil molding ran beneath the eaves, and wrought-
iron balconies sprouted from every window, designed
in curlicues and rosettes. The look was repeated in the
fanlight of what appeared to be an extra room or attic
gable that made up a partial fourth floor. Gray moss
clung to the live oaks and shuddered in the breeze, and
a large tree, currently bare, stood to one side. An elaborate fountain dominated the front yard, spilling water
onto yet more cherubs, all naked, some performing
what appeared to be sexual acts.

"Interesting," he said, noting a sign out front that
read: *The Peachtree Bed-and-Breakfast. Vacancy.*

"Perfect," he said. Wes pulled off his helmet and took
the walkway toward the house, admiring the expansive
piazza, which looked as if it could accommodate at least
one hundred guests. Antique wicker settees and rock-
ers with fat floral cushions offered seating and a great
view of the marsh and the bay beyond. Pots of pink and

white geraniums softened the look of the coral stone exterior.

Wes paused at an ornate door and studied the solid brass knocker of a naked man and woman embracing. One side of Wes's mouth turned up. Beside the door, an iron plaque dated the house back to 1850. Instead of using the knocker, he rapped on the door and waited. He was about to knock again when he suddenly heard a man cry out several times. It seemed to be coming from the back of the house.

Wes cleared the front steps, rounded the house, and raced up the driveway, following the sounds of loud, anxious voices. He paused at a waist-high wrought-iron gate and stared as an attractive redhead in jeans and a long cotton shirt chased a disheveled middle-aged man across the yard, a rolling pin poised in her hand.

"Run, you lazy good-for-nothing drunk!" the woman yelled.

The man ducked behind one of several oaks shading the backyard. "Put that thing down, Miss Annie!" he cried. "You're liable to hurt somebody."

"Damn right!" she said.

"Please don't hit him," a gray-haired woman pleaded from the back steps of the house. Beside her, a woman with long black hair and large breasts cheered Miss Annie on.

"Give him what for, Annie," she said laughingly.

The redhead chased the frightened man around the tree several times. She slammed the rolling pin against the bark twice, missing the man by a good twelve inches. Nevertheless, he continued to duck and run. "Help!" he cried. "Somebody save me!"

"Oh, for the love of—" Wes leaped the fence and ran toward the two. "Lady, stop!" he shouted.

* * *

Annie darted around the tree once more as Erdle tried to maintain a safe distance, all the while crying out for help. He ran pretty fast for someone who'd just come home from a three-day drunk, she thought. She could see the fear in his eyes as she smacked the tree again with her rolling pin. She had no intention of actually hitting Erdle, but she wasn't about to let him know that. She was so intent on her chase that she paid no heed to the chorus of voices behind her.

She was only vaguely aware of movement beside her as she raised the rolling pin high in the air and aimed once more for the tree. A disembodied hand shot into her line of vision, and her aim faltered. There was a loud, resounding *thwack,* and Theenie screamed. Annie heard a dull thud, spun around, and froze when she spied a brown-haired man sprawled across the ground. She gasped and dropped the rolling pin, then let out a squeal when it fell and bounced off the man's forehead.

"Now look what you've gone and done!" Erdle said, pointing.

Annie's eyes flew open in horror as she stared down at the handsome unshaved man in worn jeans, T-shirt, black denim jacket, and biker boots. "Where on earth did *he* come from?" she cried.

Theenie and Destiny raced down the steps and across the backyard as the stranger lay there unmoving.

Theenie gaped in horror. "You killed him!"

"Dang right she killed him," Erdle said. "If the first blow didn't do it, the second one surely did."

The man groaned and pushed himself into a sitting position. He rubbed the back of his head and winced. "What the hell?"

Annie knelt beside him. His hair was the color of Brazil nuts, thick and slightly wavy, falling just past his collar. He wasn't a local; she would have remembered him. "I'm so sorry," she said. "Are you hurt? Here, let me help you up."

Menacing brown eyes locked with hers. "Don't touch me, lady. What are you, crazy?"

"That's *exactly* what she is," Erdle said. "Mean *and* crazy."

Annie glared at Erdle. "Don't give me any lip, mister. I'm not finished with you."

"If you come near me I'm calling the cops," Erdle said. "I'm going to get me some of that hot pepper spray or maybe one of those stun guns. Or maybe I'll get me a big Doberman or a pit bull—"

"Shut up, Erdle, or I'll snatch you bald-headed!" Theenie shouted, causing the group to pause in surprise. She sniffed, folded her hands properly, and gave the stranger a saccharine sweet smile. "Excuse me, sir," she said ever so politely, "but I used to be a nurse's aide, and I think I'd better have a look at your head. Would you mind very much?"

Wes looked at her. "Are you armed?"

"I don't believe in keeping weapons. You're safe with me."

After a moment, he shrugged.

While the others watched, Theenie carefully parted his hair. "Oh my," she said. "You've already got a nasty lump. I need to put ice on it."

"What about my forehead?" Wes said, wincing when he touched it.

"It's not so bad. Erdle, help this gentleman to his feet. We need to get him inside."

"I can manage," Wes answered gruffly. He stood, towering over the rest of the group. He jabbed a finger toward Annie. "Stay away from me; you got that?"

Annie drew herself up to her full height, but at five foot two she was a good twelve inches shorter than the man. His shoulders were wide, at least twice the width of hers. "I didn't mean to hurt you. I said I was sorry."

"Sorry doesn't get it," he said. "The only thing I need from you is the name of your lawyer."

Annie gawked at him. Lawyer! He planned to sue her! She would lose everything, her home and the business she'd worked night and day for the past three years to build. She would have to try to get her old bookkeeping job back at Bates's Furniture.

"Oh dear," Theenie said. "You can't sue Annie. She doesn't have any money."

"That's right," Erdle said. "Her grandma invested all her money in one of them Viagra-like drugs, but it was yanked off the market when men started having embarrassing and prolonged erections."

Annie closed her eyes and wished she could crawl beneath something and never come out. She could feel the man's eyes on her, but she was determined to remain cool. She would deal with Erdle later. Right now she needed to try to dissuade this angry stranger from taking legal action. "Excuse me, but you were trespassing on my property, and I didn't even see you come up behind me."

Wes opened his mouth to reply, but Theenie interrupted.

"Now, now, let's not fuss," she said. "We need to see to this young man's head. Come this way, Mr. . . ."

"Bridges," he said. "Wes."

"And I'm Theenie," she replied, motioning for him to follow her to the house.

Wes glanced in Annie's direction once more before doing as he was told. The others fell into line behind him. Annie tried not to notice how nicely the man's jeans molded to his backside, but Wes Bridges was a definite ten in the rear-end department. Oh, Lord, what was she thinking? The poor man could be seriously hurt, he would probably sue her from here to Timbuktu, and she was staring at his behind. She shouldn't have spent the morning hearing about Destiny's sex life. Annie could almost smell the testosterone oozing from his pores. And she wasn't the only one looking; Destiny was eyeballing him as well.

Once inside, Theenie pointed to one of the ladder-back chairs. "Have a seat, Wes, and I'll get an ice pack."

He did as he was told, but the dark scowl on his face told Annie he was not a happy man.

"That could be *me* sitting there," Erdle said, standing just inside the door, holding the screen open as though preparing to bolt. "You could have knocked my brains out, Miss Annie!"

She turned to him. "I've never so much as laid a hand on you, Erdle Thorney. I was just trying to scare some sense into you. Some handyman you are. The yard is a mess! Have you forgotten we have an important wedding here in two weeks?"

"Somebody is actually going to marry you?" Wes asked in disbelief.

"She's already married," Theenie said, "but her husband left her three years ago."

"You're looking at one dangerous woman," Erdle said.

Annie pointed. "Out!" she ordered him. "Go pack your bags. I'm evicting you."

Erdle gaped. "But Miss Annie, you can't just throw me out. Your dear grandmother, God rest her soul, was perfectly happy with my work."

"That's before you began spending all your time in the bars."

"I'll get started on the yard work right away," Erdle said. "You just make me a list of what you want done." He hurried out the door before she could reply.

"This is a crazy house," Wes told Theenie as she placed the ice pack on his head.

Destiny gave a snort. "You don't know the half of it."

Annie noticed Wes giving Destiny the once-over, which was no surprise. Any woman who had breasts *out to there* was bound to draw attention, and the come-hither look Destiny returned obviously did not go un-noticed, because one side of his lip turned up slightly. Annie wished she'd hit him harder. "This is *not* a crazy house," she said. "You just happened to show up at a bad time."

"Annie's under a lot of stress," Theenie said, "and with good reason."

Annie clenched her teeth. "I am not stressed."

"You look stressed to me," Destiny said. "It doesn't take a psychic to figure that out."

"We have a famous person getting married here in two weeks," Theenie told Wes. "We're not allowed to say who because we don't want the media to find out, but he's more famous than Donald Trump. That's why our Annie is pulled tighter than a rubber band."

"I am *not* stressed," Annie repeated loudly.

Theenie lifted the ice pack and checked Wes's head. "Oh my, this doesn't look good. Not good at all."

"Let me see," Annie said.

Wes held up one hand as though to stop her. "Look, but don't touch."

Annie sighed and stepped closer, grimacing at the nasty-looking lump. The one on his forehead was be-ginning to swell as well. "I should probably take him to the emergency room."

"Good idea," Wes said. "I'll be able to file a police report for assault and battery."

"I don't think she really meant to hit you," Destiny said.

Annie felt herself nod in agreement, although she

suspected it wouldn't hold much water with the man. He might be the best-looking thing she'd seen in a long time, but he was bound and determined to make her pay. Instead of trying to offer him another apology, which she knew he wouldn't accept, she hitched her chin high. "Perhaps you'll think twice before getting involved in other people's business."

He frowned but didn't reply.

"I think we should call Doc Holden," Theenie said. "He'll know what to do. He's just next door," she told Wes. "Won't take but a jiffy."

Annie made the call despite Wes's objections that he didn't need a doctor.

Five minutes later the back door was thrown open by an elderly white-haired man carrying a black doctor's bag. He glanced about the room until his gaze fell on Wes. "You must be the patient."

"I prefer to use the word *victim*," Wes said, darting a look in Annie's direction.

"What'd you say?"

"Doc, you might want to turn up your hearing aid," Annie said.

He shot her a disgruntled look as he fiddled with the flesh-colored object in one ear. "You're going to be old one day, young lady." He adjusted his glasses and lifted the ice pack from Wes's head. "Oh boy, that's a nasty-looking lump. What happened?"

"Some deranged woman hit me over the head with a rolling pin."

"That would be Annie," Doc replied.

"It was an accident, Doc," Annie said.

Theenie nodded. "She meant to clobber Erdle."

"What's this bump on your forehead?"

"Another accident," Annie said.

Doc sighed and looked at Annie. "How many times have I warned you about that temper of yours?"

"I wasn't trying to clobber *anyone*."

Doc suddenly noticed Destiny. "Don't I know you?"

She introduced herself: "I write a column for the newspaper. You've probably seen my picture."

"She's the Divine Love Goddess Adviser," Theenie said. "She's psychic."

Wes sighed. "Now I *know* I'm in a crazy house."

Destiny folded her arms across her chest, which was no easy task. "Excuse me, but that was a very rude thing to say."

Doc patted Wes's shoulder. "I know it looks a little kooky around here, son, but Annie can be quite pleasant when she isn't trying to do a person bodily harm."

Annie threw up her hands. "Jeez Louise! I give up."

"Now then," Doc began, "you *do* have quite a knot back there, but that's good." When Wes arched a brow in question, the old doctor went on. "It means the swelling is probably confined to the outside, and that lessens the risk of brain injury." He pulled a penlike gadget from his bag, flicked on a light, and shined it in Wes's eyes. "How's your vision? Any blurring?"

Wes looked about the cheery kitchen with its tall white cabinets, partially wainscoted walls, and green-and-white-checkered wallpaper. "I'm fine."

"How bad is the pain?"

Wes grunted. "Feels like I've been hit over the head by a two-by-four. A couple of aspirin might help."

"You don't think I should take him to the ER?" Annie asked Doc.

"Not unless you plan on hitting him again." He reached into his bag and pulled out a small white envelope. "These tablets will help with the pain. You can take one every four to six hours."

Wes shook one of the large white tablets into his palm as Theenie went for water. "I need to escape this madhouse while I'm still able," he said.

Doc shook his head. "I don't recommend that you drive right now. Not with a head injury," he added. "And don't go to sleep, either. You don't appear to have a concussion, but we don't want to take any chances."

"What the hell am I supposed to do in the meantime?" Wes asked.

Doc shrugged. "Make Annie cook you breakfast. It's the least she can do after trying to kill you."

Annie gaped. "Hellooo," she said, waving her hands in the air. "Has anybody heard a word I've said? I was *not* trying to kill him!" She flung her hands to her sides when nobody paid attention.

Theenie handed Wes a glass of water. He gave a huge sigh and popped the pill into his mouth, but it was so large he had to swallow several times to get it down. He reached into his back pocket for his wallet. "What do I owe you, Doctor?"

Doc chuckled as he snapped his black bag closed. "Not a thing," he said. "I stopped practicing veterinary medicine a long time ago."

Wes looked up in disbelief. "You're a veterinarian?" He turned to Annie. "You called an *animal* doctor to treat me?"

"He was close by," she said defensively.

A clatter sounded from the top of the stairs leading into the kitchen. Wes looked up. "What was that?" he asked.

"I didn't hear anything," Annie said quickly.

"This house is haunted," Destiny said, drawing a gasp from Theenie.

Wes just looked at her.

Doc shook his head. "Well, I'd better get back to what I was doing," he said. He started for the door with Annie on his heels. He paused suddenly. "Wish I could remember what I was doing." He shrugged. "Oh well, it'll come to me eventually."

"Don't forget your bag," Theenie said.

"Ooopsie-daisy, can't leave that behind." Doc took the bag. "It's tough getting old," he told Wes. "My mind isn't as sharp as it used to be. Take care of that head now. I don't want to have to put you down." He chuckled as he walked out.

Annie watched him go. In the backyard, Erdle was picking up branches. She gave a hopeful sigh.

"I hope I'm not as forgetful as Doc when I get old," Theenie said.

"You *are* old," Destiny blurted, and then covered her mouth when the woman looked hurt. "I'm sorry; I didn't mean to say that. I didn't sleep well last night, what with that spirit on the loose."

"You're beginning to scare me," Theenie said.

Wes turned to Annie. "You let a crazy, senile veterinarian treat me?"

"He's not really senile," she said. "He's, um, forgetful. I don't think he's crazy, either. He was just kidding about putting you to sleep."

"That's good to know."

She offered him a tight smile. "Well now, it looks like you're stuck with us for a while. At least until we're sure you're going to be okay. How about I cook you something to eat like Doc suggested?"

Wes shook his head. "No thanks."

"Then I'll make a fresh pot of coffee," Annie offered. "Like Doc said, you don't want to go to sleep."

He gave a grunt. "Lady, I wouldn't think of closing my eyes in this house."

Chapter
TWO

Annie had just put on the coffee when the doorbell rang. She hurried to answer it and was surprised to find Jamie Swift standing on the other side, her dog, Fleas, beside her. "Oh, crap." Annie had forgotten they were supposed to meet that morning.

"Nice to see you, too, Annie."

"Sorry. It's been a bad morning." She stepped aside so Jamie could enter, and then closed the door behind her. She suddenly noticed that her friend didn't look so good. "What's wrong? Are you ill? Are you having second thoughts about getting married? That's perfectly normal, you know. A lot of brides and grooms get cold feet. Getting married is one of the most stressful events in our lives, even if you love that person deeply." She had to pause to catch her breath. It was the spiel she often gave brides.

"Do I really look that bad?" Jamie asked.

The last thing Annie wanted to do was hurt her friend's feelings. Again. "Oh no, it's just—"

"I'm on a diet," Jamie said. "I'm so hungry I could eat dirt."

"Let me make you something," Annie offered, then wished she hadn't. She did not want Jamie to meet Wes Bridges and have him recount the morning's events to her, and his belief that Annie was a threat to society.

Jamie shook her head. "I *can't* eat. I have to lose seven pounds before the wedding." She groaned. "I've never really been on a serious diet," she confessed. "Fleas and I live on double cheeseburgers, butter pecan ice cream, and my first true love: doughnuts."

"Uh-oh," Annie said. "Having trouble fitting into your wedding dress?" Annie knew Dee Dee Fontana, Max's sister and Jamie's soon-to-be sister-in-law, had insisted on flying Jamie to New York to meet her designer, a Frenchman who created gowns for the rich, the famous, and the royals.

"I fear facing that dress," Jamie confessed. "Although it is absolutely gorgeous, the material clings to every curve and is unforgiving of the slightest weight gain. And I've been so anxious about the wedding and leaving the newspaper for my honeymoon that I wasn't paying attention to how many doughnuts I was eating."

"Would you like to go over the menus at another time?" Annie asked, hoping they could reschedule.

"I'll be okay." Jamie glanced about. "Um, should I have left Fleas in the car?"

"He's safe," Annie said. "I put Attila-the-cat out earlier." Annie couldn't help but smile at the homely bloodhound Jamie had inherited when she'd purchased an old pickup truck. The dog had been part of the deal. Annie patted his bony head. "How are you this morning, handsome? You look a little sad."

"That's his woe-is-me look," Jamie said. "Since I've been on my diet we haven't had any *i-c-e c-r-e-a-m* in the house."

"Poor baby," Annie said to Fleas.

"Then yesterday he caught me sneaking my *s-u-i-t-c-a-s-e-s* from the attic. You know how he gets when I *l-e-a-v-e* him."

Annie nodded. "Okay, let's go into the dining room. Would you like something to drink? Or maybe some carrot sticks?"

Fleas slid to the floor, covered his eyes with his paws, and gave a mournful sigh.

Jamie shook her head. "No thanks. Vera has been force-feeding me carrot and celery sticks for two days. She won't even let me have cream or sugar in my coffee."

Annie chuckled. Sixty-year-old Vera Bankhead was Jamie's secretary and assistant editor. The fact that she was a strict Southern Baptist did not stop her from carrying a loaded Smith & Wesson .38 in her purse, which she had been known to use. "Well, you certainly don't want to cross Vera."

"I almost prefer her shooting me point-blank to eating another raw vegetable," Jamie said.

Annie led Jamie into the large dining room, and they took a seat at the long table, a custom-built replica of an 1820 Imperial Extending Table, only this one was adorned with bronze and gilt, as was most of the furniture in the house, with the exception of the kitchen, which had been added on long after the house was built. Numerous leaves could be added to the table so that it could accommodate thirty people. A massive Regency gilt-wood mirror almost covered one wall, reflecting light from the chandelier. On the opposite wall, a large bowfront sideboard held Annie's grandmother's fine silver and china. As a young girl, Annie had thought the dining room one of the most spectacular rooms in the house.

Until she realized that the deep red walls, black and red velvet draperies, and naked cherubs painted on the ceiling were not exactly tasteful. Not to mention the silk tapestry of women in highly suggestive poses. Unlike her mother, who considered it tasteless and downright disgraceful, Annie had learned to take it in stride.

Except for the large marble, phalliclike sculpture that had been placed beside the graceful free-floating staircase in the foyer. Annie had been twelve years old when she'd asked her grandmother why anyone would want a carving of a man's *thing* in the entryway.

The elderly woman had chuckled. "It's art, dear. And it's been in this family for many years."

Annie had broken a cardinal rule when, after her grandmother's death, she'd packed the sculpture and had it carried to the attic.

Annie noted the amused look on Jamie's face as she took it all in. "Are you sure you still want to get married *here*?" Annie said.

Jamie looked surprised. "Why wouldn't I? You have a reputation for putting on the finest weddings money can buy."

"Yes, but the guest list doesn't usually include senators, heads of state, and tycoons. Some people might find the house, um, offensive."

"If that were the case, you wouldn't have so many people wanting to marry here." She sighed. "I just hope none of the guests talk," she said. "I have never seen a man more determined to avoid the press than Max."

"People have a right to their privacy," Annie said. "Even celebrities. And Max shouldn't have to deal with TV cameras and newspaper reporters on one of the most important days of his life." She reached for a manila folder that was simply labeled: *H. Wedding*. Thankfully, it was quiet in the kitchen. "By the way, how is Max?"

"He's working hard to tie up loose ends before we leave for the honeymoon, which he still insists on keeping a surprise."

"Everyone is talking about the new polymer plant he's building," Annie said. "It's going to create a lot of well-needed jobs in this town."

Jamie nodded. "And hopefully save the lives of a few motorists. It's the same material that was used to build Max's car. He and a NASA employee experimented for a couple of years to make the product more durable, and I can tell you it's stronger than steel. A leading car manufacturer is anxiously awaiting the first sheets to come off the production line."

"You must be very proud of Max," Annie said, and then grinned. "I know it's a little soon to ask, but have you talked about starting a family?"

Jamie's smile suddenly drooped.

"Uh-oh, wrong thing to ask," Annie said, wishing she could take it back.

"I'm scared, Annie. Terrified. I don't know anything about being a wife; what on earth would I do with a child? I don't even know how to raise this dog. I mean, look at him," she said, pointing to Fleas. "He has no self-esteem."

As if trying to prove her point, Fleas managed to look even more pathetic.

"Take a deep breath, Jamie," Annie said. "It'll be okay."

Jamie sucked in air.

"Like I said, you're just having pre-wedding jitters and that's perfectly normal. And nobody says you have to have a baby. Oprah Winfrey doesn't plan on having kids, and everybody *adores* her."

"Yeah, but I sort of want a family," Jamie said.

Annie suspected as much. Jamie's mother had left while Jamie was still in diapers, and her father had not been able to fill the gap. "So take your time and stop stressing over it," Annie said. "You'll know when you're ready." She laughed. "I mean, good grief, Dee Dee's going to have a baby in how long?"

"Three weeks. But she doesn't count, because Frankie has hired three nannies."

Annie chuckled. Frankie and Dee Dee were well liked in the community because of their eccentricities and fun-loving nature. A retired wrestler, Frankie had turned his attention to politics the previous year when he suspected the local government was corrupt. He'd called on brother-in-law Max Holt to help him look into it, and they'd found more than they'd bargained for. In the end, Frankie had emerged a hero and won the mayoral election hands-down.

Annie suddenly remembered the injured man in the kitchen; she needed to get down to business. "Let's concentrate on one thing at a time," she said. "You're marrying a great guy who's madly in love with you. The fact that he's drop-dead gorgeous and filthy rich is only the icing on the cake. And speaking of cakes—" Annie pulled out a picture of the wedding cake Jamie had selected, a French pound cake with Grand Marnier buttercream frosting. It was simple yet exquisite. "I've been thinking," she said. "Since you're planning on white tea roses for the wedding, how about I tint the frosting on the cake off-white and place some of the rosebuds on top for decoration? That sort of thing is real popular now."

"Sounds beautiful."

"Great." Annie hurried on. "As for the menu, I typed up everything we agreed on so you and Max can look it over in case you want to make any changes."

Jamie reached into her oversize handbag and pulled out several envelopes. "I've received the last of the responses to the wedding invitations, so we're looking at about fifty guests. I hope you know that Max and I cut the list to the bone," she added.

"I can easily accommodate that number of people," Annie said, having hired someone to knock down the wall separating the den and oversize study when she needed the space for various businesses that held monthly meetings there. It also served well for small weddings. "I'll situate the tables near the walls in the ballroom so there will be room for dancing," she added.

Annie hoped she could do something about the water damage before the wedding. "Okay, what's next?"

"Oh, wait; I forgot to mention that Max's parents can't make it. His mother had a mild heart attack several days ago. She's getting out of the hospital tomorrow, but her doctor wants her to stay close to home. So you can scratch their names from the list."

Annie made a note to herself. "I know Max will be disappointed."

"He is. But he wasn't that close to them while growing up. His cousin Nick and his wife, Billie, practically raised him."

"Moving right along," Annie said, hoping they could wrap things up, "the minister will be here early in case you or Max would like a private moment with him. The photographer is all taken care of, and the flutist and harpist will play before, during, and after the ceremony, at least until the band starts. Well, it's not really a band, just a three-piece ensemble."

"I have no idea what I'm supposed to do when I get here," Jamie said anxiously.

"That's what the rehearsal is for. No change in number of people for that?"

"Nope."

"The florist will arrive a couple of hours early, so we'll have plenty of time to decorate."

"I just hope I fit into my dress," Jamie said grimly.

"You will. Any questions?"

"I think that covers it."

Annie checked her wristwatch. "Oh, look at the time!" She stood, hoping she didn't appear rude but knowing she needed to check on Wes Bridges, who was probably on the telephone with his lawyer that very moment.

Jamie stood as well. "I need to get back to the office anyway. By the way, how is Destiny settling in?"

"Theenie and I really like her. She's hilarious. Perhaps *outrageous* is a better word."

Jamie laughed. "Most of what she says is in fun, so don't take her too seriously." They had turned for the living room when the swinging door leading to the kitchen was suddenly thrown open and a frantic-looking Theenie poked her head through. "Trouble in the kitchen," she said. "Big trouble."

Annie darted a look at Jamie. "Gotta run." She raced into the next room, where she found Wes slumped at the table. "Oh no!" she cried. "What happened?"

"He passed out," Destiny said.

A frowning Jamie stood in the doorway, trying to make sense of what was going on. "Who is *that*?"

Annie glanced her way. Damn. She hadn't even heard Jamie follow her. "Long story."

"You wouldn't believe it anyway," Destiny told Jamie.

Annie tried to shake the man awake. There was no movement. He began to snore lightly. "Oh, great!" she muttered. "Wes, you have to wake up!" she said loudly. She shook him harder, so hard he slipped from the chair and hit the floor with a resounding thud. His head bounced once, and he groaned.

Theenie cried out in alarm and then covered her mouth, but her eyes slid side-to-side, clearly panicked. "We're going to kill the poor man yet."

"Would somebody *puh-leese* tell me what's going on!" Jamie insisted.

"We should try to sit him up," Annie said as Theenie gave Jamie a rapid-fire rundown of events. "Maybe that'll wake him."

Jamie blinked several times as though trying to digest the explanation. "I'll help."

Working together, Annie, Jamie, and Destiny managed to get Wes into a sitting position, but his head lolled to one side. Annie stood over him, bracing her feet on either side as she slipped her arms beneath his and pulled. He was too heavy, despite Destiny and Jamie trying to pull him up from behind. Annie paused to catch her breath and Wes fell back once more, dragging her with him. Fortunately, Jamie prevented his head from hitting the floor again.

Annie suddenly found herself lying flat against the man, chest-to-chest, thigh-to-thigh. Before she could make a move, Wes smiled in his sleep and enveloped her in his arms. Her jaw dropped. Whoa, mama! She couldn't remember when she'd last been this close to the opposite sex, but danged it if didn't feel good. *Too* good, she thought, his tight muscles pressed against all her body parts.

Her stomach fluttered.

Her nipples hardened.

Her gizzard quivered.

"Oh my," Theenie said, one hand at her breast as though she feared her heart would fly right out. "This won't do. This simply won't do."

Annie sighed.

Destiny and Jamie gawked.

Theenie stepped closer. "Annie, this is not proper behavior. You must get up this instant!"

Destiny laughed out loud. "You really do need to get off of him, honey. The man needs medical attention. You can lie on top of him once he's better."

Jamie grinned openly.

Annie tried to pull free, but it was useless. "He has me in a death grip." She craned her head so that she could see Theenie. "You might want to call Doc."

Theenie hurried to the telephone and dialed while Destiny and Jamie looked on in amusement.

"This is not funny, you guys," Annie told them. "He could be badly hurt. Not only that; he has already threatened to sue me."

"Doc's on his way," Theenie said, hanging up the phone. She gave Annie a funny look. "What's wrong? Why are you squirming?"

"She's copping a feel," Destiny said. She bit her fist.

"I am not!" Annie said. "I'm just, um, trying to get comfortable."

Jamie looked at Destiny. "I'm sure it's not as easy as it looks, just lying on him like that."

"I should *not* be listening to this," Theenie said, eyeballing each of them. "I know three young ladies who are going to feel terribly guilty if something happens to that poor man."

The back door swung open a few minutes later and Doc stepped in, once again carrying his black bag. "Now what?" He came to a dead halt when he spied Annie lying across Wes. "Oh boy," he mumbled. "I'm almost afraid to ask."

"He's out cold," Annie said, "and he won't let go of me."

Doc suddenly looked sheepish. "I was afraid of this."

"Afraid of what?" Theenie said.

Doc sighed. "I'm not positive, but I'm pretty sure I gave him the wrong medication."

"What did you give him?" Annie almost shrieked:

"I, well, accidentally gave him a tranquilizer. It's mostly used for large animals." He swallowed, and his Adam's apple bobbed. "Livestock."

"Oh, shit!" Annie cried. "He's going to be mad as hell when he wakes up. Wait! Maybe we shouldn't *let* him wake up. How many more of those pills do you have?"

Theenie planted her hands on her hips. "I'm going to pretend you didn't say that." She turned to Doc. "Is he in danger?"

"No, but he's probably going to be out for a while. That's not good considering he has a head injury. That and the fact he won't let go of Annie."

"Life can be hard like that," Destiny said.

Annie felt a sense of dread. "We have to get him to the hospital."

Theenie shook her head and began to pick at her fingernails. "If we do, they'll ask questions. Doc could get into a lot of trouble for dispensing medication, seeing as how he's not practicing anymore."

"Oh boy," Doc muttered under his breath.

Annie gave a huge sigh. "I'm going to lose my house. I'll have to sleep in the bus station and keep my stuff in a grocery cart."

"We'll be homeless," Theenie said. "I'll have to sleep in a cardboard box. Everybody will find out. I won't be able to show my face in Susie Q's Cut and Curl." She pulled a lace handkerchief from her pocket, put it to her nose, and sniffed. "My hair will be a mess."

Destiny and Jamie exchanged glances.

Annie looked at Doc. "Think of something fast."

"Be nice if we could wake him. Maybe we could get him into the shower and douse him with cold water."

"Okay," Annie said calmly. "Theenie, call Erdle. We'll need all the help we can get. Doc, don't you think you should check his pulse or something?"

"Good idea." Doc got down on his knees and pulled a worn stethoscope and penlight from his bag. He listened to Wes's heart, shone the light in his eyes, and took his pulse. "Everything seems normal."

Erdle came through the door and almost stumbled over his own feet. "Miss Annie!"

"Don't just stand there, Erdle, help me!" she said. "See if you can pry the man's hands loose."

Erdle hurried around behind her and tried to pull her free. "Golly, he's strong as a bull!" He pulled with all his might.

Wes opened his eyes and stared into Annie's face. His words were slurred when he spoke. "You got, um, a nice, um . . ." He frowned as if trying to come up with the word. Finally, he closed his eyes.

Annie shook him. "What?"

His eyes remained closed. "A nice ass," he said. Once again, he began to snore.

"Oh, I shouldn't be listening to this," Theenie said, covering her ears.

Everyone in the room was silent for a moment. Annie stared openmouthed at the man beneath her. So he'd noticed her after all. Her ego moved up a notch. Not that he was her type, mind you. Not that she had a type. But Wes looked, well, he looked a little dangerous, a little rough around the edges. Besides, she'd sworn off men.

Still . . . Wes made her feel sort of feminine, like she should go upstairs and put on a pair of panty hose.

Not a good sign.

Erdle managed to lift Wes's arms, and Annie shimmied out, her cheek rubbing every bone and muscle along the way, although she did her best to lift her head and not touch his crotch.

"Wow," Destiny said. "I hope it was as good for him as it was for you."

Annie shot her a look as she took a deep breath. "Okay," she said, trying to pull her muddled thoughts together. "I think it'll be easier if we drag him into the bathroom. Theenie, you hold his head off the floor so it doesn't bounce. Erdle, you grab the other arm. The rest of you, get his legs and try to shove him in the direction of the bathroom while Erdle and I pull." She waited until everyone was in place. "Okay, let's do it!"

The six of them went to work, pulling Wes across the kitchen, the hall, and finally into the bathroom. They paused in the cramped space to catch their breath. Annie pushed the shower curtain aside. "Okay," she said, "I think it would be better if we got his legs in first."

"Are we going to put him in with all his clothes on?" Theenie asked.

They exchanged looks. "Maybe we should at least strip him down to his underwear," Annie said.

"What if he doesn't wear underwear?" Theenie asked. "He doesn't exactly look the type."

"I'll check," Doc said. The women turned their backs. "Yep, he's wearing them."

"Okay," Annie said to Erdle, trying to sound businesslike and matter-of-fact, even though her pulse was going wacko. "Let's strip him down." The others, including a disgruntled Destiny, stepped from the room. Erdle and Annie managed to free Wes from his clothes, with the exception of a pair of boxer shorts adorned with red hearts.

"Get a load of that," Erdle said.

"Huh?" Annie tried not to stare at the lean, muscular body, but it would have been impossible not to look. She knew Erdle was referring to Wes's boxer shorts. "I'm sure he didn't purchase them for himself. Probably his wife or girlfriend."

"Awesome," Destiny said, peeking around the door. "It's almost worth it just to see that. Cool boxers, huh?"

Annie tore her gaze from his body. "Okay, everybody back in here. Let's get him in the bathtub."

It was not an easy task, but once they'd settled Wes into the tub, Theenie stuffed a towel beneath his head to protect it from further harm. Annie pulled the curtain closed and turned on the cold water full force. She reached in and adjusted the spray so it would hit his face. The man remained immobile. After several minutes, Annie turned off the water and looked at Doc. "He's not responding."

"Let's give it time. He should come around eventually. I hope I'm not here when he does."

Annie didn't bother to hide her annoyance. "What should we do with him in the meantime?"

"Be best to dry him off and cover him with a blanket," Doc told her.

Annie gaped. "You mean *leave* him in the bathtub?"

"I don't think we're going to be able to get him out."

Annie shook her head sadly as she moved to the linen cabinet. "This day can't get any worse."

"Unless he dies," Theenie said fretfully. "I don't know what we'll do then. Probably we'll go to jail. Which is probably a whole lot better than being homeless when you think about it," she added, only to frown. "Unless, well, you know what happens behind prison walls. We could end up in a cell with a big woman who decides to make us her *b-i-t-c-h*." She shuddered.

Destiny just looked at her. "Have you ever considered taking Xanax?"

Theenie ignored her. "I'll grab a blanket," she said, hurrying from the room.

Annie dried Wes from head to toe, all the while trying to ignore how good he looked. "His underwear is soaked," she said as Theenie returned with the blanket.

"Best to get him out of them," Doc replied.

Annie took a step back. "I'm not doing it."

"Let me do it," Destiny said.

Theenie squared her shoulders. "No, *I'll* do it," she said, surprising everyone in the room. "It's not like I haven't seen my share of naked bodies, what with being a nurse's aide and all." She looked at Destiny. "Besides, this should be done in a professional manner."

Destiny gave a grunt. "Yeah, right. You want to get a look at Mr. Big as bad as the rest of us."

"I'm not listening to that kind of talk," Theenie said, covering her ears. "La la la la la."

Destiny looked at Jamie. "Is it me or what?"

Theenie glanced at Annie. "Is she done talking dirty yet?"

Annie nodded and Theenie dropped her hands to her sides. "Okay, everybody out," the older woman said. "I have a job to do. And no peeking," she added, looking right at Destiny.

Annie followed the others out of the bathroom. She skidded to a halt. Standing on the other side of the door was her friend Danny Gilbert. She feigned a smile as her cohorts in crime scattered.

"I rang the doorbell," he said. He glanced about the room. "Why does everybody look so serious? Is something wrong?"

Annie pulled the bathroom door closed. "Wrong?" She tried to think fast. "Oh well—" She jumped as a moan sounded from the bathroom.

"What was that?" Danny asked.

Annie shot a frantic look at the others. "Um, Theenie isn't feeling well."

"Digestive problems," Doc said authoritatively. "It happens to the best of us."

Another moan. Danny looked concerned. "Is it serious?"

"Not sure." Doc chuckled. "Might have to put her down."

Annie rolled her eyes. "She'll be fine."

The bathroom door opened and Theenie stepped out, holding Wes's boxer shorts. "I'm glad to have that behind me," she said. "It wasn't as easy as I thought it would be." Her eyes widened when she spied Danny. "Oh, I didn't know we had company." She wadded the boxers in her hands.

"Are you okay?" he asked.

"I'm a little sore from all the strenuous activity, but—" She stopped abruptly as though realizing she'd said more than she should. "I think I'll just put these in the dryer," she told Annie, hurrying away.

"I really need to head back to the office," Jamie said, already backing away. "I'll see myself out." Fleas, who'd managed to sleep through the whole thing, got up, shook himself, and followed.

Annie managed to say a quick good-bye before she turned to Danny. "What are you doing here?"

He looked surprised. "Just thought I'd drop by for a cup of coffee."

"Oh." It wasn't unusual for Danny to stop by if he was in the neighborhood; he was like family. He and Annie started hanging out together years before, during the summers she spent with her grandmother. Some people mistook them for brother and sister, since they both had red hair and green eyes. "Um, gee, I wish I could visit with you," she said, slipping her arm through his and prodding him toward the living room, "but we're up to our ears in work, what with the wedding and all." She hadn't even told Danny who was getting married.

He looked amused. "Are you throwing me out?"

"No, of course not," she said, opening the door and shoving him onto the piazza. "I'm just, um, really busy right now. Bye." She started to close the door.

"Wait! I'd also hoped you might want to take in a movie this week."

"Movie? Oh, right," she said quickly. She and Danny usually grabbed a quick dinner and saw a movie every week. "May I get back to you on that?" she asked.

"Well, sure. Hey, are you okay? You seem awfully nervous."

"Nervous?" She thought she was acting pretty calm considering there was an unconscious butt-naked man in her bathtub. "I just need to go through my to-do list for the wedding; after that I'll have a better idea how long it's going to take. I'll call you."

"That's fine," he said. He turned. "By the way, whose Harley, is that? It's one mean-looking machine."

Annie wondered how she'd missed the massive chrome and black motorcycle. "It must belong to one of Erdle's friends. See you later." She closed the door and leaned against it. She gave an enormous sigh of relief when Danny pulled away in his car. She knew darn well who the motorcycle belonged to; it had Wes Bridges written all over it. That would explain his biker clothes. What she didn't know and couldn't figure out was why Wes had shown up in her backyard in the first place.

Several hours later, Wes was still out cold, and Destiny was in her room taking a nap. Annie prepared a meat loaf for dinner and iced a pan of brownies while Theenie peeled potatoes. They worked in silence, but every so often Theenie would look at Annie and shake her head.

"I know," Annie finally said. "I can't believe we have a naked man lying in the bathtub, either."

"I'll set the table," Theenie said once she'd put the potatoes on to boil.

"Thanks." Annie was grateful that both of her full-time tenants were only too eager to help around the place; it made her job a lot easier. She was only forced to hire help when her bed-and-breakfast was full. She checked on Wes, shook him lightly, but there was no movement.

Destiny came downstairs looking rested. She wore tight jeans and a low-cut royal blue blouse with gold moons and stars that did not detract from her cleavage.

"Something smells good," Destiny said. "What can I do to help?"

As Annie put the finishing touches on dinner she assigned Destiny a small task.

Erdle showed up as the women carried the food to the table. He had showered, changed his clothes, and scrubbed the dirt from beneath his fingernails, a rule Annie had put into place long ago. He took his usual chair, tucked his napkin inside his collar, and waited for the women to sit, but his eyes were fixed on Destiny.

"Please say grace, Erdle," Annie said, not because he was particularly good at it but because she thought it might put him on the path of the straight and narrow. So far it hadn't worked.

He bowed his head. "Rub-a-dub-dub, thanks for the grub."

Theenie pursed her lips. "I wish you'd learn a new prayer. That is not at all proper. One of these days the ground is going to split right open and swallow you whole."

He shrugged and looked at Annie. "I picked up all the branches, raked the leaves, and trimmed the weeds," he said proudly as they passed the food around. "We've got some leftover pine straw in the carriage house, so I'll put it out tomorrow."

Annie knew Erdle was just sucking up so she wouldn't evict him. "You'll have to stay on top of it so it stays nice. In the meantime you can start tilling that patch of ground behind the carriage house."

Erdle shifted in his chair. "That tiller is pretty old, been sitting around for years. I'm pretty sure it don't work."

"It works. I've already checked."

Erdle paused and fixed a weary gaze on her. "Tell me again why you want that land tilled?"

"I've already told you I want to plant a vegetable garden back there. It's more than large enough." Annie hoped by planting her own vegetables she would save on the grocery bills. "I need to get started right away, with the weather being so warm."

"You can't grow nothing back there. Not enough sun."

"You're wrong. It gets the morning sun."

"You're just not up early enough to notice," Theenie said.

Erdle didn't respond. Instead, he concentrated on his food.

Annie kept her gaze fixed on him. The man would stall as long as he could to keep from doing any work. "Erdle?"

"Okay," he said. "I'll get on it."

Annie was about to pin him down as to *when* he would get on it, but a sound from the bathroom startled her. She jumped from the table and hurried in that direction with Destiny and Theenie right behind. Wes was still lying in the tub, his eyes open. "Oh, thank goodness!" Annie said. "You're awake."

He didn't look happy to see her. "Would you care to explain why in the hell I'm lying naked in this effin' bathtub?"

Chapter
THREE

Annie opened her mouth to speak, but nothing came out.

Theenie peered around her. "How nice to see you awake. You're just in time for dinner."

Wes ignored her, his gaze fixed on Annie. "I asked you a question."

"Okay, but you're not going to like the answer."

"Somehow I managed to figure that much out for myself."

"It's not Annie's fault," Theenie said, beginning to fidget with her hands. "As hard as it must be for you to believe, she's had nothing but your best interests at heart since she accidentally hit you, uh, twice."

"The medication Doc gave you was stronger than we thought," Annie said, deliberately being vague. She didn't want Doc listed in Wes's lawsuit.

He stared back at her for a full minute. Finally, he sat up and rubbed the back of his head, wincing when he touched the knot. "How long have I been out?"

"All day," Annie said.

"What the hell did the man give me, a horse tranquilizer?"

Annie and Theenie exchanged looks. "It was an accident," Annie said.

Wes scowled. "*Another* accident? There seems to be a lot of that going around." His gaze narrowed on Annie. "Are you the one who undressed me?"

"I did that," Theenie cut in quickly. "I'm accustomed to seeing naked men. It used to be part of my job."

Wes seemed to ponder that before turning back to Annie. "I want my clothes, and I want them now."

Annie pointed. "They're hanging on the back of the door here. While you get dressed, I'll prepare you a plate. We're having meat loaf." She and Theenie hurried from the room.

The group was silent when Wes entered the kitchen a few minutes later, fully dressed, with the exception of his denim jacket, hooked over one finger. He leaned close to Annie. "Mind telling me what happened to my boxer shorts?"

"Oh, I left them on top of the dryer," Theenie said. She stood and hurried into the laundry room, but when she reappeared she looked confused. "They're gone." She looked at Destiny.

"What? You think I took them?"

"Well, they didn't just walk away."

The three women looked at one another, then at Erdle.

He shook his head. "I don't wear boxer shorts with hearts on them."

All eyes landed on Wes. "I got behind on my laundry, and they were my last pair. Besides, I didn't know they would be on display in a house full of strangers."

"I'm sure they'll turn up," Annie said. "Won't you join us for dinner? I know you have to be hungry."

Wes hesitated. Finally, he draped his jacket over the back of the chair and sat as everyone began passing food to him. Annie had prepared him a glass of iced tea and set it beside his plate. He stared at it for a moment.

"I didn't poison it," she said.

He took a tentative sip.

They ate in silence. Destiny finally broke it when she asked how Max and Jamie's wedding plans were going.

Theenie gasped and slapped her hand over her mouth. "We're not supposed to mention names," came her muffled reply. She cut her eyes to Erdle.

"What do I care who's getting married here?" he said with a shrug.

"Please don't discuss it with anyone," Annie told him. As she gave Destiny an update she could feel Wes's eyes on her. She looked at him, and their gazes locked for several seconds before she looked away.

A clatter from above made them pause and stare at the ceiling.

Wes glanced around the table at the anxious faces. "Are there other guests here?"

"It's just the wind rattling the windowpanes," Annie said.

"Yeah, right," Destiny muttered.

Theenie looked at Wes. "You know, our Annie puts on the most beautiful weddings," she blurted, obviously trying to change the subject. "Her clientele is growing by leaps and bounds."

"Is that so?"

"Her parties are just grand."

"I don't think Wes is interested in all that," Annie said, her face growing warm.

Theenie went on. "Annie usually does all the cooking, but Lovelle and I help. We're full-time tenants. Lovelle is away at the moment. We used to have another tenant named Dora, but she died."

Wes arched one brow and turned to Annie.

"It wasn't my fault. She was elderly and died of natural causes."

"How long have you had this place?" he asked.

Annie was surprised he was being civil to her. "The house has been in my family for generations, but I only opened the bed-and-breakfast a few years ago. This is my slow season."

He sat back in his chair and regarded her. "I might be interested in renting a room."

Everybody gaped. Erdle, in the process of swallowing, almost choked. "You'd actually rent a room from her after what happened? Man, you must be desperate."

"I only need a place for a week or two, and I hate motel rooms."

"Well, I . . ." Annie tried to pull her thoughts together. She glanced at Theenie, whose face seemed to have drained of color. Destiny looked amused.

"I can provide references," he said. "Except for that short stint in prison."

Theenie dropped her fork, and it clattered in her plate.

"Just kidding," Wes said.

"You should rent him the master bedroom," Erdle said. He looked at Wes. "It's huge. Has cable TV, a fireplace, one of those claw-foot tubs in the bathroom, and a big mirror on the ceiling."

"Wow, that sounds like my kind of room," Destiny said.

Annie managed a tight smile. "I don't normally rent it out. Only if I'm booked and have no other choice."

"Why aren't you using it?" Wes asked.

Erdle answered for her. "She moved out of it when her husband ran off with another woman."

"Thank you for sharing, Erdle," Annie said.

Wes seemed to be doing his best to swallow a smile. "How long has your husband been gone?"

Annie avoided eye contact. "Three years."

"Does he live around here?" Wes asked.

"If I knew where he lived I would serve him with divorce papers." She gave a dismissive wave. "I'd rather not talk about it."

"I'd like to see the room after dinner if that's okay."

"I have other rooms."

"Yes, but I'm willing to pay twice what you would normally charge for the master."

"Why on earth would you do that?" she asked.

"Because it offers a lot more than a motel room and because the food is good here." He almost smiled. "And I have a thing for overhead mirrors."

"Amen to that," Destiny said, drawing a frown from Theenie.

"I'd jump on that, Miss Annie," Erdle said, "seeing as how you could use the money."

Annie finally shrugged, trying to appear indifferent. "Sure." She would show Wes the room, but that didn't mean she was going to rent it to him. Annie didn't have to look at Theenie to know the woman was probably gnawing her bottom lip ninety-to-nothing.

Thirty minutes later, Annie led Wes to the second floor and into the master suite. The bronze and gilt furniture had been hand-carved along the lines of French provincial, only fancier—or ostentatious, as her mother had often remarked—adorned with hearts, curlicues, and rosettes. As in the dining room, the red walls and red velvet draperies were in keeping with the original decor. Annie had left the nineteen-inch color TV that her husband Charles had purchased for the room.

"What a shame," Wes said, looking at it.

Annie gave him a puzzled look.

He shrugged. "I don't think television sets belong in a husband and wife's bedroom, but that's just me." His gaze wandered to an overstuffed chair and ottoman near the fireplace.

"I converted all the fireplaces to gas," Annie said. "It's really nice falling asleep with a fire burning."

He turned to her. "Oh yeah?"

The look he gave her made her think of snuggling

between crisp sheets and thick blankets on a cold night, hair-roughened legs entwined with smooth ones, a warm fire painting shadows on the walls. Annie crossed her arms. It felt weird standing alone with Wes in the bedroom she'd shared with her husband for two years. "The bathroom is through that door," she said, nodding toward it.

Wes turned his attention to the lavishly carved mirror over the bed. "Nice," he said. "Did you decorate this room?"

"Oh no," she said quickly. "It was done by an ancestor. The family insisted on keeping the house as close to the original design and decor as they could. With the exception of the kitchen," she added. "The original kitchen was detached from the house, as kitchens were in most homes of that era. It burned."

"Your ancestors had unusual tastes."

"Yes."

"Where do you sleep?"

Annie tried not to let herself gaze too long into those liquid brown eyes. "Next door. And Theenie is just across the hall," she added, and then wondered why she'd felt it necessary to let him know they wouldn't be the only ones sleeping on that floor. "There are five bedrooms on the third floor, although some are small. My grandmother had an elevator installed once she began having trouble getting around, but it's slow and cantankerous." She couldn't help noticing the odd way he looked at her. Was he sizing her up? Trying to decide if she was really as crazy as he thought? She probably *was* crazy to even think of renting to him.

"I can't believe you moved out of here. Bad memories?"

He asked a lot of questions. "It just felt too big for one person."

He cocked his head to one side, studied her lazily.

"Your husband obviously wasn't a smart man. I can't imagine why he would cheat on you."

"It's quite possible he was a jerk," she said matter-of-factly.

"Well, you're still young. You'll meet your prince charming one day."

"I like my life just fine the way it is."

"Is that why you wear those big shirts? So guys won't notice you?"

He suddenly smiled, and Annie felt her toes curl. Jeez! "Yeah. I'm one of those women who have to dress down in order to keep the men at bay."

"You still look pretty damn good."

"I might have to resort to sackcloth."

He reached into his back pocket and pulled out his wallet. "You'll probably want references so the blue-haired lady doesn't jump ship the minute I move in." He fished through several business cards, handed one to Annie. "This guy will vouch for me."

"Was he your warden?"

"My banker." He gave her another card. "And this is my lawyer. I just pay him a flat fee to keep me out of the big house."

"That's always helpful. What kind of business are you in?"

"I'm a professional photographer."

She couldn't hide her surprise. It sounded so tame, and the man before her looked anything but. "How interesting. Maybe you'll show me some of your work."

"I don't think you'd approve."

Both brows arched high on her head. "Oh yeah? What kind of pictures do you take?"

"Mostly women."

"Um." She opened her mouth, closed it, and then opened it again. "Are they, uh, you know?"

"Some of them wear clothes."

Annie gulped.

"You'd make a perfect model." He reached for a stray lock of hair and twirled it around his finger. "The rich texture of your hair, slightly mussed, as though you just climbed from your bed after making love. The rosy flush I just brought to your cheeks by mentioning it."

Her scalp tingled at his touch, sending tiny ripples of pleasure down her back. Theenie was probably wondering what was taking them so long. "I don't think so," Annie said, thinking how much she sounded like Theenie. She stepped back and tucked her hair behind her ears.

"Doesn't matter. I've branched out. I like traveling to different parts of the country taking pictures of quaint little towns. 'Course, it's not as much fun as what I used to do, and it doesn't offer the fringe benefits." He winked.

Annie stared dumbly. "Do you have any questions about the room?"

"How soon can I move in?"

It was not yet nine o'clock the next morning when Annie called a meeting of sorts with Theenie and Destiny. "I've decided to go ahead and rent a room to Wes Bridges."

Destiny shrugged. "Hey, it's your house."

"Oh my," Theenie said. "Are you sure?"

"I know he looks, well—"

"He looks like one of those biker dudes," Theenie said.

"Just because he rides a Harley doesn't make him a biker," Annie said. "He's a photographer, and he has excellent references."

Destiny took a sip of her coffee. "A photographer, huh?"

Annie nodded. "He wants to take pictures of Beaumont. Because of its historic value," she added.

"What does he plan to do with the pictures?" Theenie asked.

"I don't know. Maybe he sells to travel magazines."

Annie noticed Destiny frowning. "What?"

"Something doesn't feel right."

Annie and Theenie exchanged glances.

"You think he might be lying?" Theenie said, gripping her coffee cup. "Do you sense we're in danger?"

Annie rolled her eyes. "Of course we're not in danger," she said, wishing Destiny would keep her concerns to herself instead of giving Theenie something else to worry about. "I wouldn't have rented to him unless I felt he was safe."

"He's not likely to kill us in our sleep or anything like that," Destiny said as though trying to reassure Theenie, which only caused the woman to start her lip-nibbling routine.

Annie felt the beginnings of a headache. "I've already told him he could have the room." She'd barely gotten the words out of her mouth when a door slammed upstairs. Annie and Theenie jumped.

"What in blazes was that?" Theenie said.

"It's just the wind," Annie said dismissively, refusing to meet Destiny's gaze.

"How can it be the wind when all the windows are closed?" Theenie asked. "I'm telling you, something isn't right in this house, and it seems to be getting worse. And now we've got a man moving in who could be a cold-blooded killer for all we know."

"He is *not* a killer," Annie said.

Theenie didn't look convinced. "You don't know that. You don't know that his references are valid. He could have paid somebody to lie for him. Killers do that sort of thing for each other. And remember, he even mentioned he was in prison. What if he wasn't joking? What if—"

"He's not dangerous," Annie interrupted, "and I don't think he's trying to hide anything. He told me stuff about himself that he didn't have to tell me."

"What stuff?" Destiny asked.

Annie gave a big sigh. "I wasn't going to mention it, but, well, he admitted that he used to take pictures of women. I sort of got the impression they weren't wearing much."

Theenie looked shocked. "You mean they were nude?"

Annie nodded.

"That's probably where they got that old saying: less is more," Destiny said.

"Oh my," Theenie said. "You know what that means."

Both Destiny and Annie looked at her questioningly.

"It means he probably wonders what we all look like naked."

Destiny chuckled. "Then he and I are even, because I've been wondering the same thing about him."

Annie didn't respond, but for some insane reason she wasn't crazy about the idea of Destiny thinking about Wes in the buff.

"Especially after seeing him in his underwear," Destiny added. She leaned closer to Theenie. "Why don't you enlighten us?"

Annie looked at Theenie, almost ashamed that she was as eager as Destiny for information.

Theenie blushed profusely. "I most certainly will not discuss such private matters. I was acting as a professional when I, um, undressed him, so it's not something I would have noticed."

"Oh, give me a break," Destiny said. "You may have a little age on you, but you're not blind."

"May we change the subject?" Theenie asked.

Annie nodded. "Good idea. I have more pressing matters. Has anyone seen Erdle? His car isn't in the driveway."

"I heard him go out last night," Theenie said. "Probably passed out somewhere. But if you think you're going to chase him with that rolling pin again, you're wrong. I hid it."

"I don't need a rolling pin," Annie said. "I've got my bare hands."

Annie stormed into the kitchen shortly before lunch, almost bumping into Theenie, who was watering houseplants. "Erdle is still not home," she said.

"That's it! I'm throwing him out the minute he shows up." Annie spied Danny Gilbert sitting at the kitchen table and blushed. "Oh, hi, Danny."

"Bad day?" he asked.

She shrugged. "I'm just irritated with Erdle, but that's nothing new."

"I hear you got problems with the house."

Annie glanced at Theenie.

"Well, Danny *is* a carpenter," the woman said. "I showed him the damage in the ballroom."

"You should have come to me sooner, Annie," he said. "I can take care of the floor. I even have my own sander."

"Oh, I couldn't possibly impose—"

"Don't be silly. Of course, this means you're going to have to go see that new western with me."

Annie moaned. "A western? I'd rather sit through *The Mummy* again than watch a western."

He grinned. "That's part of the deal, Anniekins. Take it or leave it."

Annie hated to ask for help, hated to put people to any trouble, but she was desperate. "Oh, all right," she said, pretending to be put out. "I suppose you'll expect me to spring for the popcorn, too."

The doorbell rang. "I'll get it," Theenie said. She hurried into the living room.

Danny was discussing what color stain he wanted to put on the floor when Theenie returned with Wes beside her. "Look who's here," she said, eyes darting about the room nervously. "He even brought his clothes."

Annie did not miss the fact that Theenie had her arms crossed as though Wes might somehow be able to see through her prim white cotton blouse. She also didn't miss Danny's raised brows. Not that she blamed him. Wes looked like the worst kind of ruffian standing there in his faded jeans, a black T-shirt, and his denim jacket. He carried a large backpack.

"You were expecting me, right?" he said.

It took a few seconds for Annie to find her tongue. "Yes, of course." She turned to Danny, who was still staring. "This is Wes Bridges," she said. "He's renting a room for a couple of weeks. Wes, this is my good friend Danny Gilbert."

Neither man made a move to shake hands. Finally, Danny nodded. "Nice to meet you."

"Same here," Wes said. He turned for the stairs and, without another word, hurried up.

Annie felt Danny's eyes on her even before she looked his way. His look was incredulous. "What?" she asked.

"You actually agreed to let that guy move in?" he whispered.

"I wasn't crazy about the idea myself," Theenie said. "Not that Annie bothered to ask my opinion, mind you, and I'm pretty sure he has a checkered past."

"It's only for two weeks," Annie said, wishing Danny wouldn't worry about her so much. Theenie said it was because he was sweet on her, even though Annie always insisted that Danny was only acting out of friendship. "Besides, he has excellent references."

"He's here to take pictures," Theenie said, giving a massive eye roll. "But I'm not going to expand on that topic in mixed company."

Danny's eyes softened. "Annie, if this is about money . . ."

She didn't miss the tender look, the genuine concern in his voice, and Annie was certain it didn't go unnoticed by Theenie. It was times like this that she wondered if the woman might be right about his feelings toward her. "You're beginning to fret as much as Theenie," she said lightly.

The front door opened and closed, followed by the sound of light footsteps. Annie looked up to find her other tenant, Lovelle Hamilton, standing in the doorway.

"I'm baaack," she announced with a flourish.

Annie smiled. "Welcome home." Lovelle was an exballerina who'd never made it big, although to hear her tell it, one would have thought otherwise. One of her claims to fame was having met Mikhail Baryshnikov at a cocktail party. She was string bean thin due to a daily dance regimen she practiced in Annie's ballroom.

"How was your trip?" Theenie asked.

"Fabulous. You know how much I love New York, having lived there most of my life. My daughter and I shopped at all the best stores, of course. I bought everybody gifts." She glanced about the room. "What's wrong? Why does everyone look so tense?"

"We have a new guest," Theenie said.

Lovelle smiled. Even at seventy-something, the woman was still striking, her makeup perfect and her platinum blond hair cut in the latest style. No blue rinse for Lovelle. "That's nice. I hope she's easy to get along with."

"It's a *he*," Theenie replied.

"Oh, goody. Is he handsome?"

All eyes fell on Annie.

"I suppose some women would consider him handsome in a rugged sort of way. I prefer a more conservative look." She punctuated her remark with what she hoped was a high-handed sniff, but the truth was she'd been thinking about Wes Bridges more than she should. Her thoughts had run amok the minute she caught sight of him in those boxer shorts.

The back door opened and Doc stepped inside. "I just stopped by to see if our patient fully recovered yesterday."

"What patient?" Danny asked.

Annie waved off the remark. "It's a long story." She turned to Doc. "He's fine. In fact, he just moved in."

"You let him move in?" Doc asked, his brow furrowing. "What about the lawsuit?"

"What lawsuit?" Danny asked. "Wait; let me guess. Another long story."

Annie nodded. "Something like that."

"Would you like a cup of coffee or iced tea?" Theenie asked Doc.

"No, I can't stay. I just learned my daughter in Tampa is having gallbladder surgery, so I'm flying down to help out with the grandkids, although they're old enough to do for themselves. Don't know how long I'll be gone."

"I hope the surgery goes well," Annie said. "Do you want me to grab your mail and newspapers while you're away?"

"The Martins already offered. It's less complicated for me to travel now that Leo is gone," he added sadly.

Annie nodded. Leo had been a stray dog eating from bags at the garbage dump when Doc had found him. Doc had brought him home, cleaned him up, and the two had lived in harmony for fifteen years before Leo died in his sleep of old age some eight or nine months ago. Annie had looked after the animal when Doc traveled; in turn, he had taken care of Peaches the few times Annie went away. "Well, you have my number," she said. "Call me if you think of something."

"Thank you." Doc started to leave and then turned. "Oh, I almost forgot. Do you need to borrow my gardener? I paid him for the whole day, but he finished up early. Man works hard and fast, unlike Erdle."

"Is he good with a tiller?" Theenie asked. "Annie wants the ground tilled behind the carriage house so she can plant a vegetable garden."

"He can do anything that pertains to yard work." Doc looked at Annie. "You want me to send him over?"

"I would love to borrow him," Annie said, delighted. Things were definitely beginning to look up. "Thank you, Doc, and have a safe trip."

He nodded and disappeared out the door.

Danny stood. "I need to run home and get my sander. Maybe by the time I get back I won't be so confused." He shook his head as he let himself out.

"I think Danny is jealous of Wes," Theenie said.

Annie arched one brow. "You're not serious."

"I've noticed the way he looks at you."

"No way," Annie said firmly. "Danny and I have known each other since we were kids. He's like a brother to me." They didn't look convinced.

Lovelle said, "You have to admit he comes around a lot."

Annie grabbed her jacket from a hook by the back door. "Have the two of you forgotten that I'm still legally married? Now, if you'll excuse me, I need to talk to Doc's gardener."

Wes unpacked the few clothes he'd brought with him. He opened the closet door to hang his jacket and found several men's suits pushed to one side. Annie obviously hadn't gotten rid of all her husband's clothes. He checked the pockets. Nothing. He moved to the window, pulled the curtain aside, and saw Annie talking to a man in denim overalls. Wes left his room and listened near the top of the stairs for a moment. The others seemed to be deep in conversation. Very quietly he made his way to the door next to his, opened it, and stepped inside.

The bedroom held Annie's scent, clean and fresh but not flowery or overbearing like some perfumes. Wes closed the door, taking care not to make a sound. The simple four-poster bed was covered with a bright quilt. Beside it, a night table held a telephone and several books. He checked the window again; Annie was still talking to the man. Wes turned and began to search the room.

Annie finished her conversation with Doc's gardener and started for the house. She heard the sound of Wes's motorcycle engine as she climbed the back steps and entered the kitchen. He obviously wasn't hanging around for lunch. She opened the refrigerator, pulled out several packages of luncheon meat and cheese and the potato and cheese soup she'd made two nights before that was popular with her tenants. She heard a noise in the dining room and decided to check it out. She pushed open the swinging door and found Theenie and Lovelle standing before an open drawer in the buffet. They jumped when they saw her.

"What are you two up to?" she asked.

Theenie looked flustered. "Oh, um, we thought we'd check the silver and see if it needs polishing."

"You polished it three days ago," Annie said.

"Yes, but we want to make sure it sparkles for the wedding."

Annie looked from one to the other. Lovelle glanced

away; Theenie began fidgeting. "You know I don't use my grandmother's silver for business functions. I have special flatware that I bought in bulk," she added, although she knew Theenie was perfectly aware of that fact. Annie noted a cardboard box on the table and looked inside. Her grandmother's serving pieces, each in its individual velvet pouch, had been placed inside. "Okay, what's *really* going on?"

"It wasn't my idea," Lovelle said.

Theenie's face reddened. "Now, Annie, I know you're not going to like this—"

"You're hiding the silver," Annie said in disbelief.

"I thought it best under the circumstances," Theenie whispered. "One can never be too careful."

"She thinks the new guest might steal it," Lovelle said.

Theenie shot her a dark look. "Traitor."

Annie crossed her arms over her chest. "Put it back."

Theenie hesitated. "If you say so, dear."

Annie was still shaking her head when the doorbell rang. She found Jamie and Max standing on the other side. "Well, hello," she said, delighted to see them.

"Hello to you, good-looking," Max said, dropping a kiss on her cheek. "If you get any prettier I'm going to have to change brides."

"See that?" Jamie said. "We're not even married yet, and he's already looking at other women."

Annie grinned at Max. She had liked him the minute they met. "He can't help himself. I'm hot stuff." She stepped back. "Come in."

"We just stopped by to drop off Destiny's mail for her column," Jamie said.

"You're in time for lunch. I'm about to heat up a big pot of my famous potato and cheese soup." She noted the sudden pained expression on Jamie's face. "Ooops, I forgot about the diet."

"I'm not on a diet," Max said, "and I love potato soup. Jamie can wait in the car with Fleas."

Jamie nudged him hard.

"You can't leave poor Fleas in the car," Annie protested.

Jamie chuckled. "He refused to get out and risk running into Peaches."

"I can put her out."

"Don't worry," Max said. "Muffin is singing Celine Dion songs to him."

Annie shook her head. Muffin was Max's talking computer, and she possessed the technology to do everything except bear children. In fact, she was more like a real-life assistant than a piece of machinery.

"I insist you stay for lunch," Annie told Jamie. "I'll make you a nice salad with fat-free dressing."

Jamie sighed. "I was afraid of that."

Destiny looked happy to see Jamie and Max. "Sit down," she said, pulling out the chair beside her, unaware that Peaches had already claimed it. The cat snarled and hissed. "Uh-oh, the cat from hell is using that chair. Perhaps you should choose another."

"I've never known Peaches to be in such a foul mood," Theenie said.

"It's because of the ghost," Destiny told her.

Max looked interested. "Ghost?"

Destiny nodded. "I'm surprised Jamie didn't mention it. You wouldn't believe what all goes on in this house." She leaned closer to Max and started to say something.

"What can I offer you to drink?" Annie interrupted before Destiny had a chance to regale Max with stories. Annie had no desire for Destiny to share with Max Holt all the craziness that went on in the house.

"I'm fine for now," Jamie said.

Max nodded. "I'm okay."

"It's like this," Destiny began.

"Are you sure?" Annie almost shouted, making them jump. "I have coffee, tea, orange juice, apple juice, diet root beer—"

They shook their heads and turned their attention back to Destiny.

". . . Two percent milk, soy. You know, I'll bet a glass of wine would be nice. I can—"

"Annie, what's wrong with you?" Jamie asked. "Why are you so jumpy?"

"It's the new tenant," Destiny said with a big grin. "You know, that half-naked guy you helped us stuff in the bathtub yesterday? He just moved in."

Max looked at Jamie. "Huh?"

Wes turned into the driveway of a modest ranch-style house, parked, and cut his engine. He removed his motorcycle helmet, climbed from the bike, and made his way toward the front door. The woman who opened it had hair the color of black shoe polish, wore a bright red caftan with matching lipstick and lime green bedroom slippers. A long, skinny cigarette dangled from her mouth.

"Wes Bridges?" she asked, talking around the cigarette. "I expected you yesterday." She had a three-pack-a-day smoker's voice; sounded like she'd been sucking on them since first grade.

"Life isn't always predictable, Mrs. Fortenberry. May I come in?"

"Yes." She stepped back and waited for him to enter before closing the door behind him. "You can call me Eve." She motioned to a lumpy chair that was the same avocado green as the dated shag carpet. Wes sat.

Garlic hung heavy in the air. Wes blinked and rubbed his eyes. The ash on Eve's cigarette was an inch long. He eyed it closely.

"I'm making spaghetti for a sick neighbor," Eve said. "Do you like garlic?"

"In reasonable doses."

"It cures all sorts of ailments, you know. May I offer you something to drink?" When Wes declined, she sat on the worn sofa across from him. She took a deep draw from her cigarette, and the ash grew longer. Finally, it fell unnoticed by her on her dress. "Now then," she said. "What have you got for me?"

"I've rented a room from your daughter-in-law."

She gave a dry hacking cough. "You work fast."

"I don't believe in wasting a client's time or money," he said.

"What do you think of Annie? Is she a kook or what? Her grandmother was a kook. Like they say, the apple doesn't fall far from the tree."

Wes looked thoughtful. "It's too soon to tell."

Puff, puff, cough. "And how 'bout that house? I ask you, have you *ever*?"

"Nope, never."

"You know it's an old bordello or, as my daddy would say, God rest his soul, whorehouse."

Wes arched both brows. "Oh yeah?"

"Before the Civil War. I read up on it a long time ago." She paused. "Did Annie mention my son?"

"I was told he left her for another woman."

"That's the cock-and-bull story she gave the police, and the reason they did such a piss-poor job of investigating. That Lamar Tevis, he's the police chief, is an idiot. He bought this fancy-schmancy deep-sea fishing boat three years ago. He's going to retire as soon as he pays it off and start a deep-sea fishing charter service. He's just biding his time until then."

"You don't believe your son left Annie?" Wes asked.

"Hell no. I wouldn't have hired you otherwise."

Wes glanced around the living room. "Perhaps we should go over my fees again."

"My check for your retainer cleared the bank, didn't it?" she said stiffly. When he nodded, she went on. "I can cover your expenses, Mr. Bridges. As I told you over the phone, my husband died three months ago. Fortunately, he had a sizable insurance policy, so I was *finally* able do something about my son's disappearance. I'll spend every dime of it if I have to in order to find out what really happened to Charles."

Wes gave her a kind smile. "Eve, your son's car was found at the Savannah airport. No luggage. He cleaned out the savings account he shared with his wife. He had enough money to fly anywhere in the world."

She looked embarrassed. "My son worked hard for that money. Do you have any idea how much it costs to keep up a place the size of Annie's? The electric bill alone would break me." She took a long drag from her cigarette. "There was no record of him getting on a plane, no paper trail, nothing. We've already been over that. The bottom line is Charles would never have stayed gone this long without contacting me. No matter what the circumstances," she added. "I spent twice the going rate to hire you because you're supposed to be the best in the business. I want my son found."

Annie and Theenie were in the process of cleaning up after lunch when Danny Gilbert arrived back with his sander. Annie insisted that he eat something before going to work. As he waited for Annie to prepare him a sandwich and heat a bowl of soup, Lovelle recounted her days as a professional ballerina.

At the other end of the table, Destiny, Jamie, and Max discussed newspaper business and chuckled over a couple of letters that had been addressed to the Divine Love Goddess Adviser.

"Some people are so loopy," Destiny said. "Listen to this one: 'Dear Love Goddess Adviser. Some months ago I discovered my husband was a cross-dresser. After the shock had passed, I decided to make the best of it, and now we share our clothes. What has me so frustrated is the fact that he doesn't *ask* if he can borrow my clothes; he just grabs what he needs out of my closet. When he returns an outfit I often find food stains on it, but he never offers to take anything to the dry cleaners. I have complained, but he doesn't listen. Could you please settle this dispute? I fear our marriage may be in deep trouble unless we can work this out.'"

Max and Jamie laughed.

"Oh, and listen to this one," Destiny said. "'Dear Love Goddess Adviser: I am probably overreacting, but I suspect my husband is cheating on me. He doesn't return home some nights until almost midnight, and he reeks of Chanel Number Five. I have found lipstick on his shirt collar, long scratches on his back, and the other night when he undressed, his underwear was on backward. Do you think I'm just being one of those suspicious wives?'"

Jamie laughed until her sides hurt as Destiny continued to read several more. Annie was happy to see her friend looking more relaxed, and the private smiles Jamie and Max shared when they thought nobody was looking would have made most women envious.

Danny finished his lunch and carried his dishes to the sink, where he rinsed them. Wes entered the kitchen, a camera hanging from his neck. All eyes turned to him, and the chatter stopped. "You must be the other new guest," Lovelle said, and introduced herself. She had met Destiny earlier.

"Nice to meet you," he said politely.

Max stood and made introductions as well. If Wes recognized Jamie, he didn't say anything. "Nice camera," Max said. "Are you a photographer?"

Wes nodded. "I've been able to get some great shots this morning. Beaumont is a beautiful town."

"It grows on you fast," Max said.

"Wes, would you care for a sandwich?" Annie asked, wishing just once she could round up everybody at the same time for meals. Seemed like she was always offering somebody something to eat; felt like she was working at the Huddle House.

"I grabbed something earlier," he said. "Nice to meet you," he told Max and Jamie as he headed upstairs, stepping aside for Theenie, who was on her way down.

"Good grief!" Lovelle said when Wes was out of hearing distance. "Where did you find *him*?"

"He sort of found us," Annie said.

"Annie almost killed him," Theenie said. "Then Doc almost killed him."

"Perhaps I should explain," Annie said. She had opened her mouth to do just that when she heard a man's voice out back shouting her name. He sounded frantic. "What in the world!" She threw open the back door and found Doc's gardener racing across the backyard, calling out to her loudly.

Footsteps sounded on the stairs and Wes hurried into the kitchen. "What's going on? Is somebody hurt?"

Annie was already on the back porch, the others behind her. The gardener stopped at the back stairs, staggered once, grabbed the porch rail. His face was ashen. He tried to speak.

Annie hurried down and touched his arm. "What's wrong?" she said. "Are you injured?" She looked for blood, didn't see any.

"It's terrible," the man managed. "Worst thing I ever seen."

"What is it?" she demanded.

"Back yonder. Behind the, um, that carriage house."

Wes pushed through the group and cleared the back steps in one jump. He was the first to arrive at the gaping hole, with Max and Danny right behind him. Wes knelt beside it, and his eyes froze at what he saw. "Holy shit!"

Max joined him. "Holy shit is right."

Wes looked at Danny. "Keep the women back."

Danny turned. "Don't come any closer, okay?" he told them.

Theenie and Lovelle came to an abrupt halt, but the others rushed forward.

"What is it?" Annie said.

Jamie blinked several times, trying to make sense of what she was looking at. "Bones?" she asked.

"It's a skeleton," Max said.

Annie gave an eye roll. "Oh, jeez, it's my grandmother's dog. She had Erdle bury him somewhere back here after he died. I'd forgotten about it."

Wes shook his head. "Sorry, Annie, but this is no dog. It's a human skeleton."

"Oh, I can't see this," Theenie said, backing away. She turned and hurried toward the house. Lovelle followed.

Annie stared back at Wes in disbelief. "That's ridiculous!"

"He's right, Annie," Max said.

"It looks human to me, too," Jamie said, and Destiny agreed.

Annie stepped closer and looked. "Oh, shit, I have a dead person in my backyard! Oh, shit. Oh, shit."

"There's some kind of cloth there," Max said.

Wes nodded and glanced over his shoulder. "Look, this is obviously a crime scene, and I'd rather not jeopardize any trace evidence." He didn't see the look Max gave him. "So I'd appreciate it if everybody would please move back."

Danny convinced the women to step away.

"It's not like I've never seen dead people before," Destiny told him. "They follow me everywhere I go."

Max and Wes were quiet as they studied the site. "Looks like the cloth was yellow at some point," Max said, "although it's hard to tell."

"There's some kind of insignia on the material," Wes said.

Max grabbed a stick. "Only one way to find out."

Destiny stood there, a knowing look in her eyes.

"Be careful," Wes whispered. "There could be hairs or fibers."

"You sound like you know what you're talking about," Max said, very gently lifting a portion of the material.

"I watch a lot of TV. Enough to know we shouldn't be doing this. Okay, hold it right there, and I'll see if I can read it." Taking great care not to disturb anything, Wes leaned forward. "Looks like a *C* and an *F*."

"Have you found anything?" Jamie called out.

"Some kind of yellow material," Max said. "Could be a shirt or a jacket. Initials *CF* on it."

Annie and Jamie looked at each other, their eyes wide and disbelieving. "No!" Annie said. "That's impossible!" She shook her head. "It can't be. It just can't be."

"Annie . . ." Jamie stepped closer, reached out.

"No!" Annie cried, and pushed her away.

"What the hell?" Wes leaped to his feet and raced toward Annie as she screamed. He shook her hard. "Annie, what is it?"

She opened her mouth, tried to speak, couldn't. Her eyes were glazed.

Wes looked confused.

Jamie looked at him. "It's a jacket. I was with Annie

when she purchased it. *CF* stands for *Charles Fortenberry.*"

"My husband," Annie choked. Her eyes rolled back in her head before everything went black.

Wes was there to catch her.

Chapter
FOUR

Police Chief Lamar Tevis studied the shallow grave closely, turning his head this way and that as if to get a better look, as one officer snapped pictures and another surrounded the area with yellow crime scene tape. Finally, Lamar stood and brushed the dirt from the knees of his khaki uniform. "It's a body, all right," he said. "I'm not an expert on this sort of thing, so I can't tell how long it has been there. Takes one of those forensic whatchamacallits for that. They may have someone at the Medical University in Charleston, but there's no telling how long it'll take them to get around to it."

Wes, who'd already introduced himself, shook his head. "I don't think you'll need a forensic anthropologist," he said, earning raised eyebrows from Lamar. "At least for the time being," he added. "Mrs. Fortenberry is certain the body is that of her husband."

Lamar glanced at Max as if seeking verification. Max told him about the jacket and initials. "Jamie was present when Annie purchased it."

Danny Gilbert crossed the yard and joined the men. "Afternoon, Lamar," he said. They shook hands.

"What are you up to these days?" Lamar asked. "Done any fishing lately?"

Danny shook his head. "Work has been keeping me busy. I'm sanding Annie Fortenberry's wood floors today."

Lamar frowned. "Uh-oh. That sounds pretty suspicious if you ask me."

"Why is that?" Wes asked.

"A woman finds a body in her backyard and claims it's her missing husband, and all she can think of is having her floors sanded?" Lamar reached into his shirt pocket and pulled out a small notebook. "I'd better write that down. Might prove helpful in the investigation."

Max and Wes exchanged looks. There was a hint of a smile on Max's lips.

"Actually, Annie is taking it pretty hard," Danny said. "She's lying down."

"I've known Annie since she was a bookkeeper at Bates's Furniture," Lamar said. "I bought several rooms of furniture there. Used to go in once a month to pay on my bill. You know Herman Bates sells good-quality furniture at reasonable prices, and he offers discounts if you buy multiple rooms."

"So what do you think?" Max asked, nodding toward the grave.

"Well, I questioned Annie when Mr. Fortenberry first turned up missing and his mother started making all kinds of wild accusations. I'll tell you, that Eve is a piece of work. But I saw no reason to suspect foul play. 'Course this changes everything. By the way, who found the body?"

"Doc Holden's gardener." Wes pointed to the man, who was sitting on a tree stump, shaking his head and muttering to himself.

"Who's he talking to?" Lamar whispered.

"He's still pretty upset," Max said.

Lamar motioned for the officer who'd finished taking pictures. "I need for you to question that fellow over there," he said, nodding toward the gardener. "And go easy on him; he looks just shy of a straitjacket."

A car pulled into the driveway. Editor Mike Henderson from the *Gazette* hurried toward them, accompanied by Vera Bankhead, Jamie's secretary and assistant editor. She held a camera.

"Oh, cripes," Lamar said. "Just what I need. Let me do all the talking."

"We heard the news on the police scanner," Mike said. "Somebody found a body in Annie Fortenberry's backyard," he added. "What can you tell us?"

Despite the grave expression he wore, it was hard for most people to take Mike seriously, not only because he was young and still had that fresh-out-of-college look, but also because he was so noticeably unorganized. He seldom ironed his shirts, and scraps of paper fluttered from his pockets when he reached for his stash of pens, which often leaked and had stained most of his clothes. He was known to chase women, and he'd had his eye on Destiny Moultrie for months. Jamie often claimed she was trying to raise him to be a *real* editor.

"No comment," Lamar said.

Mike just stared back as if unsure what to do.

Sixty-year-old Vera Bankhead planted her hands on her hips. She looked younger than her age thanks to a complete makeover the year before, which included a Susan Sarandon hairstyle, and a new wardrobe that had put Vera on the top ten best-dressed list for the women at Mount Zion Baptist Church. The fact that Vera never missed a Sunday and could quote Scripture word-for-word did not deter her when it came to getting what she wanted. She could be quite formidable.

"Cut the bull, Lamar," she said. "It's our job to report the news. You know how hard it is to come up with a decent headline in this town."

"Are you armed?" Lamar asked.

"Not at the moment."

Lamar looked relieved. "All I can say right now is yes, we do have a body, but we don't know anything yet."

"Do you suspect foul play?" Mike asked.

Vera looked at him. "That has to be the dumbest question I've ever heard. *Of course* there was foul play. Dead people don't bury themselves."

Mike's face turned a bright red.

Vera looked at Lamar. "Do you have a suspect?"

"If I did I certainly wouldn't spill my guts to the newspaper."

Vera gave a menacing frown. "Are you smart-mouthing me? Because if you are, I'll tell your mama and she'll slap you from here to Texas. She didn't raise you to talk back to your elders."

This time when Wes looked at Max he was having just as much difficulty keeping a straight face.

Lamar glanced their way. As if sensing their amusement, he hitched his chin high and squared his shoulders. "This is police business, Vera," he said, "and I'd appreciate it if you'd keep my mama out of it." He gave them a stern look. "And I don't want either of you going near the crime scene, you hear? The medical examiner will raise holy hell if he gets here and finds anything disturbed."

Vera tapped her foot impatiently. "How am I supposed to get a picture?"

Lamar pondered it. "Tell you what. You can take a picture of me *pointing* to the crime scene."

Vera sighed and shook her head. "It's shameful what you'll do to get your picture in the paper, but I guess that'll have to do for now." She raised the camera to her eyes and focused.

Lamar threw back his shoulders, sucked in his paunch, and gave a big smile, one arm outstretched, his index finger pointing to a small mound of dirt beside the open grave.

Vera lowered her camera. "What do you think you're doing? I'm not taking this picture for your high school yearbook. You need to look serious."

"Oh yeah." Lamar frowned at the camera and waited for Vera to snap his picture. "Now, if you will excuse me," he said, "I have work to do." He glanced at one of his deputies. "Nobody goes near the scene," Lamar said, cutting his eyes at Vera. The officer nodded and crossed his arms over his chest as Lamar headed toward the house.

Vera pursed her lips and looked at Mike. "If I weren't a good Southern Baptist I'd give Lamar Tevis the finger."

Annie blew her nose again and tossed the tissue into the wastebasket beside her bed. Jamie and Theenie sat on either side; Destiny and Lovelle stood at the foot. "I feel so guilty," Annie said. "All this time I've been telling people Charles left me for another woman. I never once suspected he was dead."

"Don't feel guilty, sweetie," Theenie said. "Charles probably would have left you anyway had he lived."

There was a knock at the door. Lovelle opened it. Lamar walked into the room. His gaze immediately fell on Jamie. "Your, um, editors are outside looking at the crime scene. I'd appreciate it if you'd make sure they don't mess with anything. You know how ornery Vera can be."

"Mike and Vera are professionals," Jamie said, although she knew Vera would stop at nothing to get a story, even if it meant breaking the law. And since she intimidated Mike, he would pretty much follow along. Jamie looked at Annie. "I'd like to touch base with them before they head back to the office. Will you be okay?"

Annie nodded.

Lamar waited until Jamie was gone. "Mrs. Fortenberry, I was hoping I could ask you a few questions if you think you're up to it."

"There's no need to be formal, Lamar," Annie said, offering him the closest thing she had to a smile. "Is it okay if my friends stay?"

"Whatever makes you comfortable."

"Why don't you grab that chair?" she said.

"Thanks." He picked up the ladder-back chair and placed it closer to the bed. "Okay then," he said before pulling out his notepad once more. "I understand you have reason to believe the body out back is your husband's."

"I'm positive."

Lamar looked regretful. "Well then, let me offer my sincere condolences. I know this can't be easy for you." He paused a moment. "I'm thinking maybe we could go over what happened the day Mr. Fortenberry disappeared if you don't mind."

"I don't know what more I can tell you," she said. "We covered everything when my mother-in-law filed a missing person's report on Charles three years ago."

"Sometimes people think of things later that might help," Lamar said. "I haven't had a chance to look at the file, and I want to make sure I have everything. Could you tell me again when you saw him last?"

Annie gave Lamar the exact date. "It was around six AM," she said. "Our conversation was brief because I was getting ready to drive to my mother's house in Atlanta. She'd been sick with the flu, and it turned into pneumonia. I was with her for a week."

"Did your husband appear to act differently in any way? Like maybe he was worried about something?"

"Not that I remember, but then, I was really concerned about my mom at the time, so I wasn't paying close attention."

Lamar nodded as he took notes. "Do you know of anyone who disliked your husband enough to kill him?"

A tear slid down Annie's cheek as she shook her

head. "I don't know *anyone* who would actually commit murder."

"In most cases, the killer knows the victim." Lamar paused. "I think I need to be up-front with you, Annie. The spouse is usually the first person we look at."

Annie couldn't believe what she was hearing. "Are you saying I'm a suspect?"

"Hold it right there, Lamar!" Destiny said, stepping closer, her jeweled hand on one out-thrust hip. "I happen to know a little about the law, and if you're charging Annie with murder . . ." She paused and looked at Annie. "You need to keep your mouth shut and call an attorney."

"I'm not charging Annie with *anything*," Lamar said defensively, his eyes flitting to Destiny's low-cut blouse, "but if it comes to that, I'll certainly notify her of her rights. I happen to know a little bit about the law myself."

"I'll answer your questions," Annie said. "Only I'd appreciate it if you'd take down that crime scene tape as soon as you possibly can. I'm having a big wedding here."

"Uh-oh." Lamar arched one brow and started to make a notation in his book. "That's going to look bad for you."

"It's not *my* wedding!" Annie said, wondering how Lamar could be so dense at times. She saw Destiny shake her head.

"Annie doesn't even like men," Theenie said. "She almost killed the last one who showed up at her door."

"Uh-oh," Lamar said.

"It was an accident," Annie said, giving Theenie a would-you-kindly-shut-your-mouth? look. Theenie offered a sheepish smile. Annie explained what had happened the morning of Wes's arrival. "Now the whole world knows," she said.

Lamar looked thoughtful. "I know about Erdle's drinking," he said. "Have you ever seen him get violent?"

Annie shook her head. "Never. Besides, he wasn't here at the time. An old army buddy from Mississippi rented a condo in Hilton Head that week and invited Erdle to join him. The guy even wrote out an affidavit on Erdle's behalf."

"Was anyone else in the house? Any guests?" Lamar added.

"All this happened before I turned the place into a bed-and-breakfast. Doc checked on Peaches several times while I was away, made sure she had plenty of food and water. I knew Charles wouldn't bother; he hated that cat. But Doc said he didn't bother stopping over until the day after I left because he knew I always put out extra."

"Yes, I questioned Doc at the time," Lamar said. "He claimed he didn't see anything out of the ordinary. He's so senile; if he *had* seen anything, I don't think he would remember."

Annie nodded. "His memory comes and goes, but he's ninety years old, so I'm not surprised. Now, about that crime scene tape."

Lamar looked apologetic. "I can't take it down till we're done. My men will be going over the area during the next couple of days, sifting through dirt looking for evidence. I can't have folks traipsing about, disturbing the crime scene."

"Come on, Lamar, cut me some slack here. It's going to be bad for business."

"I'll see what I can do," he mumbled, although he seemed more concerned with finishing up. "I only have a couple more questions. I'll probably find the answers in Mr. Fortenberry's file, but I want to make sure I have the name of his dentist, and if he had any broken bones that would prove without a doubt that the, um, remains are his."

"He saw Dr. Hensley. As for broken bones, I know he fractured his left wrist in high school playing football."

"I assume we'll find a wallet on him, unless he was robbed, of course. Did he carry a lot of cash on him?"

"I don't know."

"Any jewelry? A watch or wedding ring?"

"He claimed he couldn't wear his wedding ring because it caused his finger to swell," she said. Lamar didn't see her roll her eyes at the others as he jotted the information on his notepad. "He wore a Seiko watch with a gold band that I bought for his birthday, but I don't remember what kind of wallet he carried."

"Anything engraved on the watch?"

"No."

"Anything else you can think of that might help?"

"The yellow jacket with his initials, of course."

"This is a good start," Lamar said, closing his notepad. "If you think of something else, give me a call."

"Do you know how long they'll keep him?"

"I can't say for sure, since it's a murder case." Lamar stood and put the chair back in its place. He continued to stand there for a moment as though he had something on his mind. "Do you have plans to travel anytime soon?"

"Are you telling her not to leave town?" Destiny asked. She didn't wait for his reply. "See, Annie, I told you to hire a lawyer."

"I can't afford a lawyer," Annie said.

Lamar tossed Destiny a dark look. "I never said she couldn't leave town." He looked at Annie. "You haven't been charged with anything; I just wanted to know if you'd be around in case I need to ask you some more questions. And don't worry about the cost of a lawyer.

If it comes to that and you can't afford representation, the court will appoint someone."

Annie felt a sense of dread wash over her. She tried to keep the sarcasm from her voice. "Well, that certainly eases my mind."

Wes knocked on Annie's door an hour later. When he didn't get an answer, he opened the door quietly and peeked in. She was alone, lying in bed, staring at the ceiling. "Is it okay if I come in?" he asked.

"Sure."

He approached the bed. "I thought I should tell you, they've taken the body away."

"Thank God."

"I'm sorry, Annie. I know this can't be easy."

She nodded. "Charles was only thirty years old at the time of his death. I may not have liked him very much, but I never wanted him dead." She suddenly gasped. "Oh, I forgot. Somebody is going to have to break the news to his mother. I don't want her to find out on the six o'clock news."

"I'll make sure it's taken care of," Wes said. "You've got enough on your mind right now."

"Lamar said they always look at the spouse first, which means I'm the main suspect."

"Don't take it personally; it's normal procedure."

"How do you know that?"

He shrugged. "That's always been the case."

"Do you think I killed him?"

"No."

"How can you be so sure?"

"I can't see you killing *anyone,* much less dragging a body across the backyard and burying it." He smiled as if to ease the tension. "You're a bit of a runt."

"I'm stronger than I look."

"Remind me not to arm wrestle you. I'd hate to lose to a girl, especially a half pint like you."

Annie knew he was teasing her in hopes of cheering her up. "My mother-in-law thinks I'm responsible for his disappearance. She'll probably hound Lamar to arrest me."

"Did the two of you get along?"

"Not because I didn't try. But I think she was jealous. If Charles didn't call her every day she'd pout. Later, she became as resentful as Charles when I refused to sell this place."

The door squeaked. Annie looked up and found Danny peeking in. He glanced at Wes, then back at Annie. "How're you doing, sport?"

She smiled. "I'm hanging in there."

Wes seemed to take that as his cue to leave. "If there's anything I can do, please let me know."

"Thank you."

Danny stepped aside so Wes could exit. Annie swung her legs over the side of the bed. "I need to get up and start dinner."

"Don't worry about it. I've already placed an order for several large pizzas. They'll arrive by suppertime."

Annie couldn't hide her relief. "What would I do without you?"

"That's what I keep telling you. Now wash your face and come downstairs. Everybody is worried about you."

"What's wrong with my face?"

"Your eyes are swollen, and you've got black gunk under them. Matter of fact, you look like hell."

Annie winced. Lord, Wes Bridges had seen her looking that way and hadn't mentioned it. "Gee, thanks," she muttered.

"At least I'm honest."

Annie nodded. That much was true. Danny had been

the only friend to tell her the truth when she'd first suspected Charles of cheating. Most people didn't want to become involved in a couple's marital problems, but Danny felt as though she should know. "I'll be down in a few minutes," she said.

He started to leave and then turned. "Annie, I don't like to interfere in your business, but . . ." He paused. When she looked up in question, he went on. "It's Wes. I don't completely trust him. Be careful, okay?"

The light was fading when Wes parked his motorcycle in front of Eve Fortenberry's. She met him at the door wearing a frumpy dress, bedroom slippers, and holding a cigarette. She took one look at his face and stepped back as though she knew something terrible was coming. "What is it?"

"We've found your son."

"And?" Her eyes were cold and hard, daring him to give her bad news.

"Eve, I'm sorry."

Her face crumpled. "No," she said, shaking her head. She covered her mouth. Wes stepped inside and closed the door behind him.

Erdle arrived home the following morning. Annie stepped outside the minute his car pulled into the driveway. "I need to talk to you."

"You're throwing me out."

She thought he sounded surprisingly sober. "Not at the moment. Something bad has happened." She gave him the news, then said, "Lamar Tevis suspects me."

Erdle sighed. "Then I'm probably on the list, too," he said. "Everybody knows I wouldn't have given two cents for him."

"You weren't even here at the time. You have an airtight alibi."

"I forgot. Damn, it seems like it all happened about ten years ago. But you had an alibi, too. You were in Atlanta with your mother, remember?"

Annie didn't respond.

"This place is very strange," Destiny announced two days later as she joined Annie, Theenie, and Lovelle in the kitchen.

"You got that right," Lovelle said. "There aren't many places where you can find a dead body in your back-yard."

"Must we discuss this at breakfast?" Theenie asked. "And in front of Annie to boot?"

"I'm okay," Annie said, staring into her coffee cup. But she didn't look okay. Dark circles made half moons beneath her eyes, and she'd barely eaten since Charles's remains had been discovered. "I guess everybody in town knows by now," she said, nodding toward the folded newspaper beside her cup, where the morning headlines had drawn attention to the discovery. Jamie had called to apologize in advance, but Annie didn't blame her for printing it; reporting the news was Jamie's job.

Annie shoved the thought from her mind and looked at Destiny. "What's the problem?"

"Some of my lingerie is missing."

"Oh boy," Theenie said.

"I'm not accusing any of you," Destiny said hurriedly. "I already know who took them."

"Oh boy," Theenie repeated.

"Would you please stop saying that?" Lovelle insisted. "You sound like a broken record." She leaned closer to Destiny. "Who do you think took your things?"

"The spirit, to get my attention. That's the way it is with dead people."

Annie noted the fear in Theenie's eyes. "I'm sure there's a perfectly reasonable explanation," she said.

Destiny studied Annie closely. "You're in denial. This place is haunted, and the ghost has latched on to me, and you just don't want to hear about it."

Lovelle leaned closer to Destiny. "We don't really talk about it."

"Oh, I get it," Destiny said to Annie. "You're afraid it will hurt business, so you try to sweep it under the rug. There are other things about the house you're not proud of as well. Do you think people don't already know? Or *feel* it? The air is thick with . . ." She paused. "It's like a sexual undertow."

Three pairs of eyes looked at her, but nobody said anything.

"I know damn good and well I'm not the only one who feels it," Destiny said.

Lovelle leaned closer. "I've never told anybody this, but since I moved into this house I have had a lot of sexy dreams."

Theenie gnawed her bottom lip. "Well, I'll have to admit I've dreamed about Clark Gable a lot."

"Was he naked?" Lovelle asked.

"Absolutely not! Mr. Gable is a gentleman. All we've done is share a few kisses."

Annie was thoughtful as she took a sip of her coffee. She wasn't about to admit that her sex drive was in overdrive. And she'd certainly had her share of illicit dreams. She looked up and found the others watching her. She shrugged. "I hate to disillusion you guys, but I'm so tired by the time I drag myself to bed that it's all I can do to brush my teeth before climbing in."

Destiny merely gave Annie a smile that told her she knew better.

"I'm sorry your things are missing," Annie told her, "but I'm sure they'll turn up." She gave a weary sigh.

"Annie, honey, what's wrong?" Theenie said. "I can always tell when something is bothering you."

"I'm just annoyed, that's all. Two guys from the local TV station knocked on my door this morning and shoved a microphone in my face while I was still in my bathrobe."

"And you weren't wearing makeup, I'll bet," Destiny said.

Annie shook her head. "And yesterday I caught a couple of women sneaking around the backyard, no doubt looking for the grave, and the traffic has suddenly picked up because people want to see the woman who supposedly murdered her husband and buried his body in the backyard."

Theenie reached over and covered Annie's hand. "I shouldn't have hidden your rolling pin."

"On top of that, I got a call late last night from a member of the Red Hat Society. She canceled today's luncheon."

"But you've already prepared most of the food," Lovelle said.

"I can freeze some of it," Annie said.

"Did she say *why* she was canceling?" Theenie asked.

"She didn't have to. I knew this was going to happen. It's bad enough people have to read about it in the newspaper and see it on the news; that idiot Lamar still has crime scene tape stretched from one end of the neighborhood to the other. I don't blame them for canceling."

"I'm sorry I complained," Destiny said. "I didn't get much sleep last night, and I get grumpy when I'm tired." She gave a laugh. "It's not like I don't have a ton of lingerie."

Theenie suddenly brightened. "You don't have to freeze the food, Annie. You can use it tomorrow evening for the Ladies Night Out group."

Annie gave a rueful smile. "They won't be coming, either." Only she hadn't found out until after she'd spent more than one hundred dollars on two large standing rib roasts, not to mention all the other items she'd purchased. She noted the concern on the women's faces and felt guilty for burdening them with her problems. "It's okay," she said. "I'm sure this is temporary." They didn't look any more convinced than she was.

Footsteps sounded on the stairs and Wes entered the kitchen. His hair was still wet from his shower, but he hadn't bothered to shave. He looked from one woman to the other. "What's wrong?"

Theenie didn't hesitate. "Somebody is stealing Destiny's underwear, and Annie has had two cancellations." She covered her mouth and shot an apologetic look at Destiny. "I'm sorry I brought up your unmentionables. Sometimes things just pop right out of my mouth before I think."

Destiny shrugged, propped her elbows on the table, and leaned forward slightly, the cameo attached to her gold necklace sinking between her breasts. "It's okay," Destiny told Theenie. "I'm not easily embarrassed."

Wes turned to Annie. "Who canceled what?"

"It's not important," Annie said. The absolute last thing she wanted to do was tell Wes her problems.

Theenie suddenly brightened. "There's still the baby shower on Saturday."

Annie smiled and nodded. She wasn't one to let things drag her down for long. "You're right. You and Lovelle need to start thinking about the decorations." Annie knew both women got a kick out of sifting through her large cardboard boxes where she kept all sorts of decorations neatly packed and labeled; they would choose just the right items and spend hours putting them up.

Wes turned his attention back to Destiny. "You're missing lingerie?" he asked. "There's a bunch of, uh, female stuff hanging over the shower rod in my bathroom. I was wondering what they were doing there."

"See, I told you they'd show up," Annie said.

"Yes, but I didn't put them there," Destiny replied. "The ghost did it."

Wes looked at her. "What ghost?"

A sudden clatter overhead made them jump. Peaches, napping in a pool of sunlight at the window, leaped to her feet, arched her back, and hissed.

"That one," Destiny said.

Annie chuckled and waved it off. "It's just the wind."

"That's what she always says," Theenie told Wes.

"Destiny is pulling your leg about the ghost," Annie went on. "We obviously have a prankster in the house, don't we, ladies?" Even as she said it she felt a brush of cool air on the back of her neck, making her hair stand on end and sending shivers down her spine.

Dusk had settled in as Destiny stepped over the crime scene tape surrounding the still-gaping hole. The deputies had worked for two days, combing the area for evidence, before deciding they'd probably found all there was. Yet the garish yellow tape remained. Standing before the grave, Destiny closed her eyes and remained perfectly still. A cold wind whipped through the branches of the tall oaks, rustling the leaves and causing the gray moss to wave and shudder. Finally, Destiny knelt beside the hole and ran her fingers through the black dirt that would have made a perfect vegetable garden had Charles Fortenberry not been found buried there. Destiny let the dirt sift through her fingers.

"What are you doing?" a male voice asked.

Destiny turned and found a baffled-looking Erdle standing there. "You wouldn't understand."

"Nobody's supposed to go on that side of the tape."

"You plan on turning me in?" She sounded indifferent.

"You could be destroying evidence."

Destiny laughed. "If those local yokels haven't found anything by now, they're not going to."

"What makes you think you will?"

"Because my methods are different."

Erdle cocked his head to the side, studying her closely. "Chief Tevis says you're as crazy as a bedbug."

"That's because I always steal his thunder each time he hits a dead end and is forced to call on me. And because I won't sleep with him. Imagine that."

"So, were you able to get any messages from the *beyond*?" Erdle asked in such a way that made it obvious he didn't believe in her abilities.

She shook her head. "Too many people have been over it, which lessens my chances of picking up on anything. Lamar should have let me have at it first." She regarded Erdle. "You got any idea who might have killed Charles Fortenberry?"

"If I did know I wouldn't tell. Way I see it, he got exactly what he deserved."

Chapter
FIVE

It was late when Wes stepped out onto the piazza, slipping into his denim jacket to ward off the night chill. Moonlight peeked through the overhead branches, offering just enough light that he could make out the silhouette of someone sitting on the wicker swing. "Annie?"

"I couldn't sleep." She huddled deeper into her terry-cloth bathrobe and pulled the afghan around her shoulders.

"Me, neither." Wes crossed the piazza. "May I join you?"

Annie scooted to one side, and he sat down. "Would you like for me to make you a cup of hot chocolate?" she asked. "It sometimes helps me fall asleep."

"Aren't you off duty?"

She was able to make out his rugged face in the moonlight, the certain way he held his head that gave him an air of confidence. She liked that about him. That and the probing, alert eyes that not only convinced her of his intelligence but also made her feel he was always on top of things. "I like to see to the comfort of my guests," she said.

"Oh yeah?"

She didn't have to look at him to know he was smiling. "There are limits, of course," she said, unable to resist smiling back at him.

"I don't think I've seen you relax more than ten minutes since I moved in. You're always moving."

"There's a lot involved in running this place."

"So what do you do for fun?"

"Sometimes Danny and I see a movie."

"Is he your boyfriend?"

"Danny?" Annie chuckled. "No, we're just friends. I've known him for years."

"He seems protective of you."

"Yes." She wouldn't tell him that Danny sometimes carried it to extremes, that he often offered more advice than she needed. "He was there for me when my marriage hit the skids. I don't know what I would have done without his support."

"Maybe he'd *like* to be your boyfriend," Wes said.

Annie caught the teasing lilt in his voice. She laughed. "Danny would be the first to tell you I'm not looking for a boyfriend."

Wes nodded thoughtfully. "So why'd you marry this Charles in the first place? Sorry to say it, but he sounds like he was a jerk."

Annie looked at him. "You ask a lot of questions; you know that?"

"I've always been curious. You can tell me to mind my own business."

She shrugged. "Charles could be charming when he wanted, which is why he did so well in real estate." She wouldn't tell Wes how lonely and vulnerable she'd been when she met Charles, shortly after her grandmother's death. She wouldn't mention her dreams of a big family, how she'd yearned for it growing up. Those things she kept close to her heart. "It just didn't work out," she finally said, knowing she sounded like it had been no big deal when it really *had* been a big deal.

"You weren't married long."

"Two years."

"You got any idea who could have killed him?"

"No. And Lamar Tevis probably won't look too hard, since he thinks I did it. I guess he suspects the truth: that inside I'm a dangerous, cold-blooded killer."

"He's probably seen you with your rolling pin." Wes slid his arm along the back of the swing, reached for a thick strand of her hair, and rubbed it between his fingers as though testing its texture. "I think you're dangerous."

"Oh yeah?"

"Those big green eyes of yours, those cute freckles. A deadly combination, if you ask me."

"Makes it easier to snare my victims," she said lightly, although she was uncomfortable with his fingers in her hair, stroking downward, his knuckles grazing the back of her neck. She shifted on the swing. "Um, Wes?"

"You don't like that?" He pulled his hand away.

On the contrary, she liked it too much. But she had no business sitting in the dark with him and letting him touch her in a way that made her think of what it had felt like lying against him. The swing moved, and when she looked up, she found he'd slipped closer. She could feel the heat from his body. A light breeze ruffled his hair. His brown eyes looked black.

"I have to go in," she said. She gathered the afghan more tightly around her shoulders and made to get up.

"That's too bad," he said, "because I like looking at you in the moonlight."

His voice was as smooth as the velvet spread that covered her bed, and his lazy-as-a-river smile tugged at her innards. The man knew what he was doing.

"Okay, Wes, listen up," she said, still trying to keep things light between them so he wouldn't know he was getting to her. "I believe in saying it like it is."

"I like that about you."

"Um, thank you," she said.

"You're welcome."

He was trying to sweet-talk her; that's what he was doing. He'd probably sweet-talked his way into more than one woman's heart and bed, but not this one. No sirree. She had his number, could see right through him. Wes Bridges had definitely met his match.

"Now then," she said firmly. "I think I know what's on your mind, so maybe I should remind you that the absolute last thing I want or need in my life is a man."

He nodded emphatically. "That's for sure."

He was agreeing with her? "*Especially* a man who only plans on hanging around a couple of weeks and is just looking for a good time."

"Especially that."

"I don't like being tied down or having somebody tell me what to do all the time."

"Can't blame you for that."

"I like my life just the way it is, except the part about finding my husband's remains in the backyard and being the number one murder suspect." She added quickly, "But I plan to clear my name and—"

"Annie?"

"Yeah?"

"Could you just shut up for maybe one minute?"

She blinked, and without warning he dipped his head and pressed his lips against hers. Holy cow, she hadn't even seen it coming, and her mouth dropped open in surprise. Wes obviously took that as an invitation, because before she could unscramble her brain, he'd pulled her closer and slipped his tongue past her gaping lips. Jeez Louise, but the man knew his way around a woman's mouth! The kiss deepened, and she grasped his jacket with both hands, feeling as though she were riding on one of those wild carnival rides that turned her inside out and upside down and made the world around her spin all topsy-turvy as though everything was out of control.

She thought of pulling away and then decided one more minute wouldn't hurt. His lips were gentle but persuasive, and before she knew it, Annie found her tongue mingling with his. He enveloped her in his arms, and the next thing she knew, her own arms had slipped around his neck. The afghan slid from her shoulders, and she could feel his heat seeping through her bathrobe and gown, and she was straining against him wanting more. She was sorry when he raised his head.

For a moment they just looked at each other, and Annie mentally tried to pick up the pieces of her scattered brain and put them in order and find the part labeled *logical thinking*.

"Annie?"

She grappled for an intelligible word. "Huh?"

"That was dynamite."

Dynamite? Dy-nuh-mite. Eeek! "Destiny!" she almost hissed. "It's all her fault!"

"I have no clue what you're talking about, but I haven't enjoyed kissing a woman that much in a long, long time. I think we should do it some more."

Annie swayed against him. "I don't think—" But it was too late because there they were, those warm lips, stealing her self-control and turning her brain to mush again. And there *she* was, kissing him right back and thinking no man had ever tasted so good. And then her body went wacko: her nipples hardened and strained against her flannel gown and her stomach began flip-flopping like a fish out of water and way low in her belly she felt the flicker of something warm and sweet. That *something* conjured up thoughts that she had no business thinking: Wes warm and naked between her scented sheets, his big hands on her body.

Time to stop.

Annie pulled away quickly and sucked in a deep, shuddering breath. She would give her heart a few seconds to settle down, and then she would admonish him for his actions. Yep, as soon as her pulse steadied she was going to let him have it and have it good.

She sank against him.

Wes pressed his lips against her forehead. "I've half a mind to sweep you up in my arms and carry you upstairs."

She had half a mind to let him do it.

"But I know that the absolute last thing you need or want is a man in your life."

Annie's face burned as he tossed her words right back at her. Worse, she could hear the amusement in his voice, which could only mean he hadn't lost one ounce of control while kissing her and somehow she was going to have to save face.

"Thank you, Wes," she said evenly.

"Thank you?"

"For proving to me that I was right about us," she said, trying to sound sorrowful even as her heart felt as though it were beating in each ear. "Please try not to take it personally, you're a fine kisser and all, but there's just no chemistry."

"At least you gave it a chance."

She stood on legs that felt like overcooked noodles. "We can be friends."

He nodded. "Yeah, we still have that."

She turned and started for the door.

And ran right smack into a wicker rocker, stubbing her big toe. Damn! She lost her balance, fell over the arm, and her face hit the seat. Shit!

Wes was at her side in an instant, pulling her up. "Are you okay? Did you hurt yourself?"

Annie bit back the loud yowl and four-letter words that threatened to spew from her mouth as pain roiled in her toe, shot through her foot, and shimmied up her calf. Tears burned her eyes. "I'm fine," she said, managing a small chuckle. "I always bump into that chair."

"You might want to move it," he said.

Damned if he didn't sound like he was having a good time. What she really wanted to do was chew the effin' chair into a million pieces and spit it into an open sewer.

"Do you need help getting upstairs?"

Her toe throbbed inside her bedroom slipper. It would be just her luck to have broken the damn thing. She'd probably smushed it to smithereens. "No, no," she said, forcing herself to walk on it and not hobble to the door. Only later, when the surgeon was forced to amputate, would she admit to Wes that it had been a painful experience.

He opened the door for her and she stepped inside. "Good night," she said.

"Sweet dreams, Annie."

She thought she heard him laugh softly as he closed the door behind her.

Theenie was the first to join Annie in the kitchen the next morning. "Boy, don't you look nice," she said, pausing at the sight of Annie in her newest jeans and a starched pale pink oxford shirt. "And you're wearing makeup."

"I always wear makeup," Annie said, trying to sound perky despite having slept very little during the night. She had finally climbed from the bed in the wee morning hours and dragged her throbbing toe to the bathroom, where she'd found a nighttime pain reliever that had allowed her to get a couple of hours' sleep before the alarm clock blared her awake at 5:00 AM. She was still fighting grogginess and a hurting toe, but she was determined to keep it to herself. She checked the oven, where she had already put in an egg, sausage, and cheese casserole.

"You don't do your eyes up like that except on special

occasions," Theenie said. "Like when you and Danny go to a show in Charleston."

Annie entertained the thought of grabbing the sponge from the sink and stuffing it into Theenie's mouth. "It's no big deal, okay?" The casserole was beginning to bubble around the edges. Annie slid in a pan of home-made biscuits before reclaiming her chair at the kitchen table, where she'd begun making up her to-do list for the day.

Theenie joined her a moment later, coffee cup in hand. "I thought I'd never fall asleep last night," she said, batting a dainty hand against her mouth as she yawned. "Peaches kept me awake walking up and down the hall making those weird sounds in her throat that she does when she's not happy."

"Gee, I don't recall Peaches ever being happy," Annie said. As if acting on cue, the cat plopped from her chair, walked over to her now-empty food dish, and stared into it. She nudged it with her nose several times and then paused long enough as though waiting for Annie to get up and put more food in it. When Annie didn't make a move to do so, Peaches raised one paw and whacked the dish. As usual, it skidded across the kitchen floor.

"Did you remember to feed Peaches?" Theenie asked.

Annie looked amused. "Does it look like she has ever missed a meal?"

"As I was saying," Theenie began, "after about two hours of listening to Peaches growl like she sometimes does, I finally got up and carried her to your room, which was no easy task, mind you, considering how much she weighs, but I was hoping you could get her to calm down. Only you weren't in your bed. I got worried."

Annie pretended to be very interested in making her list. "That must've been when I stepped outside for some fresh air," she said in an offhand manner.

"Yes, I saw you," Theenie said.

With pen poised in midair, Annie held her breath and waited.

"With Wes."

Peaches walked over to the cabinet door. *Barn, barn, barn.*

"Kissing," Theenie said.

Annie looked at her. "You were *spying* on us?" Like they said, the best defense was a good offense.

Theenie sniffed as though she had just been insulted. "Of course not. I simply pulled the curtain aside to see if you were on the piazza, and there the two of you were, plastered together like Velcro. I don't mind telling you I was shocked." She gave another sniff.

Barn, barn, barn.

"Good morning," Lovelle said from the bottom of the stairs.

Annie jumped. She hadn't heard the woman come down. "Oh, you startled me."

"Everybody in this house is as nervous as a long-tailed cat in a room full of rocking chairs," Lovelle said. "Theenie, you don't look happy. What's wrong?"

"Oh, nothing," she said in a voice that suggested otherwise.

"That's good," Lovelle said, going to the coffeepot.

"Except I didn't get a wink of sleep last night," Theenie said.

Lovelle glanced at her. "That's too bad."

"I'm just too old to have to lie in bed and worry."

Lovelle carried her cup to the table and sat down. "Why were you worried?"

"No reason."

Lovelle turned to Annie. "I see you're already making your list."

"It's not like I don't have enough on my mind, what with Destiny talking about a spirit and Doc's gardener finding human remains in the backyard. Not to mention Annie renting a room to some biker stud who—"

"Oh, for Pete's sake!" Annie said, tossing her pen aside. She looked at Lovelle. "Theenie saw Wes and me kissing last night."

Lovelle looked pleased. "Oh, yummy, is he a good kisser? He looks like he knows a few things."

Destiny came downstairs in a flowing satin flamingo pink bathrobe and matching slippers. "Good morning," she mumbled, staggering toward the coffeepot.

"You sound tired, dear," Theenie said.

Destiny filled a cup and joined them. "Yeah, well, it's hard to rest when you've got a ghost hanging around you twenty-four seven."

Theenie nodded sympathetically. "If it makes you feel any better, almost nobody slept well last night."

"Theenie saw Wes kissing Annie on the piazza last night," Lovelle said.

Destiny shrugged. "I'm not surprised. I saw a hot romance in Annie's future when I read her palm." She looked at Annie. "Is he as good in bed as I told you he'd be?"

Theenie's mouth fell open. "You went to bed with him?" she asked Annie.

Annie felt her face burn clear to the tips of her ears. "Of course not!"

"What are you waiting for?" Lovelle said. "I can tell by the way he looks at you that he's hot for you."

"He looks at her like she's naked," Theenie said, rolling her eyes. "I knew Annie shouldn't have rented to him."

"I'll tell you what he's thinking," Lovelle said. "He's thinking he'd like to dunk his doughnut you-know-where."

"I shouldn't be hearing this," Theenie said, stuffing her fingers in her ears.

"It would do you good to get laid," Destiny said, giving Annie a hearty wink.

"La la la la la—," Theenie began loudly.

Annie was relieved when the telephone rang. She answered before it could ring a second time.

The woman on the other end of the line wasted no time. Annie just listened. "I see," she said after a moment. "Of course I understand. Please call me in the future if I can be of service." She hung up, slipped her hands into an oven mitt, and pulled out the casserole and biscuits.

Theenie pulled her fingers from her ears and looked at Annie. "I can tell by the look on your face that you just got bad news."

Annie began putting the biscuits in a cloth-lined basket. "The baby shower is off."

"That's not fair!" Lovelle said. "How can people be so rude? You've lived in this town practically half of your life. I can't believe *anyone* would think you killed your husband."

"It'll pass," Annie said, hoping she was right.

Someone tapped on the back door. Annie unlocked it and found Danny on the other side. He tousled her hair as he entered the kitchen. "Good morning, ladies." He glanced around the table at the serious faces. "Or is it?"

"It's a wonderful morning," Annie said. "The coffee is hot, and I just pulled breakfast from the oven." She poured Danny a cup of coffee, and he carried it to the table. As though following Annie's lead, all three women gave him a bright smile.

"I'll set the table," Destiny said, and went for dishes and flatware while Theenie and Lovelle continued to smile in such a way that one would have thought they'd just been handed a gift certificate to the local Family Dollar Store.

Danny smiled back and took a sip of his coffee.

"When will you be finished staining the ballroom floor?" Lovelle asked. "I need to get back to my exercise routine."

"I plan to put a couple of coats of polyurethane on top of the stain," Danny told her. "It'll be a few more days."

Annie glanced his way. "I took a peek at the floors last night. They're gorgeous."

Erdle came through the back door looking haggard. He sat at his usual place. Danny passed him the basket of biscuits. Erdle took one and bit into it.

"What time did *you* get in last night?" Theenie asked.

"I wasn't keeping track," he said.

Lovelle sniffed. "You smell like a beer can."

"It's my new aftershave."

"Aftershave, my foot," Lovelle said.

Wes came downstairs. Everybody but Erdle looked up. "Mornin'," Wes said. He glanced at Annie, and their gazes locked. "How are you?"

"Great. You?"

"Same."

"Coffee?"

He nodded. "I can get it."

"No, I'll do it."

They both reached for the cabinet door at the same time, but Annie was quicker. The door swung open and banged Wes's head. He winced and stepped back.

"I'm so sorry," Annie said. "Are you okay?"

"I'll know when my vision clears."

Annie carefully reached inside the cabinet for a mug, filled it with coffee, and offered it to him.

Their fingers brushed.

Annie felt something quicken in her stomach and let go.

Just missing her big toe, the cup fell to the floor. It

shattered and splashed coffee on the floor and cabinet doors. "Oh, look what I've done!" Annie said.

"Did you burn yourself?" Danny asked as Wes and Annie began picking up the broken pieces.

She shook her head, too embarrassed to look up. Theenie and Lovelle got up and hurried to the broom closet.

"She didn't get much sleep last night," Destiny said.

"Oh yeah?"

"It's a long story," Annie said.

Theenie and Lovelle stepped up with the broom and mop. "Annie, sit down before somebody gets hurt," Theenie said. "You, too, Wes," she added. "I'll get your coffee."

Annie and Wes did as they were told.

A door slammed upstairs. "That crazy woman is at it again," Destiny muttered. "I'd kill her if she weren't already dead."

"Like we don't have enough problems," Lovelle said, sweeping the last of the glass into a dustpan as Theenie followed with the mop. "Dead body in the backyard, dead person roaming the house, it's no wonder everybody is canceling."

"You've had more cancelations?" Danny asked Annie.

She shrugged. "No big deal. It's not like I don't have enough to do what with planning a wedding."

Something shattered overhead, making everyone jump. "Dammit!" Destiny said, bolting from the table. "She's breaking my stuff." She raced upstairs.

Erdle looked at Wes. "This is why I drink."

Wes propped his elbows on the table and said nothing. Theenie brought him a cup of coffee, and he thanked her.

"I know this is going to sound crazy," Danny said to

Annie, "and I can't believe I'm even suggesting it, but if you *really* suspect there is some kind of entity in this house, you might consider calling a priest."

"We're waiting to see if Destiny can lead her to the light," Lovelle told him. "In the meantime, be careful or she'll steal your underwear."

Danny nodded as though it made complete sense. "I'll be sure to keep them on at all times."

"That's advice we should all follow," Theenie said, tossing a look from Wes to Annie.

Erdle got up from his place, carried his plate to the sink, and rinsed it out. He placed it in the dishwasher and started for the door.

"Where do you think you're going?" Annie said. "I've got a whole list of chores for you."

Erdle sighed and reclaimed his seat.

The doorbell rang. Theenie started from the room. "Don't answer it," Annie said. "It might be another reporter."

Theenie squared her shoulders and grabbed a meat mallet from the drawer. "I'll make him sorry he ever set foot in the yard."

Wes and Danny watched with interest while Erdle rested his head on the table.

Lovelle smiled. "I'm so glad Theenie is beginning to show assertiveness."

"I just wish Doc hadn't left town," Annie said, "in case she hurts somebody."

Peaches, who'd been quiet for a while, returned to the cabinet. *Barn, barn, barn.*

Annie sighed.

Barn, barn, barn.

Annie shook her head. "I don't know which is worse, having to deal with a cantankerous cat who hates me or having to spend every spare dime I have on the upkeep of a tacky whorehouse."

"Now, Annie, you know you don't mean that," Theenie said from just inside the doorway. Max and Jamie stood beside her.

A door slammed upstairs. "Stop throwing my stuff!" Destiny shouted.

Barn, barn, barn.

"Good morning," Annie said to Max and Jamie without missing a beat. She gave them a big smile. "And good morning to you, handsome," she told Fleas. She'd barely gotten the words out of her mouth before she heard a hiss and a snarl, and a streak of orange fur flew past her. Fleas yelped and took off, and a second later there was a loud crash from the living room.

"Uh-oh," Jamie said, and turned.

"Don't worry," Annie said calmly. "Theenie, would you please make sure Fleas is okay and put Peaches out?"

"Of course, dear. Here, you can have the mallet back."

"Jamie, you and Max sit down," Annie insisted, "and I'll pour you a cup of coffee."

Max grinned. "I sort of get the feeling we dropped by at a bad time."

"We can't stay," Jamie said quickly. "Destiny called and asked if we would drop off her mail again. She sounded awful. Is she sick?"

"She's just tired."

"Annie, you don't look so well yourself," Jamie said. "Are you okay?"

Annie glanced around the room and saw what looked like pity on her friends' faces, and she crossed her arms.

"Okay, everybody listen up," she said, giving them a stern look. "I know things look bad right now, but I've been through tougher times than this." She paused. "Okay, except for my husband being buried in the backyard."

"And the part about you being the murder suspect and

all," Lovelle reminded, "which is destroying your business."

Annie wished Lovelle hadn't brought that up. "Yes," she said calmly. "But once my name is cleared everything will be back to normal. The point I'm trying to make—"

"Boy, this cat weighs a ton," Theenie interrupted, coming through the doorway with Peaches in her arms. Wes and Danny both hurried over to help her; Danny took the cat and Wes opened the door for him. "Fleas is okay," Theenie said, "but Peaches jumped on the end table in the living room and broke that statue. You know, the one that looks like a man and woman are *doing it*?" She was breathing heavily, obviously from exertion. "I never liked that statute, and I don't know why anyone would have it sitting around, but then I keep forgetting a bunch of floozies used to live here. Oh, look, Peaches scratched me."

"That cat has lost her mind," Lovelle said as more racket sounded from the second floor, "and all because we have some spirit running amok in this house."

"As I was saying," Annie began, "I expect things to calm down very soon. Certainly before the wedding," she added quickly, looking at Jamie and Max. "But in the meantime, I would appreciate it if you guys would stop with those woe-is-Annie looks, because that's going to piss me off. You really don't want to piss me off right now."

Erdle raised his head and looked around the room. "She's right. You don't want to piss her off on account of she's mean and dangerous. If you don't believe it, just ask *me*, 'cause I know firsthand."

"Erdle, do you mind?" Annie said.

He nodded and slumped over the table once more.

Wes grinned. "Well, if it's any consolation, I don't feel a damn bit sorry for you, Annie. But that doesn't mean some of us can't help. I've got a couple of friends who work for the police force in Columbia. They'll be able to advise me on what we should do, since it doesn't look like Lamar is up to the challenge."

"I'm pretty good at digging up information, if you need it," Max said.

Danny nodded. "And I can start taking Lamar fishing. If I keep him busy he won't have much time to screw up the case."

"I know what I can do," Jamie said. "I can write a huge story about this place. I'll get Vera to take a lot of pictures. Annie will have more business than she can handle."

"Lovelle and I will do whatever Annie needs us to do," Theenie said. "Right, Lovelle?"

Lovelle suddenly looked excited. "Oh, and if Annie needs money I can give a recital in the ballroom. We'll charge fifty dollars a pop."

Erdle lifted his head once more, looked around. "I'll give up drinking."

Chapter
SIX

"I hate going into this attic," Annie told Wes that evening. "It always gives me a bad case of the heebie-jeebies. I've seen a couple of bats up here." She shuddered.

He followed her up a short landing that led from the third floor to the fourth-floor attic, the only room on that floor. "I'll bet this is where Destiny's spirit spends most of her time."

Annie gulped and missed the next step. She teetered, but Wes immediately reached out and prevented her from toppling and knocking him down the stairs as well. Instead of releasing her once she'd regained her footing, he slipped his arms around her waist and pulled her against him.

Annie was very conscious of her hips pressing into his hard body. "Um, Wes?"

He nuzzled the back of her neck. "Yeah?"

Annie closed her eyes as his lips caressed her nape. Her skin prickled, and tiny shivers ran down her spine. Oh boy, she thought. The man only had to touch her, and her body went ape-shit.

"Excuse me," she said, using the same tone Theenie used when she took Erdle to task over his drinking. Wes kissed his way to one ear and nipped Annie's earlobe gently with his teeth, and she forgot what she had been about to say. Her bones started to melt.

"I want to make love to you," he said.

Instant adrenaline rush, followed by flash of heat low in her belly, followed by shaky noodle legs. Not a good sign.

Wes turned her around, looked into her eyes. "What d'you think?"

"Um." Annie gave herself a mental shake to clear her head. "We should probably think about it carefully. We don't want to rush into anything."

"We don't?"

"Definitely not. I have it on good authority that men and women who fall into bed out of simple lust only end up feeling empty or disappointed because despite meeting their sexual needs, lust does not address emotional needs. They often experience guilt, resentment, and low self-esteem. Even worse, they are at higher risk for sexually transmitted diseases. If you watched Oprah or read 'Dear Abby' you'd know that."

Wes just looked at her. "You're serious?"

"Absolutely. They offer sound advice on just about every subject, ranging from office affairs, ending relationships gracefully, to tips for getting along better with your mother-in-law and the drawbacks of body piercing, to name just a few." Annie paused to draw in breath.

Wes looked confused. Finally, he released her. "So do you want me to go into the attic first?"

"Yes, please. And check for bats."

He opened the attic door, found the light switch, and flipped it on. He stepped inside. Annie waited just outside.

"Wow, there's a lot of stuff in here," Wes said.

"Do you see anything flying around?"

"Nope. Don't worry; I won't let anything get you."

Annie peered inside the open doorway. When she didn't see any ugly black objects darting about, she stepped inside but remained close to her point of exit.

"I sorted through a ton of boxes after my grandmother died, and I donated a lot of items to the women's shelter. But that was before the bat flew at my hair. I almost killed myself trying to get out of here."

Wes lifted several sheets and peeked beneath them. "You've got a lot of cool antiques."

"My grandmother refused to part with anything that was handed down through the family. No telling how long they've been up here."

Wes motioned toward several tall file cabinets along one wall. "Is that where you keep your income tax records?"

Annie nodded. "Third cabinet, top drawer," she said. "They're filed by year and marked as backup copies." She remained where she was as Wes crossed the room, opened the file drawer, and pulled out what he needed.

"I'm assuming you and Charles filed jointly?" he said.

"Yeah." She told him what years to look for.

Annie was relieved to leave the attic behind. Returning to the kitchen, Wes set the files on the kitchen table and began flipping through one of them.

"What are you looking for?" Annie asked.

"Charles's Social Security number, credit card receipts, cell phone bills, and anything else that might be helpful."

"He charged all his business expenses on American Express."

Wes found an envelope marked: *Business Receipts*. He opened it, thumbed through them, and pulled one out. "Where is the Hilltop Steakhouse?" he asked.

"It's in Mosely, about twenty-five miles from here, on the way to Charleston."

"The two of you went often?"

"I've never been."

"Obviously he took somebody, because there are eight or ten receipts and the bills are pretty steep."

"Those were probably the nights I stayed home and ate tuna fish sandwiches."

Wes glanced up at her. "He traveled?"

Annie nodded. "His boss, Norm Schaefer, owns several real estate franchises in and out of state, so they often took turns attending monthly sales meetings, and Charles enjoyed going to various seminars, mostly geared toward sales or real estate. And there were golf tournaments and fishing trips with customers. Mostly out of town, of course," she added flatly.

Wes checked his watch and closed the folder. "There's a lot to go through here," he said, "and it's getting late. Why don't we call it a night and I'll look through the files first thing in the morning? In the meantime, I'll keep this in my room, away from the others."

Annie knew Wes would probably spend most of the night studying the files, but he was trying to spare her feelings. "Just so you know, I've gotten over Charles's indiscretions. You don't have to keep secrets from me."

"Good." He smiled. "Tell you what, Red. I'm going to need the latest picture you have of him."

"'Red'?"

"It seems fitting."

Annie hurried into the formal living room and opened a cabinet along one wall. She pulled out a photo album and flipped through the pages, quickly bypassing her wedding pictures. She found a couple of photos of Charles taken only a few months before his disappearance. She felt a dull sensation in her stomach as she studied them. Finally, she carried them into the kitchen and handed them to Wes.

He gave them a cursory glance. "Not a bad-looking fellow."

Annie shrugged. "I guess I wasn't the only woman in town who thought so." But she didn't want to think about Charles. Her big toe was hurting, and she needed to get off her foot. "I suppose I should get to bed."

"I'll follow you up."

Wes carried the files upstairs. He reached his room before she did hers. "You might want to have a doctor look at that toe if it doesn't feel better in the morning," he said once she'd arrived at her bedroom door and opened it. She frowned, wondering how he knew the toe was giving her problems when she'd been so careful to hide it.

But she had a feeling Wes Bridges knew or suspected more about her than he was letting on, and that worried her.

It was not yet 6:00 AM when Annie finished frying bacon and stirring blueberries into a large bowl of batter for waffles that she planned to serve for breakfast once her guests began waking. This was her favorite part of the day, the house so quiet she could hear the leaves on the live oaks rustling in the breeze just outside the window over her sink. She had added an extra place setting in case Danny arrived early, and she'd filled a carafe with coffee and put on a fresh pot. She poured a second cup, grabbed her notepad, and carried them to the table, where she started her daily list.

Max and Jamie's rehearsal dinner was only a few days away, and the wedding was drawing nearer. So many things to do in the meantime, she thought, even though she, with the help of Theenie and Lovelle, had managed to tackle several major cleaning projects after the Christmas and New Year's guests had gone and all the decorations had come down. The marbled entryway and pillars had been cleaned, as had what seemed miles of solid mahogany baseboards, elaborate trim, wainscoting, and floor-to-ceiling panels in the study. The porcelain tubs and sinks in all six bathrooms sparkled, and Annie had spent a solid week on her knees scrubbing the tiled floors and walls, oftentimes using old toothbrushes to get the grout clean as well.

Perhaps if she concentrated on what remained to be done she wouldn't spend so much time worrying. Not that worrying had ever solved a thing, her grandmother had told her many times after Annie had moved in and found herself tackling the expenditures and upkeep of the mansion. She wished her grandmother had worried more and spent less money so that Annie hadn't been forced to pinch every dime and nickel of her inheritance to renovate the spacious eight-bedroom mansion and prevent it from falling into total disrepair. Not only had the woman lost a bundle in the stock market; she'd also donated money to every imaginable cause.

Annie's mother, Jenna, who'd married money and profited greatly when she'd divorced Annie's father, Gunther Worthington III, had little to do with her own mother and wasn't concerned about expenditures, since the woman had always lived frugally when Jenna was growing up. However, when Jenna discovered, after her mother's death, that the family fortune had dwindled to almost nothing, she had been furious.

"So much for your inheritance," she'd told Annie. "I should have my head examined for not taking that *woman*"—as she often referred to her mother—"to court and having her declared incompetent. Not to mention that old geezer who managed her finances. All you have now is a tacky broken-down whorehouse."

There were times Annie wondered what her grandmother had been thinking when she'd made Annie promise not to sell the house, and times Annie wondered what *she* had been thinking when she'd agreed.

Annie glanced up at the sound of boots on the stairs. Wes was dressed in his usual faded jeans and a blue work shirt that emphasized his tan complexion. He paused and glanced around. "Where is everybody?"

"Sleeping. Theenie's light was still on when I got up during the night to see to Peaches. Theenie sometimes sits up late reading."

"How long have you been up?"

"Since five. I like getting up early so I can spend a few minutes by myself before putting breakfast on. The house is so quiet and peaceful this time of day."

Annie wondered if he had any idea how good he looked in the morning, fresh from his shower. Not that he looked bad in the afternoon and evening as well, she thought. The man was too damn handsome for his own good. "How about a cup of coffee?" She started to get up.

"Sit," he ordered. "I can get it myself." He crossed the kitchen, opened the cabinet, and reached for a coffee mug. He filled it and joined Annie at the kitchen table. "I see you're planning your day," he said, noting her list. "You forgot one thing."

Annie glanced down. "I did?"

"You haven't scheduled any time for R and R. When's the last time you went dancing or enjoyed a nice meal in a restaurant, where it wasn't up to you to clean up afterward?"

"I don't remember."

"Your problem is you spend too much time closed up in this house."

"You're saying I'm boring."

He looked thoughtful as he reached over and stroked her cheek. "You are the least boring person I've ever met. You've surrounded yourself with people who love you, and you obviously enjoy what you do." He pulled his hand away and reached for his mug.

"But?"

"I don't see you taking much time out for yourself.

You're always looking after other people. I guess my question is: who takes care of Annie?"

"It works both ways. These people are the closest thing I've ever had to a real family. Not that my grandmother didn't love me dearly," she added quickly, "but I was more like her caretaker."

"What about your parents?"

She smiled. "They are very nice people, but they had no idea what to do with a child. My mother much prefers me as a grown woman who will lunch and shop with her when I visit, sip expensive wine by the pool, and make sympathetic noises while she regales me with horror stories of growing up in this house. That way she doesn't have to feel guilty for staying away all those years."

"Do you see her often?"

"No, she hates this place, and it's hard for me to visit her in Atlanta with my business and all, but we usually talk on the phone once a week. Only right now she's spending a month with friends in West Palm Beach. Our lifestyles are vastly different."

"Does she know about the recent discovery in your backyard?"

Annie shook her head. "I'll tell her about it when it's all over. No sense worrying her."

"What about your father?"

Annie chuckled. "Like I said, a very nice person who *still* has no idea what to do with a child, especially a grown daughter. He lives in the south of France, sends nice checks for birthdays and Christmas, which I use to make ongoing repairs to this house."

"Brothers and sisters?"

"Nope. You?"

"There are seven of us, three girls and four boys."

"Holy cow!"

"I'm the middle child, who, according to statistics,

gets the shaft. Somebody obviously didn't inform my family of that fact, because I pretty much had it okay." He picked up his and Annie's coffee cups, refilled them, and carried them to the table.

A noise from the stairs caused them both to look up. Destiny nodded a weary "good morning" as she cleared the last step and paused, giving a huge yawn and blinking several times as though she was trying to make herself fully awake. "Coffee," she said, stumbling toward the pot.

Annie noted the tired look on her face. "Another sleepless night?"

Destiny nodded. "Dead people don't sleep. I need to check on my apartment, see when I can return." She sank into a chair across from Wes. "Not that it matters. Once a spirit person latches on to me they usually follow me everywhere. Until I convince them to go to the light," she added. She glanced at Wes. "You don't believe a damn word I'm saying. You think I'm crazy."

He shrugged. "I've noticed a few oddities around here that don't seem to have a valid explanation."

"Now you know."

"I wish there was something I could do to help," Annie said.

"Do you believe in spirits?" Wes asked her.

She hesitated. "Okay, I'm going to tell both of you something I've never told anyone, only you'll have to keep quiet about it because I don't want to frighten the others." She spoke quietly. "My grandmother used to talk to herself. At least I thought she was talking to herself, but when I finally asked her about it, she told me there was a woman, a ghost, trying to communicate with her." Annie paused and looked at Destiny. "You were right. There were many times I felt a presence. Some of my guests have reported seeing things, some sort of apparition, and sometimes I would see something out of the corner of my eye."

"I don't know why you're trying to hide it from Theenie and Lovelle. They've suspected for some time. As for your fears that it might hurt your business, I think it could draw people. Do you have this place listed on a website?"

Annie shook her head.

"Lucky for you I know someone who might be able to design one for you," Destiny said. "You've met Jamie's editor, Mike Henderson."

She nodded. "What does he charge?"

"He worships me; he'll do it for free. But you have to be willing to give *all* the facts about the house, because that's what is going to draw people."

Annie wondered how much Destiny knew.

"You mean the part about it being a brothel at one time?" Wes asked.

"How did you find out?" Annie asked. "Not that it's a secret. Most people know the history."

Wes avoided a direct answer, but he grinned. "The house pretty much speaks for itself, Annie."

She nodded. "Supposedly it closely resembles the way it looked back in the eighteen fifties. My grandmother had an old photo album of pictures taken after it was built, but I haven't seen it in years. I suspect it's somewhere in the attic." She gave an eye roll.

"This spirit was one of the women who lived here when it was a bordello," Destiny said. "Unfortunately, I can't get any information from her because she's mute."

Wes cocked a brow, and Destiny went on. "In most cases, spirits who hang around long after they've died have suffered a tragic death. Most of them are still in shock; sometimes they don't even know they're dead.

In the case of this particular spirit, she was strangled to death. She has the marks on her neck."

It was the first time Annie had heard about the marks, and she shuddered. "You're right," she said. "If you read the history of this house, you'll learn that her name was Lacey and she *was* a prostitute. She was murdered by her lover, who was promptly hanged."

Destiny pondered it. "I think she may have witnessed the hanging," she said. "That, combined with her murder, may have traumatized her so badly that she can't speak. Or," she added, "her vocal cords may have been severely damaged in the strangulation."

Wes shook his head. "This all seems pretty far-fetched. Why are you able to see the spirit so clearly and the rest of us can't?"

"Because I'm psychic and more open to this sort of thing," Destiny said. "She wants to communicate with me, but she can't, which leaves her frustrated and angry. Which is why she sometimes throws things, mostly my stuff," she added, "and that, combined with almost no sleep, pisses *me* off. I'm usually more patient with spirits.

"Anyway, I recently began having visions of what it was like back then. I see women dressed in corsets and gartered black stockings and wearing heavy rouge; I see well-dressed gentlemen following them upstairs." She suddenly sneezed. "Only the wealthy could afford to visit. Does the name Fairchild mean anything to you?" she asked Annie.

"Oh yeah. The Fairchild family settled here before the Revolutionary War. They were wealthy and highly respected. Some became politicians. There are still a few descendants living here, but most of them moved to Charleston."

"For some reason I keep seeing that name in my mind." Destiny shrugged. "By the way, the house *does* look much the same as it did back then." Another sneeze.

Annie went for the box of tissues. "Except for the kitchen and some of the furniture," Destiny added, yanking a couple of tissues from the box.

Wes looked intrigued by what Destiny had to say, but it was difficult to tell how much, if any, of it he believed. "How often do you have these, um, visions?"

"I can't predict them," Destiny said. "Sometimes they're very clear, other times they're vague and I spend hours trying to decide their meanings." Destiny sipped her coffee in silence for a moment. "Having this spirit around could work to your advantage," she told Annie.

"How?"

"Spirits are not limited by time or space. I'm willing to bet Lacey knows who murdered your husband. She probably saw the whole thing."

Annie gaped.

"Which is why I wish she would communicate with me," Destiny went on. "I probably shouldn't have yelled at her for getting into my stuff. I'll probably have to start sucking up to her if I hope to get her to cooperate. I hate sucking up to dead people."

Annie laughed. "Could you imagine me marching into Lamar Tevis's office and telling him some ghost had solved the murder?"

Destiny shook her head. "No, but if this spirit could tell us who the killer is, we might be able to point Lamar in the right direction."

Annie heard a noise at the top of the stairs. "We need to drop the subject for now. I don't want the others to know." She barely had time to get the words out of her mouth before Lovelle came down, dressed in gray slacks, a silk dove gray blouse, and a cream-colored cashmere sweater.

"Good morning, ladies," she said brightly.

"Boy, you look nice," Annie told her. "What's the occasion?"

Lovelle patted her hair. "I'm having breakfast with a friend, and then we're driving to Savannah for an art show."

Annie smiled. Although Savannah was only forty-five minutes away, she could not remember when she'd last been. "Sounds fun."

Lovelle draped her sweater over one chair. "I wish I could find my fuchsia scarf. I always wear it with this outfit."

Destiny looked up. "It's in my room. I meant to bring it down and ask who it belonged to."

"Well, how in heaven's name did it get there?" Lovelle said.

Destiny shrugged. "Probably the same way my lingerie ended up in Wes's bathroom."

"Hey, you didn't hear me complaining," Wes said. "I like having women's lingerie hanging over my shower rod. I have a thing for lacy black garter belts."

All three women looked amused. "Let me grab that scarf," Destiny said.

Lovelle looked at Annie. "This is getting out of hand. Every time I turn around I'm missing something. Yesterday Theenie accused me of taking her favorite nightgown. You've seen it, that flannel thing she wears with blue dogs and pink kittens. As if I'd be caught dead in old lady flannel," she added.

Someone knocked on the door. Annie answered it and found Lamar Tevis on the other side. "Good morning, Annie," he said. "Sorry to stop by so early, but I thought we might talk a bit." He glanced about the room. "Preferably in private."

"Is something wrong?" she asked.

"No, no. I, um . . ." He paused and cleared his throat. "I need to discuss a few things with regard to your husband's, um, remains."

Wes got up from his chair. "I'd like to listen in if you don't mind."

Annie led Wes and Lamar into a large sunroom that had once served as a sleeping porch. Windows lined the room and had offered relief during hot summer months before fans and air conditioners were invented. Wes and Annie took a seat on one of several sofas; Lamar chose a chair opposite them.

Lamar pulled his small notebook from his shirt pocket and thumbed through several pages. He wore a sad smile as he regarded Annie. "I don't suppose this will come as a surprise to you," he told her, "but all the evidence we found on or near the remains that were discovered on your property proves without a doubt that they are those of your husband." He paused as though waiting for her to take it all in. "I'm sorry, Annie."

Wes reached for her hand. "You okay?"

"Yes." But she wasn't. Not really. She felt a deep sadness that the man she'd been married to had lost his life at such an early age.

"What was the cause of death?" she asked.

Lamar hesitated. "I'll get to that in a minute, but first let me tell you what we *do* know. The coroner faxed his findings to me; in laymen's terms, your husband suffered a broken neck and head trauma."

Annie realized she was holding her breath. "Did he suffer?"

"I suppose he could have been unconscious at the time, but the head injury didn't penetrate the skull, so there's no reason to suspect that's what killed him."

"So he died from a broken neck," she said.

Lamar wiped his hands down his face. "We don't really know at this time."

"You *don't know*?" she asked.

"The coroner claims the vertebra was still intact, so

it's highly unlikely there was damage to the spinal cord or any kind of obstruction that would have interfered with normal breathing. I know we don't have all the answers, but I'm pretty impressed with what the coroner *was* able to come up with, seeing as how he's not one of those experts. I can't think of what they're called at the moment; it'll come to me."

"Forensic anthropologists," Wes said.

Annie looked perplexed. "Why wasn't Charles taken to the Medical University in Charleston, where their methods are more advanced? I thought that was the normal procedure for suspicious deaths."

"That's true," Lamar said, shifting uncomfortably in his chair, "but our coroner insisted on taking a look, since we don't get many cases like this. Some of our law enforcement people stood in on the exam, so it was a learning experience for them."

Once again, Wes and Annie exchanged glances. She frowned. "You're saying my husband's remains were not immediately sent to Charleston because the local coroner decided to use them for teaching purposes?" She didn't give Lamar a chance to respond. "Good grief, Lamar, the man isn't even a bona fide medical examiner. Did you not consider Charles's family or how anxious we might be to find out what happened to him?"

Lamar shifted uncomfortably in his chair and stared at the floor. "Annie, I'm sorry to say it gets worse." He shook his head sadly, and it was obvious he did not want to tell her.

"Why don't we stop beating around the bush here and get to the point?" Wes suggested to the man.

Lamar continued staring at the floor. "Annie, I regret to have to tell you we've, uh, lost your husband's remains."

Chapter
SEVEN

Annie sat there for a moment, unsure she'd heard Lamar correctly or even understood what he'd just said. "Would you run that by me again?" she said.

"An employee from the morgue left for the Medical University in Charleston last night with the remains, and, well, to make a long story short, the vehicle was carjacked."

"What?" she shrieked.

"You're not serious," Wes said. "How could something like that have happened?"

"A passing motorist found the driver unconscious on the side of the highway. He'd been robbed and hit over the head. The van was gone."

Annie gave an enormous sigh. "Do you have any idea what this is going to do to Charles's mother?"

"I plan to go over there and break the news to her once I leave here. I know it's a lot to ask under the circumstances, but I was sort of hoping you'd go with me."

"Forget it," Annie said. "She blames me for Charles's disappearance and refuses to speak to me, especially after I told her he left me for another woman. I seriously doubt she'd even let me in the door."

"Do you know who he was seeing?"

Annie shook her head.

"Hold it, Lamar," Wes said. "I don't think this is a good time to question Annie, but if you insist, then I'm going to advise her not to answer without an attorney present."

"I am *not* afraid to answer questions," Annie said, "and the sooner we get it over with the better." She looked at Lamar. "What do you want to know?"

Lamar glanced from Wes to her. "Would you mind describing your relationship with your husband?"

"I was planning to file for a divorce, if that tells you anything."

"Did Charles know?"

"We hadn't discussed it, but I don't think he would have been surprised. Our marriage had been deteriorating for months because I refused to sell this house. Charles obviously thought I'd change my mind if someone offered enough money, so he began looking for a buyer behind my back. He found one willing to offer top dollar for it, but I refused to budge. The marriage pretty much went to hell after that. It wasn't long before I learned he was seeing somebody."

"How did you find out?"

Annie was not going to drag Danny into it. "I just knew."

"And you can't think of anyone it could have been? A friend or co-worker maybe?" Lamar added hopefully.

"Annie has already answered that question," Wes said. "I think she's been through enough for one day. Besides, you and your officers have a missing corpse to find."

As Lamar closed his notebook and stood, he avoided looking at Wes. "I'm sorry to have been the bearer of bad news, Annie, and I appreciate your answering my questions. I'll call the minute we find, uh, you know. I'll just see myself out."

Theenie entered the room a few minutes later with Danny right behind. "Is everything okay?"

Annie stood and forced a smile she didn't feel. "He

just wanted to touch base with me, let me know how the investigation is going." She wasn't ready to discuss all she'd learned.

"Are you sure that's all it was?" Danny asked, his gaze going to Wes.

Annie was amazed that Danny could read her so well. "I wish you'd stop worrying," she said.

Danny slung one arm over Annie's shoulder as they walked toward the kitchen. "Good news. I plan to finish the floors today," he said. "But you know how I hate to work on an empty stomach, and I just happened to notice you were getting ready to make your famous blueberry waffles."

Wes arrived at Eve Fortenberry's house later that morning. She still wore her bathrobe, and her eyes were red and swollen. "I thought I'd stop by and see how you're doing," he said.

She shrugged and stepped back so he could enter. "I've been better," she said, "but that shouldn't come as a surprise." She motioned for him to sit as she sank into a lumpy chair. "Chief Tevis came by earlier."

"I figured he would." Wes paused. "You didn't mention our arrangement to him?"

"Of course not. I'm counting on you to do the job he's incapable of." She shook her head. "I have never seen such incompetence. How am I supposed to give my son a proper burial if there are no remains?" She reached for a cigarette. Her hands trembled so badly she could barely get it to her mouth to light it. "You can bet I told Lamar exactly what I thought of him." She shook her head and smoked in silence. Every once in a while she swiped at a tear. "I think I'm still in shock."

"Is there someone I can call to come stay with you?"

"No. I'm better off dealing with it in my own way." She looked at him. "Does Annie know?"

"Yeah. She was as mad as hell, but she insisted on answering any questions Lamar had, because she's as eager to get to the bottom of this as you are." It was clear Eve didn't believe him. "You know Annie has always been convinced Charles was seeing another woman."

Eve hitched her chin high. "If he was, then Annie has no one to blame but herself. She broke her word. She promised to get rid of that monstrosity of a house, and then changed her mind after Charles went to the trouble of finding a buyer."

"Are you sure that's the way it was?"

"Charles sat right there in that chair and told me the whole thing. I've never known him to lie to me."

"Annie claimed she never agreed to it," Wes said.

"And you believe her?"

"The only thing I know for certain is that Annie Fortenberry is incapable of murder."

The woman made a sound of disgust. "I should have known she'd get to you. Annie has a way with men. Believe me, I tried to warn Charles, but he wouldn't listen." She studied Wes. "You're falling for her."

"Eve, think for a minute. As much as you dislike Annie, she may be telling the truth about another woman being in the picture. What if it's true? What if that woman had something to do with your son's death? Wouldn't you want to know?"

"The only thing I know for sure is that you've lost your objectivity, which means you're not going to do me any good. But let me warn you, you're going to look foolish when Annie gets tired of you. The only thing she cares about is that house. It's all she has now that her grandmother is gone. Her own parents didn't want her."

Wes's eyes became flat and emotionless. "I only have one goal," he said after a moment, "and that is learning the truth."

Eve's grief turned to anger. "I don't need your services anymore. You're fired. You need to go back to Columbia where you belong."

Wes shook his head. "I'm not going anywhere. I intend to stay as long as it takes to find the real murderer." He stood, reached into his pocket, and handed her an envelope that had been carefully folded in half. "You'll find my note of resignation inside," he said, "as well as a full refund of everything you've paid me. I'm really sorry about your son."

He let himself out the door without another word.

Annie was throwing on her clothes when she heard Wes leave on his motorcycle the next morning. She had slept fitfully, tossing and turning, finally dozing off as dawn approached, only to awaken after 7:00 AM, two hours behind schedule. She was still buttoning her shirt as she hurried down the hall toward the stairs. She had the mother of all headaches, and she could feel the tension in her neck building, the muscles so tight they felt as though they'd snap.

Theenie was up and about when Annie rushed into the kitchen. The woman had already made a pan of homemade biscuits, scrambled a bowl of eggs, and was in the process of slicing the ham they'd had for dinner the night before.

"Goodness," Annie said. "You've already done everything."

"I figured you could use a little help, what with all that's going on. Now, sit," Theenie ordered, pointing to Annie's usual chair. "I'll get your coffee. From the looks of it, you could use some."

Annie was only too happy to oblige. Theenie poured a cup and carried it to the table. "Lovelle and I had a talk last night," the woman said. "From now on we're going to start pitching in more."

"Don't be silly. You two do enough around here as it is. Besides, it's my job. That's why you pay rent."

"You have far too many duties for one person, and Lovelle and I know darn good and well you don't charge us near enough to live here."

The doorbell rang. "Who on earth could that be?" Annie said, checking the wall clock.

"It's probably Danny," Theenie said, wiping her hands on a dish towel. "He said he'd stop by on his way to another job to see how the floor looked. I don't know why he'd use the front door, though." When Annie made a move to get up, Theenie motioned for her to sit. "I'll get it," she said.

Annie kept her seat and sipped her coffee and wondered what she'd done with the tablet she made her daily to-do list on. She had started to get up when an anxious-looking Theenie walked into the kitchen with Lamar. Two officers followed. One was middle-aged and balding, the other one much younger. He wore a buzz cut and looked as though he was fresh out of the police academy.

"Good morning, Lamar," Annie said, noting that Theenie was already gnawing her bottom lip. "I assume you're here to tell me you found what you were looking for." She was deliberately being vague since she hadn't told Theenie.

He blushed. "We're still working on it." He glanced at the toe of his shoe. "I'm here on official police business, Annie."

"Meaning?"

He raised his head. "I just came from the magistrate's house. I have a search warrant here," he said, handing her a sheet of paper. "Me and the boys need to check the premises."

Annie stared at the warrant in disbelief. "You're going to search my house? Why?"

"We're looking for anything that might help us in the investigation of your husband's murder."

"And you think you're going to find it *here*?"

"Excuse me," Theenie said, squaring her shoulders, "but this is beginning to sound like harassment to me, waltzing in here at seven-thirty in the morning."

"Just doing my job, Miss Theenie," he said.

"Eve Fortenberry is behind this, isn't she?" Annie said. "You're trying to pacify her because she flipped out when she learned you'd lost Charles's remains."

"What do you mean he lost Charles's remains?" Theenie asked in a bewildered tone. She looked at Lamar. "Did you forget where you put them?"

"I'd rather not go into it right now," Lamar said.

"You're wasting your time," Annie told him, "but feel free to search all you like."

"But don't you dare mess up Annie's house," Theenie said, looking from Lamar to the officers. "She works very hard to keep things nice and orderly around here."

"I'll need you to round up all your guests," Lamar said.

Annie frowned. "You mean wake them?"

He sighed. "I'm sorry, Annie. Please ask them to come down."

She gave him a hard look. "You're really desperate for leads, aren't you?"

Once again he looked away. "I'm as eager as you are to get this over with."

"I'll wake the others," Theenie said in a huff as she hurried toward the stairs.

Lamar and his men were quiet as they waited. Annie ignored them and poured another cup of coffee. She found her tablet and sat down at the table, where she began making her list, but her hands shook so badly she could barely hold her pen, much less write.

Destiny was the first to enter the kitchen, shrugging

on her bathrobe. Lovelle and Theenie were right behind her. "What the hell is the meaning of this?" Destiny demanded in a hostile voice. "Why would you even think of barging into Annie's place with a search warrant?"

"That's what I'd like to know," Lovelle said, also wearing a bathrobe. "What could you possibly hope to find?"

"I'll tell you what he's looking for," Destiny said. "He's trying to find anything he can so he can pin a murder rap on Annie because he has no other leads. Fat chance, Lamar."

"I would appreciate it if you ladies cooperate and remain in the kitchen while my men conduct the search," Lamar said, not bothering to address their questions.

"We'd like to start with your bedroom if you would just show us where it is real quick, Mrs. Fortenberry," the older officer said.

Annie shook her head but stood and led them to the stairs. After reaching the second floor, the officers paused at the open door to the bathroom and glanced inside. "My room is at the end of the hall," she said as they followed her.

"What's behind these doors?" the younger officer asked, nodding toward two closed doors that were on opposite sides of the hall.

"They're bedrooms," Annie answered, not bothering to stop. "Both are presently rented. This is where I sleep," she said once they'd reached her room. "Don't let the frills and ruffles fool you; it's also where I hide my murder weapons." The younger officer looked amused.

"This is the room you shared with your late husband?" the other one asked.

"No. I moved out of the master bedroom once he, um, disappeared."

"We'd like to have a look inside that room as well."

"I just told you it's rented. The tenant isn't here at the moment."

"We'll be careful not to disturb anything," he said. "You may return to the kitchen," he added politely.

Annie knew it was useless to argue, so she did as she was told. She found Lamar sitting at the kitchen table, a cup of coffee in front of him. Destiny sat at the other end, glaring. Lovelle sipped her coffee quietly.

Theenie looked at Lamar. "When I lose things, which is often, I usually have to write down each place I went that day."

"I beg your pardon?" Lamar said.

"I was referring to Charles Fortenberry's remains."

Suddenly a door slammed upstairs. Peaches raced down the stairs, her fur standing up on her back. She jumped onto one of the empty chairs and curled into a tight ball.

"Who else is in the house?" Lamar asked.

"Nobody," Annie muttered.

"I clearly heard—"

"It's the spirit," Destiny snapped. "If you don't believe it, go look. You won't find anyone up there. Anyone who is alive," she added.

Lamar just looked at her as if unsure what to say or do. He took a sip of his coffee, eyeing Destiny over the rim of his cup.

An hour passed. Annie thrummed her fingers on the table. "How much longer is this going to take?" she said, clearly annoyed. "I have a lot to do."

"And I need to use the restroom," Theenie said, getting up from the table. "I've held it as long as I can." She didn't wait for Lamar's okay before she left the room.

"This really sucks," Destiny told him. "I can't wait until you ask me for help on a case, because I'm going to have a few choice words waiting for you. And don't even *think* of asking me out again, because I'll slug you.

And by the way, I hope that new fishing boat of yours sinks. I hope you accidentally shoot yourself in the foot with your gun. I hope—"

"I think I get your point," a red-faced Lamar answered. He looked at Annie. "May I have another cup of coffee?"

"Let him get it himself," Lovelle said.

More time passed, and Annie could feel her anger rising with each passing minute. "You're wasting our time," she said, "when you could be out looking for the real killer."

The older officer suddenly appeared in the doorway. "Chief, could you come back here?"

Lamar nodded and got up from his chair. "I'd appreciate it if you ladies kept your seats," he said.

Peaches jumped down from the chair and walked to her empty bowl. She butted it with her nose until it was right at Annie's feet. Annie ignored her, and the cat walked away.

"Oh no!" Theenie said after a moment. "Peaches is digging in your favorite plant. I don't know why she insists on doing it when she knows she isn't supposed to."

Annie stared at the cat. "She does it because she knows I don't like it." Annie was tempted to ignore Lamar's order to keep her seat so she could toss the cat outside. Instead, Annie just sat there as dirt flew to the floor. Peaches paused and looked at her, topaz eyes unblinking. Annie wondered why the cat chose to pick on her. She had taken exceptionally good care of the animal. There were times the cat seemed to almost like her, those times when Annie awakened in the morning to find Peaches curled in the bed beside her. But mostly Peaches was a big pain in the butt.

Theenie patted Annie's hand. "It'll all be over with shortly. Why don't we discuss the rehearsal dinner for tomorrow night? There's an awful lot to do between now and then."

"I'm not in the mood, Theenie."

Lamar returned a few minutes later wearing rubber gloves and carrying several plastic bags. He held one up so Annie could get a close look. It was filled with cash. "You recognize this?" he asked.

"No. Where on earth did you get it?"

"There was a little hidey-hole in the master bedroom closet. Someone had cut out a piece of Sheetrock, stuffed the money inside, and put the Sheetrock back in place. There's almost thirty grand here."

Annie gasped. "Thirty thousand dollars!"

"Holy mackerel," Theenie said. She turned to Annie. "I thought you were broke."

"I *am* broke!"

"You're saying you know nothing about the money?" Lamar asked.

"That's exactly what I'm saying," Annie told him.

"As I recall, that's the amount of money your husband took from your joint savings. Now, why would he pack his bags and not grab the money?"

"Wait a minute," Annie said. "Before you just assume that's the money Charles took from our account, you might want to make sure it doesn't belong to my tenant Wes Bridges. How do we know that he didn't put it there for safekeeping? He paid two weeks' rent with cash." She knew it sounded dumb, nobody carried that amount of money around, but Lamar's suspicions didn't make much sense, either.

Lamar held up the second plastic bag. "Charles's passport," he said. "We found it hidden with the money. And this bag." He paused and held it up. "There's a one-way plane ticket to Jamaica."

Annie suddenly felt light-headed. "I didn't know

Charles had a passport. The few times we discussed traveling he said there were several places he wanted to see in this country before he traveled abroad."

Lamar took the chair beside her. "You know what I think, Annie? I think Charles was in the process of packing his bags when he ran into his killer."

Annie felt the room spin. She placed both hands flat on the table as she tried to clear her head. "I don't know what to think. And how come there was only one plane ticket? I can't imagine him going to Jamaica alone."

Lamar shrugged as though he didn't think it pertinent. "Annie, I'm going to have to take you in."

She just looked at him.

The younger officer stepped forward. "Mrs. Fortenberry, I'm going to have to ask you to stand."

"What?" Annie looked up. She blinked several times before pushing herself up from the chair. Destiny and Theenie stood as well. Lovelle sat there, looking from one to the other, eyes wide and disbelieving.

The officer pulled a set of handcuffs from his back pocket.

"Hold it right there!" Destiny said. "You so much as try to cuff her, and I'll claw your eyes out, and put a hex on you. Your wife will leave you, and your house will become infested with termites."

The man winced and looked at Lamar. "You know I can't afford to have my place treated for termites."

"Put those damn handcuffs away," Lamar said. He looked at Annie. "I don't know any other way to say this, Annie, but you're under arrest for the murder of Charles Fortenberry." He turned to the officer. "Read her her rights."

It was late afternoon when Wes Bridges stormed into Lamar's office. He found Jamie Swift and Max Holt sitting across the desk from the man. "I just heard the news. What the hell is going on here?" he demanded of Lamar.

Lamar leaned back in his chair. "Excuse me, but we're having a private conversation here."

"Let him stay," Max said.

Wes kicked the door closed and folded his arms across his chest. "What the hell business do you have arresting Annie?" he demanded.

Lamar opened his mouth to answer, but Max cut him off. "She's being arraigned late this afternoon. I'll see that she doesn't spend a night in jail."

Lamar shook his head. "Ain't no way a judge is going to agree to bail on a murder charge."

"Maybe I'll get lucky and find a good criminal attorney," Max replied.

"Not in this town you won't. The best criminal attorney in the entire Southeast is Cal Nunamaker from Hilton Head, but he only takes high-profile cases, and he charges a bundle. Anyway, he's semiretired. Spends most of his time on a private island off the coast of Florida."

Max didn't respond.

Wes pointed a finger in Lamar's face. "I'm sick of this bullshit, Tevis. You know damned well Annie didn't kill her husband."

Lamar blinked several times as though trying to regain his composure. "Just so happens I have evidence that puts her in a bad light."

Wes scoffed. "What evidence?"

"It's no secret," Lamar said, "but Annie's husband, I mean her *deceased* husband, withdrew all the money from their savings account the day before he disappeared. We found the money this morning after searching her house. There was almost thirty thousand dollars stashed in his closet. Annie suggested it might belong to you."

Wes shook his head. "I don't travel with that much

cash, and it doesn't prove anything with regard to Annie. She obviously didn't know the money was there; she assumed her husband took it and ran."

"It boils down to this," Lamar said. "Charles Fortenberry was murdered before he had a chance to get to the money, and that same person had to dispose of his body and his luggage before driving his car to the Savannah airport."

"Once again, that doesn't prove shit where Annie is concerned."

"There's more," Lamar said. "Annie went to the bank the same day her husband cleaned out the account. She'd obviously hoped to beat him to it, but she was too late."

"That's impossible," Wes said. "She was out of town. Visiting her sick mother," he added.

Lamar shook his head. "I drove over to the bank yesterday and spoke with the teller who assisted Mrs. Fortenberry, um, Annie, with her transactions the day she claimed she left town. The woman clearly remembered the incident because Annie became real upset when she learned all the money was gone. In fact, Annie was still inside the bank when they locked the door and put up the *Closed* sign. She insisted on getting all of her important papers from the safe-deposit box."

Wes shook his head. "There's been a mistake."

Lamar handed Wes a slip of paper. "Annie had to sign this when she closed the safe-deposit box. I had the bank manager check the signature. It's Annie's all right. It's dated the same day her husband withdrew the money." He leaned back in his chair and propped his feet on his desk. "Not only that; she admitted she drove to the house to confront him. She claims he wasn't there, but she can't prove it, and we don't know what *really* happened.

"Bottom line: she lied. People don't lie unless they've got something to hide, and if she lied once, what's to say she hasn't been lying all along?" He paused. "Anything else you want to know?"

Wes tossed the slip of paper onto Lamar's desk. "I think that covers it," he said. "I'll get out of your way and let you do your job."

Chapter
EIGHT

"No, Vera!" Jamie said, standing in the lobby of the police department. "I will absolutely *not* allow you to take pictures of Annie being led to the courthouse in handcuffs. Isn't it bad enough that every newspaper and TV station within a hundred-mile radius is out there?"

"How in Hades are we supposed to get a story without a picture?" Vera insisted while Mike shuffled his feet nervously. Vera placed her hands on her hips. "I know Annie is your friend, but we need this story, Jamie. This is hot, especially since they lost her husband's body. Folks are tired of hearing about Tim Haskin's bull busting through the fence every other day and how the hair dryer at Susie Q's Cut and Curl malfunctioned and burned Lorraine Brown's hair right off her head."

"Absolutely no pictures," Jamie said, "and that's final." She looked at Mike. "You can continue to write the stories, but as we discussed, I have full editorial control."

He nodded.

Max nudged Jamie. "I need to touch base with Muffin. I'll be back before they escort Annie next door."

"Good. She's going to need all the support she can get."

Max hurried to his car and climbed in. "Muffin, are you there?"

"No, I'm sipping a rum and Coke in Tahiti," replied a voice that Max had programmed to sound like

Marilyn Monroe. Muffin was Max's high-powered voice-recognition computer that ran his business empire and personal life from the dashboard of his car. Muffin had attitude.

"I need you to run a check," he said.

"Who's the lucky person?"

Max didn't hesitate. "I want everything you can get me on a guy named Wes Bridges."

"Don't make me angry, Lamar," Jamie said. "You owe Max and me."

"I'd listen to her," Vera said. "She's on a diet."

Lamar sighed. "Let me get this straight. You want me to allow a murder suspect to attend her arraignment without handcuffs. What if she tries to escape?"

"Oh brother!" Jamie said.

Vera patted her handbag. "I've got my .38. I'll shoot her in the kneecaps."

Lamar gaped.

"Vera's kidding," Jamie said.

"And we want her taken out through the back way," Max said.

When Lamar hesitated, Vera gave a grunt. "Lamar wants to get his face on TV," she said.

Lamar was prevented from answering when a white stretch limo stopped in front of the building. A moment later, the driver opened the back door and a blond middle-aged man climbed out. He wore a white tennis outfit that showed off his tanned, well-toned body. Reporters immediately surrounded him, but he merely shook his head and made his way toward the front doors of the police station.

"Holy smokes, it's Cal Nunamaker!" Lamar said. He looked at Max. "How in the world did you manage that?"

"I asked politely."

The man pushed through the glass doors of the police station and perused the group with sharp blue eyes. Max stepped forward, shook his hand, and made introductions. "Thanks for agreeing to take the case on such short notice, Cal."

Nunamaker smiled. "I came straight from the tennis court. Nice airplane you got there, Max. How did you know my favorite dish was lobster thermidor?"

"Just a wild guess."

Nunamaker looked at Lamar. "Nice to see you again, Chief Travis."

"It's Tevis," Lamar said, blushing.

Nunamaker checked his watch. "I want to see every piece of paper you have on my client. And don't tell me you've put her in a cell, because that's going to ruin my day."

Lamar cleared his throat. "We've got her in our nicest interrogation room. Matter of fact, we recently had it painted."

"And another thing," Nunamaker said, as though he wasn't listening. "I expect her to be dressed nicely at the arraignment. No jailhouse clothes or handcuffs, you got that?"

"I'm on it." Lamar hurried away.

"So what do you think?" Max said.

Nunamaker shrugged. "From what you said over the phone, all the evidence is circumstantial. There's no confession, no witness, no weapon. Hell, there's not even a body," he added with a wide grin.

"All they've got is probable cause," Nunamaker went on, "but that's all they need to arrest somebody. I called the DA from the plane. He was ready to charge Mrs. Fortenberry with premeditated murder, if you can believe it, but I threatened to make his life miserable, so he changed his mind."

Jamie gasped, suspecting that wouldn't bode well for Annie. "Can you get away with something like that?"

The man grinned. "Ordinarily he'd probably report me to the bar, but we're good tennis buddies, and he wants me to put in a good word for him at the Hilton Head Country Club so they'll offer him a membership. They don't let just anyone in. Do you play tennis, Max? You look awfully fit."

"Not as much as I used to. Do you think the judge will let her out on bail?"

"Normally he wouldn't, but he and I are tight."

"Is he a tennis buddy as well?" Jamie asked.

"No, he's my brother-in-law. I'll still have to argue the point, mostly so I get good press, but I don't foresee a problem. I should warn you, though: the bail is going to be high. Otherwise folks might think he's showing favoritism."

"No problem," Max said. "As long as he'll take a check."

"Hell, you're Max Holt. He'll take an IOU on a gum wrapper. Seriously, you and I should get together and hit a few balls sometime."

Lamar returned with a file folder in his hands, a female officer beside him. "The defendant is changing clothes," he said, handing Nunamaker the folder. "My officer will escort you back in a few minutes."

"You're a good man, Tavis."

Annie paced the room and watched the clock. Only thirty minutes left before she would have to face a judge who would probably throw her in the slammer until she was old enough to use a walker. She wouldn't be able to help Max and Jamie with their wedding. She had let them down, and she had shed more tears over that than she had over being arrested.

She jumped when someone tapped on the door. The female officer who'd been so kind to her opened the door. "Your lawyer is here, Mrs. Fortenberry."

Annie blinked. "Lawyer?"

A man in a tennis outfit stepped into the room. "Mrs. Fortenberry, at last we meet, and I must say you're about the prettiest little thing I've ever seen. I'm Cal Nunamaker, your attorney. You can call me Cal. May I call you Annie?"

She nodded dumbly. "Did the court appoint you?"

"Oh no. A friend of yours, Max Holt, hired me. I promise I'll get you out of here lickety-split. Do you have any questions?"

"You're saying I won't go to jail?"

"Absolutely not. In fact, you'll be home in time for supper."

Annie couldn't hide her astonishment. "But I've been charged with murder."

He smiled kindly. "We both know you didn't kill your husband."

"I've never killed anyone in my life."

"So I want you to wipe that worried look from your face and give me a big smile."

Annie just looked at him.

"You're not smiling," he said.

She forced herself to smile.

"That's much better. Now, you just sit tight for a few minutes, and I'll be waiting outside to walk you next door to the courthouse."

Annie nodded as the officer let him out. The woman turned and gave Annie a thumbs-up before she closed the door.

"I have never been so humiliated in my life," Annie hissed to Jamie when they exited the courthouse more than an hour later. Annie blinked several times when she saw the crowd that had doubled in size during her brief arraignment, where she had actually been charged with murder and given a court date. Several news vans waited out front, men and women stood on the steps holding microphones, and they raced toward Annie as soon as they caught sight of her. "Oh no," she said.

"Trust me, we want the publicity," Nunamaker whispered. "I'll handle everything." He stepped forward as microphones were thrust at him. "Ladies and gentlemen, I'm sure all of you know me, but for the record, I'm Cal Nunamaker, and I'm representing Mrs. Annie Fortenberry. I am only going to comment briefly on the case, and if you're nice I'll take a few questions." He gave them a movie-star smile.

"Mrs. Fortenberry is absolutely and unequivocally not guilty of the preposterous murder charge that has been brought against her by a police force that is either too stupid or too lazy to perform a real investigation." He paused to catch his breath. "Once this silly matter is behind us I plan to take measures to see that reparations are made."

"Are you saying you plan to sue?" one of the reporters asked.

"I'm planning something more formidable," he said. "My client is an honorable, law-abiding citizen, and I refuse to allow her name to be tarnished by frivolous charges that can't be backed up with solid proof."

Annie perked up when she spied a smartly dressed woman she recognized from a Charleston TV station. The woman stepped right up to Nunamaker.

"Excuse me, Mr. Nunamaker, but aren't you jumping the gun here, if you'll forgive the cliché? After all, I understand the police chief searched Mrs. Fortenberry's residence and found incriminating evidence."

"It could easily have been planted," Nunamaker said. "Chief Tavis is desperate to find a suspect after yesterday's debacle regarding the loss of Mr. Fortenberry's remains."

"Has there been any news on that?" the woman asked.

"Not that I've heard."

"From what I understand, the suspect lied as to her whereabouts the day of her husband's disappearance," the woman went on smoothly. "There's also talk of a troubled marriage and adulterous affairs. That, combined with the fact the remains were found buried in the backyard, is pretty damaging in my opinion."

"And that, young lady, is precisely why I'm representing her and you're not," Cal said, earning a dark look from her. "That's all I have in my opinion."

The reporters called out more questions, even as Annie was led away with Max, Jamie, and Nunamaker surrounding her. The crowd was so thick that Annie didn't see Wes standing at the very back.

Annie was feeling better by the time she arrived home. Cal had insisted on giving her a ride in the limo Max had sent for him. He'd gone over the case briefly with Annie, discussed his strategy, and given her his private cell phone number in case she needed to reach him. He didn't stop talking until they arrived at her mansion, at which time his mouth fell open.

"Well now, I've never seen anything like *that*," he said.

"And you probably never will," Annie assured him.

Annie barely made it to the front steps before Theenie threw open the front door. She rushed out, followed by Lovelle and Danny. "Oh, thank goodness you're home!" Theenie cried, throwing her arms around Annie's neck. "Lovelle and I have been sick with worry. I don't know what we would have done had Danny not stayed with us. And, bless her heart, Jamie called several times with an update."

Annie gave Danny a grateful look and he smiled, but she could see the deep concern in his eyes. It was the same look he'd worn as he waited with Annie during her grandmother's final hours, the look he'd worn when he told her about Charles's infidelity and afterward, when Annie realized her husband was gone, along with their savings.

Theenie pulled away slightly and reached for a tissue as Lovelle gave Annie a quick hug. "It's going to be okay," Annie said.

Theenie took Annie's hand. "Come inside, dear. We decided to hold off serving dinner until you got here."

"Welcome home, Anniekins," Danny said, leaning over to kiss the top of her head. "It's good to have you back."

Annie's kitchen had never looked more inviting to her. Theenie and Lovelle ordered her to take her seat at the table while they put the finishing touches on the meal. Although Annie had not eaten all day, she had little appetite, but she forced herself to eat so as not to hurt the women's feelings.

"Where is Erdle?" she asked.

"Who knows?" Lovelle said. "He hasn't been home all day."

"And Wes?"

"He came back a couple of hours after you were arrested," Theenie said. "He left as soon as I told him. He didn't say where he was going."

Annie wondered if he'd gone to the police station, if he'd spoken with Lamar, if he knew the truth.

Lovelle glanced up from her dinner. "Destiny called Lamar to check on you, then lost her temper on the phone, and then Danny grabbed the phone, and it went from bad to worse. You should have heard all the names he called Lamar. Even used the *F* word," she added proudly.

"I'm sorry to have put all of you through this," Annie said.

"It's not your fault," Danny said. "The good news is the ballroom floor looks great."

Annie smiled. "Thank you." She looked from one to the other and was touched to have such good friends. "By the way, where is Destiny?"

"She had to go into the office and help out, since Max and Jamie were at the police station. It probably saved Lamar's life." Theenie touched Annie's hand. "Did they lock you up with one of those, you know, *big* women?" she whispered.

Annie laughed. "No, Theenie. I never even saw a jail cell."

The woman gave an enormous sigh of relief. "Oh, thank goodness!"

"Everything is going to be okay, you guys. I promise." Annie hoped she sounded more convincing than she felt.

It was late when Max and Jamie left the newspaper office. Muffin had news for them the minute they climbed into his car.

"I have information on Wes Bridges," Muffin said.

"I'm listening," Max said.

"He used to be a cop in Columbia, graduated to detective and pretty much ran the homicide unit. Now he's a private investigator." Max and Jamie exchanged looks. "The man doesn't come cheap, but he's supposed to be the best in the business. Charles Fortenberry's mother hired him to look into her son's disappearance after she collected insurance money on her husband's death."

"That explains why he rented a room from Annie,"

Jamie said. "Eve Fortenberry suspected Annie had something to do with Charles's disappearance." She looked at Max. "I don't like it. I think we should drive over and tell Annie right this minute."

"I don't think that's a good idea," Max said.

"How can you say that? I think Annie has feelings for this guy."

"She's also up for murder. If he's that good, he just might find out who killed her husband."

"I don't want to see her hurt, Max. Again," Jamie added.

Max reached for her hand and squeezed it reassuringly. "It'll be a whole lot easier getting over a broken heart than doing prison time," he said. "I'm going to have to ask you to go along with me on this one, Swifty."

Jamie was quiet for a moment. "That doesn't mean I have to like it."

It was late when Wes arrived back at Annie's. She was sitting on the piazza, a candle burning on the wicker table beside her. "'Bout time you got home, Bridges," she said once he'd cleared the top step.

He glanced her way. "Do you make a point of sitting up until all your tenants arrive back safely?" he asked.

His tone was as cool as the breeze that whipped across her face and ruffled her thick hair. "I was worried about you."

"How was jail?"

Annie frowned. "That's a helluva thing to ask."

"Yeah? Well, I'm not feeling very sociable tonight."

He had learned the truth. She had been naive to think he wouldn't eventually find out. She should have known that even Lamar would learn that she'd withheld information. Wes crossed the piazza and reached for the door.

"I was scared," she said. "Afraid that Lamar would

think the worst if he found out I was in the bank that day."

"Well, he *does* think the worst, and now you're in a shitload of trouble. You weren't where you said you were, meaning you don't have an alibi for what, a week?"

She scooted forward on the swing. "I went to my mother's house just like I said. But when I arrived, she took one look at my face and knew something was wrong. I told her I had an appointment with a divorce attorney the following week, and she insisted that I return to Beaumont immediately and clean out the savings account. I was only planning to take half of the money, but I was too late."

"So you confronted him?"

"That was the plan, only Charles wasn't home. I was so outraged that I didn't think to check to see if he'd packed his clothes until I was on my way back to my mother's. I just figured what the hell, he was well on his way to wherever he was going."

"Lamar found the money."

"And you think I knew it was here?"

"I don't know what the hell to think, Annie. I'm having a real problem distinguishing fact from fiction."

Finally, she stood. She didn't know if she was angry or hurt at his response. "Fact," she began. "I wouldn't have spent the last few years struggling financially if I'd had that kind of money to fall back on. Fact: if I *had* found the money and Charles's passport and ticket, I would have immediately suspected something was wrong and gone to Lamar."

Wes looked at her, and the hard lines on his face relaxed. "I'm sorry you had a shit day, Annie, but look at the good side. You were on CNN."

As Annie watched him go in, she pictured throwing her rolling pin at him and it bouncing off the back of his head. Like she needed to be reminded that she had made CNN. The telephone hadn't stopped ringing since the story had first aired, only to be replayed every hour on the hour, as if the staff feared that one person in the town of Beaumont might miss it.

Annie had finally taken the phone off the hook after her mother called from West Palm Beach, having watched the whole sordid thing unfold after headlines announced that the remains of a South Carolina man were missing due to a carjacking. Not only had they mentioned Charles Fortenberry by name; they'd also given a brief history of the case, beginning with the unearthing of his bones. There was a goofy picture of Lamar Tevis standing at the site pointing toward a mound of dirt, followed by footage of Annie at her best, in an old chenille bathrobe, hair out to there, yelling and shaking her fists at a TV camera. The next shot showed Annie trying to duck behind Cal Nunamaker on the courthouse steps after her arraignment.

"I just want you to know I'm here for you, Annie," Jenna Worthington had said. "I'll catch the first plane out if you need me. I'll even sleep in that god-awful house if I have to."

Annie had thanked her but said it wasn't necessary. Still, the fact that she had offered to come had taken some of the sting out of being hauled off to jail that morning.

Annie had been hard at work since dawn, getting things ready for the rehearsal dinner and trying to sidestep Peaches, who obviously hoped something edible would come her way.

Annie looked down and shook her head. "You've already had two cans of cat food this morning. I think you have an eating disorder."

The cat meowed.

"Sorry, all I have is lettuce." Annie resumed her

work. A moment later, she heard a noise, turned, and found Peaches digging in her plant.

"No!" Annie said firmly, unaware that Wes was standing at the bottom of the stairs. She hurried toward the plant and, reached for the fat ball of orange fur, but Peaches dived to the floor in the opposite direction. Annie turned so quickly she lost her footing and fell, butt-first on the plant. It toppled over and dumped potting soil on the kitchen floor. Annie sat there for a moment, muttering four-letter words under her breath as Peaches walked to the braided rug in front of the refrigerator, slumped on it, and began grooming herself.

"Problems?" Wes said.

Annie looked at him. "What makes you ask?"

He grabbed a coffee mug, filled it, and sipped in silence. Peaches got up, walked over to him, and rubbed against his leg. Wes reached down and scratched the animal lightly behind one ear, and she began to purr. Finally, he belted down the rest of his coffee, placed the empty cup in the dishwasher, and started for the door.

He paused and looked down at Annie. "Do you need help getting up?"

"Nope. I like it here."

He nodded, unlocked the door, and opened it. "Just so you know, that plant is a goner."

Annie heard him fire up his bike, and a moment later he roared away. He no longer trusted her. At this point, she wasn't even sure he liked her. And she didn't have the foggiest idea how to make things right between them. It was her own fault. She should have told Lamar everything when he'd questioned her shortly after Charles's disappearance. But she hadn't. And that was only going to make things worse.

Erdle arrived home as Annie was serving breakfast,

and she and Theenie watched him stagger across the
backyard and upstairs to his apartment. "I guess he fell
off the wagon," Theenie said.

Annie looked at her. "You think?"

Danny pulled up in his car, climbed out, and walked
toward the carriage house, opening the door on the first
floor that led into the garage. He emerged a moment
later with the rake. "Oh, he's going to tidy the yard for
you," Theenie said. "How sweet."

Annie nodded. She would take him a cup of coffee
and invite him up for breakfast. "Yeah, he's a good
guy," she said. "I don't know what I'd do without him."

"Maybe it's high time you gave it serious thought,"
Theenie replied. "But I suspect it's too late now, since
you've already got it bad for Wes."

Max's plane touched down on the small airstrip that
afternoon. Jamie stood beside Max and Frankie as it
taxied in while Dee Dee and her personal assistant,
Beenie, waited in the stretch limo. Fleas, who'd insisted
on following Jamie from the car, had immediately
found a sunny spot on a patch of grass next to the building. He was presently sprawled on his back, eyes closed,
snoring loudly.

Max glanced at the animal. "I swear I think that dog
has sleep apnea."

"He snores louder than Dee Dee," Frankie said, and
immediately punched his fist lightly against his forehead. "Please don't tell Dee Dee I said that."

The plane rolled to a stop, and a few minutes later
Nick and Billie Kaharchek descended. Billie's children
followed them: Christie, a dark-haired beauty in a smart
dove gray business suit, and younger brother Joel, who
had the same hair color as his sister but obviously
lacked her sense of style. He wore khakis, a kelly green

dress shirt, and the ugliest plaid jacket Jamie had ever seen. He was a good two inches taller than Nick and had an easy lopsided smile.

Everyone hugged and Nick and Billie praised the smooth flight while Joel extolled the awesome in-flight cookie tray and Christie complained good-naturedly that she had probably put on five pounds by eating her weight in brownies.

"You two amaze me," Max told Nick and Billie. "You never age."

Billie laughed. Despite having a little age on her, she had maintained the youthfulness and zest for life that had drawn Nick to her some twenty years ago.

When Max had flown Jamie to Virginia to meet Nick and Billie, she had taken an instant liking to the handsome couple who had practically raised Max. Jamie was equally fond of Christie and Joel. She liked that Billie was down-to-earth and unpretentious despite having married a multimillionaire.

"Where's Dee Dee?" Nick asked Frankie, who was in the process of checking Joel's muscles and planning their first arm-wrestling match.

"In the limo. She's having problems with her feet."

"I need to give her a big hug," Billie said.

"Just don't tell her she's fat," Frankie whispered to the group.

Billie smacked his arm, and they started toward the vehicle as the last piece of luggage was placed inside the trunk. "I plan to smother her with a lot of TLC while I'm here," Billie said.

Jamie glanced in Fleas' direction. He rolled over, pulled himself up, and shook, his big ears and sagging jowls flapping from side to side. He started toward them in slow gear.

"Check out that cool bloodhound," Joel said. "I think he's following us."

"He belongs to Jamie," Max said. "Although I've agreed to adopt him after we're married."

Everyone paused and waited for the dog to catch up. Christie reached down and stroked his head. "What's his name?"

It was the question Jamie always dreaded. "Fleas."

Instead of jerking her hand away like most people, Christie laughed loudly. "Poor baby," she said. "No wonder you look depressed. Who stuck you with a name like that?"

"Not me," Jamie said, noting that Fleas was giving Christie his most pitiful look, having perfected it when he'd discovered it was usually followed by Jamie-the-sucker pulling his favorite butter pecan ice cream from the freezer. "And he always looks like a candidate for Prozac."

"What happened to his fur?" Joel asked, reaching down to pet Fleas as well.

"Hey, you guys are looking at a champion and silver-cup raccoon hunter," Max said, although the looks he received were dubious. "He's since gone into retirement, living off his 401-K now."

"Well, if you ask me, it looks like the last coon kicked some hound dog butt," Joel said.

Frankie opened the back door of the limo and climbed in next to Dee Dee as the others began opening doors, waving off the chauffeur's offer to assist. A subdued Beenie sat beside Dee Dee and nodded as Frankie made introductions, trying to talk above the compact TV set where a woman was kneeling before a toilet bowl singing the praises of a new product. Frankie hit the remote control button, and the woman disappeared as quickly as she had assured the toilet bowl stains would.

"You look wonderful," Billie said, reaching across the seat to hug Dee Dee. "Except I thought you'd have put on weight by now."

"She's already gained fifty pounds," Frankie said. He winced the moment the words left his mouth. "Although you'd never know it to look at her," he added sheepishly.

It wasn't until they were all seated that Jamie noticed Dee Dee and Beenie were behaving oddly. They had said very little, and there was tension on their faces. "Dee Dee, are you okay?" she asked.

When Dee Dee hesitated, Beenie spoke for her. "We just saw your friend on CNN."

Chapter
NINE

Annie was wearing a bright smile when she answered the doorbell shortly before 6:00 PM and found Max, Jamie, and Max's family standing on the other side. "Welcome to my home!" she called out gaily to the crowd, wondering how many of them had seen her on CNN. The only thing she had going for her was the fact that she looked one hundred percent better than she had on TV in her shabby bathrobe.

She had purposefully chosen to dress like an old-maid librarian: conservative dark gray skirt that fell below her knees, rose-colored cardigan and shell, sensible pumps, and her grandmother's antique cross pendant. Lovelle had offered her rosary, but Annie figured that would be overkill.

"Please come in," Annie said, stepping aside so the group could enter.

Jamie and Max gave Annie a hug. Jamie had called earlier in an obvious attempt to cheer Annie and make light of her CNN debut, and in the end they were laughing hysterically, just like old times.

Max began making introductions.

"I've already met our mayor and his beautiful wife," Annie said, offering Frankie and Dee Dee a warm handshake. Frankie and Dee Dee were infamously fun-loving and colorful, though Dee Dee was known to be a bit of a drama queen and prone to hysterics. And with her late-in-life pregnancy, these personality traits were becoming increasingly pronounced.

Dee Dee's bottom lip trembled when she smiled, and she didn't quite meet Annie's gaze. "I've heard so much about you," she said. "From Jamie," she added quickly.

They all knew, Annie told herself. Probably everyone in Beaumont knew by now, which explained the traffic jam out front. Theenie had caught several people snapping pictures.

"Pregnancy becomes you," Annie said. "You must be very excited."

"Yes." Dee Dee's voice squeaked and she edged closer to Frankie.

Finally, Max turned to an older couple. "This good-looking twosome is my cousin and best man, Nick Kaharchek, and his lovely wife, Billie. They took me in when I was dangerous," he added with a grin.

"He's still dangerous," Nick said.

Annie greeted them. She could see the resemblance between Max and Nick, even though the older man's face bore a few lines that gave him an air of distinction. His wife was lovely and exuded a feeling of warmth as she smiled and shook Annie's hand.

"And these are my children, Christie and Joel," Billie said.

Annie offered her hand, and the young woman shook it and gave her a quick wink that suggested Annie was all right in her book. Joel held Annie's hand longer than necessary and flirted shamelessly.

"Enough already," Billie said as she pulled him away and told him to behave. "I'm still your elder," she said, trying to sound stern and failing miserably because she couldn't quite hide her smile.

Annie noted an anxious-looking dark-haired man standing at a distance. He stepped forward and shook hands, but Annie could see that his smile was forced. "I'm Beenie," he said. "I sort of take care of Dee Dee."

"He spoils her rotten," Max said.

"I could use someone like you," Annie replied jokingly. "How would you like to come to work for me?"

"I can't!" he blurted, drawing stares from those around them. He blushed. "I mean, Dee Dee needs me. Especially right now with the baby due soon," he added. "I'm her personal assistant, so I can't leave her side. Not for five minutes, even if it means sleeping at the foot of her bed like a Chihuahua."

"Jamie was right about the house," Billie said, taking in the living room. "It's unlike anything I've ever seen. In a good way," she added.

Jamie nodded enthusiastically. "I told you you'd love it. How many people get to tie the knot in a pre–Civil War bordello?"

"Red is Dee Dee's favorite color," Frankie said. "She wants the name of your decorator before we leave, right, honey?"

"Um . . ." Dee Dee looked at Beenie.

"I don't think red is a good color for babies," Beenie said. "The person who decorated the nursery thought red was an angry color."

Annie laughed. "I suppose that explains my bad temper," she said. "Because I'm surrounded by red."

Annie had already served cocktails and hors d'oeuvres by the time Vera Bankhead arrived. "Saw you on CNN," she whispered. "I'd rethink that chenille bathrobe."

"I'll keep that in mind," Annie said. She was about to close the door when she spotted the minister hurrying up the front walk. She was glad Theenie had removed some of the more risqué objets d'art, although she suspected her grandmother was frowning down at her.

Reverend Lester Tuttle had presided over a number of weddings in Annie's house. She introduced him. He sat close to Max and Jamie, obviously wanting to get to know the couple before the wedding. Destiny entered by way of the dining room, wearing a purple ankle-length dress that hugged her curves and breasts and brought a bright blush to the minister's cheeks as they shook hands.

"I'll hang out here and see to the refreshments," Destiny whispered to Annie. "I know you have things to do in the kitchen."

Annie thanked her and hurried through the dining room and the swinging door that led to the kitchen, where Theenie and Lovelle were checking the two prime rib roasts with meat thermometers. "How do they look?" Annie asked.

"Everything is right on schedule," Theenie proudly announced. "We should be ready to serve the first course as soon as the rehearsal is over."

"Has Wes come in?" Annie asked.

Theenie shook her head. "Haven't seen him."

Annie tried to hide her disappointment as she worked to get things ready. When she was certain all was in order, she returned to the living room and led the group into the chapel. For the next half hour Reverend Tuttle instructed the wedding party as to when they would come in, where they would stand, and Annie coached Jamie and Dee Dee as they practiced walking down the aisle.

"Would you just look at me," Dee Dee said to Jamie. "I'm waddling like a duck."

Jamie and Annie lied, insisting that was not the case.

"Are you still planning to use Fleas as your, um, flower dog?" Annie asked Jamie.

She nodded. "I know it sounds totally crazy, so go ahead and say it."

"It *is* crazy," Vera said. "The craziest thing I've ever heard."

"Yuck!" Dee Dee said. "You're going to have that—"

"Don't you dare call him ugly," Jamie said.

Dee Dee clamped her lips together but shook her head sadly.

"I tried to talk her out of it," Vera said to Annie, "but she treats him like her firstborn."

Annie chuckled, noting the wide-eyed look on Reverend Tuttle's face. "Trust me: having a dog in the wedding is tame compared to some of the things couples have asked for."

"Thank you for defending me," Jamie said. "I've never had a pet before, and I know I've spoiled him, but . . ." She paused and sighed. "I think his previous owner mistreated him, so I guess I'm trying to do all I can to make up for it."

"That's so sweet," Christie said. "Mom and I are bigtime animal advocates, so we admire people who take such good care of their pets."

"I still think it's dumb," Vera said.

Afterward, while Annie ushered the group into the dining room, Dee Dee asked Jamie to show her where the restroom was located. They started down the hall.

"Psst! Psst!"

Jamie glanced over her shoulder to see who was making the sound and found Beenie hurrying toward them.

"Here comes Beenie," Dee Dee said. "The man just won't leave my side."

He closed the distance between them. "What? Why are you staring at me?"

"Because you've been sticking to me like glue since we arrived."

Beenie planted one hand on his hip. "I'm your personal assistant. It's what I do."

"I have to pee. I don't think following me into the bathroom is part of your job description."

"I think Dee Dee is asking for breathing room," Jamie said.

He looked hurt. "Okay, if you insist on knowing, this place creeps me out."

Jamie made a sound of disgust. "Oh, for Pete's sake! I don't believe you said that."

"Honey, I don't want to hurt your feelings," Dee Dee said to her, "but this place gives me the heebie-jeebies, too. Why, there's a grave in the backyard, and everybody suspects Annie killed her husband. If I weren't a strong woman I would probably faint just thinking about it." She pulled a linen handkerchief from her pocket and mopped her brow. "I might faint anyway."

"You *do* look pale," Beenie said.

"She's pale because she refuses to let the sun touch any part of her body." Jamie crossed her arms. "Annie is perfectly innocent of the crime with which she's been charged. She is no more capable of murder than we are. She's also a very good friend of mine, and I don't want her feelings hurt," Jamie added. "She has been through enough."

Dee Dee looked contrite. "I'm sorry. I don't know what's gotten into me. I am so emotional these days. I seem to cry over everything."

Beenie nodded. "Me, too."

"We wouldn't think of doing anything that might embarrass you at your wedding," Dee Dee said, and Beenie nodded in agreement.

Jamie looked relieved. "Thank you." She motioned to the bathroom door. "We need to hurry. I'm sure Annie has begun serving."

Dee Dee turned for the bathroom door, then paused and turned. "Just one question," she said. "Her husband didn't die from food poisoning, did he?"

* * *

Annie noticed Jamie ate very little dinner and refused dessert, although Max convinced her to take a tiny bite of the almond torte.

Annie smiled as she refilled coffee cups. She had specifically chosen not to serve anything chocolate, knowing Jamie would find it hard to turn down. Annie and Jamie had once shared an entire bag of Snickers candy bars. It had been well worth the stomachache they'd had afterward.

Vera looked at Jamie's plate. "You barely touched your food."

"How many more pounds do you have to lose?" Dee Dee asked.

Jamie looked proud. "I'm down ten pounds. But I don't want to eat anything fattening and risk blowing it."

"Don't be surprised if you gain back a few pounds on your honeymoon," Billie said. "I kept something in my mouth the whole time."

All eyes turned her way, and Billie blushed profusely, but nobody said anything in deference to Reverend Tuttle.

"It's this house," Destiny whispered to Billie. "I haven't stopped thinking about sex since I walked through the door."

"Jamie, you should take up horseback riding," Billie said as though hoping to change the subject. "Once Max moves his horses down," she added. "That's how Nick and I keep in shape."

Dee Dee gave a shudder. "I could never understand how you could tolerate those smelly horses."

"I must be used to it by now." Billie looked at Jamie. "Before I met Nick I didn't even know how to climb on a horse."

"She didn't know how to get off, either," Nick said. "First time I tried to help her dismount she slipped and fell on me, and we both ended up on the ground." They shared a private smile.

Annie noticed the loving exchange between the two as she began to clear away the dessert dishes. She had caught Max and Jamie looking at each other the same way, and she'd felt sad that she and Charles had never experienced that degree of intensity. She wondered what it would feel like to be madly in love with someone, to fall asleep and wake up in that person's arms year after year and still share that depth of feeling.

"Max told me it was love at first sight for the two of you," Jamie said, addressing Billie and Nick.

"I guess you could say that, considering the fact we got married after knowing each other only two weeks," Billie replied.

Vera gaped. "Two weeks! Goodness, it takes me longer than that to break in a new pair of shoes. I'll bet everybody thought you were crazy."

Billie and Nick nodded in unison. "I think sometimes you just know from the beginning that it's right," he said. "At least that's the way it was for us."

"That is so sweet," Beenie said, dabbing moist eyes with his napkin.

"We had a double wedding," Frankie said. He winked at Nick. "Remember the bachelor party and Billie jumping out of that cake half-naked?"

Annie, holding a tray of empty dessert dishes, paused at the swinging door and turned around. She didn't want to miss this one.

Billie hitched her chin high. "Excuse me, but I was wearing a T-shirt over my tassels and G-string."

"A very *sheer* T-shirt," Nick corrected.

"Mother!" Christie looked shocked. "You never told me about that."

"You should have seen the men tossing money at her," Dee Dee said.

"That is so cool," Joel said. "My mom the stripper."

"I made a gigantic fool of myself," Billie confessed. "I slipped and fell across a table of cold seafood. My hair smelled like fish for days."

"I'd like to have seen that," Max said.

"You were busy at the time," Nick reminded, "taking my Mercedes apart piece by piece."

Annie grinned, pushed through the door, and entered the kitchen. Jamie joined her a few minutes later, smiling broadly. "Everything was perfect," she said. "I can't thank you enough."

"I couldn't have done it without Theenie and Lovelle," Annie said, and was pleased when Jamie praised their efforts as well. Annie's face softened. "You're going to make a beautiful bride."

"I think I'm going to cry," Theenie said, sniffing loudly.

Jamie's smile faltered when Wes walked through the back door, but she quickly regained her composure. "We're getting ready to leave," she said. Annie had noticed the change in Jamie the minute Wes had come in and had wondered at it, but didn't have time to think about it, since her guests were leaving. She hurried out front, where they thanked her for a wonderful dinner, said their good-byes, and filed out the door. Once they were gone, Annie smiled, knowing it had gone exceptionally well.

Theenie and Lovelle helped Annie clean up. As though reading her mind, Theenie looked at her. "I offered Wes something to eat, but he said he'd grabbed something earlier. I think the man lives on junk food."

Destiny entered the kitchen. "Great dinner," she said. "I would have enjoyed it even more if *she* hadn't been there."

"Who, dear?" Theenie asked.

"The spirit. She stood across the room giving Max

goo-goo eyes the whole time. The woman has no shame."

Theenie shook her head. "Well, I hope you told her Max is soon to be married." She stretched and yawned. "I don't know about the rest of you, but I'm pooped." She cut her eyes toward the stairs. "Lovelle, are you coming up?"

"I'm right behind you," Lovelle said. They wished Annie and Destiny a good night and started up the steps.

Destiny stood there for a moment watching Annie. "Are you okay?"

"Yeah. I was nervous in the beginning, but everyone was so nice they put me at ease."

Destiny was quiet for a moment. "Annie, I know how your husband died."

Annie almost dropped the coffeepot she was filling with water. "What!"

"I saw it in a vision. He died falling down those stairs." When Annie simply looked at her, she went on. "There was an argument." She'd no sooner gotten the words out of her mouth before she sneezed.

Annie reached for the box of tissues and handed it to her. "Who was with him?"

"I don't know, but I'm certain *she* saw the whole thing."

"The spirit?"

Destiny nodded. "I've asked her a dozen times, but she refuses to communicate."

"You said she was mute."

"I've been able to pick up bits and pieces telepathically, but she won't open up completely. I don't know if it's a physical or emotional problem or both, but the woman is terrified." She paused. "Here's what I think. I'm almost certain she saw her lover hanged, but she's blocked it. She had already been through the trauma of being murdered, and the hanging was too much to bear. Until she remembers I don't think she's going to talk *or* go to the light." She sneezed twice.

Annie was trying hard to keep an open mind, but it all sounded outlandish. "Can you help her?"

"I don't know."

Annie turned back to filling the coffeepot. "Is there anything else you can tell me about Charles?" she asked.

Another sneeze. "He was definitely seeing another woman, and I'm almost certain she was somebody you knew. Although I haven't actually seen it in a vision, it's logical that the person he was arguing with pushed him. I don't know if it was this woman or if it was a jealous boyfriend or husband."

Annie heard a noise and glanced up as Wes came down the stairs.

"I was going to get a glass of ice water," he said. "Am I interrupting?"

Destiny shook her head. "I'm on my way to bed." She glanced at Annie. "Thanks again for a great dinner." She disappeared up the stairs.

Wes was quiet as he leaned against the counter and sipped his water. Annie could feel his eyes on her, and she thought it best to go upstairs. "I've locked the doors," she said. "Would you turn off the light before going to bed?" She started for the stairs.

"Annie?"

She paused and turned.

"I'm sorry for being such a . . ." He paused.

She waited. "If you can't think of a word, I'll give you my list and you can choose several from that."

"Jerk," he finally said.

"That's pretty tame and has less syllables."

He almost smiled. "I probably don't want to know. Thing is, I can understand that you were afraid, what with Charles's mother making accusations and having someone like Lamar Tevis in charge of the investigation."

Annie was thoughtful. "I just want you to know I'm not a liar by trade."

He glanced at the stairs. "I accidentally overheard some of what Destiny said. Do you believe her?"

Annie shrugged. "I believe she has visions. I don't know how accurate they are."

Wes indicated the table. "Can we talk a minute?"

He waited until Annie had taken a seat before pulling a chair out for himself. "I've been checking around. I know who Charles was seeing."

Annie sucked in her breath. She almost dreaded hearing it. "Someone I know?"

"His boss's wife."

Annie frowned. "Donna Schaefer? Who in the world told you that?"

"You sit in enough bars, you're bound to hear something sooner or later. Folks are talking about the murder, finding the body." He paused and grinned. "Losing the body," he added. "By the way, about that bathrobe you were wearing on CNN—"

"I've already put it in a box to go to the women's shelter."

"Man, you're not doing those poor women any favors."

"Could we please get back to what we were discussing?"

"I heard a guy mention he'd seen Charles at the Hilltop Steakhouse a couple of times with a pretty brunette. I already suspected it was the wife after looking over Charles's cell phone bill. He placed a lot of calls to his boss's house. During the day when he would most likely be at the office," Wes added, "but I decided to dig a little deeper just to make sure, so I got a picture of her and—" When Annie arched one brow, he shook his head. "Don't ask. I took the picture to the Hilltop, along with Charles's picture, and the bartender recognized them."

"From more than three years ago?"

"The bartender accidentally spilled a drink on your husband's favorite suit one of the times he and Mrs. Schaefer came in. Bartender said Charles made a big deal out of it, so he gave him twenty bucks to have it dry-cleaned."

"I'm stunned."

"Were you and she friends?"

"Not *close* friends, but Charles and I socialized with them now and then, and Donna and I usually planned the company Christmas party together, which was always held at the country club. She spent one Saturday here, only a few months before Charles disappeared, so we could decide on the menu and discuss decorations. She and Norm, her husband, had come to dinner here a couple of times before that, but it was pretty boring because the guys talked shop the entire time." Annie paused. "I do remember feeling disappointed that she didn't call after I'd assumed Charles had left me, but I figured she didn't want to get involved in our personal problems."

"I plan to question her, of course," Wes said.

"Then I'm coming with you." When Wes started to argue, Annie held up a hand. "I want to hear it from her own lips. The sooner the better," she added.

"We can leave in the morning after breakfast."

Jimbo Gardner shook Erdle Thomey hard. "C'mon, Erdle, you gotta wake up."

Stretched out in a booth at the back of Jimbo's Bar

and Grill, Erdle mumbled something unintelligible in his sleep. He opened his eyes, made to sit up, and groaned. "Head hurrs like hell," he said.

Jimbo handed him a glass of whiskey. "Here's a little hair of the dog," he said. "Double shot, it ought to cure what ails you."

Erdle tossed back the drink, winced, and set the glass on the table. "Wha' time is it?"

"Eight AM. I couldn't wake you last night, so I decided to let you sleep it off. But I got to start cleaning this place in time for the lunch crowd."

Erdle pressed his hands on either side of his head as though he feared it would explode. "Wha' do I owe?"

"You paid your tab last night. Don't you remember?"

"Naw."

"Man, you're shaking all over. You okay?"

"'Nother shot o' whiskey might help." Erdle slurred his words badly. "I'll pay for it."

Jimbo gave a grunt of disgust. "I'll give you one more, but that's it." He went behind the bar and filled a shot glass.

Erdle gulped it and shuddered.

"I've already called a cab," Jimbo said, "but it's going to be a while before it gets here on account Otto has several people ahead of you. You'll have to pick up your car later."

Erdle didn't put up an argument as he lay back in the booth. "Lemme know when he gets here."

Annie stared tentatively at the massive black and chrome bike. She took a step back. "I've, uh, never ridden a motorcycle before," she said, wishing Wes had taken her suggestion to use her car. "What if I fall off?"

"Don't." Wes handed her a spare helmet, then put his on. "You're not afraid, are you?"

The look in his eyes challenged her. "Of course not."

"Let me help you with the strap." He tilted her head back and fastened the strap beneath her jaw. "Okay, Red, you're all set." He swung one leg over the bike and sat on the leather seat. "Your turn. Grab my shoulders and hop on."

Annie hesitated. She should have known it would require bodily contact. She did as he said, climbing on.

Wes showed her where to put her feet and started the engine. "Which way?"

The Schaefer residence was a two-story colonial with long porches and a perfectly manicured lawn. Wes parked his bike, shut off the engine, and waited for Annie to climb off.

She looked at the house as she stood and unfastened her helmet. "Let's get this over with."

Wes rang the doorbell. A moment later a striking brunette opened it, holding in her arms what appeared to be a newborn baby. She took one look at Annie, and her mouth formed a large *O*.

"Hello, Donna."

"Why, Annie Fortenberry, you are the absolute last person in the world I expected to see."

Annie smiled tightly. Donna looked considerably older, her facial bones prominent, deep creases embedded between perfectly formed eyebrows. She had lost weight and appeared as fragile as a china teacup. "I'm sorry to bother you this early," Annie said, "but it's important."

The woman's smile faded as she caught sight of Wes, but she quickly disguised it. She hesitated, as if uncertain whether to invite them in. Finally, she stepped back so they could enter.

The oversize foyer held an antique pedestal table that

shone like a new penny, on top a crystal vase with fresh flowers and beside it the mail that had been precisely stacked, larger envelopes on the bottom, the smaller ones on top.

"Gosh, how long has it been?" Donna asked, but didn't wait for an answer. "You look great."

"I see you have a new addition to the family," Annie replied. "I didn't know you'd recently had a baby or that you were even pregnant."

Donna's eyes clouded. "We haven't kept in touch like we should have," she said. She held the baby up for inspection. "This is Kevin. He's six weeks old today," she added proudly.

Annie stepped closer to get a better look at the infant, so close, in fact, that she thought she smelled alcohol on Donna's breath. "Congratulations. He's adorable."

Donna stood there a moment as if wondering what to do or say next. "Why don't we go into the den?" she suggested. "I was just about to put Kevin down for a little nap."

Annie and Wes followed the woman to the back of the house and into a large, picture-perfect room. Annie knew that a professional had decorated the room. The French doors looked out onto a covered patio where several tables and chairs sat among lush plants. Annie and Charles had attended a number of cookouts at the Schaefers'.

"Please make yourselves comfortable," Donna said. "I'll be right back."

Annie and Wes sat on the sofa. "I think she's been drinking," Annie whispered.

He looked at her. "I thought her mouthwash smelled funny."

Donna returned a few minutes later. "May I offer you refreshments?"

"No thank you," Annie said. "We can't stay long." She thought she saw relief in the woman's eyes.

Donna smoothed her wool slacks and sat in a chair directly across from them, her back ramrod straight. "Annie, Norm and I read about poor Charles in the newspaper. We were just sick over it and everything else that has occurred since. Please accept our sincere condolences. If there's anything we can do—"

"I'm fine," Annie interrupted, thinking either Donna was a damn good actress or Wes had his information wrong. Annie glanced at Wes, who seemed to be studying the woman closely. "Donna, I need to ask you something," Annie said, "and I thought it would be best if we came by while you were alone."

The woman plucked a piece of lint from her slacks. "It sounds serious."

Annie shifted on the sofa, feeling more uncomfortable by the minute. "There is talk that you and Charles were romantically involved."

Donna looked incredulous. "Who would say such a thing?"

"I have proof," Wes said.

Donna tossed a dark look his way. "I don't believe you," she said stiffly.

He nodded and stood, as did Annie. "We'll be back," he said. "With pictures."

The color drained from the woman's face. She clutched the arms of the chair. "Wait!" she said. When they faced her once more, she looked sadly resigned, and her voice was strained when she spoke. "Please." She motioned to the sofa. "Don't leave. Not yet."

They both sat.

Donna looked directly at Annie. "Why are you doing this?" she asked. "Charles has been gone for more than three years. What do you hope to accomplish by coming here now?"

"Someone murdered my husband," Annie said simply.

"And you think that person might be me?"

"Somebody who knew about the affair could have killed him," Wes said.

"If you're insinuating that my husband killed Charles, you're wrong. He didn't know about . . ." She turned sad eyes to Annie. "The affair," she added.

"So it's true," Annie said simply. She sighed heavily, trying to take it all in.

Donna began to fidget with her hands. "Charles told me the two of you were divorcing. Norm and I were having serious problems as well. Things just sort of happened, and before I knew it, Charles asked me to leave with him."

"How could Norm not have suspected?" Annie asked, and then realized what a dumb question it was, since she hadn't either.

Donna shrugged. "Who knows? Perhaps Norm was having an affair as well. He was out of town the night Charles and I were supposed to leave together. As planned, Charles and I each spent the day getting things ready, tying up loose ends. Supposedly, he had a late-afternoon appointment for an oil change. We'd planned to drive to Atlanta, spend the night, and fly out early the next morning—"

"To Jamaica," Annie said.

"Yes," Donna said, so softly it was barely audible. She took a deep breath. "I was packed and ready at the designated time, only he never showed up."

"What time was that?" Wes asked.

"Seven PM." Annie had left for her mother's that morning.

"What did you do?" Wes asked. "When he didn't show up?"

"What *could* I do? I just assumed I'd been duped."
Her shoulders sagged; she seemed to sink within herself. "I should have known something was up. We'd
planned the trip well in advance, but Charles stopped
calling as often as he had before. Even when I knew it
was safe to call his cell, he didn't always answer. When
he did answer, he acted rushed." She gave a rueful smile.
"I knew there'd been other women . . ." She paused as
tears sprang to her eyes. "But you know how it is: you
keep thinking you're different from the others."

"No, Donna," Annie said coolly. "I don't know how
it is."

More tears. Donna swallowed. "I was desperate." It
took her a moment to pull herself together. "Anyway,
Norm and I managed to get our marriage back on track,
and a couple of years later I became pregnant with
Kevin. Things are going well for us, Annie." Her eyes
seemed to plead for understanding, even as tears ran
down her cheeks.

"I'm happy for you both," Annie said, "but the fact
remains, my husband *was* planning to leave. He'd
packed his bags. Only he never made it because somebody murdered him."

Donna shook her head. "I don't know anything about
it other than what I read in the newspaper like everyone
else. And, of course, heard on CNN."

Annie closed her eyes. Just her luck that her husband's
mistress had seen her in that damn bathrobe.

"You say your husband was out of town at the time,"
Wes said. "Where was he?"

"I don't remember. We own a couple of other real
estate companies outside of Beaumont, one in Hilton
Head and the other in Savannah, so he could have been
at a sales meeting or assisting one of the brokers."

The front door opened and footsteps sounded in

the foyer. Donna jumped at the sound. Norm Schaefer stepped into the den. He looked from Annie to Wes and finally at his wife. "What's going on, Donna? Why are you crying?"

Chapter
TEN

Nobody said anything right away. Finally, Annie stood. "Hi, Norm," she said. "It's so good to see you again." She paused and introduced him to Wes, and the men shook hands, even though Norm still looked confused.

"Wes is a professional photographer and is taking pictures of Beaumont. He's renting a room from me. I asked him to bring me over on the off chance you'd be home so I wouldn't have to bother you at the office." Annie hated to tell even more lies, but for some insane reason she didn't want to give Donna up. "Naturally, Donna and I began reminiscing about Charles, and I'm afraid we both let it get to us. I should have known better than to discuss it with a new mother who's going through hormonal changes."

Norm nodded as though it made sense. "Donna and I were both saddened to learn of Charles's death," he said as though loath to use the word *murder,* "and the charges brought against you. I don't know what Lamar Tevis is thinking. If he weren't related to half the big shots in this town, he never would have been hired in the first place."

"Honey, what are you doing home this time of day?" Donna interrupted.

"Kevin has his six-week checkup in half an hour," Norm said. "I thought I'd go with you, see how the boy is doing. Don't tell me he's napping again. You promised to keep him awake as much as possible today so he'd sleep tonight."

"It's not as easy as you think," Donna said.

Annie heard the tension in their voices and suspected the couple wasn't getting much rest these days, what with a newborn in the house.

"That boy eats every two hours like clockwork," Norm said. "By the time we finally fall asleep again he's crying to be fed."

"I have a cat like that," Annie replied. She glanced at her watch. "Wes and I should be going so you and Donna can make your appointment."

"Why did you want to see me?" Norm asked.

"Huh?" Annie blinked. "Oh well, it's probably going to sound silly. It's about Charles," she said. "I just wanted to ask you whether you know if he was having problems with anyone at work. Or any of his customers," she added, wondering if Norm would fall for her story.

"You want to know if he had any enemies," Norm said. "Absolutely not. He was well liked at the office, and a genuine asset to the company." Norm looked thoughtful. "We miss him, Annie, even after all this time."

She smiled. "Thank you. It's nice to hear. But if you think of something that might help—"

"I'll call right away," he said.

Donna and Norm walked them to the door. Norm put his hand on Annie's arm. "Annie, I don't mean to sound insensitive, but now that Charles has been officially declared dead, I want you to know he had a sizable life insurance policy. Once you get this legal business behind you, and I have no doubt you will, you'll be eligible to collect."

Wes drove the motorcycle to a small park and pulled into an empty slot. "Why are we stopping?" Annie asked once he'd cut the engine.

"Climb off. I want to talk to you."

Annie did as she was told. "If this is about Charles's life insurance policy, I know nothing about it."

"How can you not know about your husband's life insurance?"

"I mean, I knew he had it, but I don't know what Norm means by 'sizable.' Charles was in perfect health. I can't see him paying out-of-pocket for a larger policy than what his company provided."

Wes remained silent.

"Think about it, Wes. If I was hoping to collect on Charles's insurance, why would I have buried him in the backyard, where he wasn't likely to be found? If I had killed him, knowing there was money to collect, I would have put his body in his car before driving it to the Savannah airport. You can't collect insurance on a person who has been listed as missing. Jeez, even I know that. And why all these questions?" she demanded. "I feel like you're accusing me."

"Because sooner or later you may have to face a jury. You'd better get used to it."

Jimbo and Otto from Otto's Cabs managed to rouse Erdle. "Man, you look like shit," Otto said.

"I think he's still drunk," Jimbo said. "I probably shouldn't have given him anything else to drink, but he had a bad case of the shakes."

"You're killing yourself, Thorney," Otto said. "Come on; let me help you up." Together the men managed to get Erdle outside and into the cab. "You're not going to puke in my cab like last time, are you?" Otto asked.

Erdle shook his head.

Otto took his place in the driver's seat and started the engine. "I'll have you home in no time."

"My lan'lady is goin' t'kick me out for sure this time," Erdle managed weakly.

Otto gave a grunt. "I doubt it. She has too many problems of her own."

"Huh?"

Otto glanced at Erdle in the rearview mirror. "Don't you ever read the newspaper?" When Erdle shook his head, Otto went on. "She's been charged with murdering her husband."

Erdle just stared.

"Yeah, man. They took her to jail. She's out now, but there's going to be a trial and everything." When Erdle didn't respond, Otto glanced up at the rearview mirror once more. "You're sweating like a pig. Hang in there, okay?"

"Take me to the p'lice department," Erdle said.

"Say what?"

"Take me," Erdle demanded. "I got t'clear up some biz-ness. I's impor'ant."

Ten minutes later Otto pulled up in front of the police station. Erdle opened the back door, stepped out, and tripped on the curb. He fell facedown on the sidewalk. Blood spurted from his nose.

"Dammit to hell!" Otto said, slamming out of the car. He pulled Erdle to his feet. "Hold on." Otto yanked the door open on the passenger side and grabbed a box of tissues. He yanked out several and handed them to Erdle. The blood soaked through the tissue in a matter of seconds. "Here, take the box," Otto said, frowning. "Man, I ain't never seen you look this bad."

Erdle swayed. "I'm 'kay," he said. He turned and slowly staggered toward the double doors.

Inside, the dispatcher gaped as Erdle stepped up to the counter. "Sir, are you okay?"

Erdle swayed again and grabbed the ledge to keep from falling. "I need to see Tevis."

The woman sniffed. "You have been drinking."

"I know who murdered that fellow."

On the other side of the counter, an officer looked up from a file cabinet. He joined the dispatcher. "What's your name, sir?"

"Erdle Thorney. *T-h-o-r-n-e-y.*"

"And you're here to discuss a murder?"

Erdle nodded, the box of tissues tucked beneath one arm, a wad of tissue pressed to his nose. His bottom lip was beginning to swell.

"The victim's name?" the officer asked.

"Fortenberry. Y'all just dug him up the other day."

The dispatcher picked up her phone and punched a number. "Chief, you need to get out here. There's a guy says he has information on the Fortenberry case."

Tevis wasted no time. "Erdle?" he said. "What in tarnation happened to you? Do you need to go to the hospital?"

Erdle shook his head. "You arrested the wrong person. I'm the man you want."

Tevis frowned in confusion. "What are you talking about?"

"I'm the one who did it. I murdered Charles Fortenberry."

Theenie raced out the front door and down the steps the minute Wes pulled up on his bike. From the look on the woman's face, Annie could see that something was terribly wrong.

"Erdle's in jail!" Theenie said.

"In jail?" Annie groaned. "Please tell me he wasn't driving drunk! He knows better."

"No, nothing like that. You're not going to believe it. He confessed to murdering Charles."

"What!" Annie almost fell off the bike. "But that's impossible. He wasn't even here that week."

"Well, of course he wasn't," Theenie said. "Don't you see what he's trying to do?"

Annie slumped. Finally, she climbed from the bike. "He's taking the rap so the charges against me will be dropped. What did Lamar say?"

"I didn't talk to him. Delores, the dispatcher, called me with the news. She and I used to play bingo together at the VFW once a week, until people started getting greedy and buying five and six cards at a time. I can barely keep up with one card. There's just no fairness in that if you ask me."

Annie went on before the woman could go off on a tangent. "Has Erdle actually been charged?"

"Delores said he was too drunk to answer questions. Said Lamar put him in a cell to sleep it off. After Erdle threw up in the lobby."

"Oh, jeez. I suppose I should go get him."

"Won't do any good," Theenie said. "Delores says he's out cold. Said she'd call when he woke up. After Lamar questions him," she added. "You ask me, they ought to take him over to the hospital and throw him in the detoxification unit." Theenie began to fidget with her hands. "Oh, and Jamie called. I told her you and Wes were checking out a lead." She looked from one to the other. "Did you find out anything?"

"Still looking into it," Wes said.

Danny Gilbert pulled into the driveway and parked his truck. "What's going on?" he asked, making his way toward them. "How come everybody looks worried?"

Annie told him what was going on.

Danny shook his head sadly. "I'm not surprised Erdle would try to protect you," he said.

"I need to call my attorney," Annie said. All three followed her into the house, where Tchaikovsky blared from the ballroom. Annie did an eye roll. "Lovelle's practicing her dance routine." She dialed Nunamaker's cell phone number and got his voice mail. After explaining the latest events, she hung up.

The music stopped and Lovelle came into the room in a hot pink leotard and skirt. "Guess you heard the news," she said to Annie, shaking her head in disgust. "I'm beginning to think Lamar earns bonus fishing days for everybody he locks up. Too bad he can't find the real killer."

Wes excused himself and went upstairs.

"This is probably bad timing," Danny said to Annie, "but I was thinking maybe you'd like to see a movie tomorrow night. Might take your mind off your problems," he added. "I'll even buy you dinner beforehand." When she didn't respond, he leaned closer. "Annie?"

"Uh? Oh, I'm sorry. I'm just worried about Erdle. I need to drive over to the police station and find out what's going on."

"I would drive you myself if I had time," Danny said, "but I'm in the middle of a job. What do you say?"

"You should go," Theenie said. "You haven't done anything fun in a long time. Maybe Lovelle and I will go out for a bite to eat." Lovelle nodded in agreement.

Annie smiled. "Sounds great, Danny," she said, although it was the last thing on her mind at the moment. But she knew Danny wouldn't give up until she agreed, and she had promised. "I should be paying *your* way after all the work you've done," she said. "We had a deal."

He ruffled her hair playfully. "I just told you that so you'd agree to let me take care of the floors," he said, "so I'm covering it." He checked his wristwatch. "I'd better run. How about I pick you up tomorrow around five-thirty so we'll have plenty of time to eat before the seven o'clock movie?"

"I'll be ready," Annie said as Wes cleared the stairs. His camera hung from his neck.

"I'm going out for a while," he said. "Thought I'd take a few pictures since it's such a nice day."

"What about lunch?" Annie asked.

"I'll grab a hot dog if I get hungry." He started for the back door.

"I'll follow you out," Danny said, telling the others good-bye. He waited until they'd cleared the back stairs. "You got a minute?" he asked.

Wes paused and turned. "What's up?"

Danny hesitated. "I know it's probably none of my business, but is anything going on between you and Annie?"

Wes's gaze turned cool. "Why do you ask?"

"Simple. I don't want to see her hurt. She's been through a lot."

"What makes you think I'm interested in hurting her?"

Danny frowned. "Do you always answer questions with a question?"

"I appreciate your concern for Annie, but even if we were involved, I wouldn't discuss it with you."

Danny's jaw hardened. "I've already had to clean up after one man," he said. "You have no idea how hurt Annie was when she found out Charles was cheating on her."

"Yet you didn't waste any time telling her," Wes said, and walked away.

Wes parked his bike and pulled out his cell phone. He dialed a number, and a woman answered from the other end.

"Hello, gorgeous. Do you miss me?"

"Yeah, like a gunshot wound to the head," she replied.

"I need you to run a check on several people."

"And I'm going to do this because?"

Wes grinned into the phone. "'Cause you're hot for me."

"That would mean I have exceptionally bad taste in men. Give me their names."

Shortly after lunch, Annie walked into Lamar's office without an invitation and found him admiring a new rod and reel. She planted both hands on her hips and gave him a no-nonsense look that told him she was not in a good mood. "I've come for Erdle."

"Look what my brother sent me for my birthday," Lamar said, holding up his new toy. "Got a seventy-five-pound test line. Can you imagine pulling in a seventy-five-pound fish?"

"Nope. And I don't want to."

"Well, it would probably have to be a shark," he said thoughtfully.

Annie simply looked at him, thinking how scary it was to have someone like Lamar Tevis protecting the town. "I don't have all day, Lamar."

"Oh boy, I can tell you're still mad over that incident several days ago."

"Incident?" she said in disbelief. "You mean the one where you searched my home from top to bottom or the part where you arrested me for murder?"

"Aw, Annie, I was just doing my job. Do you think I enjoyed it?" He shrugged when she remained silent. "Hey, if you're here to yell at me, I may as well tell you that Jamie Swift beat you to it. She and the mayor have already given me an earful."

"Frankie Fontana visited you?"

"Oh yeah. I'll probably lose my job before this mess is over. 'Course I'll have more time to pursue my dreams."

Dreams? Lamar? Annie blinked. "That's real special, Lamar, but why did you lock up Erdle?"

"The man could barely walk when he came in, so one

of my officers suggested he lie down. He confessed to your husband's murder, but he couldn't remember the details. When he woke up he had no idea where he was or how he'd gotten there."

"So you don't consider him a suspect?"

Lamar practiced casting his rod. "I'm undecided. I know how protective he is of you. If he thought Charles Fortenberry mistreated you in any way—"

"You're barking up the wrong tree, Lamar. Again," she added. "Have you bothered to investigate the case further or are you just going to pin the murder on me and be done with it?"

"The DA was the one who insisted on bringing you in, not me. It's all about politics, Annie, but you didn't hear it from me. As for your question, the answer is yes, I am considering other possibilities."

"But I'm still the main suspect."

"Technically, yes. But you got a dang good lawyer, so I wouldn't lose any sleep over it. Which reminds me, Cal Nunamaker said he has a ton of friends who love deep-sea fishing, and that I should dock my boat over on Hilton Head because people are willing to pay whatever it costs to catch the big one, especially if it's business-related and they can write it off."

"Great. In the meantime, have you found my husband's remains? And when are you going to take down that ugly crime scene tape? I'm losing business; I've got strangers running through my yard taking video—"

"Annie, do you have any idea how much stress I'm under?" he said. "Eve Fortenberry calls some three or four times a day, yelling in my ear as loud as she can because she can't have a funeral for her son without his remains. And when she doesn't feel like yelling, she blows a whistle into the phone, and now I think I've got tinnitus. And did you know she's offering a ten-thousand-dollar reward to the person who finds her son's, um, body parts?"

"I could use ten grand," Annie said to herself.

Lamar pressed one hand against his forehead. "I've got TV and newspaper reporters hounding me day and night, crackpots calling saying aliens took Charles's remains, and now CNN wants to do a special on me. They're tired of focusing on big-city crimes and gangs. They want one of those touchy-feely stories about small towns with low crime rates, only we're going to look bad on account everybody thinks you killed your husband and buried him in the backyard. That's the kind of coldhearted big-city stuff CNN is trying to get away from. Dang, I wish this had never happened."

Annie sank into a chair and covered her face. Lamar leaned his fishing rod against the wall and paced. Annie wondered if Lamar would consider bringing in extra manpower to help with the investigation, wondered if he had even *thought* about the investigation. She sighed. "So what's the plan?"

"I'm going to let my agent handle it."

Annie looked up. "What?"

"The CNN deal. If they want me they're going to have to fight for me. They aren't the only big dog in town; know what I mean?"

Annie just looked at him, noted his gun. She wondered if he was allowed to keep real bullets in it. "I'd like to take Erdle home now."

Lamar shrugged. "You may as well. He's so hungover he can't think straight, and he's too sick to think of leaving town. I'll question him once his stomach settles."

Ten minutes later, a slow-walking, slow-talking Erdle Thorney followed Annie to her car.

"Are you out of your damn mind?" she demanded when he climbed into the front seat beside her and closed the door.

"Please don't yell," he said, leaning his head against the side window. "I've had a rotten day. I think."

"It's going to be a whole lot worse if you end up in prison for confessing to a crime you didn't commit. Not that I don't appreciate what you were trying to do," she added.

"How do *you* know I didn't do it? I had just as much opportunity as you did. I never liked Charles anyway."

"Just do me a favor and stop trying to help me, okay? I'm in enough trouble."

"How do you think Annie is holding up?" Jamie asked Destiny when she arrived at the office to pick up her mail.

Destiny shrugged. "As well as can be expected considering most of the town thinks she murdered her husband." She looked at Max. "It meant a lot to her that you retained a lawyer for her." Destiny paused and shot a glance toward the door. "Please don't just stand there." She pointed to the sofa.

Max and Jamie followed Destiny's gaze. "I take it your spirit is with you?" he asked.

"Like I have a choice? But I'm going to solve the problem once and for all. We have an appointment with a therapist in an hour."

Max and Jamie exchanged looks.

"Hold it, Destiny," Jamie said, "and let me get this straight. You're actually taking a *spirit,* an entity that no one but you can see, to a psychologist? Do you think that's wise?"

"She needs help. I can't just stand by and do nothing."

"What kind of help does she need?" Max said.

"I think she's suffering from post-traumatic stress disorder."

Max nodded as though it made complete sense. "I

know I'm going out on a limb here, but what if this therapist doesn't believe you?"

"He will. I mean, what kind of person would admit to this sort of thing unless it's for real?"

"A delusional person?" Jamie suggested.

Destiny glanced at the sofa. "Don't start shaking your head. We've already discussed this, and you agreed to go." She turned back to Max and Jamie. "Believe it or not, most, if not all, of my friends have been in therapy for years. Trust me; I know what I'm doing."

"May I borrow your muscles for about ten minutes?" Annie asked Wes when he returned from his outing.

"Sure. How can I help?"

"I need to set up some tables in the ballroom for the wedding on Saturday."

"Lead the way." He followed her toward the living room and through a door that led into a massive room with highly polished wood floors, ornate woodwork, bronzed statues, and the tallest ceiling he'd ever seen, on which fat white clouds had been painted. Wes gazed up at them, so realistic, and for a moment they seemed to be moving. He wasn't aware that Annie was watching him, a smile playing on her lips. It was impossible for him to look away. He thought he saw something in the clouds, but the harder he stared the more difficult it became.

"Don't try so hard," Annie said. "It's like looking at one of those three-D illusion pictures."

Wes relaxed his shoulders, neck, and eyes and simply waited. He had an odd sense of the clouds being alive somehow, as though something pulsed in their centers. The clouds seemed to expand and contract, the edges becoming crisp and distinct, and their roundness began to take on human forms, Rubenesque women and powerfully built men, and from behind, a radiant light somehow seemed to pass through them and purify their nakedness so that it was a thing of beauty. Wes blinked, and the forms faded once more into the clouds.

He looked to Annie for answers.

"One of my ancestors commissioned a French artist to paint something on the ceiling," she said. "He spent three years on the project. Most people can't see what's really there."

"What is it about this house?"

"I'm not sure. I just know it's important to preserve it. That's why I could never sell it."

Wes was quiet as Annie led him to an adjacent storage area where a number of tables, legs folded inside, were propped against one wall. Dozens of metal folding chairs with padded seats had been stacked around the room as well.

Annie selected seven large round tables, and she and Wes carried them into the ballroom and placed them near the wall. "I need to make sure there's enough room for dancing," she said.

Annie was breathing hard by the time they'd lugged some fifty-plus chairs into the room, placing eight at each table. "Boy, I must be out of shape," she said.

Wes looked her up and down. "Your shape looks fine to me."

"Anybody ever tell you you've got a silver tongue?"

He grinned. "As a matter of fact, I have received a few compliments with regard to dexterity—"

"Never mind," Annie said. "I don't think we're talking about the same thing."

"Perhaps it's time we should. Too bad you're already involved."

She knew he was referring to Danny, but she shrugged it off because it was difficult to explain the relationship she shared with him and because she was beginning to sense a subtle change in Danny. Perhaps it had been there all along and she'd simply been too wrapped up in other things to notice. Like with the clouds, she thought. One had to pause and look closely to see what was really there.

"The guy is in love with you, Annie."

"I can't think about that right now, Wes. Not with everything else that's going on."

"You might have to," he said. "I suspect he has been in love with you for a long time. The question is: what would he be willing to do to have you all to himself?"

Annie frowned. "Are you saying what I think you're saying?"

"It hasn't crossed your mind?"

"Not even once. Danny would never."

"People will do almost anything to protect the person they love," Wes said.

Annie suddenly laughed. "If I didn't know better I'd think you were jealous of him."

He grinned. "I'm not the jealous type, because I always get the girl in the end."

"You are so full of yourself, Bridges."

He stepped closer and toyed with a lock of hair. Annie met his gaze. "How about it, Annie?" he said softly. "How about you and me? Don't you ever wonder what it would be like?" He traced the lines of her mouth with one finger. "Think about it."

She watched him go. Holy hell, she thought. How could he possibly not know that she hadn't stopped thinking about *it* since the minute she'd laid eyes on him? It was Destiny's fault. All the woman talked about was sex. Sex, sex, sex. Anyone who thought about sex that much had a serious problem. Of course, Destiny would never admit to it; she blamed it on the house.

Annie looked around the room. With all the naked statues and titillating art filling the rooms, it was impossible *not* to think of sex. But maybe there was more to it, she thought. What if Destiny was right and there was something about the house itself that caused people to feel more sensual?

Annie walked over to one of the walls and pressed an open palm against it. She waited. She didn't *feel* any different. She tried the other palm. The wall was surprisingly warm. Why had she not noticed it before? It warmed her hand and slowly moved past her wrist and up her arm. Annie wondered if she was just imagining it, even as the tension seemed to drain from the muscles in her shoulders and on either side of her spine. Her body became loose, and she was filled with a sense of well-being. Her mind floated.

She thought of Wes. The two of them locked together, embracing. Warm and naked in her bed, Wes's hands caressing her, deft fingers seeking. And suddenly his mouth on her, tasting, and her breath becoming rapid. Her reaching out, grasping him tightly as he filled her.

"Oh my Lord!" she said, and snatched her hand from the wall.

The bearded man sitting across from Destiny read the form she had filled out. Finally, he looked up. Kind eyes peered out from beneath bushy gray brows. "Okay, Miss Doe," he began.

"You may call me Jane, Dr. Smithers."

"How may I help you, Jane?" he asked.

"I know this is going to sound strange," she began.

"Please feel free to speak your mind. You're safe here."

"I have a problem with dead people following me around. Sometimes there are more than just one of them; they just latch on to me and won't let go. It's driving me crazy."

"I'm sorry you've been having such a hard time," he said.

"The problem is *convincing* them they're dead and pointing them to the light. Like this redneck named Ronnie who got drunk and fell out of the back of a pickup truck while coon hunting," she said. "He died instantly, but he was too dumb to realize it. Followed me everywhere, even came into the shower with me. He was a pervert."

"That must have been awful for you."

"Took me forever to get rid of him. I finally lied and told him there was a strip bar on the other side of the light, and let me tell you, he hauled ass the minute I said it."

Dr. Smithers looked sympathetic and he made notes on his tablet. "Tell me about your childhood, Jane."

Destiny frowned. "My childhood? Listen, Doctor, we don't have time to go into that. I have more immediate problems. There's a new spirit following me, and I haven't had a good night's sleep since she showed up.

"She was a prostitute many years ago. She met her death violently, and that's why she's still hanging around. But I can't help her, because she won't talk. I'm pretty sure she's a mute." Destiny leaned closer. "There are other problems that I can't discuss with you in her presence because she's blocking them."

One hairy brow arched high on Smithers's forehead. "She's in the room with us?"

"Yes. I'm hoping you'll hypnotize her and help her remember these things in her past that are too painful for her to face alone."

Dr. Smithers put down his pen and studied Destiny closely. "Let me make certain I understand what you're asking," he said. "You want me to provide counseling and hypnotherapy for a spirit. So she will go to the light."

"Right. But first she has to help solve a murder. See, a friend of mine has been charged with murdering her husband and burying his body. If I could get this spirit to talk—her name is Lacey, by the way—she might be able to tell us who the real killer is. Oh, and if you could convince her to stop stealing our underwear in the meantime, that would be great," Destiny added.

He took a deep breath. "Okay, back to this friend of yours who has been charged with murder," he began patiently. "Is this person a spirit as well?"

"No, she's real."

"So you're able to differentiate between what's real and what's not?"

Destiny gave him an odd look. "Excuse me?"

He smiled gently. "I believe I can help you, Jane."

Annie was setting the table for dinner when Max and Jamie arrived. "Bad news," Jamie said. "Destiny called as we were leaving the office. She's been locked up in a psychiatric ward."

Annie, Theenie, and Lovelle just stared back at her, looks of astonishment on their faces. Finally, Theenie spoke. "I'm not surprised. I suspected her elevator was one floor short."

"I don't know what that means," Lovelle said.

"It's all my fault," Jamie said. "I knew what she was planning to do, and I didn't stop her."

"I'm equally responsible," Max said. "I should have tried to talk her out of it."

Annie finally found her voice. "What did she do?"

Jamie sighed. "She took the spirit to see a psychologist, hoping he could help her overcome her fears of what happened that traumatized her. I don't know the whole story, because Destiny and I only spoke briefly. She's pretty upset, says she's surrounded by crazy people."

"Jeez Louise," Annie muttered. "They're going to throw away the key. What else can go wrong?"

"Don't ask," Theenie and Lovelle said in unison.

"What should we do?" Annie asked.

"Nunamaker is going to take her case," Max said. "He can't do anything tonight, but he promised to check on it first thing in the morning. I personally want to know how it all came down. You can't just lock someone up without going through the proper channels." He looked at Jamie. "We need to get going."

"Are you sure you can't stay for dinner?" Annie asked.

"We're dining tonight with Max's family," Jamie said. "We wanted to tell you about Destiny because we knew you'd worry when she didn't come home tonight."

Wes came through the back door soon after Max and Jamie left. He glanced about the kitchen. "Uh-oh. How come every time I walk into this house I sense another catastrophe? A new drama?" he added.

"I don't know what you're talking about," Annie said. "Everything is fine."

"Couldn't be better," Theenie said, obviously following Jamie's lead.

Lovelle nodded. "Life is good."

"Not only that," Annie said brightly. "Dinner is ready."

"Isn't Erdle eating with us?" Theenie asked once everyone was seated at the table.

"He's probably embarrassed," Annie told her. "I lowered the boom on him after the stunt he pulled."

"Maybe it wasn't a stunt after all," Wes cut in.

All three women just looked at him.

Wes shrugged. "It's a thought. He could have had his buddy lie for him."

"I don't think Erdle could stay sober enough to get away with murder," Theenie said. She looked at Annie. "We really should get him some help."

Annie nodded. "I worry about him, too. I'll take a plate over after dinner."

"He's probably out cold and won't hear you," Lovelle said. "You'll have to climb through his kitchen window like before. Maybe this time he won't have his underwear soaking in the sink. Maybe he got rid of that mouse and you won't sprain your ankle again running from it."

"It won't be easy climbing in a window with a plate of food in your hand," Theenie said. "I would help you if I wasn't afraid that mouse was still in his house." She shuddered.

Something hit the cabinet door and everyone jumped. Peaches sat there looking at Annie. "You've already eaten," she said. Peaches began batting the door with her paw, never taking her eyes off Annie.

"We should drop that cat through Erdle's kitchen window," Lovelle said. "She'd sober him up right quick."

"That's mean," Annie said, although she grinned at the thought.

The garbage can toppled to its side and dumped trash to the floor. Peaches stuck her head inside searching for food. Annie pretended not to notice.

"I'll clean it up," Wes said, shoving his chair from the table.

"It can wait," Annie said. "Go ahead and finish your dinner."

"She's making a big mess," he said.

"Trust me. It's best to ignore her when she gets into a mood."

The garbage can rocked back and forth. Inside, Peaches kept digging, and before long all the litter was on the floor. The garbage can began to roll. It rolled through the open swinging doors and into the dining room and kept going. Something shattered in one of the rooms. The women didn't look up from their meals.

"Is there ever a peaceful moment in this house?" Wes asked.

Annie looked at him, remembering he once had referred to it as a crazy house. "All the time."

Lovelle nodded. "It's usually real quiet around here."

"Boring, you might say," Theenie added.

Wes went back to eating. "By the way, where's Destiny?"

"Locked up in a mental hospital," Annie replied, concentrating on her food once more.

Chapter

ELEVEN

It was after 10:00 PM by the time Annie showered and climbed into bed. Theenie and Lovelle had turned in early, and Wes, who'd selected a Ludlum book from a stack in the sunroom, had gone up shortly afterward. Annie set her alarm clock, turned off the light, and snuggled deep beneath the covers, not because she was cold but because she needed to feel the heaviness of the blankets on her, the sense of security their weightiness evoked.

Moonlight peeked through her window and cast a soft glow in the room. Annie had slept in this room the very first time she remembered visiting her grandmother, and it had become her own when she moved in. She'd felt safe and loved, knowing the woman was just next door. Annie had remained in her small room even after her grandmother had died. She'd closed off the grand master suite with its ornate furnishings and mirrored ceiling, slipping inside from time to time for a nap on the tall rice bed, covering herself with the woman's favorite shawl.

Shortly before Annie was to be married to Charles, she had packed her grandmother's clothes and personal items and moved them to the attic, and eventually the woman's scent had faded, replaced with Charles's Aramis cologne and Annie's simple White Linen perfume. Their lovemaking was squeezed in between *Larry King Live* and *David Letterman*. When their marriage began to sour, Charles channel-surfed during the hour-long gap and Annie spent her evenings reading magazines on "How to heat up your sex life," "How to drive your man crazy in bed," and "Satisfying him every time."

She obviously hadn't gotten it right, or so she thought at the time, because one day Charles was there and the next day he was gone. Annie moved back into her old room and read magazines on "How to survive the split," "Life after divorce," and being "Happily single."

Annie jumped when something hit her door, and she heard Peaches mewing on the other side. She thought of putting a pillow over her head to drown out the sound, but she was afraid the cat would wake the others. Annie dragged herself from her bed and opened the door, but the cat started down the hall toward the steps leading to the kitchen. Darn cat, she thought. It would be easier if she just stuffed a feeding tube down her throat.

"Peaches," Annie called out softly as she tiptoed down the hall. "Come here, Peaches." The cat made a sound low in her throat and dashed away.

Annie saw it before she felt it, something light and wispy hovering several yards away, coming toward her slowly. She froze as she caught sight of a woman's face and long swirling hair, barely visible but there nevertheless. Then, a brush of cool air against her cheek, the smell of flowers, and the feeling that something was swirling around her. The air shifted and became icy cold.

"Holy crap!" Annie staggered forward, trying to escape whatever it was, but she fell to one side, hitting her elbow on the wall. She tripped on her own feet, grasped an armchair to break her fall, and stubbed her sore toe. A multitude of four-letter words came to mind, but she was too scared to speak. She had to get back to her room. She turned and hit something solid. The ghost was bigger than she'd thought.

She was screwed.

"Annie?"

"Outta my way, Wes. Can't you see I'm running for my life?" Annie bypassed him and raced to her room, closing the door behind her. She made a mad dive under her covers.

Wes poked his head inside. "Problem?"

Annie mumbled from beneath the covers.

"What's a gust?" he asked.

Annie peered out. She could barely see him in the shaft of light from her bedroom window. "Not gust. Ghost." It was hard to talk with her teeth chattering.

Wes closed the door, walked to the bed, and pulled the covers aside. "Good thing I'm here to protect you." He slid beneath the sheets. "The things a guy has to do." He slipped one arm beneath her head. "Come closer."

Annie snuggled against him.

"You're shivering. What did you see?"

"A woman's face and hair. She just came at me, and everything got cold."

"Did she appear menacing?"

"No, but it still scared the hell out of me." Annie was quiet for a moment. "You know, I think I've seen her before. Maybe when I was a little girl," she added. "Or maybe I just dreamed of her." When Wes didn't say anything, Annie lifted her head and looked at him. "Do you believe me?"

"I think you were just trying to get me in your bed." There was a smile in his voice. "I may start hiring people to scare you so I can sleep here every night."

Annie grinned. "Sorry about the flannel gown," she said. "I wasn't expecting company."

Wes ran his finger across the material. "Feels nice."

"It's been known to send ice water through a man's loins."

"Trust me, my loins are feeling just fine. If they start feeling any better, one of us is going to have to leave."

Annie liked the timbre of his voice against her ear. She had to admit snuggling against Wes's warm body was a lot more fun than lying beneath a pile of blankets. "I'm glad you're here," she said after a moment. "I was feeling sort of lonely."

"I would have been here a lot sooner if I hadn't been afraid you'd kick me out."

"It's been a long time since I shared a bed with a man," Annie confessed.

"After one night it'll be old hat."

"You're assuming I'll invite you back."

"I'm assuming you won't let me leave."

She punched him lightly. After a moment she grew serious. "Wes, I'm scared. About being convicted of a crime I didn't commit."

"I know."

"I'm not afraid for myself, but if something happened to me, if a jury actually found me guilty and I had to go to prison, I don't know what would happen to Theenie and Lovelle. Or Erdle, for that matter," she added. She remembered how bad the man had looked when she'd delivered his dinner and a short sermon on his drinking.

"Do you trust me, Annie?" Wes asked.

Oddly enough, she did. "Yes."

"Then take my word for it: I'm going to do everything in my power to keep you out of jail."

"You don't really think Erdle killed Charles, do you?"

"I have a friend running checks on several people. So why don't you try not to worry, and let me handle it?"

Annie lay there quietly, wondering who else Wes thought might have killed her husband, but she was tired of thinking about it. All she did these days was worry; now she simply wanted to enjoy being held. Her mind drifted; the real world with its problems soon felt very far away. The only thing she was conscious of was the man beside her, his chest beneath her cheek, his steady heartbeat, and the way his long legs felt against hers.

Annie placed one hand flat against his chest, enjoying the sturdy feel of him. She ran her hand slowly across Wes's stomach, found it hard and flat. His muscles tensed beneath her fingertips. He pressed his lips against one temple. She raised her head, and he kissed her chin, the tip of her nose. He pulled back slightly, and for several seconds neither of them moved, even though Annie knew his mouth was only a breath away. Somehow she knew that Wes was waiting on her to make the next move. If she played it safe, closed her eyes and went to sleep, he would simply lie there for as long as she needed him.

But she had played it safe all her life, and look where it had gotten her.

Exactly nowhere.

Besides, who was she fooling? There was no way in hell she was going to fall asleep with Wes Bridges lying beside her.

She shifted on the bed and very tentatively touched her lips against his. They bumped noses, laughed softly. Wes's lips parted, and she tasted him.

Wes rolled to his side, and Annie found herself on her back. The kiss deepened, and Wes slipped his tongue inside, found hers, and their tongues mingled. How long they kissed, Annie couldn't have said, but it felt as if their lips had somehow fused together and she no longer knew where hers began and his left off. What had started out as tender and sort of dreamy, a kiss that she had wanted to sink deeply into and rest her tired soul in, had turned hot and urgent.

Wes pulled off her nightgown and smiled at the sight of her breasts in the moonlight. "Pretty," he whispered. He explored lower with gentle fingers. He covered her with his mouth and tasted her. Annie was almost certain her eyes crossed when he slid inside.

Afterward, he held her. Annie closed her eyes and slipped into a mindless sleep. When she opened them again, the room had lightened and Wes was nuzzling her throat. Their lovemaking was unhurried as they touched and explored and shared heated sighs until they finally shuddered in each other's arms.

The next time Annie opened her eyes, the sun shone through her bedroom window and the birds, which had mistaken the warm winter for spring, chirped and sang. Downstairs she heard someone, most likely Theenie, searching through the pan cabinet, probably in the early stages of preparing breakfast. Annie could not remember when she'd slept so soundly, and it almost didn't matter that she had awakened late. She smiled and stretched.

And froze when her leg brushed against another leg.

Her eyes popped open. Holy cow! She turned and found Wes beside her, a satisfied grin on his face.

"'Morning, Red."

"Omigod! You're still here."

He cocked one brow. "Am I not supposed to be?"

"No! The others might find out."

"Afraid they'll get jealous?"

"That's not funny. I mean, what will people think? And believe me, news spreads fast in this town. Everyone already thinks I'm a murderer; they'll think I'm loose as well."

"You are loose, but that's a good thing."

She blushed. She was no longer Wild Woman; she was Annie Fortenberry who ran a respectable bed-and-breakfast. She heard footsteps on the stairs and bolted upright on the bed. "You have to get out of here. Now!"

"Only if you'll let me come back tonight."

Annie tried not to stare, but it was damn difficult.

He grinned. "Like what you see?" He dropped a kiss on her forehead and started for the door.

"Wait!" she said. "You can't go out that way. Somebody might see you."

He paused and looked at her. "What do you suggest?"

Annie frantically searched for the gown and panties that Wes had removed the night before. She found them crumpled at the foot of the bed. She dressed quickly, feeling a bit self-conscious under his watchful eyes.

"Sexy," he said.

She didn't feel sexy; she felt desperate. She pointed to the pair of French doors that led to her balcony. "You'll have to go out that way."

"In my underwear?"

"Yes!"

Wes sighed and shook his head as he pulled the doors open and looked out. "Did you forget there aren't any stairs leading down?"

"You can climb from my balcony to yours," she said.

He shot her a look of utter disbelief. "You're kidding, right?"

"They're only about three or four feet apart. You can easily make it."

"This is the dumbest thing I've ever heard, and I've seen some pretty dumb things in my life. It's downright crazy, Annie. Are you sure all that hot sex didn't jiggle your brain?"

Annie joined him on the balcony. "Piece of cake," she said.

He stood there for a moment, studying the situation as though gauging the distance. "If I don't make it, I want to be buried with my Harley."

Annie heard voices downstairs. "Hurry!" she whispered. She held her breath as he climbed over the wrought-iron railing and planted his feet on the narrow ledge on the other side of the pickets. Taking great care, Wes held on to the wrought-iron banister and had started to step across the three-foot gap to his own balcony when a section of iron leaned toward him, yanking bolts from the stone base and taking Wes by surprise.

Annie watched in horror as the iron gave way completely. Wes twisted around and reached for the railing on his balcony, missing it by several inches. Annie screamed as he fell, landing in the thick holly hedges below.

She darted inside, raced from her room and down the stairs, almost slamming into Theenie and Lovelle, who'd obviously heard her scream and were on their way up.

"What happened?" Theenie asked.

"Wes just fell from my balcony."

The three did a little dance on the steps, trying to get out of one another's way. Annie managed to get past them. Her hands trembled as she turned the lock in the door and flung it open. She took off in a dead run.

Theenie and Lovelle looked at each other.

"What do you suppose the man was doing on Annie's balcony?" Theenie asked.

"Oh, wise up, Theenie," Lovelle said.

Annie found Wes struggling to get out of the hedges, cursing each time the spiky leaves jabbed him. Finally, he rolled out and hit the ground, giving a loud grunt.

Annie knelt beside him. The fact that his eyes were open had to be a good sign. "Are you hurt? Should I call nine-one-one?"

Wes pushed himself into a sitting position, glanced at all the pricks on his arms, and shook his head. "I think I'd like to take a hot shower."

Annie winced at the sight of his face and arms where the tiny pricks were already beginning to bleed. "I'm sorry," she said. "I didn't know about the balcony."

Doc suddenly appeared in his bathrobe, a newspaper tucked beneath one arm. "What's all the racket?" he demanded in a cranky tone. His eyes widened at the sight of Wes. "Uh-oh." He looked at Annie. "You didn't clobber him again, did you?"

In response, she pointed to the balcony outside her room.

Rounding the corner of the house, Theenie and Lovelle came to a halt. "Is he okay?" Lovelle asked.

Annie nodded.

Doc gazed down at Wes. "You need to find another place to live, son. *I* need to find another place to live. It was so much quieter at my daughter's house, even with four kids."

"What are you doing back so soon?" Theenie asked Doc. "I thought you were going to stay with your daughter while she recuperates."

"I was just in the way," he said.

"And how come you always get your newspaper and we don't?" Theenie asked.

Doc didn't answer. "You sure you're going to be okay?" he asked Wes.

"Yeah. The bushes broke my fall."

Doc grinned. "Good. I won't have to put you down."

A sleepy-eyed Erdle suddenly appeared. "I heard someone scream. What happened to him?" He nodded toward Wes.

Theenie explained. Erdle looked up and studied the damaged wrought iron, scratching his head as though trying to decide how much work he was going to have to do to fix it. "I can't believe the stuff that goes on around here," he said. "It's just one dang thing after another. I can't take much more." He wiped his hands down his face. "I need a drink." He turned and walked away.

"What's wrong with him?" Doc asked.

"We had a terrible time while you were gone," Theenie said, wringing her hands. "I just shudder every time I think about it. You would not *believe* what we've been through. And poor Annie," she added.

Doc waited. "Well, *what*?" he asked.

Theenie gave a sorrowful sigh. "I could tell you, but you wouldn't believe me."

"Well, *somebody* needs to tell me," he said loudly.

"It all started the day you left," Lovelle said, beginning with his gardener finding Charles's body. She quickly filled him in on the rest.

Doc frowned at Annie. "You were *arrested*?"

The last thing Annie wanted was for Doc to worry about her. "It'll be okay," she said. "Max Holt hired a big shot lawyer who is confident I'll get off."

Doc's ninety-year-old face suddenly took on more creases. "Are you sure?"

"Do I look worried?" she asked lightly. "My lawyer has already told me that no jury would convict me because there is absolutely no proof." Annie hated to lie, but she didn't want Doc losing sleep over her problems.

"You let me know if you need money, you hear? Or anything else," he added.

"Let me help you up," Annie told Wes. "We need to get you inside."

He stood on his own. "Am I going to have to scale the walls and climb through the attic window or am I allowed to use the back door like everybody else?"

"Your Honor, this is the craziest thing I've ever heard," Nunamaker said to his brother-in-law, who'd agreed to hear Destiny's case first thing that morning. A male nurse and a social worker had driven Destiny to the courthouse, and the social worker had handed the judge a sheaf of papers and Dr. Smithers's report.

The judge glanced over the report. "Dr. Smithers seems to think your client is dangerous and delusional." He frowned. "Something about a spirit and a murder?"

Nunamaker waved it off. "The whole thing is preposterous. Dr. Smithers only saw my client once and for a very brief period. I have highly credible witnesses who are prepared to attest to the fact that Miss Moultrie is perfectly sane."

He motioned toward Max and Jamie, who were sitting in the front row in the small courtroom. They both nodded. "Furthermore, my client is not involved with any murder, nor is she under investigation." He paused and squared his shoulders. "I resent these frivolous accusations against Miss Moultrie, as well as the unorthodox measures Dr. Smithers took to have her committed. The magistrate who signed the commitment papers never even spoke to my client."

"Dead people following her around?" the judge said. He arched one brow.

Nunamaker shrugged. "Miss Moultrie has psychic abilities. It's common knowledge that those with her gifts are more perceptive to these phenomena. Miss Moultrie donates her time to helping others through a newspaper column. She writes as the Divine Love Goddess Adviser."

The judge looked at Destiny. "So that's where I recognize you from. My wife and I read your column. Your advice always seems to be right on-target."

"Thank you, Your Honor," Destiny said, speaking for the first time since she'd entered the courtroom. "I'm very proud of the work I do, for both the living and the dead."

The judge leaned forward. "I'm not going to pretend to understand everything you do, Miss Moultrie, but you seem perfectly sane to me." He turned to the social worker. "I'm going to deny Dr. Smithers's recommendation to hold Miss Moultrie for further observation." He smiled at Destiny. "You're free to go."

"Thank you, Your Honor," she said.

The judge stood, brandishing a brand-new tennis racket in one hand.

Annie was dressed and waiting for Danny when Wes came downstairs in his denim jacket, his camera hanging from his neck. Theenie had treated the needlelike puncture wounds and applied small, round Band-Aids to the worst of them.

"Where are you headed?" Annie asked.

"I have work to do."

"Are you sure you're up to it?"

"Hey, you're looking at one tough guy here. Want to see my muscles?"

Annie would have enjoyed reminding him she had already seen his muscles and she liked them just fine, but she knew Theenie and Lovelle were taking in every word. She tried to hold back her smile as they exchanged looks, and Annie knew he was thinking about how they'd spent the previous night.

"We all have plans for tonight," she told him, "but there are plenty of leftovers in the refrigerator."

"I'll grab something while I'm out," he said, although he didn't seem to be in a hurry to leave. He just stood there looking at her, a half smile playing on his lips.

Annie tried not to remember what those lips were capable of.

"Oh, look at the time," Theenie said. "If Danny doesn't get here soon, the two of you won't have much time to eat before the movie."

Annie knew Theenie had mentioned the fact she was going out with Danny for Wes's benefit.

Wes looked Annie over. "I'd better let you go so you can fix yourself up for your big date."

Annie glanced down at her neat slacks and best white blouse. She'd even taken special care with hair and makeup. "I *am* fixed up."

"Oh well, my mistake." He winked once and walked out the back door.

"Very funny," Annie mumbled under her breath.

Danny arrived shortly after. "So how about a nice, thick steak?" he said.

"You want to know what I've been dying for?" she said. "A big, fat, juicy hamburger, onion rings, and a thick strawberry milk shake."

"You mean Harry's Place? I offer you steak and you'd rather eat grease?"

"Yeah, ain't it sinful?"

They arrived at Harry's Place a few minutes later and found the parking lot packed. "Hope we can get a table," Annie said as they made their way to the entrance. Inside they found a long waiting line.

Danny looked at his wristwatch. "We're doing okay on time as long as we don't have to wait too long to get served once we get a table." He glanced around the room. "Oh, look, there's your pal. What happened to his face?"

Annie glanced in the direction Danny was looking.

She froze when she spotted Wes sitting in a booth in the back, across from him a pretty blonde. They were leaning forward talking, their heads so close they almost touched. "Um, he fell," Annie managed, trying to keep her voice from wavering, but the sight of Wes with another woman almost made her ill. She resisted the urge to bolt out the front door.

"The guy certainly has good taste," Danny said, looking amused. "He must like 'em young; she barely looks old enough to vote. I'd ask to join them, but they look pretty intense."

"You know what?" Annie said. "I think I'd like to have a good steak after all."

It was all Annie could do to remain cheerful and attentive as they waited for their waitress, but she was determined to give it her best shot, since Danny had taken her to a nice steak house. Because all of the other tables were taken, they'd been seated at one in the bar where mostly men sat on the tall stools watching a sports program on a wide-screen TV.

The waitress appeared, and Danny ordered each of them a glass of red wine and the filet mignon with béarnaise sauce. He waited until the waitress hurried off. "If you're a good girl and eat all your vegetables, I'm going to order you your favorite dessert, Death by Chocolate."

"You're so bad," Annie said.

"I know all your weaknesses, Anniekins."

Sometimes she wished he wouldn't be so nice, and she wondered if maybe Theenie was right, that Danny wanted more out of the relationship. She looked up and found him watching her intently, his eyes telling her things he had never said out loud. Annie averted her gaze and reached for her wineglass. She raised it to her lips, and it slipped through her fingers, splashing wine across her blouse, and shattered on the table. "Oh no!" she cried, reaching for her linen napkin to blot the mess she'd made. "I'm so clumsy!"

"Watch out for the glass," Danny warned, using his own napkin in an attempt to help. The waitress arrived with a damp cloth.

"I need to run to the ladies' room and see if I can get the wine off my blouse before it stains," Annie said, and hurried away. Inside the restroom she wet a paper towel and pressed it against her forehead. Jeez, what was wrong with her? She was losing it, that's what. She was making a fool out of herself over a man. She tried to scrub the stain from her blouse, but it was no use.

She looked up, spied her reflection in the mirror, and saw the pain and disappointment in her eyes. "Boy, you really know how to pick them," she muttered to her reflection, her mind filled with the image of Wes and the blonde.

Annie had almost forgotten how bad she could hurt, and she hadn't even known Wes long. She thought of Nick and Billie Kaharchek. Love at first sight. Annie sighed. That sort of thing only happened to other people.

She arrived back at the table to find the waitress had cleared the glass from the table and delivered their food. "The stain didn't come out, huh?" Danny said.

"I'll try to treat it with something at home," Annie said.

"You'd better eat before the food gets cold."

Annie picked up her steak knife and considered falling on it. What did it matter? Her blouse was already ruined. Instead, she grabbed her fork and began the process of eating.

"How's your steak?" Danny asked.

"Great," she said, giving him an appreciative smile. She suddenly spied the wide-screen TV and saw her own reflection. The local news station was enjoying a real heyday thanks to her problems. Her smile faded.

Danny followed her gaze. "Oh, hell," he muttered. "Let's get out of here."

Annie waited until they were in his car to say anything. "It's okay, Danny," she said. "I'm getting accustomed to my new-found notoriety. Look on the bright side. I could be discovered and end up on *Star Search.* And you can tell everybody you knew me *when.*"

He shook his head. "Only you could crack jokes at a time like this."

"The least you can do is look amused. I'm using my best material."

"Do you realize there isn't anything I wouldn't do for you?"

"Of course I do. You've already proven it time after time."

"I'm not talking about sanding floors or making household repairs. I'm telling you that there are no limits, no line I wouldn't cross, to protect you."

Annie felt herself frown. "Please tell me you're not planning on doing anything dumb like Erdle did."

"We should get away," Danny said. "Spend a few days in the mountains. Theenie and Lovelle wouldn't mind. It would give us time to think. And talk," he added.

Annie looked out her side window and wondered when things had changed between them, wondered why she hadn't seen it coming despite Theenie's warnings. She had counted on Danny's friendship for so long, what would become of them now?

"Annie?"

She couldn't look at him. "You know I can't."

He gave a sigh. "I thought things would be different with Charles out of the picture. I kept hoping. But I guess deep down I knew it wasn't going to happen." He looked thoughtful. "And now there's Wes."

"I'm sorry." She finally looked at Danny.

His face was weighted with disappointment, but he didn't say anything. Instead, he reached for the key and started the car. "What do you say we skip the movie tonight?"

Annie walked into the kitchen and skidded to a halt when she found Wes sitting at the kitchen table reading the newspaper. And she thought things couldn't get worse. "What are you doing here?"

"Last time I checked, I had a room here."

"You're home early. Why are you home early? What time did you get here? And where did you get that newspaper?" She had to pause to catch her breath.

"I've been here a couple of hours, and I found the newspaper in the bushes. Have you been drinking a lot of caffeine? Is that a wine stain on your blouse?"

"Why are you interrogating me? *I* haven't done anything wrong."

Wes studied her for a moment, a perplexed look on his face. "Could we start over?"

"I want you out of here, Wes. I'm evicting you as of this moment. I'll give you all your money back."

"I don't want money. Besides, I like it here."

"This is my house, and if I say you're out, you're out." She turned and marched up the stairs.

Wes just sat there, shaking his head in confusion. Finally, he stood and started up the stairs. He found Annie in his room stuffing his clothes in his backpack.

"What the hell are you doing?"

"What does it look like I'm doing? I'm throwing you out. I should never have rented to you in the first place. You'd think I would have learned my lesson by now where men are concerned."

He shoved his face in hers. "Lady, what *is* your problem?"

"I saw you tonight. With the *blonde*. Really, Wes, isn't she a little young for you?"

He looked surprised. "She's not as young as she looks. Her brother is a plastic surgeon."

Annie grabbed his pack and lugged it from the room and down the stairs.

Wes followed.

Annie opened the door, dumped the backpack on the piazza, and crossed her arms. "See ya."

"Red, we need to talk." He closed his arms around her waist and locked his fingers together.

"Take your hands off of me!" she shouted.

"Not until you calm down and listen to what I have to say."

"What is going on here?" Theenie demanded from the doorway.

Annie turned and found Theenie and Lovelle standing there, each holding her purse. "Wes was just leaving."

Destiny walked through the back door. She paused, glanced at Wes and Annie, and then made her way to the refrigerator. She nodded at Theenie and Lovelle. "Does anybody want a sandwich?"

"How was the funny farm?" Wes said.

"It sucked; how do you think it was?"

Wes looked at Annie. "You weren't kidding."

Annie picked up his backpack, stepped out on the piazza, and raised it high over her head.

Wes hurried after her and reached for it. "Hey, don't throw that," he yelled. "My camera is in there."

They struggled.

The women huddled at the door and watched.

Erdle staggered up the back steps. "Who's doing all the yelling?" he asked. His eyes were red-rimmed, his words badly slurred. He took one look at Annie's face and staggered back. "Uh-oh, she's at it again."

"Let me go!" Annie shouted, trying to wrestle the bag from Wes.

"Miss Annie, please stop!" Erdle pleaded. "You can't keep acting like this. You're only going to end up killing someone else."

Chapter

TWELVE

All eyes turned to Erdle. Wes and Annie stopped struggling.

Annie realized her mouth was hanging. "Erdle, what the hell are you talking about?" she demanded.

He covered his mouth as though only just realizing what had come out of it. "Uh, I need to lie down." He stumbled toward the door.

Annie grabbed his arm. "Oh no, you don't. Not until you explain what you just said."

"I don't r'member."

"Then you'd better search your memory, because I'll call Lamar and have you thrown into detox if you don't finish what you started."

He looked hurt. "You'd do that?"

"Damn right. Now, start talking."

"I don't want to cause no trouble," the man said, glancing at Annie. "I could be wrong, but I thought, um . . ." He glanced down at the floor.

"What did you think?" Annie said. "That I killed Charles?"

Erdle shrugged. "I just wondered, that's all. I mean, I knew the two of you didn't get along. Far as I'uz concerned, he was a no-'count husband, and I didn't much care what happened to him. 'Sides, I figured you had a damn good reason. So I kept quiet." He looked up. "Reckon I was wrong."

Annie was clearly stunned.

Theenie had begun picking her nails.

"I think he's had too much to drink," Wes said to Annie. "Why don't I help him to bed?"

"I can make it," Erdle said. "I've had a lot of practice." He looked at Annie. "Can I go now?"

She shrugged and turned away.

He let himself out the back door.

Theenie was the first to speak. "You can't take Erdle seriously. He's a drunk."

"Who else in this room thinks I murdered my husband?" Annie asked.

Theenie gave a snort of disgust. "Don't be ridiculous."

"It never crossed my mind," Lovelle said. "I wouldn't have moved in if I had thought you were responsible for his disappearance."

"I know damn well you didn't do it," Destiny said.

Annie looked at Wes. "And you?"

"Would I be looking for the real murderer if I thought you'd done it? Erdle is just whacked-out on booze."

Annie went to the table and sank tiredly onto a chair. "My life sucks. I've got a drunk for a handyman, a crazy, senile neighbor, and a spirit in my house stealing everything."

"Speaking of which . . ." Destiny carried her sandwich to the table. "I think I'm finally gaining Lacey's trust. I had a long talk with her when they threw me in the rubber room. She stayed with me most of the time to keep me company."

Theenie gasped. "You were in a padded cell?"

Destiny's look was deadpan. "The Hyatt was full."

"She wasn't in a padded cell," Lovelle said. "They only put dangerous nutso cases in those kinds of places."

Destiny went on. "I met with a guy from the historic foundation, Mr. Hildenbiddle, this afternoon, and he gave me some interesting information. Also told me about some of your more colorful ancestors," she said to Annie. "But you already know, because Mr. Hilden-biddle said he'd shared the information with you a long time ago."

Annie's face pinked. "Okay, Destiny, you insist on airing my dirty laundry, so I may as well tell it all. Your spirit, Lacey Keating, was my great-great-grandmother, and madam of the bordello which she named Passion's Fruit. In her diaries, she claimed she got the idea because at the time there were dozens of peach trees on the property."

"Why didn't you tell us, dear?" Theenie asked.

"I didn't particularly want to share that information with anyone, but I suspect a lot of people already know."

"People aren't going to think badly of you because of what your great-great-grandmother did," Lovelle said. "My brother married a lesbian stripper, and nobody held it against our family."

Theenie looked confused. "He married a lesbian stripper? How does that sort of thing work?"

Lovelle shrugged. "Beats me."

Destiny reached into her pocket. "I don't know if this means anything, but Lacey gave it to me. I have a feeling it's significant." Destiny set a single sapphire earring on the table. Tiny diamonds surrounded the blue stone.

Annie's eyes widened, and she reached for it.

"Don't touch it," Destiny said. "I'm hoping if I hang on to it a couple of days I might get some vibes. Find out who it belongs to and why Lacey seemed to think it was important."

"Don't bother," Annie said. "I recognize it. It belongs to Donna Schaefer."

Annie and Wes remained at the kitchen table as, one by one, the others drifted off to bed. Although Annie was embarrassed that the entire household had witnessed what Theenie referred to as Annie's "hissy fit," she was still hurt over seeing Wes with another woman.

It was no wonder Erdle had suspected her of killing Charles; she *had* to do something about her temper.

But right now she needed to accept the fact that Wes did not feel as strongly about her as she did about him. She had only been a diversion.

"Annie, I can see the wheels turning in your head," he said finally. "We need to talk."

She shook her head. "It's late, and I don't want to discuss our relationship. . . ." She paused. "Correction: what I *thought* was a relationship. I'm not going to insist that you leave tonight, but I would appreciate it if you would vacate the room as soon as possible. Preferably in the morning."

"No."

She looked up. "Excuse me?"

"I'm not going anywhere. Not until your name is cleared." When she started to object, he held up his hand. "But right now, you're going to listen to what *I* have to say."

She crossed her arms. "Five minutes."

"There is absolutely nothing going on between me and the woman you saw me with tonight."

She did an eye roll. "Jeez, where have I heard that before?"

"Probably from your dearly departed husband, and by the way, I don't appreciate being compared to him. The blonde, Peggy Aten, is my ex-partner from when I was a cop."

Annie gazed back in disbelief. She remembered how nervous she'd been at the thought of him living there, recalled Destiny telling her Wes Bridges was not what he seemed. "You were once a cop and you never mentioned it to me?"

He shrugged. "I didn't see the need. I got out a while

back because I could tell I was getting burned-out after spending ten years as a homicide detective. I needed a change."

"So you became a photographer?" she said, thinking it an odd choice.

Wes gazed down at his hands for a long moment, his eyes troubled. He looked at Annie, opened his mouth to say something, and then closed it as though he'd changed his mind. "I'd rather not talk about that right now," he said. "I need to concentrate on the problems before us. I'm just asking you to trust me. And know that I have your best interests at heart."

Annie pondered it. Trust didn't come easy for her. Not when men were involved. But the concern in Wes's eyes, as well as the numerous unanswered questions about her husband's murder, told her it was best not to press him for more information.

"I wish you had told me about the cop part earlier," she said. "I would have worried less knowing I had an expert investigating the murder. Instead of someone who made his living taking pictures," she added.

He almost smiled. "Peggy was able to get her hands on some valuable information. You might be interested to know that Norman Schaefer never checked into his hotel the night of the murder. The night his wife claimed he was out of town."

"Oh yeah?"

"He was supposed to be at a real estate seminar. It wasn't listed on his expense reports, charge card, or checking account. In other words, he never showed."

"How did this Peggy person find out all of that?"

"She has friends in all the right places. The less you know, the better. If the case was to go to court and Norm was a potential suspect, Nunamaker would naturally ask him to produce proof of his whereabouts the night his wife claimed he was out of town."

"What do you think it all means?"

"It sounds suspicious as hell, if you ask me. But it gets even better. Norm had an oil change the week before your husband came up missing, and they recorded his mileage. A week later he had a small fender bender, and the mileage was included in the report. Had Norm attended a sales meeting in Savannah or Hilton Head, he would have put at least a couple of hundred miles on his car, only the odometer listed less than one hundred miles during that period."

"So he never went out of town," Annie said. "Wonder what he was doing?"

"Following his wife, maybe? I'm going to pay Lamar Tevis a visit tomorrow. Tell him what I know."

"I'll go with you."

"Maybe, maybe not," he said.

"Huh?"

"You obviously haven't read today's paper."

"No."

"You might want to take a look at the obits." He handed it to her. "Your husband's memorial service is being held tomorrow at two o'clock."

"Tomorrow?" she asked, her eyes round and wide. "Does that mean his remains have been located?"

"I spoke with Lamar. Nothing so far, and Mrs. Fortenberry isn't convinced they'll ever be found. She said she needed some kind of closure on this and if they *do* find the remains, she will have a private burial."

Annie's face drained of color, and her emerald eyes looked as though they'd turned to stone. "And she didn't bother to *tell* me? She thinks she can just plan a memorial service for my deceased husband and not *tell* me?" Tears filled her eyes; Annie was suddenly furious. "I don't believe it."

"Come with me, Annie," Wes said, getting up from

his chair. She looked dazed as he pulled her up. "We're going for a walk. We're going to practice what's called anger management. And at this moment you look like the perfect candidate."

Annie waited until he'd slipped on his denim jacket before going into the living room and pulling her lined windbreaker from the coat closet. "I hope none of my neighbors see me lurking in the night," Annie said as she and Wes stepped outside. "They'll think I'm looking to break in and kill somebody in their sleep. I'll be hauled off to jail again."

"You do look pretty dangerous in that Mickey Mouse jacket."

"Theenie, Lovelle, and I went to Disney World last year. They chipped in and bought me this." She tossed him a dark look. "Don't try to cheer me up; I'm still mad as hell."

"You have every right to be. I'm just trying to teach you ways to deal with it better. Before you discover where Theenie hid the rolling pin."

Annie sucked in the cool night air as they crossed the piazza and cleared the front steps, passing the fountain where the cherubs stood in repose. They crossed the yard and started down the sidewalk. Streetlights lit the way, and tall oaks, their massive roots jutting through the sidewalk, formed a high canopy over the cobblestone road that the residents of the historic district had refused to let the city replace with asphalt.

"I'm going to Charles's memorial tomorrow, Wes," Annie said after they'd walked a while.

"I figured as much." But he sounded worried. "I think you should maintain your distance with the woman; avoid her altogether."

"Eve Fortenberry has never liked me."

Wes tried to match strides with Annie, but she was

walking fast. "I'm going out on a limb here, but I'll bet she likes you less since you were arrested for her son's murder."

"Let her think what she likes. She has suspected me of doing something to her son since he first turned up missing."

"I wonder why?"

Annie shook her head. "I don't know. Maybe it was easier for her to think I'd done something to him than to imagine him leaving without even telling her or contacting her in all that time.

"And now it's easier for her to hate me than to . . ." Annie paused and shrugged.

"Accept the death of her son?' Wes finished for her.

"Yeah."

They walked in silence. After a while, Annie felt the tightness in her stomach dissolve, and the muscles in her neck and shoulders no longer felt like rubber bands pulled tight enough to snap. She continued to breathe in the night air. Here and there she caught the unmistakable scent of gardenia, another reminder that winter had somehow escaped them. Wes had been right to get her out; the air had cleared her head, and she felt, oddly enough, rejuvenated.

"Better?" he asked as if noting the change.

"I must be. I no longer feel like driving to my mother-in-law's and slicing all of her tires. I think I'm even beginning to feel sorry for her. Just don't tell anyone; I don't want to lose my edge." She realized they had walked quite a distance. "We should turn back," she said.

"Getting tired?"

"Not really. I've caught my second wind. I should do this every night. But that would make it seem like exercise."

They turned around and headed for the house. Wes

took her hand. "I forgot to ask. How was your evening with Danny?"

"We had a good time," she said, trying to keep her tone light. She didn't want to have to think about Danny right now. She looked at Wes, noted how dark he looked in the moonlight. Mysterious. "I'm, uh, sorry I lost my temper earlier. I haven't always had a temper. I don't even know when I got it."

"You'll work it out."

They'd arrived at the house. Wes released Annie's hand once they reached the front steps. "How does hot chocolate with marshmallows sound?" she said.

Ten minutes later Annie carried two steaming cups of hot chocolate, piled high with marshmallow topping, to the kitchen table. She'd put out a small plate of chocolate chip cookies that Theenie had made a few days before.

Wes and Annie sipped their cocoa in silence, but she felt his eyes on her. "You're staring."

"I can't help it. You look so pretty with your cheeks flushed from the walk and your hair all mussed. Like you just spent the last hour or so making love," he added, and drained his hot chocolate.

Annie felt something stir inside of her. The attraction she'd felt for him before had intensified into full-blown lust. And something else she wasn't ready to put a name to. She finished her hot chocolate and carried both cups to the sink, where she rinsed them and stuffed them into the dishwasher. She heard Wes get up, and a few seconds later he slipped his arms around her waist and kissed the back of her neck.

"How about a shower?" he said.

She turned. "You mean together?"

"It'll be more fun that way. Besides, you know what they say: it's cheaper if two people shower at the same time."

"Oh yeah?"

He stepped closer and gathered her in his arms, tilted her head up, and kissed her. He ran his hands through her hair, across her shoulders, and down her back before sliding them over her hips and pulling her closer.

Annie tasted the chocolate on his tongue, felt the strength of his arms. She laid one cheek on his chest. He felt safe, like an anchor holding her in place even with all that was going on in her life. At the same time, his kisses turned her thoughts to mush and sent logic right out the door.

After a moment, he pulled back slightly. "Is my timing off?" he asked. "I know you have a lot on your mind."

She took his hand and led him toward the stairs, where he paused to take off his boots, as though realizing they would make too much noise on the bare steps. Nevertheless, the wood creaked beneath his and Annie's feet, and she winced, hoping they didn't wake Theenie. Inside the bathroom, Annie grabbed a couple of towels and washcloths from the linen cabinet.

"We don't need washcloths," he said. "I'd rather wash you with my hands."

Annie's stomach did a little dance at the thought. She put the washcloths back. When she turned, she found him pulling off his shirt.

Wes reached for the buttons on her blouse, undoing them slowly, pressing kisses against her neck and shoulders as he pushed the material aside and let it fall to the floor. He gazed at the lacy bra she wore. "Nice," he said, cupping her breasts with his hands.

Annie could feel the heat of his touch through the fabric, and she stifled the moan low in her throat. Wes reached around and undid the clasp. He tossed the bra aside and pulled her against him once more. Skin touched skin.

He lowered his head and took one nipple in his mouth and tongued it until Annie felt it harden. He moved to the other nipple and teased it as he reached for the button on her slacks.

Annie slipped her arms around his neck and sighed as her body reacted; her lower belly warmed. Wes leaned down and pulled off her shoes. Her slacks joined the rest of her clothes on the floor. Finally, he removed her panties, and his bold stare drank in the sight of her naked body.

Annie could not help feeling self-conscious. She and Charles hadn't showered together often. Their first time in bed had not been at all romantic; he'd simply suggested they strip down and crawl beneath the sheets, where they could "fool around." His caresses had not been slow and light like Wes's. She'd felt rushed and, afterward, an enormous sense of disappointment and frustration as Charles held her in his arms stiffly for a few minutes before turning over and reaching for the remote control and turning on *Letterman.*

Wes kissed her once more, and his big hands felt like heaven on her body. "Undress me," he said against her lips.

Annie was only too happy to oblige. Her knuckles grazed his hard belly as she unfastened his jeans and tugged the zipper. Freed from their clothes, they simply stared at each other.

"You're beautiful," he said. His smile was lazy and sexy as hell.

"You're not so bad yourself, big guy."

Wes turned on the water, tested it, and motioned for Annie to step in first. He joined her and pulled the shower curtain closed.

The warm water felt good against Annie's shoulders and back. Wes wet the soap, made lather, and then spread it across her back. He put the soap aside and began kneading her neck and shoulder muscles until Annie felt them go lax. He massaged her back as he washed. Annie sighed.

"Feel good?" he asked.

She nodded. "I guess I was a little tense."

He chuckled and turned her around. "There are other ways to relieve tension, you know." He soaped her from head to toe before slipping his hand between her thighs. Annie cried out softly as he brought her to orgasm. She grasped his shoulders, buried her face against his chest, and shuddered.

"Sweet," he said.

Once she stopped trembling, Annie washed his back and hips. She soaped his chest and stomach before moving lower. He was already erect. Palms slick with soap, Annie closed her fist around him and brought him to full arousal. Wes laughed softly as he stilled her hand, rinsed himself, and turned off the water. They dried quickly and moved into the bedroom.

He wasted no time, running his tongue lazily across her body, to her center, until Annie clutched at the covers and bit back the moans that accompanied the burst of pleasure that was as powerful as the first. Wes moved over her, and she arched high as he filled her. They moved together fluidly. Annie felt her eyes tear with emotion at the beauty of their coupling, the exquisiteness of their joined bodies, and the sound of her name on Wes's lips when he lost himself in her.

Afterward, he gathered her close and they lay there quietly as their heartbeats slowed. Wes glanced down. "Why the sad look?"

"I'm just tired," she said. "It's been a long night." She couldn't tell him the truth: that she was beginning to care about him too much too soon, and that it terrified her.

* * *

Wes arrived at Lamar Tevis's office shortly after 10:00 AM and found the police chief sipping coffee and reading the newspaper, both feet propped on his desk. He looked up. "What happened to your face?"

"I cut it shaving."

"Holy cow!"

"I have information on the Fortenberry case," Wes said.

"Can I get you a cup of coffee?" Lamar asked. "We also have cheese Danish. Homemade, I might add, by our dispatcher. Yesterday it was cinnamon rolls, and the day before that—"

"No thanks," Wes interrupted.

"Grab a chair and tell me what you got," Lamar said.

Wes told him what he knew about Donna and Norm Schaefer.

"So Fortenberry was having an affair with his boss's wife. Sounds like trouble waiting to happen."

Wes reached into his shirt pocket, pulled out the sapphire and diamond earring, and placed it on the desk. "She lost this at Annie's place."

Lamar pulled his feet from the desk. "Hey, this is nice," he said, picking up the earring and studying it closely. "Are these real diamonds?"

"Yeah. I just had it checked out at the jewelry store down the street. You've got a full karat sapphire and another karat of diamonds, all high-quality stones."

"I'm confused," Lamar said. "What does this have to do with anything?"

"It puts Donna Schaefer at the house during the time Annie was away."

"Was that the only time she went to the house?"

"Mrs. Schaefer visited at Christmas, months before Charles came up missing. It was the same Christmas her husband bought the earrings. Annie said the woman loved them so much she wore them all the time.

She and Charles had planned to leave together, but he didn't show."

Lamar reached for a notebook and began scribbling.

"Here's my theory," Wes said. "Although she denies it, I think Mrs. Schaefer was angry when Charles didn't arrive at her house as planned and she drove over to confront him. They got into a bad argument, and it became physical."

"Why do you suppose Fortenberry changed his mind?"

"Maybe he met someone else in the meantime. He had a reputation for cheating on his wife."

"Did Mrs. Schaefer's husband know about the affair?"

"I've got information that suggests he did."

"Okay," Lamar said, scratching his head as though he was having trouble taking it all in. "It sounds like you might have something here. So if you don't mind, I'd like to back up and start from the beginning. Just so I get my facts right."

"No problem."

"By the way, how in the world did you get this information?" Lamar asked.

"From a very reliable source."

Annie and Theenie slipped into River Road Baptist Church and sat in the very last row. Several people glanced at them, and Annie wondered if her oversize sunglasses offered the disguise she'd hoped for. Under normal circumstances she would have sat up front with the immediate family, but the current circumstances were anything but normal. Eve Fortenberry walked into the church, pain etched into the deep lines on either side of her mouth, making her shoulders sag with the burden of it. Annie's heart went out to the woman who'd never really welcomed her into the fold despite all Annie had done to be a good wife.

On a table at the front of the church was a portrait of Charles, young, handsome, and smiling. More regret.

As though sensing Annie's deep sadness, Theenie covered one hand with hers. Annie was glad Theenie had insisted on attending the service with her. She looked about the church and saw Norm Schaefer sitting across the aisle, staring at her. He looked angry; Annie suspected he'd already been questioned. He was alone. Obviously Donna had chosen not to attend.

"Scoot down," Theenie said, interrupting Annie's thoughts.

Annie looked up. Jamie and Max stood at the end of the row. She immediately made room for them. "Thanks for coming," she said, relieved to find two friendly faces in the crowd.

Jamie reached around Theenie and took Annie's hand. "We thought you'd need a little moral support, but we have to leave as soon as the service is over. A couple of employees are out sick with the flu, so we're covering for them."

Annie smiled and nodded as a woman began singing "Amazing Grace." Afterward, people walked to the podium and told of warm and sometimes funny experiences they'd shared with Charles. Annie found herself smiling from time to time. She had forgotten that side of her husband.

Once the service was over, Annie made her way toward Eve, hoping to catch up with her before she was ushered toward the limo that had been provided by the funeral home. Annie touched Eve's shoulder lightly, and the woman turned. She had obviously been so caught up in her pain that she hadn't noticed Annie in the crowd, because her face suddenly became as cold as a barren winter ground.

"Eve, I'm so sorry," Annie began. "I can only guess how hard this is—"

"What in the name of God are you doing here?" Eve hissed. "How can you even show your face?"

Annie had never seen such contempt. "I was his wife."

"You're a cold-blooded murderer is what you are."

"We should go," Theenie said, nudging Annie.

"I did *not* kill your son," Annie insisted. "I can't believe you'd even think it."

"Go home, Annie. I can't bear the sight of you. Go back to that new boyfriend of yours that I paid for."

"What are you talking about?" Theenie asked when Annie merely stared back at the woman in utter confusion.

Eve looked at Annie, eyes narrowed. "You don't even know, do you?" When Annie shook her head, Eve almost smirked. "You poor little fool. He's a private investigator. I hired him to find out what you'd done to my son."

Chapter

THIRTEEN

"I should drive," Theenie insisted as they approached Annie's car. "You're far too upset."

Upset didn't come close to describing how Annie felt. *You poor little fool.* Eve's words echoed in Annie's head. And that's exactly what she was. Wes Bridges had been hired by her mother-in-law to look into her claims that Annie was responsible for Charles's disappearance. Renting a room in her B & B had made it easy. Sleeping with her had provided the intimacy Wes thought would make her more open to a little pillow talk.

"You haven't driven in years," Annie said. Her face and limbs felt numb and her chest tight. She gulped in several breaths. A horn blew and Theenie pulled her from the path of a car.

"Are you okay?" Theenie asked.

Annie nodded.

"Give me the car keys."

"It's a stick shift."

Theenie shrugged. "It's been a while, but I can do it. You need help getting into the car?"

Annie shook her head and climbed into the passenger seat as Theenie took her place behind the steering wheel. She started the car, and it leaped forward and died.

"Clutch," Annie said.

"Oh yeah. It's all starting to come back to me now."

Theenie tried again, and the car lurched forward. "You want me to take you home?"

"No. I can't face Wes right now. Take me to a bar."

"Come again?"

"I need a drink."

"Oh dear, I've never really been in a bar. We might look like a couple of sluts, walking in by ourselves."

"I *am* a slut," Annie said. "A fool *and* a slut."

"You're not a fool."

They drove a distance, the car bumping along as Theenie tried to reacquaint herself with a four-in-the-floor. "There's a bar," Annie said, pointing to a place called Jimbo's Bar and Grill. "Pull in."

"It looks a little rough to me," Theenie said, but did as she was told.

Annie climbed from the car and marched toward the door. Theenie had to move quickly to keep up with her. They stepped inside and blinked, trying to adjust their eyes to the dark interior. It smelled of stale cigarette smoke. The bartender, a big man in a stained white T-shirt, paused and stared. "We want a drink," Annie announced.

"Have a seat."

"Let's sit in the booth in the back," Theenie whispered, "so nobody will see us."

They headed in that direction, still trying to maneuver their way in the dark. Theenie started to sit, then gave a little yelp and jumped up. "There's a man lying here. He's probably dead. Somebody probably shot him last night and forgot to remove the body. We should leave. You don't need to be seen around dead people on account of you're already up for a murder charge."

Erdle Thorney sat up and blinked. Annie and Theenie blinked back. "What are you two doing here?" he asked.

"Annie needs a cold one," Theenie said. She and Annie took the seat across from him. Theenie began picking at her fingernails. "You look awful," she told Erdle.

The bartender arrived. "This is Jimbo," Erdle said. "He owns the place."

"I need something strong," Annie said. "I've had the worst day of my life." Well, maybe the second worst day, she thought, the first being when Charles's remains were discovered buried in her backyard.

"Give her a tequila straight up," Erdle said, "and as long as she's buying, bring me the usual."

"And you?" The bartender looked at Theenie.

"I'll just have a glass of tea."

"All we got is Long Island iced tea."

Theenie looked thoughtful. "Well, I usually drink Lipton, but I'm open to new experiences."

This brought a smile to Jimbo's face. "I'll be right back."

The front door opened, and a man stood there for a moment, silhouetted by the light streaming in from the outside. He closed the door behind him, blinked several times as though trying to see, and then headed toward them.

"It's Norm Schaefer," Annie whispered.

Theenie squinted. "I didn't know he was a worthless drunk, too."

Norm approached the booth, a menacing look on his face. He pointed to Annie. "You and I need to have a little talk."

"How did you know where to find us?" she asked.

"I followed you from the church." He looked at Theenie. "Where'd you learn to drive? I've never seen such bad driving in my life. Somebody needs to take your license."

Theenie hitched her head high and sniffed. "That would be difficult, seeing as I don't have one."

Norm gave a grunt of disgust. "You old people need to get off the road."

"Would you like to sit down?" Annie asked, trying to be polite but hoping he wouldn't take her up on her offer. She had never seen Norm act so rude, but she was determined not to make a scene.

He ignored her invitation. "What the hell did you tell the police?" he demanded, his eyes boring into hers. "They came to my office this morning and questioned me about your husband's murder. I don't like having cops show up at my place of business."

"I haven't told the police anything," Annie replied. "It's not my favorite place right now."

He sneered. "Then it must have been your biker boyfriend."

Annie hated sneers. She had an urge to slap it right off his face, but she was in no hurry to go back to jail. "Wes is not my boyfriend. He's just somebody I have sex with." The sneer disappeared, and Annie decided it was worth having Theenie and Erdle openly gape at her.

"I don't care if he's your damn plumber," Norm said after he'd composed himself. "Tell him to mind his own business or you're both going to be sorry."

"Are you threatening me?" she asked.

"Don't threaten her," Erdle said. "I'm too drunk to kick your ass."

Norm put his finger in Annie's face, and she decided she liked that even less than sneering. But she wasn't about to let him upset her; that's exactly what he was looking for, and it would be her first time practicing anger management on her own. "Did you have something else you needed to say?" she asked lightly. "Before I ask the owner to throw you out?"

"Yeah." Norm put his hands flat on the table and leaned closer. "Don't blame me because your husband had problems keeping his zipper closed."

Theenie gasped. "That's a *terrible* thing to say on the day of Charles's memorial service. Especially to his widow," she added. "Didn't your mother teach you any manners? Why, if I had children, which I don't, I would have raised them to be more sensitive to other people's feelings."

Jimbo arrived with their drinks and set them on the table. "Y'all want to run a tab?"

"That's fine," Annie said. She waited for him to leave before she addressed Norm. Instead of lashing out as she was tempted to do, she decided to take the high road. "I'm sorry that you were embarrassed by the police, Norm," she said, trying to sound sincere, "but they're questioning all of Charles's friends. That doesn't mean you're a suspect."

"She's right," Theenie said as though hoping to diffuse the man's anger. "Annie's the only one they want to fry."

With those words, Annie picked up her shot glass of tequila and tossed it back like she'd seen people do on TV. It took her breath away. "Holy crap!" she managed, and then began to wheeze.

"Bite into the lemon," Erdle said.

Annie did as he said, but it didn't help. "I can't feel my tongue."

Norm shook his head, muttered a four-letter word, and walked away.

"Here, dear," Theenie said when Annie's eyes began to roll around in her head. "Drink some of my tea. It's not bad."

Annie took the glass and gulped thirstily. Beads of perspiration oozed from her pores. She drained the glass.

"Uh-oh," Erdle said.

"It's okay," Theenie told him. "I'll order another." She motioned for Jimbo. "Would you be so kind as to bring us two more iced teas?"

"Uh-oh," Erdle said.

Two hours and three Long Island iced teas later, Theenie's head was on the table and Annie was still telling Erdle how sorry Wes Bridges was. "Did I tell you he's a private investigator hired by my mean ol' mother-in-law to snoop on me?" she said, her words badly slurred.

Erdle nodded. "I believe you mentioned it once or twice or maybe ten times." His words were equally slurred, but then, he'd drunk nonstop since Annie and Theenie had arrived.

Jimbo delivered their check. Annie picked it up, and her mouth dropped open. "Holy marolly!" She looked at him. "I believe you gave us somebody else's check. We didn't have this many drinks."

"Long Island iced tea has four different kinds of booze in it, lady," he said.

Annie looked at Erdle. "Did you know that?"

"Uh-huh. But you and the old gal seemed to like it."

Annie swallowed. That explained why she could barely see. She leaned closer to Erdle. "I don't have this much cash."

"Don't look at me. I'm flat busted."

Annie smiled at Jimbo. "My credit card is at its limit. Do you take personal checks?"

"Nope." He pointed to a big sign in bold letters that read: Absolutely No Personal Checks. Despite the size of it, Annie had to squint to see it, only to realize she was seeing double.

"Aw, c'mon, Jimbo," Erdle said. "I can vouch for her."

The man made a sound of disgust. "Look, Thorney, I don't care if she's the pope's sister; you know the rules. If I had a dollar for every bounced check I've gotten over the years, I could walk away from this dump a wealthy man."

"Well, what do you expect me to do?" Annie asked.

"Hey, I don't care if you have to go from table to table and give lap dances; it's your problem. Let me know when you figure it out."

"This is not good," Erdle said.

"You're right," Annie said. "Because I don't know the first thing about lap dancing." She recounted her money in case she'd made a mistake. She was way short. "Will Jimbo call the cops on us?" she whispered to Erdle. "I can't afford to get busted again."

"I've seen it happen," he said. "First Jimbo takes 'em out back and slaps 'em around; then he calls the cops."

"Uh-oh. I can't afford to get slapped around, either. I have to give a wedding day after tomorrow. I mean, how would it look?" She glanced at Theenie, who was snoring. "Maybe she can lend me some money." She tried to wake Theenie, but the woman didn't so much as budge. Annie shook her harder. "Wake up, Theenie, I need money," she shouted in her ear, causing the other customers to look their way.

"You're making a scene," Erdle hissed.

Annie sank into the booth. From the looks of the other customers, it was hard to believe that she could possibly say anything to offend or embarrass them.

"I have no other choice but to check Theenie's purse," Annie said. She pulled out the woman's wallet, looked inside, and frowned. "She has less cash on her than I do."

"Uh-oh," Erdle said.

"What are we going to do?" Annie asked. "We can't pay this tab."

He thought for a minute. "I'll call for backup." He slid from the booth and almost landed on the floor. He grabbed the edge of the table to steady himself. "I'll be back."

Danny Gilbert arrived fifteen minutes later. He

scratched his head and perused the threesome. "What happened to Theenie?"

"She's taking a nap," Annie said.

"So you ladies decided to drop in for a couple of drinks, huh?" he said, glancing about the room, now filled with bikers and construction workers.

Jimbo suddenly appeared. "The guy across the room wants to buy the redhead a drink," he said.

Annie was flattered. "Oh yeah?"

"I think we're leaving," Danny said. "Do you have the check?"

"Sure do." Jimbo handed it to Danny, who arched both brows. "Wow," he said, reaching into his back pocket for his wallet. "When you guys decide to tie one on, you don't mess around."

"It wasn't our fault," Annie said. "We didn't know the bartender was putting extra booze in our drinks." She looked at Jimbo as though she held him personally responsible for the condition they were in.

"They were drinking Long Island iced tea," Jimbo told Danny.

Danny looked annoyed. "Did you inform them in advance how much alcohol was in each drink?"

"I don't run a babysitting business," Jimbo said.

Danny counted out the money and handed it to him. The man didn't look pleased. "What, no tip?"

"Yeah, I have a tip for you," Danny said. "Next time tell people what they're getting when they order a drink they've never heard of."

Jimbo pocketed the money. "Just get them out of here, okay?"

"What are we going to do about Theenie?" Annie asked. "She's passed out."

"Good question," Danny said.

Jimbo gave a disgusted sigh and motioned for Annie

to get out of the booth. "Grab the old broad's purse," he said.

"Excuse me, but did you just refer to my friend as a broad? Why, you're nothing but a—"

"Annie, let's just get out of here," Danny said. "Now."

Annie reached for her and Theenie's purses and slid from the booth. Jimbo leaned over, pulled Theenie across the booth, and threw her over his shoulder. "Just tell me where you want her."

Annie fell asleep as soon as Danny helped her into the back seat of his car. "We'll pick up your car in the morning," he said, but she and Theenie were both out cold. "Guess you're not really worried about it right now," he said as he closed the door.

"What happened?" Danny asked Erdle when he joined him in the front seat. "I've never seen Annie in this condition."

Erdle told him how Eve Fortenberry had treated Annie at Charles's memorial service.

Danny looked incredulous. "Wes is actually working for Eve?"

"I don't know what's going on between them now. All I know is that Eve hired him to find out if Annie was responsible for her husband's disappearance and obviously got a great deal of pleasure announcing it to Annie at the memorial."

"Does Wes know that Annie's on to him?" Danny asked.

"Not yet. But he will the minute Annie sets foot in that house, buh-lieve you me." He paused and glanced over his shoulder at the two women. "Unless Annie is still unconscious."

Danny chuckled. "You know, I think I'd like to hang around and see that."

* * *

Annie and Theenie awoke as soon as Danny cut the engine. "Where am I?" Theenie asked. "What day is it? And how come my head hurts like the dickens?"

"It was the tea at Jimbo's Bar and Grill," Annie said. "It was spiked with tons of alcohol."

"Oh my. And it went down so easy."

The two women climbed from the car and stumbled up the front walk. The front door was thrown open by a worried-looking Wes. "You two look terrible," he said. "Where have you been?"

"They got all liquored up," Erdle slurred.

Annie walked past Wes without a word and headed for the kitchen to put on a pot of coffee. He followed. "Are you okay?"

She glared at him. "Are you asking out of personal concern or is this just part of your job?"

"What?"

"Annie knows the truth," Danny said. "Her mother-in-law gave her an earful at the memorial service."

Wes sighed and raked his hands through his hair. "I was planning to tell you."

"I don't want to hear anything you have to say. I don't even want to look at you. What I *do* want is for you to leave this house immediately."

"I don't work for Eve anymore, Annie. In fact, I gave her a full refund, including her retainer. I'll bet she didn't bother to tell you that, did she?"

"I don't care if you gave her the Hope Diamond. You're a liar and a phony, and I don't ever want to look at your face again." She staggered from the room and up the stairs.

"I think she means it," Danny said. "I'd start packing if I were you."

"That's going to make things real convenient for you, isn't it, Gilbert?"

"Don't blame me, friend," Danny said. "You managed to screw up all by yourself."

When Annie opened her eyes the sun had gone down and her bedroom was bathed in shadows. She could barely make out Danny's form in the corner chair. "Is he gone?"

"Yes. I stayed with him while he packed so he wouldn't be tempted to knock on your door."

"Thank you."

"How do you feel?"

"Like I should be in ICU."

Danny moved to the bed, sat down, and took her hand. "Listen, I've got some time off, so I'm going away for a while."

"How long is a while?"

"Actually, I've had a job offer in Charleston."

"I didn't know."

"I'm supposed to report to work in a couple of days."

"So you've already decided."

He nodded. "I think a change would be good for me."

"How will I reach you? Will you still have the same cell phone number?"

"No, I'm going with a different plan." He paused. "How about I call you once I find a place to live and get settled in?"

"That'll be great. Charleston's only a little more than an hour away. I can come on a Saturday or Sunday morning and stay all day."

"Yeah." He reached up and mussed her hair. "Be good to yourself, Anniekins."

Annie watched Danny leave through her bedroom door, and instinct told her he would not be calling anytime soon, if at all. She sat in the growing darkness, knowing she had never felt more alone. Wes was gone, and one of her very best friends had just said good-bye.

She had a choice: she could either sit in bed and feel sorry for herself or move on.

She would move on, because that's the way she was.

Annie entered the kitchen some minutes later, once she'd run a brush through her hair and brushed her teeth. She needed to eat; maybe the food would absorb whatever alcohol remained in her stomach. She found Theenie, ice pack pressed against her head and a bottle of Extra Strength Excedrin in her hand. Her other hand held the phone to her ear. She glanced at Annie.

"Thank you for calling," Theenie said. "I'll be sure to pass the news to Annie. . . . No, she's not mad at you." Theenie hung up.

"I hope that wasn't Doc. If he sees us like this he'll put us down for sure."

"Guess what?" Theenie said as she opened the bottle in her hand.

"I could use a couple of those," Annie said. "Maybe three."

Theenie shook two tablets into her palm and passed the bottle to Annie. "That was Lamar Tevis on the phone just now. And guess what?"

"Okay, *what*?"

"Donna Schaefer just confessed to murdering Charles. The charges against you have been dropped."

Chapter
FOURTEEN

Wes checked into a motel, grabbed his knapsack from the bike, and went inside the room. He dropped his bag on the bed, switched on the TV set, and went into the bathroom, where he threw cold water on his face. In the mirror over the sink a tired, haggard man looked back at him. Wes paced the room, picked up the remote, clicked on several channels, and turned off the TV. Finally, he kicked off his boots and lay down on the bed.

He awoke shortly before 11:00 PM with an empty stomach.

Some ten minutes later Wes pulled into a diner where a neon sign flashed the words: *We Never Close*. Inside, a jukebox wailed a Patsy Cline song, competing with the loud, steady hum of voices and occasional laughter.

Wes glanced about, noted the full booths, and took a seat at the long counter. A TV set anchored to the ceiling played the eleven o'clock news. He tried to listen once the Patsy Cline song came to an end, but Jimmy Buffet took her place.

A young waitress with hair that had been bleached one too many times sauntered toward Wes, the gleam in her eyes making it clear she liked what she saw. Her uniform was short, the top button undone, giving Wes an unimpeded view of plump, youthful breasts. "What'll you have?" she asked.

He averted his gaze. "Large milk and a stack of pancakes."

"Want hash browns with that? We're running a special."

"No thanks."

She stood there for a minute, tapping a pencil against her bottom lip. Her mouth was slick with gloss. "You're new in town, aren't 'cha?"

He glanced up at the TV. "Yeah. Just visiting."

She smiled. "I saw your bike when you pulled in. Awesome. I love motorcycles, but I've never ridden on one."

Wes kept his eyes glued to the TV. "Will my order take long? I'm in a hurry."

"No problem. I'll put a rush on it." She scribbled something on her pad and turned.

Wes blinked and straightened on his stool when Lamar Tevis's face suddenly flashed on the screen. "Hey, wait, can you turn up the volume on the TV real quick?"

"We're not supposed to."

Wes smiled. "Please."

She ambled toward it, reached for the remote control, and turned it up a notch. Lamar's face disappeared, was instantly replaced with a photo of Donna Schaefer, followed by what appeared to be a home video of her leaving a hospital with a baby wrapped in a blue blanket tucked in her arms. She pulled the blanket back, and there was a close-up shot of the baby, red-faced and squint-eyed, his tiny fist pressed to his mouth. A smiling Norm Schaefer stepped into the frame, wearing the look of a proud new father.

Wes strained to listen, but the jukebox drowned out the sound. "I still can't hear the TV," he told the waitress when she delivered his milk.

"You wouldn't be able to hear a freight train coming through with that music blaring," she said. "Just hold on." She disappeared through a swinging door. In less than a minute, the jukebox died. Several people began to complain.

"I'm sorry," the waitress shouted, arms flailing as though she had no idea what was going on. "I'll bet the dang thing blew another fuse."

Wes grinned and slapped a ten-dollar bill in her palm.

Annie, Theenie, Lovelle, and Destiny were crowded around the TV set in the sunroom as the newscaster gave the latest details on the investigation of the murder of Charles Fortenberry. Jamie and Max had called only minutes ago to let Annie know the local news station was airing a news conference.

All four women were quiet as they watched Lamar step up to a microphone while one young officer in the background did his best to make sure the camera got a shot of his face. He smiled, waved, and mouthed the words, *Hi, Mom*.

"Ladies and gentlemen," Lamar began in an authoritative voice. "As you know, this office has been investigating the murder of thirty-year-old Charles Fortenberry, who was found buried in his wife's backyard less than two weeks ago. Mr. Fortenberry had been missing for more than three years. Thanks to the hard work of my excellent investigative team, we have solved the case. In record time, I might add."

"Excellent investigative team, my butt," Jamie muttered.

Lamar glanced down at his notes. "At approximately three PM today, thirty-five-year-old Donna Schaefer, a lifelong resident of Beaumont, was admitted to Beaumont Memorial Hospital for fatigue and depression. A staff physician immediately saw her, and our office was contacted. Mrs. Schaefer gave a statement to me from her hospital bed, admitting that she was responsible for the death of Charles Fortenberry."

"Well, now we know," Theenie said.

"Mrs. Schaefer's husband has retained an attorney," Lamar went on, "so I'll answer a couple of questions, and then I'll give him the microphone."

"Chief Tevis," one of the reporters called out. "Does this mean Mr. Fortenberry's widow has been cleared of murder charges?"

"Yes." Lamar pointed to a reporter nearby.

"Has anyone located the missing remains?" another reporter asked.

Lamar looked uncomfortable. "I'm sort of hesitant to talk about it until I am one hundred percent certain, but the van was very recently discovered abandoned less than one hundred miles from here in Baxter County. It has been searched, and it is my understanding that it is indeed the van, and the contents inside are intact. I'm waiting for verification from the Baxter County sheriff."

"Oh my gosh!" Annie said. "Lamar finally did something right."

"Chief Tevis," a female reporter called out. "Does anyone know at this time the actual cause of death to the victim?"

A camera swung in the woman's direction.

"She's the reporter from Charleston," Annie said.

Lamar hesitated. "Well . . ."

"Isn't it true Mr. Fortenberry's injuries were not life threatening?"

Lamar looked surprised. "We don't know that for sure."

"I understand the medical examiner was unable to state the cause of death," the woman continued.

"Boy, she's a real ballbuster," Destiny said, drawing raised brows from Theenie.

Lamar was clearly flustered. "We don't have all the answers right now," he said. "That's why the remains were being sent to the Medical University in Charleston to begin with. I have nothing more to say." He stormed away from the microphone.

Lamar was replaced by a balding man with oversize glasses who wasted no time getting started and spoke quickly. "My name is Randolf Pierce, and I've been retained to represent Mrs. Schaefer in this case. I met with her only briefly before she made her statement to the police. I do not share Chief Tevis's optimism that this is a cut-and-dried case, so to speak; this investigation is ongoing."

The camera flashed to a frowning Lamar.

"Because we still have many questions, most of which will have to wait until my client's condition is stable, I will not be answering questions specific to the case." A disgruntled murmur rose from the crowd. "All I'm prepared to say is that Mrs. Schaefer is being treated by a fine group of doctors, and it will be up to them as to how long she remains in the hospital and when she can answer further questions." He paused and looked through the crowd. "I would like to say, on my client's behalf, that she willingly came forward and insisted on talking to the police, despite serious medical problems. Thank you for your time."

Several reporters voiced questions, but they went ignored as Pierce stepped away from the microphone.

The telephone rang and Lovelle rolled her eyes and picked it up. She immediately put her hand over the mouthpiece and looked at Annie. "It's Wes. He says it's important."

Annie took the phone and gently placed the receiver in the cradle.

Wes was waiting for Lamar in the reception area the next morning when he came in at seven. "I need to talk to you," Wes said.

"Hey, did you see me on TV last night?" Lamar asked.

"Yep."

"How about that smart-aleck woman from Charleston? Boy, I ripped her a new one, didn't I?"

"Oh yeah."

Lamar checked his watch. "Now, where is Delores? She's supposed to bring in sausage biscuits. I'll spend the rest of the day fighting heartburn, but it's worth it. By the way, several of my friends taped the news conference last night in case you want to watch it again. You know, in case you have company or something. Let's grab a cup of brew and go into my office."

Wes waited until they had their coffee and were seated in Lamar's office before he pulled out his wallet, flipped it open, and handed it to the other man.

Lamar arched both brows. "A PI, huh? I should have known."

"Before that I was a cop. Worked homicide for a number of years."

"Someone from Beaumont hired you for a job?" When Wes hesitated, Lamar handed him his wallet, got up, and closed the door. "Everything you say stays in this room."

"Eve Fortenberry contacted me a few weeks ago," Wes said. "Asked me to look into her son's disappearance."

Lamar reclaimed his seat. "I'm not surprised. She's taking it pretty hard." He stared into his coffee cup for a long time. He looked sad. "The more I look at this case, the more questions I have."

"Such as?"

"Fortenberry was alive when Donna Schaefer left the scene; she saw him blinking his eyes. But like I said, he didn't die from injuries sustained in the fall."

"Fall?"

Lamar nodded. "When he didn't show up she drove over and confronted him. Even went into his bedroom to see if he'd packed, which he hadn't. Hell, I don't know if he changed his mind about leaving or if he met someone else. Sure can't ask him." He shrugged. "Anyway, she says the whole thing was an accident. Charles told her he didn't love her and never had. They got into some kind of tussle, 'cause she said she left a bad scratch on his face.

"So he told her to get the hell out, and when she wouldn't, he stomped out of the room toward the stairs. She caught up with him and grabbed his arm to stop him from leaving. He struggled to pull free and fell. She flipped out and ran."

"Does Mrs. Schaefer know she wasn't responsible for his death?"

"She's in the psych ward and in no condition to talk. She was a mess when she came in, but it was obvious she was trying to hold herself together long enough to get it all out. It must've been eating at her." He shook his head sadly.

"So what do you think killed him?" Wes asked after a moment.

"Don't know. At first I wondered if he could have had a heart attack, but he had a complete physical less than a month before his death, and he was in excellent health. We also don't know who buried the body. Mrs. Schaefer swears she didn't do it."

"Are you thinking there was more than one person involved?"

"Had to be. Fortenberry was six foot two and weighed one-eighty at his last physical. And get this. Mrs. Schaefer has back problems from a car accident some years ago. Has to see one of them chiropractors every so often," he added. "Bottom line is, nobody is going to convince me that some one-hundred-and-ten-pound weakling with back problems dragged that body from the house, across the backyard, and buried it."

"You're wrong," Wes said. "The bottom line is we still have a murderer out there."

Annie was hard at work in the kitchen when someone knocked on the back door. She washed her hands and dried them, then hurried to answer. She was surprised to find Wes standing there. Okay, maybe *surprised* didn't aptly describe her, because her stomach gave an immediate lurch and her heartbeat quickened. Not a good sign. Definitely not good. Best to get rid of Wes fast, before some other body part went haywire on her. She started to close the door, but he pressed one hand against it, holding it fast.

"We need to talk."

She wished he didn't have to look so good. "When pigs fly, Bridges." She tried once more to close the door, but he continued to block it.

"I'm prepared to stand here as long as it takes."

The determined look on his face told her he meant it. "This is a bad time, okay?" she said. "The wedding of the century is being held here tomorrow, and I've got a ton of work to do." She gave him a tight smile. "Now, why don't you run along? Surely you can find somebody to spy on."

"I'm not going to apologize for renting the room under false pretenses," he said. "I'm a professional, and I was hired to do a job, namely find out what happened to your husband."

"Which meant snooping on me," she reminded. "You got a lot of nerve coming here, you know that?"

"You're still mad at me."

"Duh. If I weren't practicing anger management I'd

pull out my rolling pin. I might just have to have a relapse and do it anyway."

"Put yourself in Eve's place."

"No thank you. The woman is nutso." But she *had* put herself in Eve's place as much as she could, and her anger and resentment toward the woman had cooled. Not all of it, though.

"Her son and only child had been missing more than three years when she hired me, Annie. She was sick with worry."

"And positive I was behind his disappearance. That stinks. At least I don't have to feel guilty for all the mean things I've said about her."

"I think some of the blame should fall on her son for telling her how unhappy he was in his marriage."

"Don't worry; I've said plenty of bad things about Charles, too."

Wes looked like he might smile and then seemed to think better of it. "What would you have done differently, Annie? Had it been your son? And knowing Lamar Tevis was in charge of the investigation," he added.

"I certainly wouldn't have accused *me*."

"It took me about five minutes after meeting you to realize you weren't responsible for his disappearance. I would have decided sooner had I been conscious."

"I think that would have been a perfect time to tell the truth."

"I wanted to."

"What you wanted was to get me into bed."

"That, too."

Annie glanced at the clock on the wall. "Are we done yet?"

He stepped closer. "Darlin', we haven't even started."

Her toes tingled at the endearment, at the look in his eyes that made her stomach feel like warm taffy. "I'm busy, Wes."

"I have to tell you something," he said. "About Charles."

Annie couldn't hide her irritation. "I'm tired of talking about Charles, okay? I just want to get on with my life."

"Donna Schaefer didn't kill him, Annie. I think someone else came in after she left. Probably the same person who dragged him to the backyard and buried him."

Annie felt a chill race up her spine. "Norm?"

"Could be. I want you to be careful. He's already mad because I pulled him into the investigation, and because you made him look stupid at Jimbo's. Erdle told me."

"I can take care of myself," she said.

"You won't have to. Danny is so lovesick over you he'll come running every time you call."

"Danny is gone."

Wes's brows drew together. "Gone where?"

"He had a job offer in Charleston."

"Where in Charleston?"

"I don't know," she said impatiently. "He just left, okay? I don't have any way of reaching him." She felt a lump in her throat. "Can we not talk about it right now?"

"Annie—"

"Look, I'm not mad anymore, okay? And I appreciate your giving me the heads-up about Norm. But I really have a ton of work to do, and I just need to be alone for a while." What she needed was to be away from him. So she could think.

Wes nodded. "I'm, uh, on my way to Columbia," he said. "Something came up with a case that I thought was over and done with."

Annie felt a sinking sensation in her stomach. He was leaving. "I see," she said, keeping her voice even.

"I'll be back."

"Of course."

"I'm coming back because I don't want to be away from you."

She tried to look away, but she couldn't let go of his eyes, and the thought of him leaving, even for a day, made her want to reach out to him and ask him to stay.

"My timing is probably way off, but I want you to think about something while I'm gone, Annie," Wes said softly. He reached into his pocket and pulled out a small velvet jeweler's box.

Annie's stomach dived to her toes and her lips went numb. "Oh, shit. Oh, shit. Oh, shit." She looked at his face. "Is that what I think it is?"

He smiled. "Only one way to find out."

Annie started to reach for it and then snatched her hand away. "Um, I don't think—"

"Afraid?" he said gently.

All the air had been sucked from her body. She gulped in a mouthful. "Terrified," she managed.

"Take a chance, Annie. Take a chance on me. On us."

"It feels like things are moving so fast."

"I think sometimes you just know," Wes said.

She had heard those words before. Annie opened her mouth to speak, but no words came out.

"Why don't you think about it?" He set the box on the table. "You know how to reach me."

When Lovelle and Theenie came downstairs some time later, they found Annie sitting at the kitchen table staring at the box.

"Holy cow, is that what I think it is?" she said, echoing Annie's own words.

"I think so," Annie said, "but I'm afraid to look."

Theenie put a hand to her mouth. "Wes asked you to marry him?"

"Uh-huh."

"Well, what did you say?" Lovelle demanded impatiently.

Annie was prevented from answering when Destiny plodded down the last couple of stairs, groaning aloud. "I'm exhausted," she said. "I was up half the night talking to Lacey, but I *finally,* after Lord knows how many hours, got through to her."

"How did you manage that?" Theenie asked.

"Well, the name Fairchild kept popping up in my mind, and I kept getting a funny feeling about it, so I did a little research and discovered the Fairchild family lived in this area when the house was a bordello. I suspected Jonathan Fairchild was a customer. I managed to get a picture, and when I showed it to Lacey she became agitated. Finally, she pointed to the marks on her neck."

"So he killed her?" Theenie asked.

Destiny nodded. "I don't know why. Maybe he had a thing for Lacey and resented her sleeping with other men. Or maybe he just got rough with her. It'll probably come to me later, but the good thing, once Lacey saw that picture, she suddenly realized she was dead. And *then* she remembered her lover being hanged, and she couldn't wait to go to the light. I hope they're happy, because I'm so far behind with my mail I'll never get caught up."

"You mean she's really gone?" Lovelle said, sounding disappointed.

"Yup. Now I'll be able to get some sleep." Destiny sighed. "Damn, I'm good."

"I'm going to miss her," Theenie said. "It was so nice having a spirit in the house. And kind of sexy, too, what with her stealing our underwear."

"Cotton underwear is not sexy, Theenie," Lovelle said. "Face it."

Theenie ignored her. "At least we know she's finally at peace."

"I need coffee," Destiny said, "and lots of it." She started for the coffeepot, paused, and looked at Annie. "You haven't said a word. What's wrong?"

"She's contemplating," Theenie whispered, stepping aside so Destiny could get a look.

Destiny crossed the room and stared down at the box. "Hmm, let me guess."

"She's afraid to open it," Lovelle said.

Destiny frowned. "That's nonsense. A jar of pickles is hard to open, a stuck window is hard to open, but we're talking jewelry here. I can rip that lid off with my bare teeth from the other side of the room. Come on, Annie, give it up."

Annie knew she would have to look sooner or later. She took a deep breath and lifted the lid. The ring flashed at her.

"Oh my Lord!" Theenie said.

Lovelle sighed. "Boy-oh-boy."

"*Very nice,*" Destiny said. "A full karat, great clarity, no visible flaws, perfect Tiffany setting. I take it Wes gave it to you?"

Annie nodded. Her heart was pounding so loud she was certain Doc could hear it next door. "I can't think. I must be in shock."

"It's beautiful," Lovelle said.

Theenie began picking her nails. "Yes, but it's likely to snag on the blankets when she makes the beds."

"So, does this mean you're engaged?" Destiny asked. "Um."

"Not that I'm surprised," Destiny said. "I've been having visions. Max and Jamie aren't the only ones getting married in this house. I didn't want to say anything on account I wanted it to be a surprise. When is the big event? No, don't tell me; I already know. You're going to be a May bride. Better start making plans."

"I didn't give him an answer," Annie said. "He just left the ring here and told me to think about it."

"At least try it on," Lovelle said. "See if it fits."

Annie was tempted. Finally, she pulled the ring from the box and slipped it on her left finger. All three women leaned forward to get a closer look.

"That's one big rock," Theenie said.

Annie nodded. "It's a little loose."

Destiny waved the remark aside. "It can be sized. I think you should wear the ring while you're considering your answer, though. Do you get to keep it even if you say no?"

"Why would I do that?" Annie asked.

"You can always put it in a different setting. I should know these things after five marriages."

Theenie looked at Lovelle. "If she marries Wes, we'll have to move. You know how newlyweds are."

Lovelle nodded. "They stay naked a lot." She looked thoughtful. "That might not be a bad thing, seeing how Wes is so hot."

Theenie's mouth flew open. "Lovelle, I don't believe what I just heard come out of your mouth!"

"Hey, old ladies have needs, too. That's why they make adult toys."

"I shouldn't be hearing this." Theenie pressed her hands to her ears. "La la la la la. Is she done yet?"

"Nobody is moving anywhere," Annie said. "Besides, I can't get married right now; I just buried my husband."

Theenie nodded. "Oh yeah. You're supposed to be in mourning."

Destiny took a sip of her coffee. "See, that's the thing about diamonds. They go with any color. Especially black."

"Do you love him?" Lovelle asked.

All eyes went to Annie. She suddenly felt a lump in her throat. "Yeah. I just need to think."

Lovelle patted her on the back. "Well, now that things have settled down, your mind will be clearer."

Annie and Destiny exchanged looks. Neither of them spoke. Annie went back to work. Destiny refilled her coffee cup and sipped in silence. Peaches stretched and yawned in one of the chairs and jumped to the floor. She walked over to her bowl and swatted it hard. Water sloshed over one side as the bowl sailed a good three feet. Nobody noticed. Peaches walked over to the cabinet, sat, and stared at Annie. Finally, Theenie and Lovelle disappeared into the sunroom to watch their favorite morning show.

Destiny sneezed. "Donna Schaefer didn't kill him."

Annie went on with her work but said nothing.

Peaches rubbed up against the cabinet, never taking her eyes off Annie.

"She only thinks she's responsible for his death because he was alive when she ran out." Destiny wiped her nose.

Peaches smacked the cabinet with her paw. *Barn, barn, barn.*

Annie looked up and gazed out the window over the sink.

"Somebody came in afterward and did it. I just have to figure out who." Sneeze, sneeze. *Barn, barn, barn.*

Peaches took several steps back and hurled herself against the cabinet and then slumped to the floor, tongue lolling from her mouth.

Destiny gaped.

Annie glanced at the cat, turned, and continued to stare out the window. "She's faking."

* * *

It was late in the afternoon when Annie allowed herself to take a break. She poured a glass of iced tea and decided to drink it in the sunroom. As she made her way through the house, she smiled. Theenie had polished the antiques until they shone like a dime, and Destiny had run a damp mop over the wood floors and vacuumed the rugs. The tables in the ballroom wore crisp white tablecloths and were set just so, thanks to Lovelle.

Annie wasn't sure how she would have managed without their help; she'd spent the entire day preparing hors d'oeuvres, baking traditional wedding cookies, as well as layers for the French pound cake that she would later frost and decorate. Salad plates, asparagus, stuffed cherry tomatoes, champagne, and wine were chilling in the restaurant-size refrigerator at the back of the large walk-in pantry. She had wanted to get as much food preparation behind her so she could concentrate on the main course tomorrow. The two women she often hired for large occasions would arrive an hour before the food was to be served so that she would be able to concentrate on last-minute details.

Everything was under control.

Yeah, right. Her guts had not stopped shaking since Wes had arrived bearing an engagement ring and the latest news on Charles's death.

She missed Wes. Her bed had been a lonely place without him the night before. She longed to have his arms around her because he made her feel safe and cared for, something she had only recently begun to realize that she'd spent most of her life craving. She missed his smile, the laughter in his eyes that told her he refused to take life so seriously. She missed the tender looks and kisses, and the taste and smell of him.

And she regretted sending him away that morning

instead of admitting that somehow, in just two weeks' time, she had fallen in love with him, too.

"Annie?"

She jumped at the sound of Theenie's voice. "I didn't hear you," she said.

"Are you okay?"

"Yeah. I'm just trying to think of everything I need to do before tomorrow. Right now I'm on break."

Theenie followed her to the sunporch, where they each claimed a chair. "You're thinking of Wes."

"He deceived me."

"He was hired to do a job. Once he was convinced of your innocence, he began looking elsewhere."

"He's probably all wrong for me, Theenie."

"That's what I thought at first, but I've since changed my mind. He loves you, Annie. He's sincere. Lovelle agrees."

"It just happened so fast."

Theenie patted her hand. "You can schedule dinner parties and luncheons and weddings, but you can't put love into a time frame." She suddenly frowned. "Where's your engagement ring?"

"Huh?" Annie glanced at her hand. "Holy crap, it's gone!"

"Okay, everybody calm down," Destiny said an hour later, after all four of them had searched every nook and cranny for the ring.

"Calm down?" Annie cried. "What am I going to tell Wes?"

"It has to be here somewhere," Lovelle said. "It didn't just walk off."

"Annie, think," Theenie said. "When was the last time you noticed it?"

"I know I glanced down at it a number of times after

I first put it on," she said, "but then I got busy. What if it slipped off and fell down the sink?"

"That has been known to happen," Destiny said. "Does Erdle know anything about plumbing?"

Annie nodded. "He makes most of the repairs around here. When he gets around to it," she added.

"His car is in the driveway," Lovelle said. "I'll go get him."

"Give me the box the ring came in," Destiny said. "I'll go into the living room where it's quiet so I can concentrate. Maybe something will come to me."

Annie grabbed the jeweler's box and handed it to her. "Good luck."

Erdle staggered in through the back door a few minutes later, followed by Lovelle. "He's drunk, of course," she said.

Annie gave an enormous sigh of disgust. "What else is new?" She looked at him. His clothes were badly wrinkled; his hair stood in tufts. Lovelle had obviously awakened him. He held a plumber's wrench in one hand. His eyes widened at the trays of food sitting on the counter and kitchen table. "Wow!" He belched. "I've never seen so much food."

Annie had already cleared the cabinet beneath the kitchen sink. "Did Lovelle tell you my ring may have slid off my finger and gone down the drain?" she asked.

He scratched his head and blinked several times. "She might have mentioned it." He gazed back at the food. "What's all that?"

"Stuffed grape leaves, Roquefort grapes, wedding cookies, and . . ." She paused, wondering why she was bothering to answer. "I'm in a hurry."

"Why would anybody want to eat grape leaves?" he asked.

"Erdle, would you please—"

"Can I just have a couple of those cookies? I haven't eaten in a while."

Annie sighed. "Okay, but please hurry."

Erdle studied the tray of cookies carefully. "Eenie-meenie-miny-mo—"

"Oh, for Pete's sake!" Theenie said. "Just grab one and be done with it."

"Annie said I could have two."

Annie leaned against the counter and pressed her fingers to her temples. She could feel a headache coming on, but she was determined not to lose her temper.

Erdle selected a cookie from each tray and popped one of them in his mouth. "Hey, that's good."

The doorbell rang. "That's probably Jamie," Annie said. "She's dropping off her wedding dress."

"I'll get it," Theenie said, and hurried from the room.

Erdle made for the sink as he tossed the second cookie in his mouth and chomped down. "Ouch, damn!" he said, his hand flying to his jaw. "You must have put a rock in this one."

Annie frowned. "Huh?"

"I think I just broke a tooth on something hard." He pointed into his open mouth.

Annie sighed. Was there no end to all the craziness? She looked in Erdle's mouth. "Open wider," she said. He made an unintelligible sound and his mouth widened a smidgeon. Annie caught a flash of something gold. "My ring!" she cried, causing Lovelle to jump. Peaches sprang from the chair and hid behind a plant. "Don't swallow!"

Startled, Erdle immediately gulped, and the ring became lodged in his throat. He grabbed his neck with both hands. "Argh!" he said.

"Did you swallow it?" Annie shrieked, unaware that Theenie, Destiny, Jamie, and Vera were standing in the doorway with Fleas in tow. Peaches hissed and arched her back and then darted from behind the plant, claws bared. Fleas gave a yelp as Peaches raked one paw across his face. A howling Fleas turned and bounded from the kitchen with Peaches on his heels.

Erdle wheezed as he tried to suck in air.

"He's choking!" Lovelle said.

Annie grabbed him from the back and immediately began performing the Heimlich on him. Lovelle reached for a tumbler of orange juice on the counter and shoved it at him.

"Don't drink it!" Annie said.

Clearly panicked, Erdle ignored her, raising the glass to his lips and chugging. He swallowed and belched loudly.

"You swallowed it!" Annie yelled.

"Huh?" He blinked back dumbly.

She grabbed his shirt and shook him, almost causing him to drop the container of juice. "You swallowed my engagement ring!"

Theenie and Lovelle gasped.

"Spit it out!" Annie ordered, still shaking him.

"Miss Annie, stop!" he said.

"What's going on?" Jamie asked, trying to make herself heard over the commotion.

Theenie turned to her. "Wes gave Annie an engagement ring. She lost it. I think Erdle just swallowed it."

"Why would he do something stupid like that?" Vera said.

"It wasn't my fault," Erdle said, trying to catch his breath and pull free from Annie. "It was in the cookie."

"You and Wes are engaged?" Jamie asked Annie, clearly shocked.

Theenie and Lovelle managed to pull Erdle free of Annie's grasp. "Stop it, this instant!" Theenie told her. "You're supposed to be practicing anger management."

"He swallowed my ring!"

"It's not his fault," Theenie said. "The ring obviously slipped off your finger while you were making the cookies."

"Why didn't you tell me you and Wes had become engaged?" Jamie demanded.

Fleas tore through the kitchen and raced up the stairs, Peaches right behind him, snarling and hissing.

"It's not official," Annie said. "I'm still thinking about it." Something shattered upstairs, but it went ignored.

Erdle bolted toward the back door, but Annie was faster, throwing herself in front of him. "Oh no, you don't! I'm taking you to the emergency room to have your stomach pumped out."

The color drained from Erdle's face. He looked at Lovelle. "Do you have any vodka to go with the rest of this orange juice?"

Suddenly an earsplitting whistle pierced the air and everybody stopped in their tracks to see where it had come from. Vera pulled the whistle from her mouth. "Okay, I've listened to just about all I'm going to put up with," she said, "so I want everybody to shut up and do as I say." She pointed to Erdle. "Sit."

"Yes, ma'am." He pulled out the nearest chair and sat.

She looked at Jamie. "Go find those crazy animals and do something with them or I'm going to call the animal shelter and have them both picked up and you won't have a flower dog in your wedding."

Jamie nodded and raced up the stairs, calling out for Fleas.

"Now then," Vera said. "As I see it, there are only two ways to get to that ring, but having the poor man's stomach pumped out seems a bit extreme, so we'll have to take a different approach, if you get my drift."

Theenie nodded. "Why didn't I think of that? I have just the thing." She hurried up the stairs with the speed and agility of a woman half her age.

"Would somebody tell me what's goin' on?" Erdle asked.

"You'll find out soon enough," Vera told him.

Theenie returned, slightly out of breath, holding a large bottle. "This'll do the job," she said.

Annie stepped closer. "What is it?"

"Castor oil. My mother used to make us drink it when we got, um, *clogged up*. Once Erdle drinks this I guarantee you'll get your ring back, although it'll take a few hours at least. I want him to drink the whole bottle just to be sure."

"The *whole* bottle?" Annie asked.

"It won't hurt him," Theenie said. "Doctors used to have people drink this stuff all the time before certain tests."

"The *whole* bottle?" Annie repeated.

"Yep." Theenie uncapped the bottle.

"Oh no, you don't!" Erdle said, jumping from his chair. "You've lost your danged mind if you think I'm going to drink that nasty stuff."

Annie planted her hands on her hips. "You're going to drink it if I have to personally pour it down your throat."

"No way," he said, starting for the door.

"Let me take care of this," Vera said, pulling her Smith & Wesson .38 from her purse. She trained it on Erdle. "Maybe this will change your mind."

Everybody froze, including Erdle. "Lady, are you crazy? Put that thing down before you hurt somebody."

"Put that gun away, Vera," Jamie said from the bottom of the stairs. She held a hissing Peaches several feet in front of her, obviously trying to escape being clawed. "Have you forgotten all you had to go through after you shot the last person?"

Erdle swallowed and slid his gaze to Jamie. "You're

saying this won't be her first homicide?" His voice squeaked.

"I haven't shot anybody in months," Vera said. "I only do it as a last resort."

Without taking his eyes off her, Erdle reclaimed his seat. Theenie handed him the bottle of castor oil. He took a sip and gagged. "Blah! That's the worst stuff I've ever tasted in my life! I can't go through with it."

Vera pulled the hammer back on the pistol. Erdle quickly took another slug. He shuddered and made a face; then, taking a deep breath, he turned the bottle up and drained it. "Satisfied?" he asked Vera.

She nodded, put the hammer in place, and stuffed the gun in her purse.

Jamie looked at Annie. "May I put the cat outside? Fleas won't come out from under your bed."

"Of course," she said. "Oh, and I'll make sure Peaches is out when you arrive tomorrow."

Jamie looked relieved as she headed toward the back door with the cat.

"The forecast is calling for rain," Theenie said. "Peaches is scared of the rain."

"It's not going to rain on Jamie's wedding day," Destiny said.

Annie shrugged. "Well, if it does, I'll ask Doc to babysit. Peaches likes Doc. He used to feed her and change her litter box when I went out of town."

"Can I go now?" Erdle said wearily. "I feel sick."

Annie closed the distance between them. "Don't you *dare* throw up, Erdle Thorney!" she said in a threatening voice.

"My stomach doesn't feel so good," he whined.

"That's because you've introduced it to something other than booze," she said.

"I'm gonna be sick," he wailed.

"Stop it!" Annie said, feeling as though her nerves

would snap. "I swear, Erdle, if you throw up I'm going to take Vera's gun and shoot you myself."

"You're a crazy lady," he said, leaning dangerously to one side. "And mean as hell to boot. That's how come I know you killed your husband. And all this time I been protecting you. Even buried the body so nobody would find out. Crazy and mean is what you are."

Chapter

FIFTEEN

Several gasps filled the room as Erdle's head fell back and he began to topple. Annie shrieked but caught him before he hit the floor. Jamie hurried over to help her. Very gently, they laid him on the floor, and then they looked at each other.

"He's out cold," Jamie told her.

"Did you hear what he said!" Annie cried. "He said he buried Charles."

"I heard," Theenie said. "I think we should call Lamar."

Jamie shook her head. "Not yet. We need to try and get more information out of him." She paused. "Let's get him to the sink and stick his head under cold water."

"Here we go again," Destiny said as she hurried over to help.

Theenie and Lovelle cleared the sink and counter as the three younger women dragged the man over. Annie pushed his head into the sink and Theenie turned on the cold water full force. Erdle came up coughing and sputtering. "You're trying to kill me!" he said to Annie. "So I don't tell what I know."

"Erdle, you idiot!" she shouted. "I didn't kill Charles. This is the last time I'm going to tell you." He didn't look convinced. "Do I *look* like a murderer?" she demanded.

"Do I look like a grave digger?" he replied, water streaming down his face. He blinked and rubbed his

eyes. Lovelle hurried away and reappeared with a bathroom towel. Annie dried his hair while the others held
him up. Vera pulled a chair across the room, and Annie
and Jamie lowered him onto it as Destiny shoved a cup
of black coffee in his face.

"Drink," Annie said.

Erdle blew into it and cautiously took a sip.

Once Annie was sure he could sit up on his own, she
released him. "Start talking, Erdle, and don't stop until
you've told us everything."

His gaze went to Vera. "Is she going to shoot me?"

Vera planted her hands on her hips. "No, but I'll
pistol-whip you if you don't start moving your jaws."

He gave a sigh and looked at Annie, his face beaded
with sweat. "I saw him. Charles," he added. "He was
laying at the foot of those stairs, deader'n all get-out."

"*When* did you see him?"

"Same day you left for your mama's. Act'ally, it was
late that night."

"You told Lamar you were with your army buddy that
weekend."

"I lost my keys and had to borrow his car so I could
drive back and get my spare set. I keep them under the
stairs to my place. My friend was passed out. He has a
drinking problem, if you know what I mean."

"I think we can relate," Destiny said, giving an eye
roll.

"Only reason I came in the house was 'cause the back
door was standing wide open. Charles's car was in the
driveway, so I figured I'd let him know in case somebody had broken in or something. I stepped inside the
kitchen and turned on the lights and that's when I found
him. He had a bad scratch on his face, so I thought—"

"You thought I'd scratched him and pushed him down
the stairs," Annie finished for him.

His look was sheepish. "I reckon I wasn't thinking straight."

Annie wasn't interested in his apology at the moment. "Then what?"

"I dragged him out in the yard and buried him where I figured nobody would look. After I checked his pockets to see if he had anything important on him," he added. "Then I drove his car to the airport and hitched a ride back. When I arrived back at the motel some hours later, my friend was still passed out."

"What did you do with Charles's belongings?" Annie asked.

"I packed his bags and hid 'em. Raked leaves for two days once I came home. Burned his stuff with the leaves. Didn't find no money. Didn't know he'd hidden money in a hole in the closet."

"You're certain he was dead when you found him?" Jamie asked.

"Yep. Somebody smothered him. There was a pillow next to the body."

Annie closed her eyes and took a deep breath.

"That's all I know," Erdle said.

Jamie rubbed Annie's back, obviously trying to comfort her. "You didn't see anyone else on the property?" Jamie asked.

Erdle shook his head. "I told you everything. Can I have a sandwich? I don't want no more of those cookies."

"I'll make it," Jamie said. "Annie, you sit down before you fall down."

"Would you like a glass of brandy?" Lovelle asked.

Annie shook her head and took a seat at the kitchen table. "I don't drink anymore."

Once Jamie had served Erdle, she made room for him at the table so he could eat his sandwich. "Why don't we go into the living room and give Erdle a few minutes to himself?" she suggested.

Vera pointed a manicured finger at Erdle. "You move, you die."

He nodded.

"Come on, dear," Theenie said, helping Annie from the chair.

Annie did as she was told, following the women, her arms and legs feeling weighted.

"Don't you think we'd better go ahead and call the police now?" Theenie asked Jamie.

Jamie shook her head. "I don't think Annie is in any position to speak to them at the moment."

Annie was glad Jamie was there to take charge of the situation, because her brain had shut down on her.

Lovelle glanced over her shoulder as if to make sure they were alone. "Does anyone happen to know if it's against the law to bury somebody who is already dead?"

"Of course it is," Vera said. "You can't just go around burying folks wherever it suits you. You probably have to buy some kind of permit."

Jamie looked thoughtful. "I hate to say it, but I think the murderer is still on the loose. I don't believe Donna Schaefer *or* Erdle put that pillow over Charles's face."

"That's what I'm thinking," Annie said.

"Annie, would you like for me to call Wes?" Theenie asked. "He always seems to know what to do."

She shook her head. "I don't want to have to explain about the ring what with all this other going on."

"I can solve that little problem," Destiny said. "Wal-Mart sells cubic zirconia rings that look like the real enchilada. I can probably find something similar to the ring Wes gave you. Trust me, he won't notice the difference."

Theenie nodded. "Good idea. We only have to fool Wes for six or eight hours. Until, well, you know."

"I won't be long," Destiny said, hurrying out.

"I'd like to discuss your, um, engagement when you're feeling better," Jamie told Annie.

"Don't worry; Wes is a good man," Theenie said. "I would have put up a fuss if I didn't think so. I need to have a little talk with Erdle. He's going to have to stay here tonight. It'd be best if he slept on a cot in my room so that when the time comes, I'll be there. Remember, I was a nurse's aide," she added, not for the first time. "May I get you something, hon?" she asked Annie.

Annie shook her head. "I'll help you break the news to Erdle in case he gives you any problems."

The women returned to the kitchen. Theenie told Erdle the plan.

"I'm not sleeping under the same roof with a bunch of crazy women," he said, his eyes darting at Vera as though he feared she would whip out her pistol again.

"You are *not* going to leave this house until I get my ring back," Annie said. "I expect you to stick to Theenie like glue until you, um, *deliver.*"

"I'll need a few items to ensure a successful and antiseptic retrieval," Theenie said.

"Say no more," Annie replied, hoping Theenie would not share. "Just take whatever you need."

"Why don't we start wrapping these trays of food and putting them away?" Lovelle suggested. "We can store the nonperishable items in the butler's pantry so we'll have room in the refrigerator."

"Vera and I will help," Jamie said, "but first I need to see if I can get Fleas out from under the bed." She hurried upstairs.

Annie was thankful she hadn't frosted Jamie's cake yet; she wanted it to be a surprise. With the help of the others the food was quickly put away. Annie heard Jamie grunting and groaning from the stairs and saw that she was doing her best to carry her dog down the stairs.

"You're going to throw out your back," Vera said, "and you won't be worth a flip on your honeymoon."

"I probably shouldn't be listening to stuff like that," Theenie said.

Jamie put Fleas down and held his collar. "I hate to be a pest, Annie, but do you have any peroxide?"

"I'll get some," Theenie said.

Annie suddenly noticed that Fleas had blood on one side of his nose and hurried over. "Did Peaches do that?"

"I don't think she likes bloodhounds," Jamie said, trying to make light of it so Annie wouldn't take on those worries as well.

"I'm so sorry," Annie said, rubbing the dog on his bony head. "Peaches is old and ornery like Doc."

Theenie returned with the peroxide and a handful of cotton balls. As Jamie and Annie held the dog still, she cleaned the wound. Fleas whined and moaned and scratched himself fiercely with one leg. "Peaches got him good," Theenie said. "Look how deep the scratch is. Good thing Doc isn't here; he'd insist on putting the poor thing down."

Lovelle nodded. "Yeah, Doc's a snarly old man, but he can't stand to see something suffer."

Jamie and Vera left once the kitchen was clean and Jamie had helped Annie carry a rollaway bed from the attic to Theenie's room so Erdle could stick close to the woman. They'd been gone less than ten minutes when a jubilant Destiny returned bearing a ring that strongly resembled Annie's engagement ring.

Annie held her hand out for all of them to see. "What do you think?"

Lovelle studied it closely. "I can tell the difference, but I'm with Destiny. I don't think Wes will notice." She yawned. "I'm exhausted. Why don't we call it a night?"

As tired as she was, Annie forced herself to take a

shower before climbing into bed, but two hours later she was still staring at the ceiling, her mind racing. Every time she closed her eyes she saw Charles lying at the bottom of the stairs, a pillow pressed against his face. She drew comfort thinking perhaps he'd been unconscious at the time.

She picked at her tired brain, trying to find answers to the questions that plagued her until sheer exhaustion forced her eyes closed. She awoke once after a bad dream, but when she couldn't remember the details, she turned over and went back to sleep.

In her next dream she was twelve years old, visiting her grandmother for the summer. They were standing on the back porch gazing down at the stray tomcat that showed up every morning for scraps of food.

"What's his name, Granny?" Annie asked the first time she saw the scrawny animal.

The woman chuckled. "I call him Lover Boy on account he spends his nights chasing females and getting into fights with the other male cats. Last time he got into a fight he showed up missing half his hair."

The old woman tossed a handful of chicken bones on the ground, and the cat pounced on them as though he hadn't eaten in days. After that, Annie made a point of collecting table scraps and only ate half her oatmeal in the morning so Lover Boy got enough to eat.

Then one morning Annie stepped out the door with her oatmeal bowl and found Lover Boy curled beside the bottom step. He looked up at her, his eyes glazed, his fur matted with dried blood. Her breath caught in her throat when she noted half of one ear had been torn away. She raced into the house for her grandmother.

"Go get Doc," the old woman said after she'd checked the cat.

Doc took one look at the ailing feline and shook his

head sadly. "He's bad off, Annie. Afraid I'm going to have to put him down."

Tears streamed down Annie's cheek as she watched Doc carry Lover Boy away.

Annie bolted upright in the bed. Her cheeks were wet from crying. She reached for the telephone and dialed Wes's cell phone number. No answer. She hung up and climbed from the bed, dressed quickly, and then made her way down the hall toward the kitchen stairs. At the back door she paused to unbolt it and slide the chain free. She winced as it creaked open, reminding her she needed to take an oil can to the hinges. She closed it behind her and started across the backyard where Annie's grandmother had long ago pulled up her boxwood hedges so she could admire Doc's rose garden.

Wes opened his eyes when he heard his cell phone ring from the other side of the room, but it took several minutes for him to locate it. By the time he found it tucked in the pocket of his jeans it had stopped ringing. He switched on the lamp beside his bed and rubbed his eyes, trying to force himself awake. Finally, he punched a button on his phone and scrolled down, searching for the last number listed on his screen.

Despite the late hour, the downstairs lights burned brightly on the first floor of Doc's house. Having knocked several times as hard as she could, Annie gave up. She suspected Doc was watching TV in his den and couldn't hear her at the door. She lifted the flowerpot beside his door and reached for the key beneath it.

Inside, the TV blared from the den. Annie found Doc asleep in his recliner, an old quilt draped over him. She turned off the TV, and he jerked and opened his eyes. He frowned at the sight of her. "What's wrong?" he asked.

"We need to talk. It's important."

"What is so important that you have to barge into my house at two o'clock in the morning?" he said, his face red and mottled from sleep. He sounded out of sorts.

"It's about Charles," she said.

"Oh, good grief. Don't you watch the news or read the paper? They found the lady who did it."

"Donna Schaefer didn't kill him, Doc. Charles was alive when she left."

"How do you know?"

Annie sat on the nearby sofa. "Erdle came in later that night and found Charles dead, a pillow next to the body. He thought I'd killed him in one of my dumb temper fits, so he tried to cover it up by burying Charles in the backyard."

"Erdle buried him? Seems I remember he was gone at the time."

"He came back for something later that night. He took care of everything nice and neat."

"Why are you telling *me* this?" Doc said.

"You were pruning your rosebushes during that time, remember? From your garden you can see my backyard. And then you like to sit in your lawn chair with your cognac and look at them, sometimes for hours. You once said that's when you do your best thinking."

"Annie, would you get to the point? I'm an old man. I could pass on before you finish your story."

"You saw Donna Schaefer arrive at my house and then run out later. So you went over to investigate. Am I getting it right so far?"

Doc remained silent.

"You found Charles lying on the floor unconscious. You never liked Charles. You knew he had been cheating on me for some time, didn't you? Danny probably told you. You thought Charles was no better than an old tomcat. So there he was, lying there, helpless and unconscious. You went into the living room and got a pillow and—"

"No," Doc said, indignant. "What kind of person do you take me for? A coldhearted killer?" he asked. "Is that what you think?"

"Then tell me."

Doc pulled off his glasses, rubbed his eyes, and blinked several times. He stared straight ahead for a moment. "That's not the way it happened, Annie. Not at all." He sighed heavily.

"You're right about me sitting in my lawn chair. I sat in it until it was dark, then realized I was getting hungry. Before I could get up, I saw this woman pull up in her car and go into your house. The lights flashed on in your bedroom, and I could hear them arguing. The woman started yelling and carrying on something awful. Finally, I got enough of it and started for my back porch. Then I heard her scream, and she came tearing out of the house like the wrath of God was after her. I could hear her sobbing. She got into her car and left."

Once again Doc became quiet, as though he had slipped into another place. Annie sat quietly and waited. She heard a sound from the next room, saw a shadow. Saw Wes.

"I didn't go over right away," Doc finally said. "I thought of calling the police but decided against it. I came inside the house and cleaned up. Made myself a sandwich. When I went back out I noticed the back door was standing open, and I wondered why Charles had not closed it. So I walked on over.

"I found him lying at the bottom of the stairs. I knelt beside him, and he opened his eyes. I asked him if he was in pain. He said his neck was hurting him real bad, said he'd heard it snap and was afraid he'd broken it. I told him not to move." Doc paused and looked at Annie.

"See, I know about neck injuries and what they can do to a person. I had a friend who spent twenty years in a wheelchair begging to die. Twenty years is a long time to wait to die, Annie. I told Charles to rest, that I'd look after him. He closed his eyes, and I went into the next room for the pillow. I had no other choice but to put him down."

Wes stepped into the room and went to Annie. Doc didn't seem surprised; he didn't even look up. He just stared at the blank TV screen, the wrinkles more prominent on his tired face.

Wes slipped his arms around Annie's waist. "You okay?"

She nodded. "How did you know to come here?"

"Stuff just started falling into place in my head today," he said. "When I saw your number come up on my phone, I knew you needed me."

She leaned against him. "Thank you."

Wes held her for a moment longer before releasing her. "You look exhausted, and tomorrow is the big day. Go home and get some sleep. I'll stay with Doc."

Annie nodded. She could not remember ever feeling so tired, and she knew whatever Wes decided to do, it would be the right thing. She stood.

Doc looked up. "I want you to know something, Annie. I *need* you to know. I would never have allowed you to go to prison for something I'd done."

She nodded. "I know." She touched his shoulder on her way out.

Annie and Jamie both held their breath and watched Fleas amble up the aisle in the large meeting room that had been decorated and turned into a wedding chapel of sorts, complete with a festooned arbor. Fleas wore a special collar that was adorned with white tea roses and baby's breath. As Annie had suspected would happen, some of the wedding guests raised an eyebrow as others chuckled or laughed out loud. Fleas paused halfway, turned, and looked at Jamie, who prodded him on with a single nod. He made his way toward the altar and sat, and Jamie grinned. Max looked proud. The minister simply gazed down at the dog as though he didn't know quite what to make of the whole thing. In the front row, Vera shook her head sadly.

Annie turned to Dee Dee, stunning in a kelly green sheath of raw silk. Diamonds and emeralds adorned her ears and throat and flashed each time she moved. Annie was almost certain the guests would not notice Dee Dee's ballerina-style bedroom slippers. "Okay, Dee Dee, you're up," she said.

Dee Dee put on a bright smile and took two graceful steps before she jerked to a halt and clutched her stomach. "Uh-oh!" She turned, her eyes wide in disbelief, her mouth forming a giant *O*.

Annie and Jamie gaped at Dee Dee's stained bedroom slippers, then at each other.

Nearby, Beenie covered his face with his hands. "I knew she'd wait until the most inopportune moment."

Annie motioned for Lovelle, who grasped Dee Dee's hand. "Come with me, hon," she said.

"But who's going to be matron of honor?" Dee Dee asked.

Jamie looked at Annie. As if reading her mind, Annie shook her head. "I'm wearing a uniform." Her black skirt and starched white blouse matched the outfits her two assistants wore.

"You'll have to go," Dee Dee told Beenie, who wore a winter white tux.

"Me!" he cried. "I don't know anything about—"

Dee Dee shoved her bouquet at him and gave him a hard push through the double doors.

Beenie struck a pose and started up the aisle on his

tiptoes, pausing and smiling at the guests as he literally floated toward the front like a swan.

Jamie did an eye roll. This could only happen at *her* wedding.

"I'm sorry," Dee Dee said to Jamie. "When you get a chance, please tell Frankie I need to go to the hospital." Lovelle quickly ushered her away.

"Time to go," Annie said, releasing her hold on Jamie's elbow as the guests stood and waited for the bride. Annie had never seen a lovelier bride. Beenie had outdone himself on Jamie's hair and makeup, tucking tiny sprigs of baby's breath at her crown. "Don't forget to smile."

Jamie took a deep breath and started down the aisle. Suddenly she wasn't so nervous. She remembered to walk slowly as Annie had taught her and smiled at the guests, nodding here and there at those she recognized. Her gaze sought and found Vera's; the woman stood proudly on the front row, tears streaming down her face. Jamie blew her a kiss and mouthed a silent, *I love you*. Beside Vera, Billie, Christie, and Joel were all smiles. Jamie winked at them. As she neared the front, her gaze sought out Max, and the tender and loving look on his face almost stole her breath. She wondered what she had ever done to deserve him.

The crowd reclaimed their seats as Jamie took her place next to Beenie, who was doing his best to catch Frankie's attention and cutting his eyes toward the back of the chapel. The minister cocked his head to one side as though trying to figure out what Beenie was doing there.

Sitting in the middle of the second row, Frankie arched his brows, and then, as though suddenly realizing something was amiss, the six-foot-six retired wrestler–turned–mayor stood and tried to make his way to the end of the row. "Excuse me," he said a little too loudly as one wedding guest after another was forced to stand in order to accommodate his exit. He stepped on a woman's foot, and she gave a yelp, even as he apologized profusely.

"Ohmigosh!" Beenie said, and nudged Jamie. "Dee Dee forgot to give me the ring." Before Jamie could respond, he stepped closer to the minister. "Could you hold off just a second? I'll be right back."

Jamie watched in amazement as Beenie hurried up the aisle, only a few feet behind Frankie.

Jamie could feel Max's eyes on her. She glanced his way and shook her head sadly as Frankie knocked loudly on the door to the bridal salon, right next to the crowded wedding chapel.

"Dee Dee, are you okay?" Frankie called out. "Open the door."

Jamie sighed and looked straight ahead.

The door opened. "My water broke, Frankie!" Dee Dee cried. "My dress is ruined, and it took the designer weeks to find the exact match for these earrings."

"I'm sure he wrote down the color, sweetheart," Frankie told her, "but I can always buy you different earrings."

"Beenie, what are *you* doing here?" Dee Dee demanded. "You're supposed to be up front with Jamie."

"You forgot to give me the ring!"

"Oh no!" she cried. "Here it is."

Dee Dee suddenly shrieked loudly. Inside the chapel, the guests craned their necks in order to see what was going on.

"I think I just had my first contraction," Dee Dee cried. "I don't like this, Frankie! I was told there would be no pain. I did *not* agree to pain."

"Hang on, sweetheart, I'll carry you out to the car."

Beenie raced up the aisle and took his place next to Jamie. "I have the ring," he whispered.

She nodded. "Yes, we heard the entire exchange," she said, giving him a tight smile. "Every last one of us," she added as chuckles and muffled laughter sounded from the crowd. She glanced at Max and Nick, who were staring straight ahead. She saw their shoulders move and knew they were doing their best to keep from bursting into hearty guffaws.

"Uh-oh," Beenie said, glancing down. "This is not good."

Jamie followed his gaze. Fleas was half-sprawled on the floor beside her licking himself.

The minister cleared his voice, squared his shoulders, and gazed about the crowd. "What is marriage?" he asked. "To answer that question I'd like for us to ponder Scripture from the Book of Genesis."

Jamie and Max looked at each other and shrugged.

Ten minutes later, Jamie's eyes had glazed over, and her feet were killing her. Beside her, Beenie could not stop yawning, and Fleas had rolled onto his back and was snoring loudly.

"And so God saw that it was not right for Adam to be alone," Tuttle continued in a droning voice, "so He put Adam into a deep sleep—"

"This guy is putting me into a deep sleep," Beenie whispered to Annie, trying to stifle yet another yawn. "I wonder if Dee Dee's baby has started preschool yet?"

Fleas snorted and snored.

"And God took from Adam a rib and from that rib He created woman so that Adam could have a help-mate." Tuttle smiled. "And so I ask you again, what *is* marriage?"

Beenie's hand shot up. Jamie pulled it down. "It's a rhetorical question," she whispered.

"Today, I have the honor of joining another man and another woman together, just as it was meant to be from the very beginning. But first, let us bow our heads and offer up a prayer for this very special couple."

Annie closed her eyes and prayed Tuttle would get on with it.

The minister closed the prayer and looked from Max to Jamie. Tuttle raised his book, adjusted his glasses, and began to read. "Dearly beloved . . ."

Suddenly Max's cell phone rang. Jamie and the minister looked incredulous.

"I'm sorry," Max whispered. "It's my emergency line."

Jamie blinked rapidly. "Do you have to answer it *now*?"

"Muffin is the only one who calls this line. And only if it's urgent." He pushed the button. "This better be good, Muffin," he said, and listened.

Jamie glanced over her shoulder and saw the dark frown on Vera's face as well as the surprised looks of those surrounding her.

Max hung up. "The hospital just called the cops on Frankie."

Jamie gasped; Nick frowned.

"Dee Dee arrived at the hospital screaming like a banshee. Frankie immediately spotted her doctor, wrestled him to the floor, and put him in a headlock. Took a half-dozen security men to pull him off," Max added. "He's in restraints and Dee Dee has gone ballistic."

Jamie closed her eyes.

Max looked at Tuttle. "Could we get on with it? Jamie and I are needed elsewhere."

"And I need to use the little boys' room," Beenie said.

From her place in the back row Annie covered her face with both hands. She felt ill. The wedding was not going well; in fact, whatever could go wrong *had* gone wrong. She glanced up as Wes took the chair next to her.

"Sorry I'm late," he whispered so softly that Annie had to lean closer in order to hear. "I've been with Doc at the police station the entire time. Lamar wants to talk to Erdle ASAP. I told him Theenie had ordered Erdle to stay in bed because of a stomach virus." He arched one brow. "What's wrong? You look pale."

"The wedding is a bust."

His eyes softened. "I'm sorry, Red."

"I suppose I should look on the bright side. Things can't possibly get any worse." Annie had barely gotten the words out of her mouth before she spotted Peaches heading down the aisle. Annie instantly froze. "Who let the cat in?" she hissed. Peaches sat down and looked around at the crowded room as though curious.

Tuttle spoke from the front. "Jamie, do you take Max to be your lawfully wedded husband? To love—"

"I do," Jamie interrupted, causing the minister to look up in surprise.

"Quick, let me out," Annie whispered to Wes, trying to think of a way to reach Peaches without drawing attention. If only she had food! She slipped from the row, bent her knees—no easy task in her tight black skirt—and duckwalked toward the cat. She was almost close enough to grab Peaches when all at once the animal's ears spiked and she arched her back. Annie reached for her, but the cat slipped through her fingers and made a mad dash toward the front.

"And, Max," Tuttle went on, "do you promise to love and cherish Jamie and place her above all others?"

"I do," Max said, smiling tenderly at Jamie.

Fleas looked up only a split second before Peaches flew into him. The hound yelped loudly, startling those up front, who turned and stared in amazement. Fleas tried to escape, but Peaches was relentless. Flowers flew in every direction. Fleas howled and rose on his hind legs, trying to climb into Jamie's arms. His toenails sank into the delicate fabric of her dress, causing it to rip in several places. Jamie cried out when one of his nails scratched her.

"I knew that crazy dog would mess up everything!" Vera said loudly.

Fleas turned his head, obviously recognizing Vera's voice, and he bounded toward her. Vera shrieked as the hound jumped onto her lap.

Annie hurried toward the front. There was no use trying to be inconspicuous now. Peaches saw her coming and ran beneath a chair. Annie fell to her knees and crawled on all fours, even as Vera tried to push Fleas off her lap.

"I now pronounce you man and wife," Tuttle said quickly.

A burst of applause rose from the crowd as Max pulled Jamie into his arms for a long kiss, and when they turned around, the guests bolted to their feet and cheered loudly. Max hurried over to Vera, swept Fleas from her lap, and planted a kiss squarely on her mouth. Vera became flustered and began patting her hair in place.

Annie managed to grab Peaches and scramble up the aisle and out of the room, where she found Lovelle waiting. She thrust the cat into the woman's arms. "Torture her before you kill her."

Lovelle smiled sweetly. "I'll have her drawn and quartered, dear." She grunted as she lugged the cat away. "Why don't we grab a bite to eat, Peachums?" she said.

Jamie and Max joined Annie, and Jamie threw her arms around her. "I'm sorry we turned the wedding into a circus," she said, "but we played before a great crowd, don't you agree?"

Annie noted the guests spilling through the doorway,

still cheering. "Is Fleas hurt?" She looked at the cowering dog, still in Max's arms.

Max grinned. "Only his pride." He winked and managed to pull an envelope from his pocket and hand it to her. "We have to go, Annie. Got to spring Frankie from the slammer."

Jamie kissed Annie on the cheek, and the two left through the front door.

Annie was relieved to see the rest of the guests leave. Somehow, despite all that had occurred, they had enjoyed themselves immensely, and although everything else had turned out crazy, dinner had been perfect. Jamie had since called. Max had convinced Dee Dee's doctor not to press charges against Frankie, but only after Frankie agreed not to sic Snakeman and his boa on the doctor as he'd threatened. Dee Dee was still in labor, but she was feeling no pain and having a grand time watching the Home Shopping Network on TV and placing orders as fast as she could.

Now, sitting in the swing on the piazza and enjoying the night air, Annie began to relax for the first time in weeks, even though she had concerns, some a result of what had occurred that day.

Erdle had still not delivered the ring.

Nunamaker, who had agreed to take Doc's case, was fairly certain the man would not spend time in prison, not only because of his advanced age, but also because Doc had acted out of mercy when he'd ended Charles's life.

Nunamaker had already discussed Erdle's part in the case, and the DA was considering probation, on the grounds that Erdle agreed to enter a six-month alcohol treatment facility, attend daily AA meetings, and submit to random drug and alcohol tests.

Danny had surprised Annie with a call shortly after

the food had been served and had given her a temporary number where he could be reached, and they'd teased each other and laughed together like old times.

Annie was thankful their friendship had survived, and it made her even more determined to visit Eve Fortenberry in a few days and try to make peace.

The screen door opened and Wes stepped out bearing a plate with wedding cake. She had been too anxious during the wedding to notice the prick marks were already beginning to fade.

"You're missing all the goodies," he said, sitting down beside her.

Annie groaned. "After all the cooking I've done, I don't even want to look at food."

"This is the best cake I've ever tasted. Erdle must be feeling better, because he ate three huge pieces."

"He did?" Annie felt hopeful. Wes still didn't know about the missing ring, and those "in the know" had agreed there were some things that simply weren't worth sharing.

Wes finished his cake and set his empty plate on a nearby table. "So what do you think about serving this kind of cake at our wedding?"

"Assuming I'll marry you, of course."

"Assuming I won't change my mind by May."

"*May?*" She blinked. "Have you been talking to Destiny?"

He shook his head. "She left with that young senator. The one she said looked like Andy Garcia."

"What about your company in Columbia?" Annie asked.

Wes shrugged. "I can move my office to Hilton Head. There are a lot of rich people there. Couples with money like to cheat on each other, and they can afford the best hotels. I hate sitting in the parking lots of dumpy motels, you know?"

Annie hesitated. "We probably should discuss Theenie and Lovelle."

He grinned. "Hey, I love those two ladies. It wouldn't be the same if they moved out. It's bad enough Destiny chased off the ghost."

Annie leaned against him and gazed at the peach tree, surprised that it was already in full bloom. Either it had blossomed overnight or she'd been too busy to notice. The man beside her was a different story; he'd managed to insinuate himself into her life, her bed, and all her waking thoughts despite all that had happened. Not only that, he'd stuck by her. Despite the evidence against her, he'd been convinced all along of her innocence. Heck, he was even willing to marry her, knowing she had a temper.

It had to be love.

Sometimes you *did* know when it was right, she thought. Maybe she had known it the first time she'd laid eyes on those ridiculous boxer shorts.

"May works for me," Annie said.

"Great." Wes smiled. "It just so happens I know of this bed-and-breakfast that puts together awesome weddings. Only we're going to hire someone else to do the work." He pulled her close and kissed her.

"I can't think of a place I'd rather be married," she said, leaning against him, enjoying his arms around her waist. Annie spied Peaches skulking about in the yard, darting looks her way, obviously aware that her owner was still furious over the debacle with Fleas. Probably wondering if she was going to miss a meal over it, Annie thought.

The cat walked over to the peach tree and climbed to the lowest branch, which was no easy feat for a twenty-two-pounder. All at once, Peaches went limp and fell to the ground with a loud thud. She rolled over several times and came to a dead halt on her back, all four legs pointing skyward, head lolling to one side, tongue hanging out.

"I think I'll have a slice of that cake now," Annie said.

"I'll get it for you." Wes stood and went inside the house.

Annie sat there for a moment, enjoying the quiet. Suddenly she shivered as a gust of cool air swept over her, raising goose bumps along her arms and sending tingles along her backbone. Something moved just outside her peripheral vision, and she turned quickly. Nothing there. She felt her gaze drawn to one of the ball-room windows. The drapes parted, and Annie could feel someone watching her intently, a sense of knowing that she had experienced many times before.

Only nobody was there.

Epilogue

"Stop running, dammit!" Annie shouted the next morning as Erdle dashed down the back steps.

"He sure runs fast for a no-good drunk," Theenie said.

Erdle ducked behind one of the massive oaks. "You are *not* going to make me drink any more of that nasty stuff!" he yelled, pointing to the new bottle of castor oil in Theenie's hand. "I'm calling Lamar to come take me to jail."

Annie planted her hands on her hips. "You are *not* leaving this house with my ring in your, um, system. Don't make me get my rolling pin."

"You're a crazy lady, you know that?" he shouted. "Mean *and* crazy. And you wonder why I drink."

From the back door Destiny and Lovelle watched. "I can't believe Dee Dee was able to deliver a nine-pound baby boy and Erdle can't pass a one-karat ring," Destiny said. "Men can be such wimps."

"We'd better go out there and give the girls a hand," Lovelle said. The two started down the steps.

"Oh, good, we've got backup," Theenie said.

The four women circled Erdle, who clung to the tree as a drowning man would to a life raft. Theenie uncapped the bottle. "You three grab him, and I'll pour it down his gullet."

Suddenly Erdle's eyes widened. He winced and

grabbed his stomach. "Argh." He doubled over and groaned.

Theenie put the cap on the bottle and patted his arm. "Follow me, dear," she said. Erdle nodded and staggered across the yard, sweat beading his brow. "And don't worry about a thing," Theenie said, "because I'll take good care of you. Did I tell you I was once a nurse's aide?"

Destiny turned to Annie. "Looks like it's just a matter of time."

FULL
BLAST

Many thanks to Jen Enderlin aka SuperJen for giving us a great book idea! Special thanks to Eric Hughes for coming up with the title for this book.

ONE

Jamie Swift had been in the newspaper business long enough to realize it was a lot like being a waitress. You had to meet the needs of those you served—the rich, the poor, the in-between, even the crazies who complained no matter what you did. And like a waitress, you had to hope the tips were good. A big tip could make all the difference. A big tip in her case meant headlines, and she was in the business of finding headlines. But they didn't come easy in a small Southern town where life was, for the most part, uneventful, even predictable. She had to scramble for newsworthy events.

So here she was, once again, sitting at her desk, sifting through stories, looking for a new slant or an idea to make it more interesting to the reading public. She was so intent on what she was doing that she jumped when someone tapped on her door.

Sixty-year-old Vera Bankhead rushed into Jamie's office and closed the door behind her. "You are *not* going to believe this!"

Jamie glanced up. "What is it?" she asked, straightening in her chair and trying to work the kinks out of her neck from sitting in one position for so long. She had come in early, hoping to work undisturbed. "You got a good tip for me?" she asked the woman before her. "Give me a headline, and I'll kiss the ground you walk on."

"This is even better." Vera paused, as if to add a little drama to what she was about to say. The hairpins had popped out from her gray beehive hairdo, and her glasses were askew. She shoved them high on her nose and glanced about as if to make certain they were alone. She eyed the large plate-glass window overlooking the courthouse square where automatic sprinklers were doing damage control to a parched lawn brought on by a record-breaking July heat wave. Vera marched over and snapped the blinds closed.

Jamie arched one brow. "This must be big."

"It's bigger than when Lorraine Brown caught her husband doing the nasty with Beth Toomey on a sofa in the back office of the VFW Hall."

"Wow. Wasn't she jailed for going after them with a letter opener?"

"Yeah, and Tom refused to bail her out until she signed an agreement stating she wouldn't do him bodily harm afterward. She kicked his butt anyway the minute they released her."

"So tell me."

"You're not going to believe it," the woman repeated.

"Vera, out with it already!"

Vera held up a white paper sack. She reached into it and pulled out a brownie. "Taste it."

Jamie's mouth watered at the sight of the chocolate goodie. "I really shouldn't. I've already had three doughnuts this morning. I can barely button the top of my jeans."

Vera gave her *that* look, the one that said she wasn't going to take no for an answer. And Vera could be fierce. Although she still worked as Jamie's secretary, fear and intimidation had prompted Jamie to promote her to assistant editor of the *Gazette*, as well. That and the fact Vera carried a .38 Smith and Wesson in her purse. Jamie was almost sure she wouldn't pull it on her; Vera was the closest thing she'd had to a mother, but it was best to humor her.

"Okay, okay." Jamie reached for the brownie and tasted it. "Yum, that's good." She finished it off in three bites.

"Do you feel any different?" Vera asked, eyeing her closely.

"Yeah, I want another one. I can always buy larger jeans."

"This isn't just *any* brownie," Vera said in a conspiratorial whisper. "There are rumors floating around that Lyle Betts is putting aphrodisiacs in them."

Jamie arched one brow. Lyle Betts owned Sunshine Bakery, and was considered a pillar of the community. He was president of the Jaycees, coached Little League, and played Santa Claus for the children's unit at the hospital every year. "No way," she said.

Vera crossed her heart. "As God is my witness."

Jamie pondered it. Vera was a strict Southern Baptist; she only lied when absolutely necessary.

"Do you have any more?"

"Yeah, I bought extra. I figured we should do a little experimenting. We'll eat a couple more, and then compare notes."

"Oh, Lord," Jamie said, as Vera divvied them up. The last thing she needed was to start feeling horny. It had been three weeks since she'd laid eyes on sexy and mysterious Maximillian Holt, the man who blew into her life from time to time just long enough to turn her world upside down and inside out. The same man she had already voted most likely to climb beneath the sheets with first chance she got.

"I've already had three," Vera said, "and I don't feel a thing except for a little indigestion. Chocolate does that to me."

"I'm sure it's just a bunch of hype to sell brownies,"

Jamie said, hoping she was right. Lately she'd been having X-rated dreams where she and Max played starring roles. They did things she was certain were illegal in most states.

"And get this," Vera said. "Maxine Chambers quit her job at the library and just opened a lingerie shop right on Main Street. And guess what she named it? Sinful Delights."

Jamie couldn't hide her surprise. She couldn't imagine the prim librarian doing such a thing.

"And that's not all," Vera went on. "Folks say she's got a whole display of unmentionables hanging in her window where God and everybody can see them. She just undraped it today. Elbert Swank said his jaw fell open so hard when he saw them that he almost lost his dentures on the sidewalk out front. I would have given anything to see that."

"A new lingerie shop," Jamie mused. "Imagine that." She tried to keep her excitement at bay. Beaumont needed a good lingerie store, a place where cotton panties and practical bras weren't the order of the day.

"Of course I got my information secondhand so I'll have to get over there and check it out personally. You know how I am about getting my facts straight."

"Maybe she'll advertise with us," Jamie said. "We can always use the business."

"Oh, pooh. We're going to make money on that new personals section you started. How many people have written in so far?"

"We must have about ten total; seven from men, three from women. Pretty good for a small-town newspaper, don't you think?" Jamie had hoped the ads would bring in well-needed revenue and attract more readers. It was too early to tell, but she remained confident.

"I'm keeping my fingers crossed," Vera said. She stepped closer. "One ad in particular caught my attention," she almost whispered. "It was in yesterday's paper. The heading read 'Ready, Willing, and Able.' Sounds like a winner to me, seeing as how most men in my age bracket have a little trouble in the *able* department."

Jamie laughed out loud. "Vera Bankhead, I am *shocked*!"

Vera grinned. "Hey, even a woman my age has needs."

"Perhaps you should respond to the ad."

"What if he's ugly? You know I can't abide an ugly man. Maybe you should give me his name first."

Jamie shook her head. "You know the ads are strictly confidential."

"I'll bet I could figure out who he is. I know everybody in this town."

Which was why Jamie had insisted on handling the personals section, she reminded herself. She kept the ads locked in a file cabinet in her office. As much as she loved Vera, it was a well-known fact the woman was the biggest gossip in town. Jamie shrugged as though it made no difference. "I would see that your letter reached him."

"I'll have to think about it."

Jamie sighed wistfully. "Well, one thing is certain. Love is definitely in the air in the town of Beaumont, South Carolina. I think it's romantic." Jamie had only recently come to realize just what a romantic she was, and she knew Max Holt was responsible. She had begun to daydream about their relationship, had begun to wonder where it was going. She wanted him in her life permanently, and that scared the hell out of her.

"Sounds more like L-U-S-T to me," Vera replied. "It's the heat. Everybody in town is acting strange. If they start eating these brownies, they're going to be out of control."

Jamie didn't want to talk about lust because, once again, it brought Max to mind. Max, who was too gorgeous for his own good and knew it. Max, who clearly lusted after her but kept his true feelings to himself. Not that she didn't have a bad case of lust, as well; it's what drew them together like iron shavings to a magnet, what made her skin literally ache for his touch.

It had been that way from the moment they'd first laid eyes on each other, when Max had come to Beaumont to aid his brother-in-law, now the mayor, in an attempt to clean up town corruption. Max had ridden in on his white horse, or in his case, a two-million-dollar car with enough technology to run a small country. Max's investigation had dragged Jamie right into the middle of it; she'd found herself dodging bullets from hit men, almost getting blown to smithereens by a car bomb, and landing in the path of a monster-size alligator.

Okay, so maybe she was exaggerating the size of the alligator, but all alligators looked big when you were treading water and happened to be in their path.

Most women with half a brain would have grabbed their purses and said, "See ya," but not Jamie. She had followed Max to Tennessee to find the person responsible for hiring the hit.

Simply put, Max was a philanthropist with brains and money, and as long as there was a cause or an injustice, he would be there, come hell or high water.

"My stomach feels funny," Vera said. "I think I ate too many brownies."

Jamie looked up. "Yeah?" She wouldn't tell Vera she was having a bad case of butterflies. The woman would attribute it to the brownies, but Jamie knew better. She was thinking about the last time she and Max were together in what could only be described as a compromising position. Sooner or later, things were bound to come to a head.

She and Max couldn't go on this way forever, but she was afraid to hope for more. She could fantasize all she wanted about a lasting relationship, but Max did not impress her as a man who could be tied down to any woman for very long.

"It's probably all in my mind," Vera said. "Lyle Betts most likely started the rumor just to get people into his bakery." She glanced about the office. "Where is Fleas, by the way?"

"Huh?"

"Are you even listening to me? Where is your dog? You know, that ugly hound you bring to work with you every day because he sulks if you leave him at home?"

"He's at the vet. And he's not ugly."

"I hope he's getting his anal glands expressed. I can't live with that flatulence problem much longer."

Jamie had *inherited* Fleas, a wrinkled, forlorn-faced bloodhound some weeks back. At the time she had desperately needed a vehicle, and, trying to save money, had bought a rust bucket of a pickup truck. The car salesman, who claimed the dog was attached to the truck, had knocked fifty bucks off the price of the truck as an incentive for her to take the dog. They were bonding rather well, or at least as well as could be expected with a dog that had chronic gas.

"He's being neutered today," Jamie said. "Poor thing," she added. "I'll bet Dr. Adams has his nuts on a chopping block as we speak."

Vera shuddered. "I don't even want to think about it."

They were interrupted when someone tapped on the door. "Pardon me," a female voice said.

Vera and Jamie glanced toward the door. Jamie felt her jaw drop to her collarbone. Vera gaped, as well.

"I'm sorry to disturb you," the woman said, "but there was nobody out front."

Jamie continued to stare. The woman had coal-black

hair that fell to her waist. Sparkly blue eye shadow colored her lids, and her lashes were long enough to paint the side of a barn. "May I help you?" Jamie managed.

The woman stepped into the room. Her skirt was short and tight; her low-cut blouse, emphasized perfect oversize breasts. Jamie decided either God had been very generous in the boob department or the woman was stuffed to the gills with silicone.

"My name is Destiny Moultrie," she said in a husky voice. "I'm here about the job."

Vera tossed Jamie a suspicious look. "What job? You've decided to replace me, haven't you? You'd rather have some Elvira–Erin Brockovich look-alike with big knockers sitting out front."

"I don't know anything about this," Jamie said, holding out both hands. She looked at the woman. "What job?" she asked, echoing Vera's question.

"The advice columnist. You've been turning it over in your mind for weeks."

"I have?"

Vera looked at Jamie. "You have?"

Jamie shifted in her seat. "Um, well—"

"You never mentioned it to me," a very peeved Vera interrupted. "You've always come to me with your ideas."

The woman looked from Vera to Jamie. "I didn't mean to cause friction. Perhaps we should discuss this in private, Miss Swift."

Vera took offense. "*Miss Swift* doesn't keep secrets from me. I know more about what's going on around here than anyone else." She tossed Jamie a dark look. "At least I thought I did."

Jamie couldn't mask her confusion. "Vera, please, not now."

But Vera was not deterred. "First, you take the personals section away from me because you don't trust me, and now *this*. I should quit. I should hand in my resignation and go on one of those senior citizens' cruises that serves seven meals a day. I could meet a nice widower, and sow a few wild oats. I still have a few oats left, you know."

"Vera—" Jamie fought the urge to crawl beneath her desk. They were acting anything but professional. But she knew better than to argue. In Vera's mind, Jamie was still an unruly kid who'd never been properly disciplined by her father.

"Seven meals a day?" Destiny said. "That's a lot of food. I would bust right out of my clothes."

"You're *already* busting out of your clothes," Vera said. She turned to Jamie. "On second thought, I'm *not* quitting, because I've been here longer than anyone, and I'm not going to risk losing my benefits. Furthermore, you *can't* fire me. It was your daddy, God rest his soul, who hired me, not you." She gave a huff and marched from the room, but not before slamming the door behind her.

"Uh-oh, I blew it," Destiny said.

Jamie turned to her visitor. She was intrigued. "Please sit down, Miss Moultrie," she said, using her professional voice. She smiled serenely, as though it were an everyday occurrence for her secretary to pitch a fit. Okay, so it *was* an everyday occurrence, she reminded herself. Vera was probably out front right now polishing her .38.

"Please call me Destiny," the woman said. She took one of the chairs directly across from Jamie's desk. "I'm sorry for barging in like this, but I sensed you would be making a decision soon, and I wanted to be the first to apply."

Jamie merely looked at her.

"You *have* been thinking about starting an advice column, right?" Without warning, the woman smacked her forehead. "Oh, man, I hope I'm not in the wrong place."

"The wrong place?" Jamie realized she was repeating a lot of what was being said.

Destiny pulled out a small notebook and flipped through several pages. "Is your middle name Leigh?"

Jamie nodded. "Yes. It was my mother's first name." Now why had she gone and given out personal information to some stranger she'd probably never see again?

"Yeah, I know about your mother. She walked out when you were still in diapers."

Jamie arched both brows. "Excuse me, but I don't see the point of all this."

Destiny looked up. "Sorry. I shouldn't have mentioned the part about your mother. I know you still find it painful at times."

"What else do you know?"

"There's an old tire swing hanging in your backyard, am I right?"

Jamie snapped her fingers. "I've got it. You're a private investigator, aren't you? Who hired you, and for what reason?"

"No, I'm not. Just answer this one last question. Do you have a bar of Dove soap in your lingerie drawer?"

Jamie felt the color drain from her face. "Who are you? How do you know about the soap?"

"I just do."

Jamie leveled her gaze at the woman. Her astonishment had an edge of anger to it. "Tell me more about the soap."

"Are you sure?" When Jamie nodded, she went on. "The scent reminds you of your mother, even though you remember little else about her."

Jamie felt the goose bumps rise on her arms. She was quiet for a moment. "I'm going to ask you again. How do you know this?"

The woman sighed. "I'm psychic. Sort of."

Jamie did a gigantic eye roll. "Sort of? What does that mean?"

"I have visions, and I'm right a lot of the time, unless I'm under a lot of stress, then I might make a mistake now and then. It's a simple case of performance anxiety; sort of like sex. But I get it right more often than not."

Jamie sighed. It was really turning out to be a weird morning. First Vera with her brownies, and now she was conversing with a woman who claimed to be psychic. She had time for neither because she had to concentrate on getting a newspaper out. "Miss Moultrie, um, Destiny—"

"I'm working on getting better," Destiny said. "I practice every night." She paused. "You don't believe in psychics, do you?"

"Not exactly."

"See, I knew that." The woman licked the tip of her finger and drew a short imaginary line in the air as though marking her success. Turquoise rings circled every finger, bracelets jangled on her wrists. "There are a lot of phonies out there. Some claim to be one hundred percent accurate. There's no such thing."

"I wasn't, um, looking for a psychic. Just an advice columnist." There. She'd gone and admitted it.

"You've already got 'Dear Abby.'"

"My column was going to be for locals only. To sort of complement—"

"Your new personals section," Destiny said. "People would be more intrigued by a psychic. And I've got the perfect name for it. 'The Divine Love Goddess Advisor.'" She pulled out an envelope and handed it to Jamie. "Why don't you look over my résumé and give it some thought. I wouldn't be able to start for a day or two since I just moved here and have to unpack. But I travel light."

Jamie shifted uneasily in her chair. "Why Beaumont, South Carolina?" she asked. "This town isn't exactly a booming metropolis. And the *Gazette* is rather small."

"I was sent here for a reason," Destiny said. "I'd never even heard of this place, but it came to me in a vision. So I used a small pendulum, and Beaumont came up on the map. I had to use a magnifying glass to see it, but now I'm sure I'm in the right place. Well, pretty sure."

Jamie simply nodded. She figured it was best to humor the woman until she could get rid of her.

Destiny smiled. "I know it's a lot to take in, but you can rest easy, my column will bring in many new readers."

"You know this for a fact?"

"Yep. I also have a very good feeling you're going to hire me. This interview is just a formality."

Jamie had no intention of hiring her. The last thing she needed was some kook working for her. "I'll have to think about it. I'll keep your résumé on file in the meantime."

"I know you have doubts," Destiny went on as though she hadn't heard. "And I don't blame you. This newspaper is very important to you after what you've been through. You've struggled for so long to keep it going. I admire your tenacity, Jamie, but you have to stop comparing yourself to your grandfather."

Once again, Jamie felt the tiny hairs on her arm prickle. "What do you know about my grandfather?"

"He started this newspaper from nothing and did extremely well. He passed it on to your father when he died, but your father didn't fare so well. He never wanted to be a newspaperman to begin with."

"You're pretty good," Jamie said, "but this is a small town where everybody knows everybody's business. You'd only have to ask around to get your information." Even as she said it, she wondered how the woman had found out about the soap in her dresser drawer. She decided to humor her. "While you're at it, tell me this. There's this man in my life."

"Yeah, I know all about him. He sort of saved your behind when you had financial problems so he's a silent partner. You're afraid of falling in love with him, but I would advise you to follow your heart."

"How does *he* feel?" Jamie surprised herself by asking.

Destiny looked thoughtful. "He's hard to read." Suddenly, she sneezed.

"Bless you," Jamie said.

Destiny's eyes watered, and she sneezed again. "You'll have to forgive me. This always happens when I start picking up on stuff. Do you have a tissue?"

"Don't you know?"

"Look, I can't be expected to know *everything.*"

Jamie reached into her side drawer and pulled out a small box of tissues and handed it to her, just as Destiny let out another sneeze.

"I have to go before it gets worse." The woman stood and wiped her eyes. "Oh, by the way, I'm not going to charge you for my services. I've been married five times so I get plenty of alimony. This is just a hobby."

"Five husbands, huh?"

Another sneeze. "Yeah, and I'm not even forty years old. A girl has to work fast to rack up that many husbands in such a short period."

Jamie sat back and studied her. "Didn't you know the marriages were going to fail?"

Sniff, sniff, sneeze. "I was in love with them at the time, so what could I do? How about you call me when you're ready for me to start? My new number is on my résumé." She made for the door, and then paused. "This man you're thinking about?"

Jamie remained silent.

"He's going to be back in your life very soon."
Jamie perked. "And?"
"Fireworks."
Jamie arched one brow. "Fireworks?"
Destiny smiled. "Fireworks."

TWO

Vera eyed Destiny suspiciously as she stepped into the reception area. "It was very nice meeting you, Vera," Destiny said, dabbing her nose with a tissue. She sneezed several times as she made her way toward the front door. She opened it, and then turned. "By the way, I'm sorry you're having car trouble."

Vera hitched her chin high. "Excuse me? There's not a darn thing wrong with my car."

Destiny shrugged. "Whatever." She hurried out.

"What was all *that* about?" Vera demanded when Jamie stepped out of her office. "Am I fired?"

"Don't be ridiculous, you'll still be here when I'm dead and gone. I was thinking about starting an advice column now that our personals section is doing so well."

"Why wasn't I told?"

"Because I haven't made up my mind."

Vera frowned. "Then how—"

Jamie was beginning to feel weary. "Destiny Moultrie is psychic. Or so she says."

Vera pursed her lips. "Oh, good grief, you don't believe in that hocus-pocus, do you?"

"She was very convincing, but, no, I think it's all a crock." That didn't mean she didn't feel uneasy about some of what Destiny had told her.

"Hogwash, that's what it is," Vera said. "And that woman needs to get on allergy medication. One of these days she's going to sneeze too hard, and those T-I-T-S are going to pop a button, and somebody is going to get hurt."

Jamie waited until after lunch to check on Fleas. The vet's assistant assured her the surgery had gone well. "You can pick him up in the morning," she said. "We'll give you a list of things to look out for during his recovery. You're going to have to make sure his stitches don't pull free, and he's not going to be able to go for walks for about ten days."

"That shouldn't be a problem," Jamie said, "since all he does is eat and sleep."

Jamie hung up a moment later. Stitches? Recovery? She did a mental eye roll as she imagined Fleas lying on her sofa with an IV of ice cream dripping into his veins. Once again, she reminded herself she was not the perfect pet owner. But what could she do? The animal refused to eat the healthy dog food she bought for him. He preferred cheeseburgers, fries, butter pecan ice cream, and Krispy Kreme doughnuts. And Jamie, who practically lived on junk food, ate the same things.

She told herself that despite their bad eating habits, as best she could figure, they were close to getting in the four food groups.

The rest of the day passed quickly for Jamie, approving layouts for the newspaper and getting it to print. She had begun working for her father at the newspaper— performing small jobs after school like emptying wastepaper baskets and keeping pencils sharpened— since first grade, earning three dollars per week. Looking back, she realized he'd preferred bringing her to the office instead of leaving her with a babysitter.

As she'd grown, so had her duties, and, until she'd gone off to college to study journalism, she'd worked in every department, earning little money but loving the work so much that she would have done it for free. She'd earned extra cash by selling subscriptions, which her father claimed she had a knack for, what with her big blue eyes, blond hair, and winning smile.

"You're like your grandpa," her father had told her not long before he'd died. "You've got ink running through your veins. You love this newspaper as much as he did. You'll do well by it."

Jamie smiled fondly at the thought, the good old days, when she and her father had worked side by side in order to make deadlines. And thinking of her father brought Destiny Moultrie to mind once more. The woman was about as strange as they came, but just thinking about all she'd known of Jamie's life gave her a bad case of heebie-jeebies. Jamie's father had *not* wanted to be a newspaperman, and the paper had suffered as a consequence. Jamie had begged and pleaded for permission to leave college in order to relieve him of some of the work, but he had absolutely refused to let her quit. Somehow his staff, all of them as devoted as Vera, had been invaluable in seeing that the paper made it to print on time.

Jamie couldn't help but wonder how Destiny had managed to get as much information as she had, but she knew there had to be a logical explanation. There were gossips in town who would be only too happy to share what they knew.

Except for one thing, she reminded herself, the soap in her drawer. That couldn't be explained.

Jamie and Vera headed out the front door shortly after five P.M. Jamie lingered beside Vera's car, in no hurry to go home to an empty house. She hadn't realized just how much she'd come to depend on Fleas's company.

"You headed any place in particular?" she asked Vera as the woman slid into the driver's seat of her old Buick.

"We usually have church on Wednesday night," Vera said, "but we're having Vacation Bible School so that's out. Maybe I'll bake a cake for my sick neighbor. What about you?"

"Oh, I've got a million things to do," Jamie lied. "You know me, busy, busy." Jamie tried to think of what she could do to pass the evening.

Vera closed her door and rolled down the window. "This car is hotter'n Hades. Next car I buy is going to have a decent air conditioner."

Jamie continued to stand there. "Well, then, you have a nice evening."

Vera nodded, stabbed her key into the ignition, and turned it. Nothing happened. "What in the world? It was running fine this morning." She tried again. The car didn't respond.

"Uh-oh," Jamie said. "Sounds like you're having car trouble. Sounds like the starter."

Jamie's eyes widened. The two women locked gazes. "Uh-oh," she said.

"Don't be ridiculous," Vera said, as if reading her mind. "It's just a coincidence."

An hour later, Jamie led Vera into her garage where a red 1964 ½ Mustang convertible sat. With the exception of the color, it was an exact replica of the one Jamie had received from her father as a graduation present years before, only hers was white. Even though she'd spent a lot of money maintaining it, she still drove it with pride and wouldn't have thought of replacing it. It was in that very garage that Jamie had helped her father rebuild old cars, and each time he sold one, he'd tucked the money into her college fund.

Vera stepped up to the car and ran her hand along the hood. "It looks like it just rolled off the showroom floor. Are you sure Max won't mind if I borrow it? I mean, he bought it for you. It was a gift."

Jamie shrugged. "He only bought it because it was his fault mine was riddled with bullet holes." Luckily, it had since been repaired.

Vera shook her head sadly. "Do you know how strange that sounds? How many people send their cars to a body shop with bullet holes? That is precisely why I think Max Holt is the wrong man for you. I appreciate what he did for this town, but trouble seems to follow him everywhere."

Jamie figured it was best not to get into a debate with Vera over Max. Not that Max couldn't charm Vera's Hush Puppies right off her feet, mind you, but nobody had ever been good enough for Jamie as far as Vera was concerned. It didn't matter that Max was filthy stinking rich and turned every female's head between the ages of eighteen and eighty; he was a moving target for con men, bad guys, and the mob.

What Jamie also wouldn't tell Vera was that Max was more dangerous to her heart than any other body part. The three weeks she'd gone without seeing him seemed like forever. She knew he was a busy man— his company, Holt Industries, had offices all over the world—but surely he could have found time to pick up a telephone.

"So, you wanna take it for a spin?" Jamie said, chasing Max from her thoughts.

Vera opened the door. "Oh, Lord, it's a stick shift. I haven't driven one of those in years."

"All you need is a little practice."

Twenty minutes later, they were cruising Main Street with the top down, Vera grinning like a sixteen-year-old who'd just gotten her driver's license. "Hey, I'm pretty good at this," she said, shifting the gear into first after pausing at a stop sign.

Jamie grinned, as well. "See, I told you you'd pick it up in no time."

Vera glanced at her. "I don't look silly, do I? I mean, me driving around in such a snazzy car at my age. I'm no spring chicken, you know."

Jamie looked at her. Vera's beehive had already lost its hairpins and fallen to her shoulders, but the excitement in her eyes made up for her mussed hair. "You look great. And, no, you do not look silly." If anything, she looked younger.

The woman hitched her chin high. "I want to take it around the courthouse square again. Maybe I'll see somebody I know."

Jamie smiled at Vera's enthusiasm. She had to admit it was more fun riding around town with her than sitting home alone worrying about Fleas.

Vera circled the square. The downtown area had received a face-lift in the past couple of years. Each shop owner had painted his or her store in what was referred to as an historic color. They'd added awnings and massive flowerpots out front, hoping to draw business from the strip mall on the outskirts of town.

Jamie knew the town well. Despite changes to the outside, the Downtown Cafe still served the best coffee in town, and she knew the regulars who gathered first thing in the morning for the $2.99 breakfast special of eggs and bacon and the best homemade biscuits she'd ever tasted. There was Coot Hathaway's doughnut shop where you could buy glazed doughnuts straight from the oven and sticky buns that stuck to the roof of your mouth and chocolate mocha doughnuts that were her personal favorite. And nobody made better sandwiches than Donnie Maynard, who owned the local sandwich shop. He bought his bread fresh from Sunshine Bakery, and his meat-loaf sandwiches, served cold, always drew a crowd. He used a secret ingredient that he swore he would take to his grave, and no matter how hard folks tried they couldn't figure it out.

The courthouse square was as quaint as it had been in Jamie's younger days. People still fed pigeons or read the daily newspaper or gathered in small groups to catch up on the latest gossip. The Garden Club had replaced the old shrubbery with new—in late spring, the azaleas blazed with color in every imaginable hue. Fall brought with it colorful mums, and pansies were planted in winter. Even the bandstand had been given a fresh coat of white paint.

"Oh, look!" Vera said. "There's Robyn Decker and Betty Hamilton from my Sunday school class. Wait'll they get a look at me in this hot car." Vera braked and tapped the horn several times, and the women looked up. They gaped in surprise and hurried over. Both wore lightweight jogging outfits and sneakers.

"Vera, is that you?" Betty said. She was tall and slender and wore a mop of short gray curls that had obviously been sprayed into place because not one strand strayed.

"What in heaven's name are you doing in that car?" Robyn asked. Her hair was the same light gray, on the frizzy side, tucked back with hair combs. She was on the heavy side. A sheen of perspiration coated her forehead.

"I'm taking a test-drive," Vera said, winking at Jamie. "Ya'll want to cruise with us?"

The two women looked at one another. "Sure," Betty said. "It's too hot to try to get our exercise."

Jamie had to agree. Not only was it hot, the humidity hung over the town like a woolen blanket. She got out of the car, and pulled back the seat so the two women could climb in. "Fasten your seat belts," she said, once they'd settled themselves and Jamie reclaimed the front seat.

"You sure you know how to drive this thing?" Robyn asked.

"Vera drives it like a pro," Jamie told her.

They shot off, and the women in the back seat giggled like teenagers. "Hey, maybe we can pick up some guys," Betty said.

Robyn Decker gasped. "Why, Betty Hamilton, I don't believe what just came out of your mouth. You know we can't fit any men into this back seat, what with the size of my rear end." More giggles.

"Holy marolly," Vera called out. "There's Maxine Chambers's new store." She whipped the Mustang into a parking slot directly in front.

All four women leaned forward as if trying to get a closer look from where they were sitting. Finally, Jamie opened her door.

"Where are you going?" Vera asked.

"I want to check it out."

Double gasps from the back seat. "What if somebody sees you?" Betty said.

Jamie shrugged. "Aw, come on, ladies. The ground is not going to open up and swallow us just for looking."

"I don't care if the ground does swallow me up," Vera said. "I figure it's worth it." She pulled the seat forward, and the two in back reluctantly climbed out.

All four women hurried to the front of the store and gazed at the window display.

"Oh my," Betty said. "I can't believe a proper Southern woman like Maxine would fill her window with unmentionables. What are our young people going to think? It might be dangerous. It might raise the testerone level in some of the boys, and that could spell trouble."

"Testosterone," Jamie corrected. "And I seriously

doubt it's something they've never seen before. You know how inquisitive boys can be."

Vera eyed the merchandise. "I don't think I would even know how to wear some of this stuff."

Jamie perused the items in the window, making a mental list of what she planned to buy. "Maybe Maxine provides a list of instructions." But she was as surprised as the others that Maxine Chambers would actually open a sexy lingerie shop. Maxine had always been on the prudish side.

"What are those lacy things hanging over there?" Vera asked. "Between the garter belts and the see-through bras."

Jamie followed her gaze. "Those are thong bikini underwear."

Vera arched both brows. "They don't look as though they would do much good in covering your behind. Why, if a cold wind blew up your skirt—"

"Oh, Lord, ya'll are *not* going to believe who is heading our way," Robyn said.

Betty turned. "Oh, heavenly days, it's Agnes Aimsley and her grandson. The jig is up."

Jamie turned as Agnes, frail and white-haired, inched her way toward them. Her sneakers looked out of place with her prim dress. The man beside her, a twenty-something preppie type, had her arm tucked through his protectively. His brown hair was cropped short, and he wore oversize tortoiseshell glasses that had gone out of style long ago.

Vera looked grim. "Agnes teaches our Sunday school class," she told Jamie. "You may have heard she had a heart attack last year. She's such a devout Christian that she'll have another one if she sees what's in Maxine's window."

"We're talking de-vout," Betty emphasized. "If she dies, Jesus is going to have to move over and let her sit next to God. I'll bet that's her grandson. I hear he's one of those religious fanatics. I hear he can be a real cuckoo clock at times."

"Hello, ladies," Agnes called out pleasantly. "I see you're taking advantage of the nice weather the good Lord has provided."

"Um, hello, Agnes," Vera said.

Jamie tried to suppress a smile as Vera, Betty, and Robyn backed against the store window, no doubt attempting to block it from Agnes's view.

"Have ya'll met my grandson, Brent Walker? He's visiting for the summer while on break from Emory University where he is studying to be one of God's messengers."

They all shook hands. "Very nice to meet you, ladies," Brent said politely. He glanced up at the sign hanging over the window. Agnes looked up as well.

"'Sinful Delights,'" she read aloud, and suddenly smiled. "I didn't know we had a new chocolate shop in town. I hope they sell Godiva, that's my favorite. Scoot over, I want to see."

She and Vera did a little jig as Vera tried to stop her from looking past her.

"Believe me, Agnes, you're better off not knowing," Betty said.

Jamie cleared her throat and tried to remain straight-faced. The grandson looked confused.

"Perhaps we should move on," Brent said, as if taking his cue from the looks on the women's faces.

Agnes wasn't deterred. "Would you ladies please step aside so I can see what's in the window?"

It was like the parting of the Red Sea, Jamie decided, watching Vera, Betty, and Robyn clear the way so Agnes could step closer. "Oh my," she said. Her eyes glazed over in shock.

Brent's face turned a deep red. "What is the meaning of this?" he demanded. "Who would open such a place?"

Vera started to answer, but he cut her off and pulled a small tablet from his back pocket.

"I demand to know the name of the owner."

"Maxine Chambers," Betty supplied. "Actually, we're shocked, as well."

He scribbled the name on his pad. "This place looks like something straight out of Sodom and Gomorrah. I'm going to have a talk with this Chambers woman. I feel it's my Christian duty."

"Would somebody please explain what *those* are," Agnes said, pointing to a pair of underwear.

"They're edible undies," Jamie said, only to have Brent glare at her. Jamie shrugged. "Well, she asked."

"Edible undies?" Agnes said. "I don't understand." Suddenly, as if a lightbulb had gone off in her head, she gasped and covered her breast with both hands as if to keep her heart from leaping out. "Oh my."

"Let's go, Gram," Brent said, taking her by the arm. And not a moment too soon. Agnes swayed and fell into a dead faint.

Brent caught her in his arms. "Somebody call 911!"

"Well, thank God it wasn't a heart attack," Vera said when she dropped Jamie off at her house two hours later, after sitting in the ER waiting on word of Agnes's condition.

"It was probably a good idea that her doctor decided to keep her overnight for observation anyway," Jamie said. "I'll tell you, that grandson of hers is a nut."

"Yeah, he's a real fruitcake," Vera said, putting the gear into neutral. "Oh, by the way, you're not feeling a little weird, are you?"

"What do you mean?"

"You know, from eating those brownies?"

"You mean horny?"

Vera rolled her eyes. "Yeah, that."

Jamie decided she wouldn't tell Vera she got horny every time she thought of tall, dark, and drop-dead gorgeous Max Holt. "Yeah, I'm feeling a little frisky," Jamie confessed, although she suspected it was just her imagination. "I'm thinking maybe a cold shower is in order."

Vera sighed. "I'm thinking the same thing. Must be my wild oats acting up."

Jamie arrived at work the next morning, just as Destiny Moultrie climbed from a cream-colored Mercedes. The woman hurried over.

"I know I promised to give you a day or two to think about the column," she began, "but I'm anxious to get started."

Moultrie was dressed in silk khaki-colored slacks and a matching jacket that hung open to expose a tight purple bustier that barely contained her breasts. "Cleavage" seemed to be Destiny's middle name.

"I'm really busy," Jamie said.

"I was hoping we could talk it over this morning. And I'd like to discuss another matter with you. It's pretty important."

Jamie did a mental sigh. That meant all the doughnuts would be eaten by the time she got to the small kitchen in back, but she figured she at least owed Destiny the truth. She had no intention of hiring a psychic for her column, even if there was to be a column, which she hadn't decided on one way or the other.

"I can only afford a few minutes," she said.

"I knew you'd say that." Destiny followed her to the front double-glass doors.

Vera looked up the minute they stepped inside. Her gaze immediately fell on Destiny. "How did you know I was going to have car trouble?"

Destiny shrugged. "I just had a feeling. I didn't want you to find yourself stranded."

"You didn't tamper beneath my hood, did you?"

"Vera!" Jamie said. "That was not a nice thing to say."

"It happens all the time," Destiny said. "People don't want to believe in things they can't see."

Vera gave a grunt. "So what's it going to cost me to get my car repaired?"

Destiny shrugged. "I have no idea."

Vera looked at Jamie. "See, I told you there was nothing to this psychic stuff."

"What I meant to say," Destiny began slowly, "is I have no idea how much a new engine costs."

"A new engine!" Vera cried.

"Man, that's going to cost you," Jamie said, then caught herself. What was she thinking?

"New engine, my foot," Vera said. "There's not a darn thing wrong with my engine."

"Maybe we should step into my office," Jamie said, motioning Destiny inside.

The woman followed. Jamie paused at the door and glanced back at Vera. "Has Mike come in yet?" Mike Henderson was Jamie's fresh-out-of-college editor. She was trying to raise him to be a real newspaperman since he was organizationally challenged and spent much of his time chasing women.

"He's covering the city council meeting, and then he has an appointment to interview the new high school football coach."

Jamie nodded and closed the door. She turned and almost bumped into Destiny.

"I have something to tell you," the woman said.

Jamie took the chair behind her desk and motioned for Destiny to sit. "What is it?"

"Last night I had a vision. You were in it. There was a man with you."

Jamie perked up and thought of Max. "Oh, yeah? Were we naked?" She slapped her hand against her forehead. Now why had she gone and said something like that? The last thing she needed to do was encourage the woman.

"It wasn't that kind of vision," Destiny said. "This man was in uniform, and he was asking you a lot of questions."

Jamie remained quiet.

Destiny didn't seem deterred by her silence. "The situation was, um, dire, because I had this heavy feeling in my chest afterward."

Jamie figured any woman with Destiny's breasts would have a heavy feeling in her chest. She sighed. "Okay, Destiny, I'll play along. Who was asking these questions and what were they?"

"I don't know." At Jamie's look, Destiny went on. "Hey, I'm doing my best here, okay? I can't give you every little detail." All at once she glanced to the chair beside her. "Shut up, okay? I don't need your help."

Jamie's eyes widened as she followed Destiny's gaze to the empty chair. "Uh, Destiny, who are you talking to?" she asked.

The woman didn't hesitate. "His name is Ronnie. He's from the spirit world. He doesn't have enough sense to know he's dead. Follows me everywhere."

Jamie gripped the arms on her chair as chills raced up her spine. Time to bolt, she told herself.

"He's just an old redneck, don't worry, he's harmless." She glanced back at the empty chair. "Yes, you heard me right, Ronnie, you *are* a redneck. Anybody who gets sloppy drunk and falls out of the back of a pickup truck doing sixty miles per hour is a bona fide redneck in my book." She looked at Jamie. "That's how he died. He's kinda between worlds."

"Oh, well, that certainly explains it." Jamie glanced

at the door. It would take her less than three seconds to reach it if she ran like hell.

"Hey, I know it sounds crazy," Destiny said, "but that's the way it is. I have dead people show up all the time. They don't usually stay long. So, when do you want me to start?"

Jamie blinked. "Huh?"

"The job? I got a lot of my stuff unpacked last night so I'm ready to roll."

Jamie decided the woman had enough problems so she tried to let her down easy. "I'm thinking maybe I should hold off on the column," she said. What Jamie was actually thinking was that Destiny needed to be hauled off in a straitjacket.

"I suggest you announce the new column in your newspaper as soon as possible."

"Well, like I said—"

Destiny sighed in exasperation. "Dammit, Ronnie, would you *please* stop yakking and let me finish this conversation?" She shifted in her chair and regarded Jamie. "Look, I don't have all day. Let's do this. Run the announcement. If you don't get a substantial amount of responses, I promise I won't bother you again."

Once again, Jamie glanced at the chair beside Destiny. "Does he follow you everywhere?" she asked, thinking it would be best to have all the facts before she reported the woman to the authorities.

"Who, Ronnie?" Destiny sighed. "Hell, I can't even take a shower without the pervert getting in there with me. But don't worry; as soon as his pea brain realizes he needs to move on, he'll be out of my life." She rolled her eyes. "Dead people," she said on a sigh. "They can be such a pain in the ass." All at once, she sneezed. "Uh-oh, gotta run before I go into a sneezing frenzy." She stood and made for the door. "I'll call you later."

Jamie stopped her. "Um, Destiny?"

She turned. "Yeah?"

Jamie almost felt sorry for her. "How about I call you when I've made my decision? In the meantime, don't tell Vera about your friend, okay?"

"Vera, I need to run an errand," Jamie said, shortly after Destiny left. "I won't be long."

"No problem, I'll hold down the fort."

Jamie picked up her pocketbook and left the building, hurrying down the street toward Maxine Chambers's shop. She couldn't wait to see what was inside. She opened the door and stepped in, and was greeted by the smell of lavender.

Maxine was standing behind the counter. She had changed her mousy brown hair to a flattering red and wore makeup, something she had never bothered with when she'd worked at the library.

"Well, Jamie Swift, it's wonderful to see you again, only this time we don't have to whisper like we did at the library."

"I just came by to offer my congratulations on your new store," Jamie said.

Maxine smiled. "Well, you're the first. Everyone else is shocked that I would do such a thing, and some preacher wannabe is calling constantly, accusing me of corrupting the town. And get this; he wants to meet with me so he can pray for my soul. I told him to take a hike."

Jamie knew Brent Walker had been the one to call. "I'm sure it's going to take time for some folks to adjust. I'd just ignore him." She glanced around. "Now then, why don't you show me around? I've been dying to come in."

"What did you have in mind?"

"I'm not sure. Something a little sexy." She thought

of the edible underwear. "Without going overboard," she added.

"Come on and let me show you my new European lace collection. They're elegant but simple. Sexy *and* classy," she added.

Jamie followed her to an aisle where Maxine held up the most beautiful bras and panties she'd ever seen. "Oh my," she said.

"Aren't they lovely?" Maxine said proudly. "And look at this baby doll sleepwear in satin. Think how nice that would feel against your skin."

Jamie ran her hand against the material. "I've never felt anything so nice."

"I agree," Maxine said. "This is top-of-the-line. Oh, and I've got these beautiful teddies and body suits. Aren't they wonderful? And you've got just the figure for them."

"Why, thank you, Maxine." Jamie paused and studied the woman. "I don't mean to be nosy, Maxine, but what made you decide to open a lingerie store?"

The woman smiled. "I guess I'm the last person in the world people would expect to find running a store like this, but it's always been a secret fantasy of mine. So one morning I woke up and reminded myself I wasn't getting any younger, and that's when I started getting serious about it. Unfortunately, I haven't had a lot of customers since I opened."

"Then you'll have to let me write an article about your store," Jamie said, "along with a nice advertisement. It'll be my celebration gift to you."

"Why, thank you, Jamie. That's very kind of you. You know, I've always liked you. You were so careful with your library books. You never dog-eared the pages like some folks, and you always brought them back on time." She sniffed. "Not all people respect books like you do. Why, I could tell you stories—"

"Show me what else you've got," Jamie said, wanting to change the subject. Maxine probably did have a lot of stories, but she didn't have time to listen to them.

Maxine gave her a complete tour of the store. In the end, Jamie selected a number of items from the European collection.

"Good choice," Maxine said, "and since you're one of my first customers, I'm going to give you a ten percent discount." She rang up the merchandise, then wrapped the bras, panties, sleepwear, and body suits in tissue paper and put them in a beautiful lavender-colored bag.

Jamie handed her a check. "Why don't we meet for lunch early next week so we can talk about your store?" she said. "In the meantime, I'll send my editor over to get a picture of you for the ad."

Maxine looked pleased. "Well, now, I think that would be quite nice. You just call me when it's convenient."

"I'll check my calendar and get back to you." Jamie left the store a few minutes later with her purchases and walked by the bakery, thinking how good a brownie would taste right about now. She didn't really believe they contained an aphrodisiac, but on the off chance they did, she'd better steer clear of them. Her libido was giving her enough trouble these days.

And that made her think of Max. She wondered when she would see him again. At the same time, she questioned why she had allowed herself to become so involved. She knew very little about the man except that he was a gazillionaire who owned a whole slew of companies and had dated his share of celebrities. She knew he'd once been married, but that it hadn't worked out, and it was probably one of the reasons he wasn't in a hurry to marry again.

What she didn't know was how she felt about their situation. After an engagement gone badly, Jamie had pretty much decided marriage wasn't in the cards for her, at least not in the near future. But now she was beginning to have second thoughts, and it was all because of Max. Knowing herself as she did, she was aware that she wasn't cut out for the short-term flings Max was accustomed to. She wanted more.

Damn. She had tried so hard not to fall for him. She had fought her growing attraction to him every step of the way, only to realize that she was beginning to entertain thoughts of a possible future with him.

As she saw it, she had two choices. She could try to get the man out of her system and wonder for the rest of her life if anything would have become of them or she could continue to wait.

Neither option sounded particularly appealing.

THREE

Happy Paws Veterinary Clinic was decorated with vinyl chairs and floors, obviously to make it easier to clean up after nervous cats and dogs. Which explained the strong disinfectant smell, Jamie thought upon entering the reception area shortly after lunch. Some furry friend had either suffered a sudden loss of bladder control or heaved up a helping of meat chunks. From somewhere in back, a cacophony of barking persisted.

As Jamie waited for the receptionist to get off the telephone, she studied the large bulletin board that served as a lost-and-found center. Another bulletin board listed a variety of puppies and kittens to sell or give away.

She thought of adding Fleas's name to the list. Owning a pet was more trouble than she'd thought. Only, she couldn't think of a person who'd want to take on a dog with emotional problems and missing hair.

When the receptionist hung up the phone, she smiled at Jamie. "Oh, you're Fleas's mommy, aren't you?" the woman said in a voice that sounded too small and squeaky for someone who appeared to be at least one hundred pounds overweight.

"That's me," Jamie said.

"Hold on one sec, hon, and I'll get him."

Fleas did not look happy to see Jamie, but then the sagging brown skin and folds along the hound's face and jowls gave him a perpetual look of sadness and discontent. This time it seemed to be mixed with outright annoyance.

Oh, great, she thought. He's pouting.

"Okeydokey," the receptionist said. "His heartworm test was negative, so you can give him his first dose today, then he has to take one every month. You'll need to mark your calendar."

"He won't eat it," Jamie said dully. "Unless I can hide it in his ice cream."

The woman laughed as though it were the funniest thing she'd ever heard. "Oh, dogs love them," she insisted. "It comes in a meatlike treat."

"Can I put it between a hamburger bun with cheese on top?"

More laughter. Which was rather annoying for Jamie since she was serious.

"And then there's the flea preventive. You'll want to apply it once a month. It'll be easier to remember if you do it at the same time you give him his monthly heartworm medicine. I gave you a six-month supply of each. That's what people usually request." She hesitated and looked about the room as if to make sure nobody was listening. "Have you ever owned a pet, hon?" she whispered.

Was it that obvious? Jamie wondered. "This is my first, um, experience."

"There's a booklet inside his goody bag. It'll give you all sorts of information. And you can call us if you run into problems."

Jamie pulled out her checkbook and pen. "How much do I owe?"

"Well, now, let's see." The woman pulled up the information on the computer. "He had a full exam, we clipped his toenails, took blood for the heartworm test, performed the surgery—" She looked up. "We expressed his anal glands. I have to tell you, it wasn't pretty. Our technician had to go home for the rest of the day." She burst into giggles. "Just kidding."

Fleas sank to the floor and covered both eyes with his paws.

Jamie tightened her grip on the pen as she prepared to write the check. This was going to be bad.

"Oh, and there was a charge for anesthesia, of course, and his nerve pills."

"Nerve pills?"

"You mentioned he had a bad case of separation anxiety. Don't worry, Dr. Adams started him on a teensy-weensy dose, but it should take the edge off. Try giving it to Fleas with peanut butter. It's easier that way."

Jamie looked at Fleas. The dog had serious emotional problems, including shell shock from his coon-hunting days.

The woman behind the counter looked up from her computer. "Okeydokey, it comes to four hundred and eight dollars."

Jamie's eyes almost popped out of her head. She looked at Fleas. "You realize I paid less than that for the truck."

Fleas rose up on his front legs and shook hard. His long ears flapped annoyingly. Finally, he sat back on his haunches and began to lick himself.

Jamie cringed.

Police Chief Lamar Tevis was waiting for Jamie when she arrived back at the office, Fleas on her heels. The serious look on the man's face told her something was wrong. He held his cap in his hands, and his sandy-colored hair was still flat from wearing it. Vera was on the telephone. She shrugged at Jamie as though she had no idea why the chief of police wanted to see her.

"Hello, Lamar," Jamie said. "May I help you?"

He glanced at the bloodhound beside her. "Wow, that's about the ugliest dog I've ever seen. Is he a stray?"

"He belongs to me," Jamie said.

"Sorry, I didn't know he was yours. How come he's missing hair on his back?"

"A raccoon attacked him."

"I didn't know you liked to hunt coons. Why, me and my buddies—"

"It happened before I, um, came into ownership." Jamie saw that Lamar was still staring at her dog as though he were ugly. She hitched her head high. "Actually, he's pure bloodhound. Comes from championship bloodline," she added. It was a lie she told often.

"No kidding. What's his name?"

This was the part Jamie hated most. "Fleas."

"Uh-oh." Lamar stepped back.

"He doesn't actually *have* fleas, somebody just named him that. So what brings you to this neck of the woods, Lamar?"

Lamar glanced at Vera, then back to Jamie. "Perhaps we should talk privately. No offense, Vera."

Vera hung up the telephone. "Like I won't find out," she said. "So you can just kiss my royal behind, Lamar."

"Spoken like a true Southern Baptist," Lamar said with a chuckle.

"Any word from Mike?" Jamie asked, wishing her editor would check in more often. He was probably sweet-talking one of the counter girls at Dairy Queen.

"He called while you were out. Said he was working a hot story and would be in shortly. He wouldn't give me the details, he was acting real secretive and all. You know how dramatic he gets."

Jamie nodded. "Pray for a decent headline." She led Lamar inside her office and closed the door. He waited for Jamie to sit before he took the chair in front of her desk. Fleas plopped down beside Jamie's feet and gave a huge sigh.

"I guess you haven't heard the news," Lamar said. "Luanne Ritter was found murdered in her home late this morning. Suffered a fatal blow to her head," he added.

"Oh my God!" Jamie said. Luanne Ritter owned Ritter's Loan Company.

"Yup. That's where your editor has been all morning. At the murder scene," he added. "I didn't want to say anything in front of Vera. Not until I gave you the news."

"Do you have a suspect?"

"It's too early to tell. Her neighbor, Elaine something-or-other—" He paused and reached for notes. "Elaine Brewer is her name. Anyway, she went over to Luanne's house to borrow some coffee, knocked several times, but there was no answer. She found the door unlocked and almost tripped over Luanne's body on the kitchen floor. Coroner said Luanne had been dead at least ten or twelve hours. Sounds a little suspicious to me," he added.

"Oh, yeah?"

Lamar leaned closer. "Get this. The neighbor drinks decaf. Luanne drinks only regular coffee. I'd think after being neighbors for ten years this Brewer woman would have known. We've taken her in for questioning."

Jamie just looked at him. Lamar was a good honest man, but he wasn't the smartest investigator she'd ever met. "This is unbelievable," Jamie said.

Lamar glanced up quickly. He looked defensive. "You don't think I'm making this up, do you? The murder, I mean? My men will vouch for me. Your editor, too."

Jamie blinked. "What I meant was it's hard to believe someone just murdered Luanne in cold blood."

"I have the body to prove it. I can take you over to the morgue if you want to see for yourself."

Jamie did a mental eye roll. "Let's start over, Lamar. What can I do for you?"

Lamar reached into his shirt pocket and pulled out a small section of newspaper. He unfolded it and handed it to Jamie. "This was on Luanne's night table. Nobody knows about it except the responding officer and me. I'd like to keep it that way for now." He pretended to zip his lips. "Get my drift?"

Jamie found herself looking at a copy of her personals section that had been cut out of the newspaper. She glanced at Lamar. "You're not thinking my personals section had something to do with Luanne's murder?"

"There may be nothing to it, but I thought you should know." He leaned back in his chair and crossed one leg over the other. Fleas sat up and began to scratch. Lamar watched, an uneasy expression on his face. "Luanne wasn't very popular in this town," he went on, "what with her line of work. Way I heard, she could lean pretty hard on someone if they were late on their loan payment."

Jamie shook her head as she continued staring at the ads. Her hands trembled. "It has to be business related, Lamar. I think this—" She paused and held up the section of newspaper. "This is just a coincidence."

"Could be. I've sealed her place of business, and we're planning a full investigation. Like I said, I don't want this ad stuff getting out. I just wanted to make you aware." He took it from her, refolded it, and stuffed it into his pocket. "Also, I need your help."

Jamie knew where he was headed. "You know I can't give you the names of those who've submitted an ad without a court order."

"No judge is going to give me an order to look into

every name on your list," he said. "All I'm asking is that you keep an eye out for anything that looks suspicious. In case we have some kook on our hands."

"Yes, of course."

"I do have one other question. Did Luanne run an ad?"

"No."

Lamar shifted in his seat. "She had a message on her answering machine from a man regarding an ad. Said he'd call her back. Unfortunately, Luanne didn't have caller ID, and the tape must've been old because the voices weren't that clear."

"She must've answered his ad."

"She had another call from a fellow who claimed he was a man of God, said he wanted to meet with her immediately. He didn't leave his telephone number, told her he'd call back. Once again, it was hard to make out the message."

"Wonder why he didn't leave his name," Jamie pondered aloud.

"We also found religious literature stuffed inside her mailbox so he obviously knew where she lived."

"Was there any indication of forced entry?"

"No. Luanne opened the door for the person who killed her, so whoever it was must've not presented a threat. She might have opened the door for a preacher. This is all speculation, of course."

Jamie nodded. She thought of Agnes Aimsley's grandson, Brent Walker, then pushed it aside. Brent might be a bit on the kooky side, he might even leave religious material in Luanne's mailbox, but he wasn't a murderer. But she kept quiet, knowing how quickly Lamar could get sidetracked.

"By the way," Lamar said. "Where's Max Holt?"

Jamie would have loved nothing more than to say, "Jeez, last time I saw Max he had my skirt shoved to my waist and his hands on my thighs." Instead, she shrugged. "Who knows? He's a busy man."

"He's your partner."

"Max is my *silent* partner, Lamar. I run the newspaper."

"Max is good at this sort of thing. Investigative work," he added.

Jamie was not surprised by the remark. Lamar had witnessed firsthand just how good Max was when he'd almost single-handedly discovered who was involved in the town's corruption, which had bled taxpayers of their dollars for years. "You thinking of hiring him on as a deputy?" she asked, grinning, if for no other reason than to lighten the mood.

Lamar grinned back. "I tried, but he turned down the job. I reckon he has bigger fish to fry."

Despite her attempt at flippancy, Jamie could feel her stomach knotting. "Lamar, tell me you don't really think Luanne's murder is connected to my personals section, because if you think it is, I'll stop running the ads immediately."

"Then we risk losing the killer *if* it's connected. Are you going to help me?"

"I'll do what I can legally."

"That's all I'm asking," Lamar said. He left a few minutes later.

Jamie reached for the telephone. It was time to call Max.

Max Holt was in the boardroom of Holt Industries when he received Jamie's call. He immediately excused himself and hurried into his private office. "What's up, Swifty?"

Jamie had not forgotten the sexy pitch of his voice, or the teasing lilt he often used with her. Just hearing his voice again did all sorts of soft and fuzzy things to her insides. And that reminded her of how little she knew about the man. He moved in mysterious circles, dined with royalty, and made business deals that ended up on the pages of the *New York Times*.

"Max, do you have any idea what I had to go through to reach you?" Jamie said. "I had to bypass a receptionist, a secretary, and your personal assistant, all of whom insisted on knowing my business with you."

"What did you tell them?"

"I said I had a small oil-rich country for sale and that you might be interested in buying it."

He chuckled. "Well, I'm glad you were able to reach me. What's up?"

Jamie wondered how he could sound so casual when every nerve ending in her body was tingling at the sound of his voice. She wondered if he'd thought about her these past weeks. "I have a problem on my hands," she said. She told him about the personals section she had started, Luanne Ritter's murder, and the fact Police Chief Lamar Tevis suspected the two might be connected. She figured, as her partner, Max should know. Okay, so maybe there was more to it than that. It was a good excuse to call him.

"And here I thought you were calling to say you missed me," Max said. "You and I have some unfinished business, you know."

Jamie felt a thrill of delight race up her backbone at the thought. They had come so close the last time. She shook her head, trying to push the image from her mind. "Max, this is serious," she said, wondering how he could just pick up where they'd left off after three weeks of no word.

"Does Lamar Tevis have proof the two are connected?"

"No. But what if they are?"

"Don't assume the worst before we have time to look into the facts," he said. "Listen, I'm driving down tomorrow for Frankie's surprise birthday party. I can't believe my brother-in-law is reaching the big five-oh."

Jamie had received her invitation the week before. Jamie had met Frankie and his wife, Dee Dee, when they'd moved to Beaumont some ten years prior, after Frankie had retired from wrestling as Frankie-the-Assassin. They'd become fast friends, but it was hard to believe Max and Dee Dee were brother and sister. "Of course I'm going," she said.

"My schedule will be tight," Max said, "but I can swing by your house and pick you up on the way."

Jamie took her time in answering. It was no surprise that Max would just assume she would attend the party with him. And on a Friday night of all nights when most reasonably attractive single women had dates. She almost preferred cutting her tongue out with her dull letter opener than telling Max she was dateless.

Be cool, she told herself.

"I, um, didn't know you were coming, Max, so I sort of made other plans," she said, then wanted to smack her own mouth. Her and her dumb pride, she thought. But Max had a way of bringing out the worst in her when it came to male-female stuff.

"Oh, yeah?" He sounded more amused than annoyed. "Well, if we put our heads together I'm sure we can think of a way to ditch him. I have to get back to a meeting and wrap things up here so I can leave, but do me a favor. Wear that blue dress you wore the first night I met you."

Jamie heard a dial tone. She hung up. She felt something nudge her foot and glanced down at Fleas who was watching her. "Okay, so I made up that part about having a date," she said. "Sometimes things just fall out of my mouth before I have time to think about them. Especially when it comes to *that* man," she added.

The dog thumped his tail against the floor.

"It's complicated with Max and me," she went on. "I never know where I stand with him." She couldn't tell Fleas the truth, that she couldn't get Max out of her mind, that she was just itching for the chance to be alone and naked with him. It wouldn't be fair to discuss sex in front of the poor animal since he'd just been neutered. Not that she could imagine Fleas interested in chasing a female dog, since it would take effort on his part. And Fleas was allergic to effort.

Jamie gave a huge sigh. Suddenly, her thoughts took a drastic turn, and she snapped her head up. Holy cow! Destiny Moultrie had warned her she would be talking to a man in a uniform, and it would be bad. She had been right on the money. Jamie picked up the telephone and dialed the woman's number. Destiny answered on the first ring.

"We need to talk," Jamie said.

"I demand to know what's going on," Vera said, standing in the doorway of Jamie's office. "And I'm not going to take no for an answer."

Jamie noted the determined look on Vera's face. "You're not armed, are you?" she said.

Vera pressed her lips into a grim line and ignored Jamie's question. "You've never kept secrets from me. Why was Lamar Tevis here? What'd you do now? Are you in trouble with the police?"

Jamie gave a sigh. Why did the woman always assume she'd done something wrong? "Luanne Ritter was murdered."

Vera's brows shot up in surprise. "No kidding? Well, I'm sure she had it coming."

"Vera!"

"Nobody liked her anyway. Folks only borrowed money from her when they were desperate. And Luanne liked to talk. If someone's credit rating was low, she blabbed it all over town. Why, I heard that one of Luanne's employees roughed up a couple of customers who fell behind on their payments. And to think, Luanne's husband, God rest his soul, was such a nice man. If he knew how Luanne treated her customers, he'd have reached right out of his grave and snatched her bald-headed."

"Well, now, that's something to think about," Jamie said, not knowing how to respond.

"I'm telling you, that woman was no better than a loan shark. So why did Lamar come to you?"

Jamie didn't meet her gaze. She didn't like lying to Vera. "Um, Mike was on the crime scene, and Lamar doesn't want vital information printed in the paper."

Vera suddenly looked indignant. "Why didn't Mike call me? I'm the assistant editor. I should have been there to take photos."

"I suppose he felt he had to move fast since it was a murder investigation." Jamie was proud that Mike had made it to the scene. He was a good editor, but his poor time-management skills and sexual exploits had interfered with his work in the past. He now made a concerted effort to get to work on time.

Vera didn't look placated. She sniffed, a definite sign of annoyance. "Well, I have to leave for a hair appointment," she said. "Helen is going to cover the phones. Besides, I want to be the first to tell everybody at the beauty shop about Luanne."

Five minutes later, Mike rushed into Jamie's office. As usual, his clothes looked as though he'd slept in them. His light brown hair was mussed, as though he'd finger-combed it on his way out of the house. "Have you heard the news?" he asked.

"Yes. Lamar was here earlier."

"I'm going to get right on the story. We're going to have a kick-butt headline. Oh, and you're not going to believe this one. They were hauling Luanne out of her house on a stretcher, and the body bag slipped. Luanne hit the ground."

"Oh, jeez. Please don't mention it in your article."

"Lamar almost had a stroke."

"So did Vera when she found out you didn't call her to take pictures."

"Uh-oh. Maybe I should leave town for a couple of days," he said. "By the way, are you going to Frankie Fontana's birthday party tomorrow night? It's the talk of the town, what with him being the new mayor and just turning fifty and all."

"Yeah, I'm going."

"You should take me with you. I could get pictures for the society column."

Jamie hadn't thought of that. Frankie's wife.

Dee Dee, would go all-out for the party, and the photos would fill up space. With the exception of Luanne Ritter's murder, there just wasn't enough going on in Beaumont these days. "You'd have to rent a tux."

"I've already got one. Come on, Jamie, I need a night out. My life is as boring as yours."

"My life is not boring."

"Whatever. So, what do you say?"

Jamie pondered it. At least it meant she wouldn't have to show up alone. Not that she'd ever let that stop her before, but this was different since she'd already told Max she had a date. She had to save face. "Okay, you can go as my escort."

"Your escort? Oh, I get it. You couldn't find a date."

Jamie gave him a look.

"Hey, I understand. It's not like I've never had to scramble to find someone to go with me at the last minute. It's harder for women to go alone, though. They tend to look desperate."

Jamie drummed her fingers on her desk. "Mike, don't you have an article to write?"

"Hello?" a voice called out.

Jamie looked up to find Destiny standing in the doorway. Mike looked, as well. "Well, hello to you," he said, straightening his tie and squaring his shoulders as if to make himself appear taller. "May I help you?" His eyes were fixed on her breasts.

"I'm here to see Jamie."

He went on as if he hadn't heard. "I'm her editor, Mike Henderson." He rubbed a hand over his head, smoothing out his rumpled hair. "You've probably seen my byline."

"Destiny Moultrie," she said in her husky voice. "And, no, I haven't had the pleasure of reading your articles. I've just moved to Beaumont."

"You just moved here?" he repeated. "Well, then you probably haven't had a chance to dine at our best restaurants or see the sights. I could—"

"I don't eat out much," Destiny said. "I'm a vegetarian."

Mike smiled broadly. "A vegetarian? Well, now, isn't that a coincidence. It just so happens I'm a vegetarian, too."

Jamie tried to suppress a smile. Mike lived on fast food and probably wouldn't recognize a zucchini from a cucumber. "Um, Mike, about that article—"

"Yeah, yeah." He reached into his pocket. "Here's my business card, Miss Moultrie."

"Call me Destiny," she said, taking the card.

"If you should find yourself in need of a tour guide, I'm the man for the job. Oh, and use my pager. That's quicker."

"Thank you, Mike."

He was still smiling as he backed from the room and closed the door.

"Nice man," Destiny said to Jamie.

"Yes, Mike can be very, um, charming," Jamie said. She motioned for Destiny to take a seat. "Thank you for coming right over," she said. "I have something I want to discuss with you."

"Have you decided about the job?"

"I'm still thinking about it." She paused. "Something terrible has happened." Jamie debated whether or not to tell her about Luanne and decided to hold off.

Destiny leaned forward. "Oh my, what is it?"

"I was hoping you could tell me."

Destiny shook her head. "I haven't had any more visions if that's what you're asking."

"Nothing about the man in uniform who was supposed to question me?"

"No, nothing. Why?"

Jamie leveled her gaze on the woman. "I was questioned by the chief of police this morning about a murder that took place last night."

Destiny simply looked at her. "I'm not surprised. Who was the victim?"

Jamie told her what she knew.

Destiny listened carefully. "I'm not getting anything on it, but that doesn't mean it won't come to me later." She suddenly glanced behind her. "Ronnie, I asked you to wait in the car."

Jamie looked up at the vacant spot behind her. "Your dead spirit came with you?"

"Sorry. Just ignore him."

Jamie nodded as though it were an everyday occurrence to have a dead spirit in her office. "Destiny, I don't know anything about psychic ability; in fact, I don't really believe in such things."

"I know that, but I hope you won't let it stand in the way of giving me a job. I am perfect for it. I have feelings for what people really need help with. I *can* help them, Jamie. I've done this sort of thing before with a lot of success."

Jamie considered it. If an advice column pulled in more readers, it could only mean more revenue for the newspaper. "Tell you what. I'll announce the new column in an article and see if we get any responses. If we get a significant number, the job is yours. As long as you realize I have editorial control on what goes out," she added.

"Are you going to announce to your readers that I'm psychic?"

"The jury is still out on that one." Jamie wasn't sure how the citizens of Beaumont would accept it.

"Don't forget, I want to be referred to as the Divine Love Goddess Advisor. I think it's catchy, don't you?"

Jamie didn't have a clue. Probably folks would laugh her right out of town. "You realize I'm going out on a limb here."

"I won't let you down," Destiny promised.

Vera walked through the door two hours later. Jamie sat back in her chair and stared, her mouth agape. "Wow!" The gray was gone, and her hair cut in a flattering style.

Vera preened. "Susie colored it, added a light frosting, and then cut it. She says this haircut is the rage in Hollywood. Susan Sarandon and Sharon Stone are wearing this style. Mitzi, the cosmetologist, did my makeup. Of course, I ended up buying fifty dollars' worth of foundation, powder, and eye shadow from her, but she showed me how to use it to enhance my best features."

"You look great," Jamie said and meant it. "In fact, you look ten years younger."

"That's what everyone said. It sort of made up for the fact they already knew about Luanne Ritter. News travels fast in this town." She paused. "Um, Jamie, would you mind if I kept the Mustang for a few more days? It's going to cost a fortune to fix my old car."

"What's wrong with it?"

"Don't ask."

"It's the engine, right?"

"Yeah, but that doesn't mean your psychic friend is on the up-and-up."

"You're saying it's just another coincidence?" Jamie asked.

"I'm saying my car is old, and the engine was bound to give out sooner or later."

Jamie just looked at her.

"Frankly, the car is not worth what it would cost to replace the engine so I need to look around, see if I can find something affordable."

"You're welcome to keep the Mustang as long as you need it," Jamie replied.

"You're a doll. By the way, I hear your friend Dee Dee is throwing a big birthday party for Frankie tomorrow night. You plan on going?"

"I wouldn't miss it."

"Who are you going with?" Vera asked.

Big pause. "Mike."

"*Our* Mike? What's wrong, couldn't you find a real date?" She didn't wait for Jamie to respond. "Well, I don't blame you for not wanting to go alone. Not with people still talking about your broken engagement and all."

Jamie felt her ego plunge to her toes. "That wasn't my fault." Which was true. She'd broken up with Phillip

Standish because his mother had been the ringleader of the town's corruption scandal. "Besides, I didn't love him." That was true, too. She'd simply wanted to belong to a real family for once. Security and predictability had been important to her at the time. Seemed those days were gone forever. Her life was about as predictable as a tornado. And that tornado had a name: Max Holt.

"Oh, nobody is blaming you," Vera said. "It's just, well, I don't want folks feeling sorry for you. I wish you could have found a better date than Mike. I mean, he's so young. He can't be more than twenty-four or five."

"I'm hoping he'll look older in his tux," Jamie said.

"I'm hoping he'll remember to wash behind his ears."

Leave it to Vera to make things worse, Jamie thought. "It's not a *real* date, okay? He's just acting as my escort. Besides, he wanted to go so he could snap some pictures for the society column." Jamie regretted the words before they left her mouth. Snapping pictures was supposed to be Vera's job.

"I've already heard about the birthday cake your friend Dee Dee chose for Frankie," Vera said, as if she were more interested in the latest gossip than she was in snapping pictures. "Lyle Betts baked it if that tells you anything."

Jamie leaned back in her seat. "Oh, yeah?"

"The way I heard it, Lyle has an *adults' only* book to order from. The cake is supposed to be of a naked woman."

Jamie chuckled. It sounded like something Dee Dee would do; she could be outlandish at times. Which was why some of the more genteel families had had trouble accepting the couple when they'd first moved to Beaumont. Dee Dee had arrived wearing rhinestone outfits, and Frankie had shocked the town when he'd invited his old wrestling buddies for a visit. Jamie had taken them under her wing and invited them to all the social events, and the two had become a hit. It was a known fact they could liven up even the dullest party with their presence. And when Frankie had run for mayor, promising to clean up town corruption, he'd won hands down.

"And get this," Vera said. "People are lining up at Lyle's bakery to buy brownies. Wouldn't surprise me if half the women in this town ended up pregnant before long," she added with a knowing look.

Jamie promised herself to steer clear of the brownies.

The following night, Jamie slipped on her blue silk dress, and checked herself in the mirror. Her makeup and hair were perfect. She had taken a long bubble bath, slathered herself with lotion from head to toe, and then given herself a manicure and a pedicure. She tried to convince herself it had nothing to do with Max.

She'd even tried to convince herself that her trip to Maxine Chambers's lingerie shop had nothing to do with Max, but beneath her clothes she wore a body suit that was designed to make a man's tongue fall to the floor. The fact that she'd spent close to two hundred dollars in the shop had almost caused her to swallow her own tongue.

The doorbell rang at precisely six forty-five. Jamie opened the door and found Mike on the other side. He wore a baby-blue tux that was outdated, and at least one size too small. Ruffles peeked out from his sleeves. "Oh, jeez," she said.

"I know it's a little snug," he told her. "My parents bought it for my high school prom. I guess I've filled out."

"You look fine," Jamie told him, not wanting to hurt his feelings. She knew he tried to help his parents financially from time to time, and odds were he couldn't afford to rent a tux. Probably nobody would notice his white socks anyway. Besides, it wasn't a date. Mike was going as part of his job.

"Hey, you look gorgeous," he said, taking a long look. "You should dress up more often, and you wouldn't have so much trouble finding a date. Hey, speaking of gorgeous, what's your friend Destiny doing tonight? I'm here to tell you, that woman is hot. You should fix us up."

"Don't you think she's a little, um, mature for you?" Jamie asked.

"Age is not an issue with me. I'm taking you out, aren't I?"

Jamie shot him a dark look. "May we leave now?"

Jamie did not see Max among the crowd of people when she and Mike came through the door at Frankie and Dee Dee's, and her heart sank. What if he'd been unable to get away? Or maybe he'd had a better offer in the way of female companionship. Max Holt would naturally have his share of offers. Jamie pushed the thought aside. Max would not renege on a promise to be at his brother-in-law's fiftieth birthday party. She craned her head, trying to see above the tall heads in the room.

Max spotted Jamie the minute she stepped through the front door. He smiled at the sight of her so-called date, who immediately headed toward the dining room where the buffet was set up. His smile broadened when he noticed she was looking for him, but he was hidden from view at his place beside one of the round, floor-to-ceiling columns inside the house. He simply stood there for a moment watching her. Finally, he moved toward her until he was standing directly behind her.

"Looking for someone?"

Jamie felt the hairs stand on the back of her neck at the sound of his voice. Every nerve in her body sprang to life as she turned and found herself looking into Max Holt's handsome face. For a moment all they could do was stand and stare at each other. It was as though all the people in the room had evaporated.

"Hello, Max," she said, trying to sound cool. But cool wasn't easy, what with her heart beating like a conga drum in her chest. Damn, he looked good in his black tux, which, unlike Mike's, was simple and elegant and probably tailor made. Of course, the man looked good no matter what he wore.

Max was all male—sinewy muscle, gorgeous olive complexion, hard jaw. He was as polished as they came, with an underlying air of danger that oddly made her feel safe in his presence.

His smile was slow and lazy as a winding river. "You amaze me, Swifty. I thought you couldn't get any prettier. I was wrong."

Jamie offered him a benign smile, meant to make him feel as though she were immune to his charm. "Thank you, Max. Coming from a world-renowned womanizer I consider that quite a compliment."

He grinned. "So, who's the boy?"

"Excuse me?"

"Your date?"

"You know Mike Henderson. I hardly think he qualifies as a boy. He's, um, not exactly a real date, he just escorted me. He's here to take pictures for the society column."

"If he were any younger, I'd have to report you to the authorities."

"Same old Max."

"Tell you what, Swifty. I'm going to be a gentleman about this, seeing as how you probably think I took you for granted. I assumed you wanted to see me as badly as I wanted to see you. But let's get something straight." His tone dropped, and there was a slight huskiness to it. "You leave the party with me."

FOUR

Jamie's stomach quivered at the thought of going anywhere with Max. "I don't know if that's wise."

He stroked one finger down her arm. Her skin prickled.

"There you go again," he said. "You're thinking too much." He gave her a private smile. "You're wearing the blue dress. I can't wait to see what's under it."

Jamie gulped. Yikes, the man was seducing her right there on the spot. And damned if there was anything she could do about it because her tongue had suddenly become plastered to the roof of her mouth.

And now, here she was, wondering what *he* was wearing, if anything, beneath that dignified-looking tux.

"I need a drink," she said, if for no other reason than to change the subject. Max knew what he did to her, and he was probably enjoying every minute of it.

Max motioned, and a waiter appeared instantly, carrying a tray of white wine in tall, long-stemmed glasses. "Would you like a glass of chardonnay?" the man asked.

Jamie concentrated on keeping her hand steady as she reached for one of the goblets. She could feel the perspiration beading her upper lip, and she hadn't put any tissues in the small bag she'd chosen to bring.

"Are you hot?" Max asked.

Jamie tried to play it down, suspecting Max was enjoying her discomfort. "There are too many people crammed into this place. I think your sister invited half the town."

"Dee Dee does have a way of going overboard," Max said, looking about the room.

Mike returned balancing a plate stacked high with food, camera dangling from his neck. "Hi, Max. Hey, nice tux. I'll bet you didn't rent it in Beaumont." He looked at Jamie. "Why is your face all sweaty?" He didn't give her a chance to answer. "I haven't eaten all day. I hope I don't make a pig of myself." He bit into a finger sandwich. "Wow, check out the brunette who just walked through the door. The one in the red dress," he added. "I should go over and introduce myself. Maybe she'll let me take her picture." He winked at Jamie. "Don't tell Destiny. I'm saving myself for her." He hurried away.

Jamie shook her head as she caught the amused look on Max's face. He pulled a handkerchief from his pocket. "May I?" When Jamie merely shrugged, he very carefully mopped her forehead and upper lip. "There now, good as new."

Jamie drained her glass. "I should find Frankie and wish him a happy birthday."

"Great, we can go together."

Dee Dee Fontana and her assistant Beenie appeared out of nowhere. "Oh, Jamie, I'm so glad you could come!" she cried, hugging her tightly. "You too little brother." She and Max hugged, as well.

"You look beautiful," Jamie said, noting Dee Dee's ankle-length, Kelly-green cocktail dress. It set off her green eyes and red hair. Jamie was certain Beenie had handpicked the outfit for her; he'd long ago tossed her slinky rhinestone garb, before husband Frankie had been elected as town mayor. Beenie was dressed in Ralph Lauren, his dark hair combed straight back, emphasizing a perfect oval face.

"Frankie will be thrilled to see you," Dee Dee said in her Betty Boop voice that gave the former beauty queen a childlike quality most people found endearing.

"We wouldn't have missed it for the world," Jamie said, and then wished she had used a singular pronoun. She didn't want anyone, least of all Max, to think she was his date for the evening. "You look gorgeous as always," she told the woman quickly, hoping no one had caught the slip. Dee Dee seemed to sparkle. Well into her forties, she passed for thirty, thanks to a plastic surgeon in Hilton Head that she kept on call.

"Where *is* Frankie?" Max asked.

Dee Dee giggled. Coming from anyone else, it would have sounded silly, but Dee Dee's little-girl quality and naïveté made people, especially her husband, want to take care of her. "He and several of his old wrestling buddies are at the bar. Snakeman, Big John, Choker, and Dirty Deed Dan flew in to celebrate with us."

Jamie recognized some of the names as Frankie's old wrestling buddies. Snakeman had toured with a twenty-foot boa during his wrestling days. "Is there a snake in residence?" Jamie asked, hoping that wasn't the case.

Another giggle from Dee Dee. "No, the snake died a while back, and Snakeman decided not to replace him because it made traveling difficult. The snake was just part of the show."

Jamie tried to hide her sigh of relief. The last thing she wanted was something wrapping itself around one of her ankles.

Dee Dee offered them a conspiratorial grin. "Wait till you see the cake I ordered."

Beenie rolled his eyes and tapped his fingers against his lips. "It's designed to look like a naked woman. It starts at the shoulders and ends at her navel, and get this, she's wearing a nipple ring. Tacky, tacky, tacky."

Dee Dee pretended to pout, something else she pulled off very well. "You didn't think the one that looked like a man's buns was tacky."

Beenie struck a pose. "Now that was a work of art." He shrugged. "Besides, I like men's buns." He went on. "Anyway, as I told Dee Dee, this is *not* the time or place for such decadence. We have visiting dignitaries, and they will probably be offended. I would have chosen something elegant but simple. Less is always more."

The waiter came by. Jamie grabbed another glass of wine. Max grinned.

"Oh, Beenie, stop acting like an old maid and loosen up a bit," Dee Dee said. "It's not going to kill you to have a little fun now and then."

Jamie couldn't help but smile as Dee Dee and Beenie continued to fuss. Dee Dee had hired Beenie away from an exclusive spa in Hilton Head. They were inseparable, but they tended to argue like brother and sister.

"And guess what else we ordered from the bakery?" Dee Dee said in a conspiratorial whisper. "Aphrodisiac-laced brownies. Everybody in town is shocked that Lyle Betts is making them, but he claims he can't bake them fast enough. Isn't that a scream?"

Jamie wasn't about to tell her she had already tried them. "Oh, here's the birthday boy now," she said as Frankie joined them. Standing well over six and a half feet, with a barrel of a chest, Frankie Fontana struck an imposing figure. Jamie had not known Frankie in his wrestling days, but as a teenager, Max had seen him in the ring a number of times and assured her he had been quite formidable. Now, having been retired more than ten years, Frankie wore a good-natured smile and easygoing attitude that made him appear as harmless as a kitten.

"Glad you could come," Frankie said, pumping Max's arm enthusiastically and giving him a hearty slap on the back. He hugged Jamie lightly as though realizing his own strength.

"Happy birthday," Jamie said and Max seconded it.

Frankie grinned from ear to ear, looking much like an overgrown kid despite his graying temples. "I guess Dee Dee told you about the cake. Snakeman is going to remove the nipple ring with his teeth, and then we're going to have arm-wrestling matches in the kitchen. Better place your bets while there's still time."

Beenie looked aghast. "Do you realize the lieutenant governor is here?" he hissed.

"Yeah, he's the one taking the bets," Frankie said.

Dee Dee patted her husband's hand. "Well, I'll put my money on you any time, sweetie," she said. He kissed her lightly on the lips although it was obvious he would have preferred something more passionate. Twenty years of marriage had not dampened their desire for each other.

Frankie looked at Jamie. "I'm especially glad to see you. Dee Dee has a dilemma."

"Frankie's right," Dee Dee said. "I need to find a cause."

"A cause for what?" Jamie asked.

Dee Dee giggled. "You know, a cause. Now that Frankie's the new mayor, I think I should make some sort of contribution to this town."

"That's a wonderful idea," Jamie told her friend. "You could volunteer at the hospital."

"Eeyeuuw!" Dee Dee shuddered.

"Dee Dee doesn't like being around sick people," Frankie explained. "We wouldn't want her to catch any germs."

"There's a telephone number in the phone book for people wanting to volunteer their time," Jamie offered. "You could call them and see what they need. I'm sure you'll find something that interests you."

Dee Dee suddenly brightened. "I could work for a hotline service. You know, help people out who have personal problems. I'm a good listener."

Jamie and Max exchanged looks. Jamie couldn't imagine Dee Dee trying to solve anyone's problems. God bless her, but Dee Dee's answer to everything was a new piece of fine jewelry or a shopping trip to New York.

"I don't know about the rest of you, but I'm hungry," Frankie announced. "Let's grab some grub."

A few minutes later, Max and Jamie carried their plates and glasses of wine to one of the love seats adorned in faux leopard. Dee Dee had decorated the room in a jungle theme, complete with animal-skin sofas, banana plants, and wooden giraffes. Max sat close enough so that their thighs touched. It didn't go unnoticed by Jamie.

"Max, we really need to talk," she said, trying to ignore the tingling that started at her hip bone and spread right down to her painted toenails. Her stomach took a nosedive as she imagined his hair-roughened thighs touching hers without benefit of clothes. Lord, what the man did to her!

"You smell nice," he said.

"Thank you." She didn't want to think about how good he smelled. She tried to remember what she had been saying before he'd touched her and her mind had taken leave. "I'm, uh, really concerned about Luanne Ritter's murder and that the personals section may be connected to it. I told Lamar I'd pull the ads, but he disagreed. He's afraid if the murder had something to do with the ads, we might lose the killer. I think it's too risky."

"Give me a few more details," he said.

Jamie told him about her conversation with Lamar, trying not to leave anything out.

"We're going to have to work fast, Swifty," he said.

"We'll have to work at night, after the office is closed. Nobody is supposed to know. Not even Vera."

"What about the production staff?"

"They never come up front. Besides, even if they did, they'd have no idea what we were working on."

"You have records of the people who've written in?"

Jamie nodded. "I keep them locked in my office for confidentiality's sake. Vera pitched the fit of all fits when I told her she wasn't privy to the information, but you know how she loves to gossip." Jamie paused. "By the way, I lent her the red Mustang. Her old car gave out on her."

He grinned. "Does she drive it with the top down?"

God, if only he wouldn't smile like that, Jamie thought. She could handle almost anything but those bone-melting smiles. "Yes. She even got a new haircut so the wind wouldn't mess up her hair so badly."

"I can't wait to see that." He glanced around the room. "Tell you what. We'll wait until the birthday cake is served, then slip out and drive to the office." He suddenly smiled. "Unless you need to get your date home in time for his curfew."

Jamie shot him one of her looks.

Frankie's cake was rolled out on a serving cart an hour later, and the guests gathered around and sang "Happy Birthday," even as some gasped at the sight of the naked figure of a woman with size-D breasts. Frankie blew out his candles and hugged Dee Dee as everyone clapped. Snakeman made a production of removing the nipple ring with his teeth and received rousing applause.

"Speech!" someone shouted from across the room.

Frankie laughed. "I'd have thought you guys had heard enough of my speeches during the mayoral campaign," he said. "Okay, but I'll make it short. First of all, I'd like to thank you all for being here to share my birthday. Dee Dee and I are very lucky to have so many friends. And because we consider all of you friends, I would like to make an important announcement."

Max and Jamie looked at each other and shrugged.

Frankie paused and smiled tenderly at Dee Dee. She beamed. "After all these years, my wife and I are expecting a baby."

Everyone clapped. Jamie looked at Max. "Well, there goes that perfect figure she's worked so hard to keep," she said, knowing Dee Dee went bananas if she gained a pound.

Max merely grinned. "Sounds like she and Frankie have been eating brownies."

Max and Jamie left the party shortly afterward, but not before they'd offered Frankie and Dee Dee their congratulations.

"I'm going to be an uncle," Max said, his tone incredulous, as they pulled away from the Fontana house, which was really an estate. An estate on which sat a salmon-colored house that Frankie claimed was pink and caused a lot of snickering from his wrestling buddies who referred to it as the Pink Palace.

Jamie still couldn't believe the news. "Dee Dee is going to have to give up her rigid dieting. She's eating for two now."

"Hello, Jamie," a voice called from the dashboard. "What's this about Max being an uncle?"

Jamie smiled. "Hey, I've missed you, Muffin," she

said to the voice-recognition computer that ran Max's business from a dashboard that was more complicated than most jets; thanks to a team of first-rate computer whizzes. Max had hired them away from top government contractors, and with his help, they'd created the car's instrumentation using state-of-the-art equipment.

Spread out among luxury automotive goodies like a tachometer, an altimeter, and a global positioning satellite system were a highly enhanced PDA, a keyboard, a digital speech-recognition module, a photo-quality printer, fax, satellite phone, HDTV display screen, and a full video-conferencing suite, all operated by a high-powered computer that was smaller than an ashtray. "She" had a Marilyn Monroe voice, but because she was constantly fed information from a team of experts, she was the only one capable of matching Max's genius.

Not only that, Max had created in her technology that was able to make judgment calls, not based on data but on simple human emotion. His competitors, including the federal government, claimed it couldn't be done. Now they wanted to buy that technology.

"Dee Dee's pregnant," Jamie said at last.

"Uh-oh."

"My thoughts exactly," Max said. "We can expect drastic changes in the Fontana household."

"Wait a minute," Muffin said, "I thought she was going through menopause."

Jamie smiled, although she was still stunned by the news. "You ever heard of a change-of-life baby? It happens."

"How's she taking the news?"

"She looked thrilled," Jamie said, "and I think she'll make a wonderful mother. Dee Dee is very softhearted. And Frankie is going to enjoy spoiling the little tyke."

"I'm going to start looking into all the best baby books," Muffin said. "I'll get every piece of data I can, then Dee Dee and I will talk."

"I can't wait to see her in maternity clothes," Jamie said. "I'm sure Beenie will insist on the best designer money can buy."

Max gave her one of his slow easy smiles. "You sound a little exuberant there, Swifty. Sounds like you wouldn't mind having a little bambino of your own. You might need to give it some thought, what with that ticking biological clock thing that women worry so much about."

"My clock is ticking just fine, Max," she said, "and no, I don't think I'm ready for motherhood. I can't even raise a dog properly, but at least he won't be sitting in some therapist's office thirty years from now complaining what a crummy job I did."

"Ah, Jamie, you'd be a great mom," he said.

"Really?" The sincerity in his voice touched her.

"Excuse me," Muffin said. "I think we're missing something here. A father, maybe?"

Max and Jamie locked gazes. "How *is* Fleas, by the way?" Max asked.

Jamie thought he'd done a clumsy job of changing the subject. "I just had him neutered."

"See, that makes you a responsible pet owner," Max said.

"Uh, Muffin," Jamie began, "back to love and marriage and baby carriages, how's your love life?" Muffin had been having an on-again off-again online romance with a laptop computer at MIT. Max had also programmed Muffin with a personality. She had attitude.

"We're sort of taking a break from each other," Muffin said. "I think I intimidate him. I think he's chatting with someone else."

"He'll be back," Max said. "A smart man never walks away from a good thing."

Jamie felt his eyes on her, but she didn't dare look his way. As she had told Fleas, their relationship was complicated. "I suppose you told Muffin what's going on in Beaumont," she said, realizing she had been the one to change the subject this time. Each time things got too personal between them, one or both of them backed off. Besides, if Max started sweet-talking her, they'd never make it to the newspaper office.

"Yeah, what do you think?" Muffin asked.

"I think I'm going to feel guilty for the rest of my life if my personals section is involved in that poor woman's murder."

"You can't take everything Lamar Tevis says as fact," Muffin said. "We're not dealing with Colombo. Do you have backup info on the people writing the ads?"

Jamie felt herself nod even though she knew Muffin couldn't see her. "Yeah, I have to keep the letters on file in case someone gets a response."

"Anybody else have access to them?" Muffin asked.

"Not even Vera."

"Oh, man, I'll bet that pissed her off. So, here's what we do," Muffin began. "You give me the names and any other pertinent info, and I check them out. If I find anyone who looks suspicious, we'll take a closer look."

Twenty minutes later, Max pulled into the parking lot of the *Beaumont Gazette*. A cream-colored Mercedes was parked in one of the slots. "Boy, you must've given somebody on your staff a really good raise," he said.

"Oh, no, that's Destiny Moultrie," Jamie said with a sigh as the woman climbed from her car. Destiny had not picked a good time to show up. "She's going to be our new Divine Love Goddess Advisor."

Max frowned. "Come again?"

"I'll explain later."

Destiny raced around to the passenger door as Jamie climbed out. The woman was wearing her bathrobe and bedroom slippers. "Oh, thank God I found you," she cried. "I drove by your house, but you weren't home. I figured I'd check here just in case."

Jamie could see the woman was upset about something. "Um, Destiny, this is my partner, Max Holt."

Jamie didn't miss the knowing look in Destiny's eyes as she looked his way. "It's about time you showed up," she said. Max arched both brows in question, but Destiny turned to Jamie and grasped her hands tightly. Jamie was surprised to find them icy cold.

"I had a vision." Destiny glanced to her side. "Ronnie, get lost, this is important."

Jamie winced inwardly. Just what Max needed to hear, she thought.

"The name is Max Holt, not Ronnie," Max told her.

"Destiny isn't talking to you," Jamie quickly said. "Ronnie is from the spirit world."

"Actually, he's between worlds," Destiny said. "He doesn't know he's dead, so he follows me everywhere."

Max simply nodded as though it made complete sense. "Okay."

"I've been eating garlic pickles all day," Destiny told Jamie.

Which explained her breath, Jamie thought.

"I know it sounds crazy, but when I eat garlic pickles I dream a lot." She looked from Jamie to Max. "Sometimes I have waking dreams or visions where I see things."

"Destiny claims she's psychic," Jamie told Max. She wasn't sure what kind of reaction she expected, but she was surprised when Max merely smiled politely.

"Nice to meet you, Destiny."

"Same here." Once again, she turned to Jamie. "Anyway, I awoke about an hour ago, and—" She paused and shuddered. "I saw this woman. Her skull was crushed."

"You're right, Destiny," Jamie said. "A woman *was* found dead this morning. Remember, we discussed it."

"No, Jamie. You don't understand. I'm talking about another woman. A second victim," she added. "It hasn't happened yet."

FIVE

Jamie felt a sense of fear, a feeling of dread wash over her. Then she reminded herself she didn't believe in psychics. Yes, but Destiny had told her things, things that couldn't be explained. She suddenly realized Destiny was shivering, despite the warm night. "How do you know these women are not one and the same?" Jamie challenged.

Destiny sneezed. "I just do. The second woman will put up a fight. There will be scratches on the killer's arms."

"Did you see the victim's face or the face of the killer in your vision?" Max asked, surprising Jamie.

"Believe me, I tried."

"This sounds a little far-fetched," Jamie said, no longer knowing what to think about the woman's predictions.

"It's true," Destiny said.

Max looked thoughtful but remained silent.

Jamie wanted to send Destiny on her way, but the woman appeared too upset to drive. "Destiny, we need to get you inside," she said. "You don't look so good."

Max followed them. Jamie noticed he didn't seem a bit skeptical when Destiny announced that Ronnie was right behind her. Jamie turned and eyed Destiny suspiciously. "If you're so certain this murder is going to take place, why can't you see the killer?"

Destiny paused and looked at her. "I'm blocked, okay? Everything is murky. I don't know where or when the murder is going to take place, but one thing is for sure—" She suddenly sneezed. "It's only a matter of time."

It wasn't until Jamie had gotten Destiny inside and sat her down in the small kitchen with a fresh cup of coffee that she stopped shivering. "All I keep seeing is this poor woman," she said. "Fighting for her life," she added, followed by another sneeze.

Jamie grabbed several tissues and handed them to her.

Max leaned in the doorway listening. Jamie gave him a cup of coffee and he quietly thanked her, all the while watching Destiny closely, as though trying to make up his mind about something. Jamie wondered if he was trying to decide whether Destiny was the real thing, and she couldn't help feeling surprised. Did Max actually believe what she was saying? Of all the people in the world, Max Holt struck her as the last person on earth who would believe in psychics.

Jamie joined Destiny at the table. She had her eyes closed. "What are you doing?" Jamie asked.

"Looking for a face," Destiny said. "All I'm getting is a view of her, the victim, from her shoulders down. Struggling and fighting for her life."

"Is she wearing something unusual?" Max asked. "Maybe something with a monogram on it?"

Jamie glanced up quickly. Was Max merely trying to humor her?

"I'm not getting anything." A fat tear rolled from Destiny's left eye and slid down her cheek. "There's no use trying to force it. It either comes to me or it doesn't."

"What about the garlic pickles?" Jamie asked.

Destiny shrugged. "That's something my grandmother used to do. It sometimes works, but not always."

Jamie tried to think, tried to open herself up to what she was hearing. What she knew about psychic phenomena was next to nothing. But she was certain Destiny believed somebody was about to die.

Max put down his coffee cup. "Jamie, may I have a word with you?"

Jamie looked at Destiny.

"I'm okay. Besides, I need a minute to myself."

Max and Jamie didn't speak until they'd reached her office and closed the door. "Max, I know all this sounds and looks strange, but—"

"Not really."

Jamie couldn't hide her astonishment. "Are you saying you believe in this sort of thing?"

"I don't disbelieve. I think there are some things in this world that can't be explained. And I believe the woman saw something. She's obviously hysterical."

"She spooks me, Max. I mean, she shows up in my parking lot in her bathrobe with stories of visions and murder and some guy named Ronnie from the spirit world. You don't think that's strange?"

"Have any of her predictions come true?"

Jamie told him about Destiny's vision concerning Lamar. "I want to believe her, but she has a ghost following her around, for Pete's sake. I don't know whether to take her seriously or call a doctor."

Max put his hand on Jamie's shoulder. "Listen, I'm not saying she's the real thing, but I think she bears listening to. That doesn't mean I'm not going to put Muffin on the case. I think we should use every possible means to catch the killer before he strikes again. If what Destiny says is true," he added.

"I'm scared, Max," Jamie said. "I honestly can't bear the thought of my column being responsible for Luanne Ritter's death. I don't care if everybody in this town *did* hate her; she was still a human being. And the thought of somebody else getting killed is more than I can handle."

Max took her in his arms. "Then we'd better get to work."

Jamie unlocked the file drawer in her office and pulled it out. She found what she was looking for right away. She joined Max and Destiny.

"Max and I thought maybe you could look through some of these ads and see if you get a feel for them."

Destiny looked doubtful. "I've never been real good at psychometrics, but I'll give it a try."

Max slid forward in his chair. "Jamie, before you get started, I'd like for you to make a copy of the ads so I can fax them to Muffin."

"Sure, Max. It won't take but a couple of minutes. Please help yourself to more coffee if you like. Also, there are soft drinks in the refrigerator and maybe a couple of stale doughnuts." Jamie hurried into the reception area where the copy machine and fax were situated along one wall near Vera's desk. She felt like she had stepped into a bad science fiction movie.

When she returned, she found Max and Destiny talking softly. He seemed genuinely interested in what she was saying. "Here are the copies." Jamie handed them to Max, and showed him to the fax machine. "Call me if you need me."

He nodded and went to work.

Finally, Jamie joined Destiny on the sofa. "Okay, here's what we've got."

"There's only one problem, Jamie," Destiny said.

"Even though I've never been really good at this sort of thing, it works better if the object is handled by the original person only."

Jamie gave her a blank look. "Come again?"

"In this case, the actual author of the ad." She reached for one of the sheets of paper. "The way psychometrics works is that you feel the energy from the person who touched the object."

Jamie tried to hide her skepticism. "You're saying since I was the last one who touched these ads they will hold my energy?"

Destiny nodded. "At least some of it. What we can do is look at the ads and see if anything stands out. Maybe something will come to me. It might help later in a vision, who knows?"

Max returned and reclaimed his seat. "Okay, I faxed the info to Muffin, and she's already at work on it."

"I'm afraid we're not having much luck," Destiny said. Jamie nodded in agreement. "We're just looking through the ads, seeing if anything sounds unusual or, um, ominous. For example, the heading on this ad reads 'Looking for discreet relationship. Must be open to new experiences.'"

"You're right, that's scary," Max said.

Jamie realized he was teasing her. "We don't know what it means," she said. "'Open to new experiences' could mean he's into kinky stuff."

Destiny pondered it and finally shrugged. "Or maybe he just likes sailing or horseback riding," she said. "That could be one way of looking at new experiences."

"But why would he insist on discretion?" Jamie asked. "Doesn't that sound a little paranoid?"

Max shrugged. "It could mean he doesn't want people to know he found a date through a personals ad. That doesn't mean we don't check him out, though."

"How many ads do you have there?" Destiny asked.

"Only seven, since I just copied the ones from the men. I have all their addresses and phone numbers. The way it works is, they pay for the ad, which includes a couple of dollars extra for postage, and when I get a reply I forward it to them. It's a new feature, of course, and I'm hoping it'll catch on. As least I was until I heard about Luanne Ritter's murder."

"Did you happen to notice any return addresses from those who responded to the ads?" Max asked.

"There weren't any," Jamie told him. "They obviously wanted to keep it confidential. Small town and all," she added.

"Take a look at this ad," Max said after a minute.

Jamie shuffled through the pages. "Yeah, I remember that one."

Destiny leaned forward and read, "'Till Death Do Us Part.'"

"Did you not think that sounded strange when you read it?" Max asked.

Jamie shook her head. "No. It could simply mean this person is looking for a lifetime partner, which is what a couple of the ads say. Now that someone has been killed it sounds pretty menacing, and we definitely need to check it out."

"Don't you have anyone who sounds like a guy I'd want to meet?" Destiny asked, surprising them both. "Hey, I'm new in town; I wouldn't mind meeting a nice guy. He'd have to be open-minded, of course."

Jamie almost welcomed the change of subject. "My editor Mike Henderson has a crush on you."

"Oh, yeah?"

"He's a little young."

"Young is nice. Two of my husbands were old and died on me. It's such a hassle planning a funeral."

Max cleared his throat. "I believe we have work to do, ladies," he said.

Jamie nodded. "Okay, this ad reads, 'Don't Pass Me By,' and another one, 'Walking on Sunshine.'" She suddenly chuckled. "Oh, listen to this. 'Offer Good for a Limited Time.'"

Even Max chuckled at that one.

"They all seem to be searching for the same thing," Jamie said. "A woman looking for a good time who might be interested in a long-term relationship." A sheet of paper fell to the floor. "Oh, I almost missed one. Listen to this. It reads, 'Deeper Than the Night.'"

"That sounds nice," Destiny said.

"Yeah, listen to his ad. He says, 'No matter what path you choose, keep it simple, but throw your heart into it.'"

Destiny sighed. "Wow, that's deep." She glanced to an empty space in the room. "Oh, stop acting jealous, Ronnie. Remember, you're dead? It's not like I can go bowling or coon hunting with you." She rolled her eyes at Jamie. "That's Ronnie's idea of a good time, if you can believe it. At least the last guy that attached himself to me had a little class. He was an English professor."

Jamie just stared at her.

"How old is this guy who claimed to be deeper than the night?" Destiny asked.

"Thirty-five and never been married."

"Which means he doesn't have children," Destiny said. "Believe me, I've had my share of stepchildren. I should take the ad home and put it beneath my pillow tonight. Maybe something will come to me. You should give me his name and address. I could drive by his house; see if I get any vibes."

"These are confidential."

"You didn't mind letting me hold them a few minutes ago," Destiny objected.

"That was different. I was seeking your, um, professional opinion. If you want to meet this guy, you'll have to go through the proper channels like everybody else. Only, I'd hold off until we look into the murder."

Max checked his wristwatch. "It's after midnight. We need to go home and get a good night's sleep. By morning, Muffin will have a lot of the information I requested, and we can start from there."

They left the building a few minutes later, once Jamie had locked up. Destiny pulled away in her Mercedes as Max helped Jamie into the passenger's side of his car. He joined her in the front seat a moment later.

"Max, we need to talk about Destiny," Jamie said. "I know she sounds convincing, but surely you don't believe in the supernatural."

"I simply try to keep an open mind," he said. "I've seen and heard of instances where psychics have taken investigators right to the crime scene. In fact, I was personally involved in one of those instances."

Jamie looked at him. "You were involved with a psychic?"

"The son of a close friend of mine was kidnapped for ransom five years ago. A woman just appeared at his front door with all the information the police needed to find the boy. They still call on her from time to time."

Jamie felt the goose pimples rise on her arms. "But what about this Ronnie, this dead spirit that Destiny claims follows her everywhere?"

Max grinned. "Yeah, that's pretty strange, but from what I've read, and this is only what I've read, some people get lost between worlds when they die suddenly or violently because they're confused and don't know they should go to the light."

"The light?" Jamie shook her head. "Max, do you know how that sounds?"

He laughed. "Yeah, I know, but there have been cases reported. Some priests believe in it. Why do you suppose exorcisms are performed? It's believed that a dead spirit can attach itself to a live human. I read all this stuff when I was a kid. I was really fascinated with that sort of thing."

"You're really scaring me now." Jamie said shuddering. "I don't think I want to talk about it anymore."

"I know it all sounds far-fetched like you said, but I believe the woman in your office tonight saw something that frightened her. I don't think she was faking it."

"I've lived in a small town too long," Jamie said. "I believe in what I can see. Could we change the subject?"

"Yeah." Max looked at the dashboard. "Muffin, are you there?" he asked.

"Yes, and I've been listening to every word. I'm with Jamie. This whole thing gives me the creeps."

"Then let's talk facts. You got anything yet?"

"Do you know what time it is?"

"I know it's late, but—"

"So, go to your hotel and get a good night's sleep. I should have something for you in the morning."

Jamie was glad they were headed in a different direction. That's exactly what she wanted to hear: facts. "You're not staying at Frankie and Dee Dee's?" she asked.

Max shook his head. "I need a place to work while I'm in town, and I wouldn't be able to think straight with Frankie and his wrestling buddies around. Besides, I'm not into arm wrestling."

"Where are you staying?"

Max shrugged. "Where am I staying, Muffin?"

"You have reservations at the Carteret Street Bed and Breakfast."

"It's really nice," Jamie said. "Probably not as nice

as you're accustomed to," she added, suspecting Max had stayed in some of the best hotels in the world. "But you should be comfortable there."

"You have a suite on the first floor," Muffin said. "It has a sitting room, courtyard, and private entrance on the east side. Guaranteed late arrival; you'll find a key waiting for you beneath the doormat."

Max looked at Jamie. "You should stay with me tonight."

"Uh-oh, here it comes," Muffin said. "I'm outta here."

"I can't stay with you," Jamie replied. "I know the owners. I went to school with their daughter. I wouldn't feel right."

"I have my own private entrance, remember?"

It sounded so tempting. And Jamie hated to waste the body suit she'd spent forty bucks on. And in all honesty, she wasn't sure she wanted to stay by herself after hearing about dead spirits and exorcisms. But she had a dog to care for.

"You're going to have to show me how to get to the place anyway," he said. "I'll get lost."

Jamie looked at him. "Oh, puh-lease. You could find your way to Mars in this car, Max."

"Yeah, but—"

"Why don't you ask Muffin for directions to the Carteret Street Bed and Breakfast?"

"Because she doesn't have beautiful blue eyes like you." He stopped at a red light. "C'mon, Swifty, what d'you say?"

She sighed. "Oh, Max—"

"You're doing it again, Jamie. You're thinking too much. You're doing the 'what-if' thing."

She knew he was right. It was time she stopped doing so much thinking and just enjoyed being with Max because, well, in all honesty, she wanted him as much as he wanted her. And it wasn't like she had to stay all night. She could go home later and let Fleas out. Later, after she got over her case of the heebie-jeebies.

"Turn left at the light."

SIX

Carteret Street Bed and Breakfast was a massive, two-story Colonial with verandas on both floors. Oversize rocking chairs and baskets of ferns gave it a welcoming look. Once Max had parked his car and grabbed a bag from the trunk, Jamie pointed him toward a narrow, flower-laden path where old-fashioned street lamps lit the way. They found themselves standing at the door to his room. Sure enough, a key had been placed beneath the doormat. He unlocked the door, opened it, and motioned for Jamie to go through first.

Fresh daisies sat on a highly polished cherry coffee table. The rust-and cream-colored furniture was comfortable looking while maintaining a look of simple elegance. The ornate crown moldings and woodwork were a deep mahogany, and repeated in the oversize fireplace. A tasteful rug covered heart-pine floors. Max opened a set of French doors and found a sink, small refrigerator, and microwave.

"Nice," he said. "Where's the bedroom?"

Jamie's stomach dipped to her toes. "Through that door."

He took her hand in his and led her in that direction. An old four-poster rice bed and matching highboy, both in cherry, greeted them. The comforter was pure linen, as were the curtains. Jamie had visited the bed-and-breakfast several years ago when it had been redecorated, and she had praised it in an article. She was glad Mrs. Hobbs had given Max the nicest suite.

The Hobbses were an older couple—short and stout as teacups, as Vera liked to say, but Mrs. Hobbs was worse than Vera when it came to gossip. Vera did most of her gossiping on the church lawn after Sunday services; Myrna Hobbs preferred holding court at the local Piggly Wiggly grocery store, where she could often be found picking up food items for her guests. Vera claimed Myrna exaggerated, that a soul couldn't believe a word that came out of the woman's mouth. Vera believed in sticking to the facts.

Max reached for Jamie.

"I, um, thought maybe you'd like to see the garden first," she said quickly. "It's really very nice. Mrs. Hobbs hired a man who designed a garden at one of the old plantations in Charleston."

Max suddenly smiled. "You're nervous, aren't you, Swifty? You're remembering last time. I have to tell you, you're all I've thought about the past few weeks."

She smiled. "Really? Gee, I wish I'd known." Jamie hated to bring up the fact he hadn't contacted her in the three weeks since that time, but she figured it needed saying. It had to be the wine talking. She'd had three glasses at Frankie and Dee Dee's, which was well over her quota.

"I was out of the country most of that time. I'm not real good at sending postcards." When she didn't say anything, he went on. "I guess I could do better." He sighed and raked his hands through his hair. "Do you still want to look at that garden?"

Jamie opened the French doors leading from the bedroom. Taking Max's hand in hers, she led him down a brick walkway and across a small footbridge that covered a pond. Once again, old-fashioned street lamps lighted the way. Jamie was glad Mrs. Hobbs had left them burning for Max's arrival.

"The pond actually has goldfish in it," Jamie said. "Huge ones."

Max studied his surroundings with only a hint of interest. "So, can you tell me the names of these plants?"

"Sure." Jamie glanced around. "That tree is a hemlock. And the plants growing beneath it are hosta plants. Or plantain lilies as they're sometimes called," she added. "They're shade plants." She pointed. "And that's caladium, and growing next to it is ostrich fern." She caught sight of Max's grin. "What?"

"How do you know this?"

"Just because I never have time to mow my lawn or weed my flower beds doesn't mean I don't know about plants. I planted a whole bunch of daylilies around the pickup truck in the backyard to try to make it look more attractive."

"Did it work?"

"No. But you know how attached Fleas is to that truck."

"Does he sleep in it?"

"Are you kidding? He has this giant pillow that I bought for him so he can sleep on the floor in my bedroom, but when I wake up each morning I find him sprawled across the foot of my bed."

"That's going to present a real problem for us."

Jamie's stomach fluttered. "I think he's become somewhat spoiled since you last saw him," she said, changing the subject.

Max stroked her arm. "I'd like to go inside and spoil you."

More fluttering. "Okay, but you didn't get to see the entire garden."

This time, Max captured her hand and led her

through the French doors into the bedroom. A breeze blew in from the doorway, bringing with it the scent of magnolia. Moonlight dappled the room. Max pulled Jamie into his arms and kissed her.

Jamie leaned against him, delighting in the solid planes of his body and his scent. He offered more than a mere distraction from spending part of the evening talking about bogeymen, and she had been waiting for this moment all evening. No, she had been waiting much longer than that. Common sense had told her it was sheer folly, but her heart refused to listen. She returned Max's kisses with a hunger that surprised even her.

Max cupped her hips in his hands, pressing her flat against him so there was no doubt that he was as eager for her as she was for him. He slid his fingers through her hair, anchoring her head between his palms as he kissed her more deeply. Jamie clung to the jacket of his tux.

She slipped her arms around his neck and tilted her head back, parting her lips beneath his so his tongue could explore the inside of her mouth. Max's hands moved to her breasts, warming them through the clothes she wore.

"I want you, Jamie," he whispered. "I have since the first time I saw you."

Damned if she didn't want him too. She just wasn't sure she could get him out of that tux quickly enough. "I need to use the powder room first," she said.

He gazed down at her, a promise in his eyes.

Jamie slipped from his arms and stepped inside the bathroom, purse in hand. An old claw-foot bathtub dominated the room. The mahogany woodwork had been softened with beige linen wallpaper and ivory towels. Still a bit rattled, Jamie checked behind the shower curtain, and then told herself she was being silly. From the next room, she heard soft music and realized Max had turned on a radio. She swayed to the sound as she reached for the zipper of her dress, slid it down and shrugged out of it. She gazed at her flushed face in the mirror, noted the worry lines on either side of her mouth.

She wished she weren't so edgy.

She reached into her purse for the minibottle of Kahlúa that she had stuffed into her pocketbook before leaving the house that evening. Dee Dee had given it to her, as well as a raw-silk jacket, when she and Beenie had returned from a shopping trip in New York. Jamie had suspected things might turn romantic with Max before the evening was over, and she'd hoped the Kahlúa would settle her nerves. She opened the small bottle and took a sip. What if she was making a mistake? What if she fell head over heels in love with Max, knowing how reluctant he was to make a long-term commitment? What if? Oh, the hell with it, she thought. She drained the small bottle.

Bravery had never tasted so good. She could feel her shoulder muscles relaxing, and the knots loosening in her stomach.

It was about time she took a few chances in life.

Max undid the knot of his bow tie and walked into the sitting room. He opened the small refrigerator and reached inside for a container of bottled water. He turned and started for the bedroom when a light tap at the door stopped him. He unlocked it and opened it, finding a squat, gray-haired woman on the other side. She held a tray of food.

"I hope I'm not disturbing you, Mr. Holt," she said quickly, "I know it's terribly late—I've been up watching old black-and-white movies, and I heard you come in and thought you might enjoy a light snack from the kitchen."

"You must be Mrs. Hobbs," Max said, backing away so the woman could enter.

"Yes, but you can call me Myrna." She set the tray on the coffee table. "I trust you've found everything you needed."

"Everything is fine."

"I hope you like croissants. I also brought several cheeses and grapes. Fruit and cheese always go together so well, don't you think?"

"You wouldn't happen to have a bottle of champagne handy, would you?" Max asked.

Mrs. Hobbs sniffed. "I don't keep alcoholic beverages on the premises, Mr. Holt. I guess it comes from my strict Baptist upbringing, but I've always been a teetotaler. My husband accuses me of being far too prim and proper, but I'm afraid it's a little late in life for me to change."

"I understand, Myrna, and I respect your beliefs. Thank you for bringing me the snack." The woman didn't seem to take the hint.

"Tell me, Mr. Holt," Myrna said, her eyes bright with curiosity. "What's it like being a big-time celebrity with all that money?"

Max laughed and shook his head. It didn't look like Myrna was in a hurry to leave.

Jamie had freshened her makeup and sprayed perfume in places she was certain would shock Vera's church friends. She fluffed her hair, hoping it gave her a wild, untamed look.

She turned for the door, felt her head swim. She was loose as a goose. Maybe she shouldn't have drunk the whole ounce of Kahlúa, especially since she'd had more than her share of wine at Frankie and Dee Dee's party. Not only that, she'd barely touched her food.

Oh, well, it was too late to worry about it now. Besides, she was single and over twenty-one, and if she wanted to act a little wild and crazy every now and then, so be it. Max accused her of thinking too much, of being too predictable.

Let him get a look at the new Jamie Swift.

The music was coming from the alarm-clock radio on the bedside table; Johnny Mathis singing "Chances Are." The bed was empty. Jamie wondered why Max wasn't already naked and in it. Maybe he'd sensed just how nervous she was and wanted to take his time. She turned for the short hall leading to the sitting room, almost tripping over her own two feet.

Okay, so she was a little tipsy.

"'Chances are,'" she sang off-key as she started down the hall, failing miserably at her attempt to walk straight. Finally, she called out. "Okay, here I am, ready and willing." She stepped inside the sitting room, did a little dance routine, and then froze when she found Max standing at the door with Myrna Hobbs.

The woman looked Jamie's way, and her mouth formed a gigantic O.

"Jamie, I'm sorry you're so embarrassed," Max said, once he'd packed her inside his car and pulled away from Carteret Street Bed and Breakfast.

"I'll get over it."

Max shook his head. "I can't believe Myrna Hobbs kicked me out of my room."

Jamie wasn't surprised. "Oh, that's nothing. Myrna will beat it to the Piggly Wiggly the minute they open tomorrow. By noon, everyone in town will know what happened." She did a massive eye roll. "Did you hear what that woman called me, Max? She called me a drunken floozy."

"Yeah, well, I think I got it across to her that I didn't appreciate it."

Jamie had to admit it was true. Max had called Myrna Hobbs on the carpet for that one, which was why the woman had asked him to leave the premises. "Thank you for defending me."

He grinned. "I'll have to admit, you *did* sort of look like a drunken floozy, but I liked it. You looked cute."

Jamie groaned.

"Hey, I think it's great you've loosened up, Swifty." He gave a low whistle. "And that thing you're wearing under your dress," he added. "Where can I buy you ten more just like it?"

So he'd liked the body suit. At least one good thing had come of the evening.

A voice sounded from the dashboard. "Excuse me? What are we up to *now*?"

Jamie put her finger to her lips in an obvious attempt to stop Max from telling Muffin what had just occurred. He smiled and turned down the volume switch. "Wait a minute. You're worried about what my computer will think of you?"

"Muffin is not just *any* computer," she whispered.

Max turned up the switch.

"Hello?" Muffin called out. "Is anyone home?"

"I'm here," Max said.

"Why'd you hit the volume switch?"

"None of your business," he said, grinning.

Silence. Finally, "Don't piss me off, Max. You need me. I make you look good."

"Yeah, yeah, yeah. I need the name of another hotel. Something with a work station so I can go online. You know the routine."

"What was wrong with the last one?" Muffin asked.

"Too stuffy. See what you can find."

Jamie was only vaguely aware of the conversation between the two. She didn't feel well, her stomach was churning and her head hurt, no doubt from the alcohol she'd consumed. She was glad when Max turned into her driveway. She waited until the safety bar rose before reaching for the doorknob. "Well, I'd invite you in, but I have to go throw up."

"Rule number one: never mix your alcohol."

"Jeez, I could have used that information earlier."

Fleas nudged Jamie awake the next morning at five A.M. She rubbed her eyes and looked at him. "Gee, thanks for rescuing me from the possibility of sleeping late on a Saturday." Since becoming housemates with the bloodhound, she rarely slept until the alarm clock sounded during the workweek, and she never slept late on weekends.

"This must be what it's like to have kids," she grumbled, knowing Fleas probably had to go to the bathroom. After that he would want something to eat. She sighed.

The doorbell rang. Max, no doubt. The man was like a vampire. He could live on four hours' sleep. She stumbled from the bed and into the living room. Her head hurt, and her eyes felt gritty. She checked the peephole, and sure enough, Max stood on the other side.

She opened the door. How could he look that good in the morning? "What?"

"How's your head?"

She noted the amused look. "I think a couple of aspirin might help. Is that why you stopped by?"

"I know you don't like getting up before seven," he said. "That's why I brought coffee and doughnuts. To sort of soften the blow."

"Chocolate doughnuts?"

"Chocolate mocha cream."

Damn the man for knowing her every weakness. She opened the door. He stepped inside and followed her into the kitchen, staring at her wrinkled sleep shirt. "I was kind of hoping you'd still be wearing that black thing this morning," he said, setting down her coffee and the folder he carried under one arm.

Jamie reached for the aspirin bottle beside her sink. She popped two in her mouth and followed it with a sip of water. "I burned it," she said.

"God, please, no."

"Okay, I'm *thinking* about burning it."

"Don't do it, Jamie. Burn that shirt instead."

She took a sip of her coffee. Naturally, Max knew just how she liked it. He grinned at Fleas and the two reacquainted themselves, Max giving the animal a hearty rub on the head. "Have you taught him any tricks yet?" he asked Jamie.

She looked into the bag of doughnuts and pulled one out. Fleas licked his chops. "Yeah, he's learned to wait until I leave the house before getting on my sofa so he doesn't get yelled at."

"Good dog." Max offered the dog a sympathetic look. "Sorry to hear she had your gonads cut off, guy. You're looking a little depressed."

"Speaking of his unmentionables, he needs to go out." Jamie unlocked the back door, opened it, and Fleas ambled outside as though he had all the time in the world. "Don't pee on my rosebush," she said, as he hiked his leg on a small bush of tiny yellow tea roses.

Max chuckled. "Yeah, you've trained him real well."

Jamie carried her coffee and doughnut to the kitchen table and sat down. "Not that I'm not thrilled to see you, Max, but is there a specific reason you felt you had to visit the minute the sun came up?"

He grabbed his folder and joined her. "Yeah, Muffin has all kinds of information for us. I figured you'd be interested."

"I'm all ears," she mumbled.

"Remember the ad that read 'Till Death Do Us Part'?"

"Yeah, that was spooky," Jamie said.

"He's a minister who performs a lot of marriage ceremonies. He obviously doesn't believe in divorce."

Jamie glanced up quickly. "A minister? Lamar said someone called Luanne saying he was a man of God. Max, we could be on to something."

"That's why I told Muffin to dig deeper."

"Anything else?"

"All the men are either single or divorced. We've got an auto mechanic, a dentist, a chef, and—" He paused and chuckled. "Remember the ad that read 'Offer Good for a Limited Time'?"

"Yeah."

"He's a car salesman."

Jamie laughed. She had finished her doughnut and was debating having a second, but she wouldn't rush. She didn't want Max to think she lacked discipline. She sipped her coffee, counted to ten.

"Just get the doughnut and be done with it," he said, as though reading her mind. "I bought extra."

Jamie got up, grabbed the bag and carried it to the table. "I don't normally eat more than one, but—"

"Save it, Swifty. This is me you're talking to. I've seen you go through a dozen doughnuts in two days flat."

She frowned at Max but took a bite from the second doughnut nevertheless. "I was under a lot of stress at the time. So the guys you mentioned seemed to check out okay?"

"Yeah. Their ages vary, but most of them just want to meet someone who likes to go to a movie or dine out, that sort of thing."

"Um, what about the guy Destiny and I thought was so cool. You know, the ad that read 'Deeper Than the Night'?"

"I was waiting for you to ask about him. What do you know about Samuel Alister Hunter, or Sam Hunter as he's called?"

Jamie arched both brows. "I didn't recognize the name until just now, but then I'm not used to seeing his full name. And I can't tell you much about him except that he was a hunk in high school. Unfortunately, I was in middle school at the time so I didn't stand a chance. He went off to college, and eventually went to work on Wall Street. I haven't seen him since. I had no idea he'd returned to Beaumont."

"He just moved back. He's semiretired after making his money in the stock market, but he's looking to buy land which he plans to develop."

"No kidding? I wonder if he's still a hunk."

"Control yourself, Swifty. You're hot for me, remember?"

"I should probably try to set up a date with him," she said. "Just in case he's the murderer," she added.

"You're a brave and admirable woman," Max said, "to put yourself in harm's way in order to protect others."

"That's me, Max, brave and admirable. Willing to risk life and limb for the safety of others."

Max leaned back in his chair and regarded her with a half-smile. "You didn't sound so brave last night when we were discussing the supernatural."

"I hope we're not going to get on that subject again," Jamie said.

Fleas scratched at the back door. Jamie let him in, gave him a doughnut and poured him a bowl of milk.

"That's the most ridiculous thing I've ever seen in my life," Max said. "He should be eating meat."

"He has a cheeseburger every day for lunch." Jamie put on a fresh pot of coffee, hoping it would ease her throbbing head. She leaned against the cabinet.

"Back to the subject of Sam Hunter," Max said. "We don't really know much about the guy, and he returned to Beaumont three days before running his ad."

"Why would a guy with his looks be interested in someone like Luanne Ritter?" Jamie pondered aloud.

"Maybe he didn't know her."

"That's hard to believe, everybody knew Luanne."

"What did she look like?"

"She was so-so," Jamie said, trying to think of a nice way to describe the woman.

"I've got all the addresses, information, everything. We need to check these people out. You're going to have to arrange a date with them. Quickly," he added.

"I can't date all these men that fast," Jamie said.

"You're only going to contact the ones who allowed their phone numbers to be printed," Max said. "Unless you want to tell them that you were processing their ads at the newspaper office and liked what you saw. Maybe we can enlist Destiny. She can contact half of them. Besides, she already knows what's going on."

"That's a great idea," Jamie said, sarcasm slipping into her voice. "Ronnie can chaperone."

"Yeah, well, we'll have to talk to her about bringing Ronnie. We don't want to spook these guys. But I think between the two of you, we'll be able to get the job done quicker. I'll be close by, of course."

"We're not going to be able to find out who the murderer is in one date," Jamie said.

"You're right. We're going to have to watch them. If I have to call in some of my people, I will."

"We don't have a minute to waste, Max. We need to get to work on this immediately."

He stood, crossed the distance between them, and pulled Jamie against him. "It's still early. We could toss out that shirt."

Jamie's stomach fluttered in response. He had a point there. It wasn't even eight o'clock. Murderers usually waited until after dark to strike. She was about to respond when the doorbell rang several times.

"So much for that idea," Max said, releasing her with a sigh.

Jamie hurried into the living room and peered through the peephole. "Oh, damn. It's Vera," she called out to Max. "She's probably already heard the news. Myrna works fast."

SEVEN

Jamie reached for the doorknob and opened it. "Good morning, Vera. Max and I were just having coffee and doughnuts. Won't you join us?"

The woman stepped through the front door. "I just ran into Myrna Hobbs at the Piggly Wiggly. Were you really drunk and doing the hootchy-kootchy in one of her suites last night?"

"Aw, Jamie was just having a little fun," Max said, coming up behind her. "Mrs. Hobbs overreacted."

"Yeah, I was just having a little fun," Jamie echoed.

"At least you're being honest with me," Vera told her, "which is a good thing. I couldn't bear the thought of your being a slut *and* a liar."

Jamie rolled her eyes. "I'm not a slut. There aren't enough eligible men in this town for me to be a slut, even if I wanted to."

Vera looked at Jamie. "Well, for your information, I slapped Myrna's face and told her she'd better never make another derogatory comment about you as long as she lived."

"Good for you," Max said.

"You actually slapped her?" Jamie asked. "In the Piggly Wiggly?"

"Yeah, the security guard threw me out of the store, threatened to have me arrested if I didn't leave. I can't afford to go to the slammer because I have to teach Sunday school for Agnes Aimsley tomorrow. She's still in shock after seeing all those unmentionables hanging in the window of Sinful Delights." Vera had to pause to suck in a deep breath.

"Myrna Hobbs will think twice before she decides to pull me over in frozen foods and start talking trash about you. I told her it was okay if I called you a slut, but she'd better keep her fat mouth shut."

"Thank you for defending me," Jamie said. "I think."

Vera shrugged as if it were no big deal. "Look, I know you're all grown-up, but if you insist on sleeping around, you're going to have to be discreet. I hope you're on the pill and practicing safe sex. I probably should have had this talk with you long before now. I probably shouldn't have fed you all those brownies."

Max regarded Jamie. "You never mentioned you were promiscuous."

Jamie pressed the ball of her hand against her forehead. "Vera, could we talk about this later? I have a small headache."

"She's hungover," Max said. "She mixed wine with Kahlúa."

"Yeah, Myrna mentioned you had an alcohol problem," Vera said. "You might want to get help with that."

Fleas came up beside Jamie and nuzzled her leg as though he sensed she was in need of his support. Jamie sighed. "Would you guys give me a break? I have less sex than this dog, and he's been neutered. And I'm *not* an alcoholic."

"She's in denial," Max said, obviously enjoying the whole thing.

Vera turned to him. "Now that we've got that settled, I want you to come outside and look at this Ferrari I'm test-driving. I thought maybe you'd take a ride with me, see what you think."

Max shrugged. "Sure."

"You're test-driving a Ferrari?" Jamie said incredulously. "Why?"

"Because I'm thinking of buying it. I can buy a Ferrari if I want to."

Jamie had just realized Vera was wearing Capri pants. Vera, who never wore anything other than dresses. "Do you have any idea how much they cost?"

"Yeah, but it's ten years old, and the guy is going to cut me a deal. I'm thinking I need something a little sporty. I'm thinking I need to reinvent myself. I've signed up for a class on line dancing. I might meet someone. All the men at church are on their last legs." Vera started out the door, then paused and glanced over her shoulder at Jamie. "You might want to change into something else. That shirt you're wearing isn't very flattering."

By the time Max returned, Jamie had showered and changed into shorts and a cotton T-shirt. She wore only a hint of makeup, and had pulled her wet hair into a ponytail. Luckily, her headache had dulled.

Max paused when he saw her. "Damned if you don't have the best set of legs I've ever seen on a woman. No wonder you have such a reputation with men."

Jamie gave him one of her looks. "Tell me Vera isn't really going to buy a Ferrari," she said.

"I think I convinced her not to. The mileage was too high, and it's kind of beat-up. I told her I could probably find her a good deal on a car if she'd give me a few days, but I think she's having a good time looking. Now, why don't we get to work?"

"Okay, I'll call Destiny and see if she can help," Jamie said, although she wasn't thrilled at the prospect.

Destiny arrived an hour later. "Here are the ground rules," Max said, addressing both women. "You meet the guy in public, and you carry a cell phone that I will provide for each of you, complete with a GPA."

"What the heck is a GPA?" Destiny asked.

Jamie answered. "It's a device that lets Max know where we are at all times."

"You two have done this sort of thing before, haven't you?" Destiny asked.

Jamie nodded. "Yeah, and we always get the bad guy in the end." She paused. "Um, Destiny, Max and I didn't want to bring this up, but it might be distracting if you start talking to Ronnie on your, um, dates."

Destiny turned to the empty chair beside her. "Did you hear that, Ronnie? We're trying to find a killer. You're going to have to keep your mouth shut." She paused. Finally, she turned to Max and Jamie. "He promises to cooperate if I'll hang out with him at the bowling alley afterward. That's Ronnie's idea of a good time." She rolled her eyes.

"Okay," Max said. "Muffin, my assistant, was able to get much of the information we need. The guy with the 'Till Death Do Us Part' ad is a minister. We just found out he does a lot of marriage counseling, even has a little wedding chapel and provides everything a couple needs for the auspicious occasion, right down to the flowers and catering. He's very antidivorce and insists on counseling couples for an extended period of time before he'll agree to marry them. He accepts fairly large donations for the sessions, and the use of his chapel. I think Jamie and I should check him out just in case. We could pose as an engaged couple."

"That'll never work," Jamie said. "He'll see right through us."

"Not if you act like a real fiancée," Max said. "You're going to have to be nice to me, hold my hand, and simper at me a lot. That's what engaged couples do. It isn't until after the marriage that they learn to dislike each other."

Jamie just looked at him. Leave it to Max to make marriage sound like a prison term.

"Aw, come on, Swifty, it'll be fun," Max said, as though he hadn't realized he'd made a blunder. He reached for a cell phone in his pocket and punched a button. "Muffin, why don't you see if the Reverend Heyward can schedule us after lunch," he said. "In the meantime, Jamie and I are going to check out one Larry Johnson, author of 'Offer Good for a Limited Time.'"

"I'm on it," Muffin said. "What else?"

"Just hold tight." Max turned to Destiny. "I want you to call the dentist. He takes Saturday-morning appointments. Can you fake a toothache?"

She shrugged. "I've faked orgasms, that's gotta count for something. Besides, my wisdom teeth have been bothering me for months. I can kill two birds with one stone."

Larry Johnson owned and operated Beaumont Used Cars and reminded Jamie of a weasel with his beady, close-set black eyes. He held a hand-flex exerciser in one fist and pumped it furiously as he questioned Max about his Porsche look-alike. "That didn't come off an assembly line," Johnson said.

"You're right," Max said. "I had it custom designed."

Johnson changed the flex device to his other hand before taking them on a tour of the lot.

"My therapist advised me to use this," Larry told Jamie when he caught her staring. "I work out every morning at the local gym. It's supposed to help with stress."

"Does it?"

"No." He chuckled. "The only thing that works is a double shot of scotch straight up."

Jamie and Max pretended to find his words amusing. "I can certainly relate to that," Jamie said, thinking it was a good way to break the ice. They needed to get a fix on the guy, and in order to do that they needed good rapport. "I prefer Kahlúa," she added with a grin.

Larry smiled at her but didn't let up on his flexing. "That's a girlie drink."

She batted her lashes, something Dee Dee would have done with ease but which she found taxing. "So, I'm a girl."

Larry paused and gave her a long, hard look. "Yeah." He cleared his throat. "So, do you folks see anything you like?" It was obvious Larry had seen what he liked.

"I want to take a second look at the white Chevy Corvette convertible," Max said.

Larry nodded. "Good choice. Just so happens that's my old car, and I took damn good care of it. Low mileage, too," he added. He hitched his shoulders high. "Just bought me a brand-new one. Unfortunately, it's about the only nice thing I own since my divorce. Child support payments, you know? But I'm real proud of it. Got a security system on it that'll wake the dead."

They walked over to the used Corvette, and Max climbed in. "You mind if I take it for a test drive?"

"No problem, pardner." Larry dropped the keys into Max's hand. "It runs like a charm."

"I'll stay here and wait for you," Jamie said, giving Max one of her looks. She glanced Larry's way. "I might just find something on the lot I like."

The comment seemed to fly right over Larry's head, Jamie noticed, but then he probably thought she and Max were a couple. Jamie figured she could change that easily enough. She looked at Larry. "You got any coffee inside?"

"Sure."

Max took off in the Corvette, and Jamie followed

Larry inside a small building. The dark paneled walls were adorned with pictures of race cars. Jamie noted a nondescript woman sitting before a computer. "This is my secretary, Mabel," Larry said. The two women nodded, and Mabel handed Larry several messages. "Come into my office and I'll pour you a cup of java," he told Jamie.

"Actually, Larry, I don't care for coffee," Jamie said once he'd closed the door behind them.

"Well, then, we'll just chat until your, um"—he glanced at Jamie's ring finger, which was bare—"until your significant other returns."

Jamie sat on a fake-leather couch. "Max and I are just friends. You know, good buddies."

"Oh, well, that's nice." Flex, flex. "You can never have too many friends in this crazy world," he said. "Me? I'm a loner."

"Sometimes it's good to have someone to talk to after you've ended a relationship. I speak from experience."

"Sorry to hear that, Jamie. Is it okay if I call you Jamie?"

She nodded. "I know what you're feeling right now because I've gone through it. The pain and emptiness." She sighed heavily. There were times she thought she would have made a damn good actress. "The loneliness," she added.

He was flexing triple time. "I can't imagine a woman with your looks being lonely. Maybe you should get out more."

Jamie gave a grunt of disgust. "Most of the men in this town are either married or downright ugly. It's not every day a woman meets a guy who owns his own business and is attractive to boot."

He nodded. Finally, he jerked his head up as though a lightbulb had just gone off inside. "Oh, were you talking about me?"

Jamie wagged her finger and made a tsking sound with her tongue. "You're playing games, Larry. I don't like games."

He sat up straighter in his chair. The man's eyes registered interest. "Maybe you and I can get together for a drink sometime. Soon," he added, after a few seconds.

"How about this evening?" Jamie asked.

He looked surprised. "Well, sure. I usually leave here around six. I could meet you in the lounge at the Holiday Inn around six-fifteen. They have happy hour until seven-thirty. Free food, half price on drinks." He gave a self-deprecating smile. "That's usually where I eat my dinner. Not that I can't afford to take a lady someplace nice once in a while and buy her a real meal," he added quickly. "Why, we could—"

"The Holiday Inn will be fine, Larry. Six-fifteen," she added.

The Corvette reappeared, and Max climbed from it. Jamie watched him walk toward the building. She wondered if Max had any idea just how good-looking he was, how no men came close in comparison.

Jamie and Larry rejoined Max. "What'd you think of the car?" Larry asked.

"I like the looks of it," Max said. "Let us talk with our friend. If she's interested, we'll bring her over."

"I look forward to hearing from you," Larry said. He winked at Jamie. He seemed so excited at the thought of meeting her later that he didn't even bother with a sales pitch.

Max and Jamie climbed into Max's car and pulled from the car lot. "I'm meeting Mr. Johnson for a drink at six-fifteen," Jamie said. "The lounge at the Holiday Inn."

"Boy, you work fast," Max said. "I didn't even have time to get the VIN number off the car so Muffin could check it out. No wonder you've got such a reputation in this town."

Jamie rolled her eyes.

Muffin came on. "Make sure you don't get into Larry Johnson's car," she warned Jamie. "He's got a couple of DUIs on his record."

"Hmm," Max said. "And I'd stay away from the Kahlúa tonight, Swifty, or you'll be doing the hootchy-kootchy on the tables at the Holiday Inn."

Jamie looked at him. "Go ahead and have your fun. I, on the other hand, have a job to do." She paused. "Speaking of which, have you heard from Destiny?"

"Yeah, she's waiting to see the dentist."

Dr. Kevin Smalls, a thirtysomething man, was almost completely bald, and his belly tugged at the buttons on his shirt. The examining room was decorated in a pale blue-green; obviously to make patients feel less anxious, but it wasn't working on Destiny as she drummed her long nails against the arm of her chair.

"Just relax," the dental assistant said and smiled. "We haven't lost a patient yet."

Finally, Dr. Smalls pulled the small mouth mirror from Destiny's mouth. "Okay, I'm done here. I'll meet you in my office." He got up and left the room.

Destiny was shown to his office a moment later. Smalls shook his head sadly. "It's no wonder your wisdom teeth have been bothering you, Miss Moultrie," he said. "You know, most people have them extracted at a much earlier age."

"Really?" Destiny asked, not looking too pleased. She glanced around the office, her eyes resting on a bag of golf clubs.

"They're crowding the back of your mouth. I suggest we set you up with an oral surgeon as soon as possible."

"Do you play golf, doctor?" she asked.

He glanced at the bag of clubs. "When I have time. My wife and I share custody of our children so my weekends are pretty much taken up with them."

"So, what do you do for fun?" she asked.

"Well, I hadn't really thought much about it."

"Maybe it's time you started taking care of your own needs. You could start by inviting me to lunch."

Max and Jamie grabbed an early lunch at Maynard's Sandwich Shop where Donnie Maynard convinced Max his meat-loaf sandwich was the best thing in the world next to indoor plumbing.

"I'll give it a try," Max said.

"Make that two," Jamie told Donnie and wondered if Max had ever eaten a meat-loaf sandwich.

Max paid for the order, and they carried their drinks to a table. The walls inside the shop were of old brick, the tables and chairs battered and scarred, yet sturdy. Max took a sip of his iced tea. As if noting the curious look on Jamie's face, he arched one brow. "What?"

"When's the last time you had meat loaf?"

"Are you kidding? My cousin's wife, Billie, used to cook it all the time."

"The people who practically raised you?" she asked, remembering he'd mentioned them before.

"Right. I was sixteen years old when I moved in with them. Nick taught me everything I know about the newspaper business and horses; Billie taught me to focus my energy."

"You lost me on the last part."

"I was pretty much a juvenile delinquent from the age of five."

"Too smart for your own good, I'll bet."

"Nick was instrumental in breaking my bad habits by having me muck the stalls each time I got into trouble. You ever mucked a horse stall?"

"Nope. Don't want to, either."

"Builds character."

Their sandwiches arrived. Jamie thanked Donnie and waited until he walked away before saying anything. She knew that Max's parents had pretty much given up on their son; that the only attention he'd gotten was from the servants and during his summer vacations with his cousin Nick. "Do you ever see your parents?"

"I swing by now and then if I'm in the vicinity. They're older and have more time for me than they used to." He took a bite of his sandwich and nodded his approval. "Hey, this is good," he said.

Jamie bit into her sandwich, as well. As usual, Donnie had outdone himself on the meat loaf. "He has a secret recipe. Neither love nor money will get him to part with it." But her thoughts were elsewhere. She pondered what Max had just said about his parents having time for him now. There had been no bitterness in his voice. He'd obviously come to terms with their relationship. "What about Nick and Billie?" she asked. "Do you see them often?"

"I usually spend holidays with them. They have two kids; Christie and Joel." He chuckled. "Well, they're not really kids anymore, Christie is probably about thirty, and Joel is a couple of years younger. They both work for the newspaper. We're all pretty close." He smiled.

"Why are you smiling?" Jamie asked.

"I'm thinking about Billie. She goes all out decorating the house for Christmas, and every year she swears it's going to be her last. Somehow, she ends up doing even more the next year." He paused. "You would like her. She's simple and down-to-earth. So is Nick."

"I'll bet they're proud of you."

Max looked surprised. "Thank you. I believe that's the nicest thing you've ever said to me."

"Well, look at all you've accomplished, Max."

He shrugged. "Nick taught me to go after what I wanted. The only time he disagreed with me was when I told him I was getting married. He and Billie didn't feel I was ready. It didn't take me long to realize they were right."

"Is that why you're dead set against marriage now?"

"Let's just say I learned my lesson. I'm in no hurry to repeat that mistake."

"Don't you think you're being a little harsh?" Jamie asked. "I mean, look at Frankie and Dee Dee. After twenty years they're still madly in love."

"I'd say they're the exception, as are Nick and Billie."

They concentrated on their lunch after that, although Jamie realized she didn't have much of an appetite. She wondered how long it would be before Max became bored with her and moved on, and the thought was not a pleasant one. But she couldn't think about that right now because she had to work with him to solve Luanne Ritter's murder.

In the meantime, she needed to protect her heart.

Once they'd finished lunch, they thanked Donnie and headed out the door. Muffin was waiting for them.

"Good thing I don't take lunch breaks or we wouldn't get anything done," she said.

"What's up?" Max asked.

"The Reverend Heyward claimed he was much too busy to see you, but I was able to get you in at two o'clock, once I hinted that a hefty donation would change hands."

"Great," Max said. "That'll give us time to check out a couple of addresses." Max reached for a folder beside his seat. He handed it to Jamie. "How about looking at the ad entitled 'Open to New Experiences' and giving me the address," he said. "You know, the guy looking for a discreet relationship?"

Jamie flipped through the file of names and printouts that Muffin had supplied. "Here we go. John Price, age fifty-five, new to Beaumont, recently opened his own accounting firm. He lives on the edge of town. I know the area. Just stay on this road until you hit the main highway."

Max followed her directions, and they ended up in a rural area. They found the house, a two-story frame with NO TRESPASSING signs on the property, and a Doberman pinscher on a long leash that was attached to the porch rail.

"Well, now, Mr. Price obviously doesn't want company," Max said. "What else have we got on him?"

Jamie glanced back at the file. "Like I said, he's new in town, lived here about three months," she said. "Been divorced about a year from his second wife. He has a daughter by his first wife; she's in college. No police record. He left a high-paying position in Atlanta to come here. He's renting the house."

Max picked up a pair of binoculars and trained them on the man's residence. "Interesting. He's installed a fairly expensive security system on a piece of rental property, and he's got a man-eating creature guarding the front door. Wonder what he's got guarding the back?"

"I'm not going to go look," Jamie said. "I don't want to arrive at my date with half my face ripped off. Besides, he's accustomed to living in a large city where the crime rate is high."

Max looked at her. "Or maybe he's hiding something. Muffin, do what you have to do, but I want to know if Mr. Price is at work today. I want to have a look inside."

Jamie gaped. "You're not going in there?" When Max didn't respond, she went on. "See, this is why I should never have called you. I should have let Lamar Tevis handle it. You remember Lamar Tevis, our chief of police? He's the man who's going to throw you behind bars for breaking and entering."

"Just for the record, Max," Muffin said, "I want you to know I'm taking Jamie's side on this." She paused for a few minutes, and then came back on the speaker. "Mr. Price is with a client," she said.

Max grinned. "Perfect. Now, here's what we're going to do."

EIGHT

Jamie watched Max slip around the side of the house and disappear. The dog out front barked ferociously. "I hate this," she said to Muffin. "Max has absolutely no respect for the law. He's either hacking through firewalls or breaking and entering, and I can't believe I always find myself in the middle of it. One day we're going to get caught, and they're going to lock us up and throw away the key."

Three minutes later, Muffin came on. "He's in." Then, a quick, "Uh-oh."

Jamie's heart leaped to her throat. "What is it?"

"There's another Doberman inside. A mean one."

"Holy Toledo!" Jamie cried. All at once, the dog out front began barking out of control.

"Hang on, Max," Muffin said. "I'll cover you."

"What's going on?" Jamie demanded.

"I just blasted both animals with an ultrasonic frequency that should draw their attention for a few minutes. Max and I have done this sort of thing before. Max," Muffin said. "Are you okay?"

Jamie's nails bit into the palms of her hands. "Put him on the speaker," she said. "I want to know that he's okay."

Max came on. "I managed to lock the dog in the bathroom. I'm going to search the place."

"Oh, boy," Jamie said. "Muffin, how do you plan to get him out?"

"Same way I got him in."

Jamie counted the minutes. "How long has he been in there?"

"Less than five minutes," Muffin said. "There's nothing we can do but wait."

"I wish I hadn't quit smoking," Jamie said. "I could use a cigarette about now."

"Don't worry," Muffin told her. "Max is good at this sort of thing."

Jamie watched the clock on the dashboard. The next ten minutes seemed to drag on forever. Once Max was finished searching the house, he alerted Muffin, and she hit the dogs with the high-frequency sound once again. Max emerged from the house looking calm. He started the car and pulled away. "The place is clean," he said. "I didn't find anything out of the ordinary, but that doesn't mean we're not dealing with a killer."

Jamie leaned her head against the seat and closed her eyes, waiting for her heartbeat to return to normal.

Once Max had driven a distance, he looked at her. "Are you okay?"

"I am now."

"So you were worried about me, huh?"

She just looked at him.

Max grinned. "Muffin, Jamie was worried about me. That says a lot about our relationship."

"What relationship?" Muffin asked.

"Thank you, Muffin," Jamie said, "for not feeding his enormous ego. He knows darn well why I was worried. I don't look good in stripes, and if I go to prison, what's going to happen to Fleas? Nobody wants a dog with emotional problems and missing hair."

"You guys need to stop arguing," Muffin said. "You have an appointment with the Reverend Heyward in half an hour. You're supposed to be in love."

* * *

The Reverend Joe Heyward was a big man, standing well over six feet, with a broad chest that made Jamie think of Frankie. He looked to be in his early sixties. "So you two are thinking of getting married," he said, once Jamie and Max had joined him in his office. The paneled walls were adorned with pictures of happy brides and grooms.

"Yes, sir," Max said. "We're in love."

"Madly," Jamie said.

"Sometimes, love is not enough," the reverend replied. "There are trials and tribulations in this world that can tear a couple apart unless they are determined to work on their relationship every single day, every single hour, every single minute. You must be one hundred and fifty percent dedicated."

"Wow, that sounds like a lot of work," Max said.

"It certainly is," the reverend replied. "Otherwise, you'll end up in divorce court like half the couples in this country, and—" He paused and leaned forward. "I do not believe in divorce." He clasped his hands as if in prayer. "What God hath joined together let no man put asunder. Till death do you part," he added.

"We agree, don't we, honey?" Max said to Jamie.

"Huh? Oh, right."

The reverend went on as though he hadn't heard. "I was married to my wife for thirty years before the Lord took her. Do you think it was always easy? No, it was not. Oh, she looked real nice when I first met her, all dolled up at the church social. Prettiest thing I'd ever seen. But people change over the years, and you have to accept change."

The man pointed to Jamie. "She's a beauty right now, but what are you going to do when she gets fat and starts nagging with every breath? 'Cause you can count on that happening, son. Women love to nag. They can nag in their sleep. You fantasize about putting a pillow over their face and shutting them up for good." He paused and cleared his throat, as if realizing he'd made a blunder. "Not that I would ever consider such an act, mind you."

Jamie almost shivered at his last sentence. The man sounded off his rocker. Why on earth Luanne had contacted him was beyond her; the woman had obviously been desperate for male attention. Was he the one who'd called her the night of her murder? What if he'd decided to stop by and meet Luanne personally? Would she have opened the door if he'd mentioned he was a minister? So many unanswered questions.

"This marriage business sounds tougher than I thought it would be," Max said. He looked at Jamie. "And you *do* eat a lot of doughnuts. You keep that up, and you're going to be the size of a freight train."

"That's how big my wife was," Heyward said.

Jamie gaped at Max. "I don't eat *that* many doughnuts. And I don't nag."

"Oh, yes you do," Max told her. He looked at the Reverend Heyward. "And she can be disagreeable at times. It's not always easy."

"I'm not disagreeable," Jamie said. "You're just stubborn and arrogant."

Heyward shook his head sadly. "I can see that we have our work cut out for us." He reached for his appointment book. "Let me see when I can fit you in."

"Would you mind if we get back to you?" Max said. "I need to check my calendar." He handed the man a hefty cash donation.

Heyward's eyes widened at the sight of the money. "I suggest we begin as soon as possible, maybe meet a couple of times a week. Call me as soon as it's convenient. And don't be discouraged; a good solid marriage makes for a lot of happiness. As a matter of fact, I hope to marry again one day soon. I'm definitely in the market for a good wife."

Max was grinning when he and Jamie climbed into the front seat of his car a few minutes later. "What do you think?"

"I think the man is wacko. I don't think many women are going to jump at the chance to become the next Mrs. Heyward. And that business about putting a pillow over someone's face to shut them up." She shuddered. "I don't like it."

"I wouldn't mind knowing how his wife died," Max said.

"Muffin, are you there?" Jamie asked.

"Yeah, what's up?"

"How did the Reverend Joe Heyward's wife die?"

"She choked on a chicken bone," Muffin replied.

Jamie rolled her eyes. "No, seriously."

"I'm telling you, the woman choked on a chicken bone."

Jamie sat there for a moment. She felt Max's smile before she glanced over and saw it. "How can you possibly think that's funny?"

"Well, he said she was as large as a freight train. I'll bet she could put back a whole truckload of fried chicken."

"Max, that's not one bit funny." Nevertheless, Jamie could feel the corners of her mouth twitching. Max reached over and tickled her.

"Lighten up, Swifty. We're not letting Heyward off the hook that easily."

"I don't like being tickled."

"I plan to find all your ticklish spots before long," he said.

Jamie tried not to let her mind run amuck. "So what's next?"

Max didn't hesitate. "I think we need to pay Lamar Tevis a visit and see if he's got the tape of the phone messages Luanne received the night of her murder. Muffin, call the police department and see if the chief is in."

Lamar greeted Max with a handshake. "Good to see you again, Max," he said. He nodded at Jamie and invited them to sit. He reclaimed his chair. "Now, then, may I ask *why* you want to hear the tape?"

Jamie answered. "A minister ran an ad with me, Lamar, and you said a man called Luanne claiming to be a man of God. She must've contacted him and left her telephone number."

"Well, like I told you, the tape must've been old and worn because the voices aren't very clear. But I'll be glad to play it." He popped a small cassette into his answering machine and pushed a button. There were several brief messages, along with a lot of crackling on the tape. They were followed by the voice of the man who claimed to be a man of God and needed to meet with Luanne immediately.

Jamie felt the hairs rise on her arms. She looked at Max.

"It's not Heyward," he said.

"No, but I think I recognize the voice. It sounds like Brent Walker."

Lamar stopped the tape. "Who is Brent Walker?"

"Agnes Aimsley's grandson. He's visiting her from the seminary."

"Are you sure?" Lamar asked.

"Could you play the tape again?" Jamie asked.

Lamar did as she requested. He cut off the machine once the tape ran out. "What do you think?" he said.

"I've only met this Walker guy once, and you're right, the voices aren't very clear, but I'm almost positive it's him. I can't imagine why he'd be calling Luanne, though. He didn't run an ad."

Lamar leaned back in his chair. "I reckon I'll have to pay him a visit and find out."

"I'm curious," Max said. "Was Luanne robbed?" Lamar looked at Jamie. "We haven't released this information, so this is off the record."

"Of course."

"I think it was made to look like a robbery," he said. "Her jewelry box was cleaned out, but she was wearing several expensive rings. A burglar would have noticed."

The lounge at the Holiday Inn was doing a good business when Jamie arrived. Obviously, the free hors d'oeuvres were a big plus; people were lined up at the two tables that had been set up with chafing dishes. Larry Johnson was sitting at the bar. He looked surprised to see Jamie, as if he'd expected her not to show.

He stood as she crossed the room. "You dressed up," he said. "I'm flattered."

"Of course I did," Jamie said. "I wanted to look my best."

"You succeeded very well. Would you rather get a table?"

"A table would be nice," Jamie said, thinking he would be more open to conversation if they had privacy. She needed him to feel comfortable with her.

Larry grabbed his drink and led Jamie to a table that was situated in a dark corner. A cocktail waitress appeared a moment later. Jamie ordered a club soda and lime; Larry a double scotch.

"I thought you liked Kahlúa," Larry said, once the waitress left them.

Jamie noted he looked disappointed that she hadn't ordered a drink. After what Muffin had said about his drinking history, she suspected Larry preferred hanging with boozers, and, despite all the ribbing Jamie had received about how she'd acted at Myrna Hobbs's place, she seldom touched alcohol. But once again, she needed Larry to feel comfortable around her or he wouldn't say what was on his mind.

"Actually, I love the stuff," she said, "but I'm still recovering from a hangover I got at a friend's birthday party."

He grinned. "I hope you don't mind if I have another."

"No, please, I insist."

"I'm afraid I'm not in the greatest mood tonight," he confessed. "I received a call from my ex-wife, and we got into it over the telephone so I closed the dealership at five and got the hell out of there."

Jamie hoped it meant he'd had time to belt back several scotches. "I take it the split was not amicable."

He gave a grunt. "Hardly. She got everything, including the house, and I'm paying child support out the ass. My apartment is crap, and I barely have any furniture. All I have to show for years of hard work is a decent car."

"I'm sorry." Jamie didn't know the man well, but she suspected he'd gotten exactly what he deserved. "I'm sure you feel a lot of animosity toward your ex right now, but perhaps it'll pass in time."

"Don't count on it. She put the screws to me. But I'm here to tell you, she's going to get hers."

Jamie caught the menace in his voice. "What do you mean?"

His answer was guarded. "As they say, what goes around comes around, know what I mean?" He suddenly looked apologetic. "I'm sorry. I have no right to unload on you. I invited you here for a good time."

"I *am* having a good time," Jamie said. "I don't get out much."

He looked doubtful. "A woman with your looks? I find that hard to believe."

"Remember, I mentioned I was involved with some-one for a while? He didn't like to go out much."

"I go out every night." Larry shrugged. "Here, mostly, but it's better than sitting at home. The ex got the only decent TV set, too. I was mad as hell over that one. A guy shouldn't have to give up his TV."

They were interrupted when the cocktail waitress ap-peared with their drinks.

Larry shoved several bills at her, told her to keep the change, and she walked away. He stirred his drink. "My ex claims I have an anger problem, among other things. The judge ordered me to get counseling on an-ger management if I wanted to see my children. I think that sucks." He raised his glass, but it slipped from his hand, and his entire drink spilled on him, soaking the front of his shirt. "Oh, shit, now look what I've done."

Jamie tried to help him mop the spill with a napkin, but it was useless.

"I've got to get out of this shirt," Larry said. "It's sticking to me." He looked at her. "I only live a couple of miles from here. Why don't we run by my place, let me clean up, then we can grab a bite to eat someplace. I'll take you to a real restaurant so you can show off that nice dress."

Jamie hesitated. Max had specifically told her and Destiny not to leave a public area with the men.

"Hey, this isn't a pickup, okay? I just want to get out of this wet shirt."

Jamie knew Max would be mad as hell if she left the premises with Larry, but what could she do? If she re-fused to go, she might lose her one chance of finding out whether he had ever met Luanne Ritter, much less visited her the night of her murder. He certainly had an anger problem, and his alcohol abuse made him a walk-ing time bomb.

Besides, she owed Max for having scared the life out

of her when he'd broken into John Price's house. "I'll follow you in my car," she said.

They left the lounge. Jamie climbed into her car and followed Larry from the parking lot, wondering if Max could see her from his vantage point at the other end of the lot. She grabbed her cell phone and punched in Max's number. He answered on the first ring.

"Okay, Max, I know you're not going to like this, but I'm following Larry Johnson to his place so he can change shirts." She explained about the spilled drink.

"Bad idea," he said. "I specifically told you—"

"I know what you told me, but I think I'm on to something here. This guy looks suspicious."

"All the more reason to turn your car around and head in the opposite direction. I don't want you alone with him."

"Listen, Max, I can't see him intentionally killing Luanne Ritter, but he has serious problems. I think he feels he can talk to me."

"Oh, so you think you're going to get a full confession out of him?"

"Not exactly, but—"

"Turn your car around, Jamie," he ordered. "It's not worth the risk. I'll follow you to Frankie and Dee Dee's."

"No way, Max. Not when I'm this close. Trust me on this one, okay? And call Frankie and Dee Dee and tell them we can't make it for dinner. I'll be dining with Larry."

She hung up the phone in order to avoid arguing with him. The cell phone rang. She knew it was Max. She ignored it, knowing he would never agree to let her enter Larry's apartment. But she was determined to find out what she could. Besides, something told her she had nothing to fear with Larry Johnson. As long as she played along, she reminded herself.

Finally, the cell phone stopped ringing.

Five minutes later, Jamie followed Larry into the parking lot of a generic-looking apartment complex. She parked beside his car and climbed out. He hit a button on his key chain, and his Corvette beeped. "I don't trust the teenagers around here," he said. "If I ever catch them messing with my car, I'm going to take a crowbar to them. Matter of fact, I keep one behind the seat of my car and another one beside the front door in my apartment."

Jamie suppressed a shiver. Luanne Ritter had died from a blow to the head. She tried to make light of it. "A crowbar would certainly scare me away," she said with a laugh. At the same time, she wondered what Larry's wife had found appealing about him. "Yes, sir, a crowbar would definitely get my attention," she added, causing him to grin.

She followed Larry to a door and paused beside him while he unlocked it. He opened it, stepped inside and flipped on a light switch, then motioned for Jamie to enter. "It's not much, but it's home."

Jamie followed him into a sparsely furnished living room. Larry had obviously found a good deal on fake-leather furniture because the couch and chair matched those in his office. The apartment smelled of stale food and booze. Sure enough, there was a crowbar leaning against the wall beside the front door. "It's not so bad," she lied. "A few pictures on the wall, and the place would be really homey."

"I'm not much of a decorator."

No kidding, she thought.

"Hey, and I'm sorry about the mess, but I wasn't expecting company." He grabbed a pile of clothes from the sofa. "Have a seat."

Jamie sat down. He went about turning on more lights, then headed into the kitchen and made himself another scotch. "My shirt is plastered to me," he said.

"Would you mind if I grabbed a quick shower and changed? Then I'll take you to dinner."

"No problem," she said.

He hurried into the next room. Several minutes later, Jamie heard the sound of running water. She stood and tiptoed into the bedroom and immediately started searching through Larry's dresser drawers. She was looking for jewelry. If Larry had indeed killed Luanne and tried to make it look like a robbery, he could very well have hidden his stash until he could dispose of it. A man with his financial problems would probably try to sell it when he felt it was safe.

If he'd been the one, she reminded herself. *If* the murder was actually tied to her personals ads. There were a lot of ifs, but Jamie knew she wouldn't have any answers unless she checked.

Nothing unusual in the drawers. Jamie glanced at the closet. She sometimes kept money tucked inside an old coat pocket. She heard a noise and turned.

Larry was standing in the doorway, a towel draped around his midsection.

She froze. Damn, damn, damn.

"Why are you in my bedroom?" he asked.

Jamie stared back at him for a full minute as she tried to find her tongue. She had been so engrossed in her search that she hadn't heard the sound of the shower being turned off or the bathroom door opening. Finally, she smiled. "Why do you think?"

"I should have known Jamie would pull something like this," Max said, having followed her car to Larry's apartment complex and watched her enter through one of the doors.

"What are you going to do?" Muffin asked.

Max stared at the door to the apartment. He noted Larry's Corvette out front. "She thinks she's so smart.

Let her figure it out." He sat there for about twenty seconds. "Dammit," he muttered. He opened his car door and climbed out.

Larry smiled at Jamie and stepped closer. "Why am I surprised?" he said. "I knew we had chemistry the minute I laid eyes on you."

Jamie wanted to tell him she felt about as much attraction for him as she did for an eel. "Yes," she said in a husky tone meant to sound sexy. "I felt it, too."

"We don't have to go out," Larry said. "Besides, I'm hungry for you."

"Yes. I mean, no," Jamie said hurriedly. "On second thought, I think we should still go out. Someplace romantic," she added. "We shouldn't rush things."

"I could order pizza. Is that romantic enough?"

"Um, I was sort of hoping for soft music and candlelight. Maybe we could go dancing."

"Baby, we don't need all that." He suddenly pulled her against him. "Why put off the inevitable? You want it as bad as I do." He dropped his towel to the floor and pressed himself against her.

Jamie's skin crawled. The last thing she wanted to see was a naked Larry Johnson. He pulled her face close, studied her with those beady eyes. Oh, hell, he was going to kiss her, she thought.

He lowered his head, and their lips touched. Jamie felt herself stiffen.

"Relax," he whispered against her lips. "I'll go slow."

Jamie closed her eyes. It would be easier to let him kiss her if she didn't have to look at him. She braced herself. Think; think. His kiss deepened, and she started bargaining with God.

Please don't let him stick his tongue in my mouth. I'll even start going to church with Vera if I have to.

Larry pressed his tongue against her lips, trying to prod them open. "Come on, baby," he crooned.

Jamie's heart sank to her toes. She flattened her hand against his bare chest, hoping to push him away gently, when, all at once a loud siren split the night. They both jumped.

"Sonofabitch!" Larry yelled. "Someone is messing with my car."

Jamie's head spun. "What?"

"That's my alarm system. Some asshole is trying to break into my car." He searched the room frantically and grabbed a pair of pants. He danced about, trying to get his legs into his slacks. He didn't bother zipping them as he raced from the room.

"Oh, thank you, God," Jamie whispered as she heard the front door of the apartment being flung open. She hurried into the living room, grabbed her purse, and ran out. She stood there for a moment, disoriented. Finally, she bolted toward her car.

And bumped into Larry and his crowbar.

"My car's okay," he said, and then gave her a funny look. "Where are you going?"

"I just remembered I have to go home and feed my dog."

"Feed your dog?" he said in disbelief. "Can't that wait?"

"He's hypoglycemic. If he doesn't eat every four hours, his blood sugar level drops and—"

"Lady, what the hell are you talking about?" Larry scowled and began flexing his fists. "You get a man hard enough to break concrete blocks, and then you come up with this bullshit story about having to go home and feed your dog? What's with that?"

Jamie suspected he was on the verge of erupting. "Larry, things were getting out of hand. It's my fault. I haven't, well, you know, it's been *sooo* long since I've been with a man, and I'm really attracted to you, but I need more time. I don't want to do something I might regret later, you know? Especially since—" She paused, hoping she sounded convincing. "We might want to keep on seeing each other."

His facial muscles relaxed. "You're worried I won't respect you in the morning, is that it?"

"Something like that. You know how it is."

He seemed to ponder it. Finally, he nodded. "Okay, then, I can wait. I'll call you."

"No. I'll call you. Just give me a couple of days."

He flexed a fist. "Well, okay."

Jamie covered the short distance to her car, climbed in, and punched the lock.

Max was waiting near the entrance to the apartment complex. He drove forward slowly as Jamie approached in her Mustang. She followed him for several miles before he pulled into the parking lot of the Piggly Wiggly supermarket. He slammed out of his car.

The look on his face told her she was in deep doo-doo. She rolled down her window. "Max, I—"

He jerked her car door open. "Get out."

Jamie gave a huge sigh but did as he said. "Okay, go ahead and yell at me so we can get it over with."

"Just what the hell were you thinking?"

"I was trying to get information." She wasn't about to tell him she'd ended up in Larry's bedroom.

"You're off the job."

NINE

Jamie blinked furiously. "Excuse me?"

"I'm calling in my own people. It's too dangerous, and I can't trust you to follow directions."

"You *can't* pull me off the job," she almost shouted. "I'm the one who called you. Besides, who are you to talk about taking chances when you broke into John Price's house today? At least I didn't break any laws."

"I knew what I was doing or I would never have gone in," Max said. "You acted irrationally by entering Johnson's apartment when we don't know if he's the killer or not. Jesus, Jamie, the man could have overpowered you. You're not thinking straight because you're emotionally involved in this."

"You're not taking me off the *job,* as you call it, but you're right—I *am* emotionally involved. My personals section could be connected to Luanne Ritter's murder. *That's* why I took the chance I did. If Larry Johnson killed Luanne, I want to know."

"At the risk of causing harm to yourself?" he asked.

"If I had felt threatened by him, I would never have gone in. Besides, I got out before anything happened, didn't I?"

"I got you out by tripping the alarm system in his car."

She wasn't about to tell him how grateful she was for that or let him see how shaken she was over her ordeal. "It's a moot point now," she said, raising her voice. "I'm safe."

"You need to settle down."

"I *can't* settle down. Nobody in this town seems to care that a human being died. They keep thinking of the Luanne Ritter who ran a loan company and wasn't liked. Well, she may not have been the most popular person in town, but she didn't deserve to die. I don't know how I'll live with myself if my newspaper is involved."

"Well, you just might have to face that fact, so get over it."

"Gee, thanks."

"I'm being realistic. If you want to spend the rest of your life beating yourself up over something you had no control over, then do it."

"I shouldn't have called you. I should have let Lamar handle it."

"Then why *did* you call me?"

She hesitated, and her voice broke when she answered. "Because I was afraid Lamar couldn't handle the job. I knew you could. Satisfied?"

Without warning, Max pulled her against him. For a moment, he simply held her, waiting for Jamie to calm down. He sighed heavily. Finally, he pulled back so that he was looking into her eyes. "Look, I'm sorry I got angry with you, babe, but I was worried as hell. Promise me you won't try anything like that again."

"I have to know the truth, Max."

"And we're doing everything we can." He released her. "Did you see anything in his place that looked suspicious?"

She told him about the crowbars. "He carries one in his car. If we could get our hands on it—"

"No way," Max said. "If he looks like our man, I'll have Lamar Tevis check him out and send the crowbar to the crime lab. Also, I'm going to have Muffin check his and Luanne's telephone records."

"Luanne's picture was recently in the newspaper. We

could take it to the Holiday Inn and show it around. See if anybody remembers her being there with Larry."

"He might find out, and we'll blow our cover. We just need to have him watched closely for the next couple of days until we can rule out the others. I suppose I could put Destiny on it."

"That's fine." Jamie had no desire to lay eyes on the man again.

Max checked his wristwatch. "We still have time to make dinner at Frankie and Dee Dee's."

Jamie was glad he hadn't canceled. She needed the diversion after what she'd been through. "I'll follow you."

Vera Bankhead stared at herself in the mirror as she tried on the new dress. On the bed behind her were two new pantsuits she'd purchased, as well.

Vera reached inside the little pocket of her purse and pulled out the ad she had cut out of the newspaper that day. "'Open to New Experiences,'" she read aloud. She often talked to herself, a result of living alone most of her life. "'Interested in discreet relationship with woman in fifties,'" she continued. "Okay, I'm a tad older, but I look pretty good, and I can be as discreet as the next person. Lord knows I wouldn't want my preacher finding out that I was responding to a personals ad."

She hurried into her living room where she kept her old Remington typewriter. She typed the address on a plain white envelope and chuckled. "Jamie will never suspect a thing," she said.

Max and Jamie arrived at Frankie and Dee Dee's house around eight P.M. to find Dee Dee in tears.

"It's because of the lobsters," Frankie said miserably. "We had a tank installed in the kitchen. You may have noticed it when you were here for the party. Anyway, I had a bunch of lobsters flown in from Maine, and we were going to have them for dinner tonight, but Dee Dee—"

Dee Dee interrupted. "The chef was going to drop them live into a pot of boiling water, Max." Her bottom lip trembled.

"Honey, how do you think they cook lobster?" Frankie asked.

"Well, there *are* more humane ways to prepare them," Max said, "but I'm sure your chef knows that."

"I don't want to hear about it!" Dee Dee cried, palms pressed to her ears. "I want them sent back. Or find homes for them."

Max and Jamie exchanged looks. Jamie tried to imagine where one would find a good home for a lobster. It wasn't like they could drop them off at the local animal shelter and hope someone would adopt them.

Beenie had his arms crossed and was tapping his foot impatiently. "Well, I, for one, had my heart set on a nice lobster dinner, but Dee Dee said there will be no murders committed in this house so we'll all probably end up eating bologna and cheese sandwiches."

"I'd rather have a big old rare steak anyway," Snakeman said. "Come on, Big John. You and me can run to the store and pick up a load of 'em."

"I guess that will be okay," Dee Dee said. "Since the cows are already dead."

Jamie walked over to her friend. Dee Dee looked delicate in a cream-colored georgette dress that fell to her ankles. "Honey, I don't care what we eat as long as it doesn't distress you. You're just feeling a little sensitive now that you're pregnant, and you have every right."

Dee Dee sniffed. "I told them I wouldn't mind eating the lobsters once they grew old and died. I'm trying to cooperate."

"Does anyone know the life span of a lobster?" Beenie asked sarcastically.

No one had heard the chef come into the room. "This is nonsense, waiting for a lobster to die before we can cook him," the man said. "A lobster must be alive when you cook him or he's no good. I can put them in the freezer to numb them before I drop them into boiling water."

Dee Dee burst into tears.

"Scrap the lobster," Frankie said. "Snakeman is going to buy steaks."

"This is a crazy house," the chef muttered under his breath and pushed through the swinging door leading to the kitchen.

"Would you like to go upstairs and lie down for a while before dinner?" Jamie asked Dee Dee.

Beenie softened at the sad look in Dee Dee's eyes. "Of course she would. Come on, honey, you need to rest a bit, and then I'll repair your makeup."

"The rest of the guys are in the game room playing pool and darts," Frankie said to Max. "Why don't we join them?"

Beenie very gently placed a lavender-scented satin eye mask over Dee Dee's eyes as she half reclined on a settee, holding her Maltese, Choo-Choo, against her breasts. "I know everyone thinks I'm being foolish," she said, "but the thought of killing those poor lobsters is more than I can bear." She sniffed. "I was beginning to think of them as pets."

Beenie caught Jamie's eye and shook his head sadly. "Our Dee Dee has been feeling out of sorts all day," he said. "Tired and weepy," he added. "She was real upset over that woman's murder."

"That poor woman," Dee Dee said, removing her eye mask. "It's all I can think about."

"We're all very saddened by it," Jamie told her, "but I'm sure the police are doing everything they can to find the killer." She offered Dee Dee the closest thing she had to a smile and changed the subject. "You'll be relieved to know that Muffin is already doing research on pregnancy and child care. She's ordered a few books for you. By the time this baby comes into the world we'll all be experts."

Beenie did a quick repair job on Dee Dee's eyes. "I just hope I don't gain a lot of weight," Dee Dee replied. "You know how I am about my weight."

"Oh, pooh," Beenie said. "For once in your life stop worrying about your waistline. Besides, that new fashion designer I selected assured me you'd be the best-looking pregnant woman in town. In the country, even," he added. "You know what I think? I think a lot of celebrities out there will have their own designers trying to copy your style."

Dee Dee seemed to perk up at the thought.

"And of course the baby's nursery will look like something off a magazine cover," Beenie said. "I'm talking to interior designers who have been commissioned by the biggest names in show business."

"It sounds so exciting," Jamie said. "I can't wait."

Dee Dee touched her still flat tummy. "Eeyeuuw, I'm going to look like I'm carrying a giant melon," she said suddenly. "I won't be able to let Frankie see me in the buff."

"I've heard that a lot of men find pregnant women very sexy," Jamie said.

"But some women never totally regain their figures after having a baby," Dee Dee pointed out.

"That's not going to happen," Beenie said. "Your plastic surgeon can perform liposuction as soon as you deliver the baby. We'll have him on standby."

Jamie suppressed a shudder. It sounded rather drastic.

"And what do I know about being a mother?" Dee Dee said. "I've never raised anything but a Maltese." She sat up. "I have to speak to Muffin."

"Now?" Jamie asked.

"Yes. She always has the answers to all my questions, and I have a lot of questions."

"You want me to come with you?" Jamie asked.

"Yes. You can take notes." She glanced at Beenie. "You want to come?"

"No, I'm going to join the guys. I get hot being around all that testosterone."

So you're saying you've been experiencing morning sickness for some weeks now?" Muffin said a short while later.

Dee Dee sniffed. "Yes. It isn't very pleasant."

"Your doctor has probably told you to keep soda crackers on your night table, right?" Muffin replied.

"I have trouble keeping them down."

"The nausea should go away after the first couple of months," Muffin told her. "There are medications to help you through it if you like."

"I just hate taking anything while I'm pregnant," Dee Dee said. "What bothers me even more is the fatigue. I get up in the morning and several hours later I'm ready for a nap."

"It happens to a lot of women," Muffin told her. "The first three months or trimester, as it's called, is the worst. Odds are, once you get into your fourth and fifth month you'll start feeling better. Of course, you're going to be the size of a refrigerator."

"Eeyeuuw!" Dee Dee cried.

Muffin chuckled. "Just kidding."

"Hey, pregnant women are cool," Jamie said. "Once you start getting big, everyone opens doors for you and waits on you like a princess."

Dee Dee seemed to ponder it. "But people already do that."

Muffin spoke up. "Hey, I'll bet Frankie will start buying you more jewelry."

Jamie looked up from her notes. "Muffin, what a materialistic thing to say."

Dee Dee looked at her. "Maybe if I play my cards right I'll get that new ten-karat solitaire from Tiffany's I've been wanting." She looked thoughtful. "This pregnancy thing might just end up being the best thing that's ever happened to me, and when it's all over, I'll have a precious little baby boy or girl. It's a win-win situation."

"Do you plan on breastfeeding?" Muffin asked.

"Eeyeuuw, I hadn't thought of that." Dee Dee was quiet for a moment. Finally, she looked at Jamie. "What do you think?"

"Don't ask me, I can't even raise a bloodhound properly. Maybe you're trying to make too many decisions at once. You've barely had time to get used to the thought of being pregnant, much less buying maternity clothes, decorating a nursery, and deciding whether you should breastfeed. You need to relax."

"How come Frankie isn't worried about these things?" Dee Dee asked. "I feel like I'm going through most of it alone."

Jamie grinned. "He's too happy to be worried. The woman he loves more than anything in the world is going to have his baby. He's passing out cigars."

"Are you happy for me, Jamie?" Dee Dee asked.

"Of course I am. Why wouldn't I be?"

"It's silly, but I just wanted to make sure I had your support. And because I'm a little nervous. I want to be the best mother I can be. I never thought I'd feel like this about a baby. It's a miracle that I got pregnant after all these years, and I don't want to botch it."

Jamie reached across the seat and hugged her. "Dee Dee, you are going to be a wonderful mother. And Frankie will be a great father. I think this is one lucky baby."

"How far along are you?" Muffin asked.

"Six weeks."

"Well, that'll give us plenty of time to learn everything we can about babies," Muffin said.

Dee Dee smiled almost dreamily at Jamie. "You know, I never thought I would be facing motherhood, but this would more fun if you were going through it with me. I mean, you're my best friend. We'd have a blast if we were both pregnant at the same time. We could shop together."

Jamie almost swallowed her own tongue. "Um, maybe I should just concentrate on raising Fleas right now."

It was shortly after eleven p.m. when Max and Jamie arrived back at her house. Fleas was spread-eagled on the sofa. He didn't move as they came into the house.

"That's some watchdog you've got there," Max said.

Jamie walked up to the animal, hands on hips. "Excuse me, but are you supposed to be on the sofa?" she asked.

The dog didn't budge.

"Okay, play your games, but Max and I are going to have ice cream."

One of Fleas's eyes popped open. He raised his head.

"I figured that would get your attention," Jamie said, going into the kitchen.

Max followed. "You don't really feed him ice cream, do you?"

Jamie was already pulling a carton of butter pecan

from the freezer. "Yeah. He won't go to bed for the night without his treat."

Fleas climbed from the sofa and walked into the kitchen. He sat and waited, watching Jamie's every move. She dipped ice cream into his doggie bowl, and then put some in bowls for Max and her. Fleas had eaten his by the time they carried their bowls to the kitchen table. For a moment, Jamie and Max enjoyed their dessert in silence. Max looked at her.

"I'm sorry I came down so hard on you earlier," he said. "I almost lost it when you went into Larry Johnson's apartment. I think he's dangerous."

"Or he could just be angry because he had to give up everything in the divorce. He's hard to figure, but it's obvious he doesn't have much respect for women. Still, I have a hard time believing he's a cold-blooded killer, but then I can't imagine anyone murdering another human being." Not that she hadn't witnessed killing during their trip to Tennessee, she reminded herself. She'd watched the FBI gun down two notorious mob figures, and she still had nightmares about it from time to time.

"Johnson definitely has two things against him," Max said. "Anger and booze. That can make for a deadly combination. Also, if he has financial problems, he might have taken Luanne Ritter's jewelry."

"Assuming, of course, that he killed her," Jamie added quickly.

They finished their ice cream. Jamie picked up the bowls and carried them to the sink where she rinsed them out. She didn't hear Max get up, but all at once she felt his arms slide around her waist.

"I really missed you while I was away, Swifty," he said, his mouth at her ear.

Jamie tried to suppress the shiver that raced up her backbone and reached for the towel to dry her hands. "I missed you, too, Max," she said.

He turned her around so that she was facing him, and the two gazed at each other for a moment. Finally, Max kissed her.

Jamie could taste the ice cream on his tongue as he explored her mouth. She slipped her arms around his neck and drew him even closer. She had been waiting for Max to kiss her for most of the evening, and now she opened her mouth wider to receive him.

Max broke the kiss and studied her. "Remember that unfinished business back in Tennessee?"

Jamie blushed in spite of herself. Her with her skirt shoved high on her hips, Max's mouth on her, tasting. "Yes." The word was little more than a whisper.

"I'd like to finish it."

He took her hand and led her to her bedroom. He walked over to the nightstand and switched on the light. At Jamie's look, he smiled. "I want to be able to get a good look at you." He pulled her into his arms once more; this time there was a look of sheer determination on his face. Jamie welcomed his hands on her breasts and closed her eyes as her nipples contracted, despite the clothing that separated them. She gave in to the wonderful sensations his touch created.

Max reached around and unzipped her dress, kissing each shoulder as he bared it. He released the garment and it fell to her feet. Jamie kicked off her heels and was left standing there in her bra and panties, the ones she'd bought at Sinful Delights.

"Jesus, Swifty," Max said, his voice suddenly husky. "I'd like to know where you buy your lingerie."

She smiled coyly and reached for the buttons on his shirt, but her fingers trembled as she undid them. Finally, she pulled the shirt free, and Max stood there with his chest bare, looking better than anything she'd ever laid eyes on. She ran her hands over him. Her stomach fluttered. If she'd known he looked this good, she would have jumped into the sack with him sooner.

Max reached around and unfastened her bra. He tossed it aside and pulled her into his arms. Skin met skin. Jamie's body responded immediately.

Max cupped her breasts in his hands and then he lowered his head and kissed the spot between them. Jamie held his head tightly against her as she felt her insides swoop upward. Max's hands suddenly appeared at her hips. He kneaded the flesh before pulling her against him where she could feel his hardness. Something hot flashed low in her belly.

Jamie whimpered his name as he buried his face against her throat. "Oh, Max."

"I know, Jamie. I know." He picked her up and carried her the short distance to the bed.

Jamie reached for his belt, fumbled with it until she was able to unfasten it. "I could use some help, Holt."

He grinned and pulled off his socks and shoes. Finally, he unzipped his pants. It took only seconds for him to dispense with them. His boxers followed. Jamie's breath caught in her throat at the sight of his lean but slightly muscular body.

Max joined her on the bed, pulled her into his arms once more, and kissed her deeply. He pulled back slightly. "Birth control?" he whispered.

"We're covered," she managed.

He removed her panties and sought the area between her thighs with his fingers. Jamie pressed herself against his hand.

Max teased her with his fingers, even as he continued kissing her. He began to inch his way down her body, kissing her abdomen, her tummy. He parted her thighs to receive his tongue.

The doorbell rang.

Max jerked his head up. "What the hell?"

Jamie blinked furiously, trying to awaken her dulled senses. "I wonder who that could be."

"Ignore it."

She sat up. "I can't ignore it, Max. It's almost midnight. Something must be wrong. It could be Vera."

He gave a huge sigh, climbed from the bed, and reached for his slacks. "This had better be good." He tugged them on and zipped them.

Jamie grabbed her bathrobe. She hurried into the next room, Max right behind her. Fleas was on the sofa sleeping soundly. Jamie shot him a dirty look as she made for the door. She checked the peephole. "It's Destiny."

"You're kidding. What's she doing here?"

Jamie opened the front door. Destiny was dressed in skintight faux-leather shorts and a rhinestone tee that was molded to her oversize breasts.

"Don't you ever check your answering machine?" the woman asked frantically. Her eyes darted to Max then back to Jamie.

"I was out all evening," Jamie said. "I only returned home a little while ago. Do you know what time it is?"

"Of course I do," Destiny said. "I wouldn't be here if it weren't important. I've lost Ronnie."

TEN

Jamie gaped at Destiny. "You're serious, aren't you?"

"Of course I am. I feel responsible for him. I was wondering if he was over here."

"Why would he be here?" Jamie asked.

"He likes the two of you. He told me. He especially likes your hound because he had one similar. Ronnie used to be an expert coon hunter," she added, shaking her head sadly. "I can't let him go off on his own because, well, because he needs my help. I'm the only one who can convince him to cross over to the other side. To the light," she added.

Jamie gave a massive eye roll. "I don't believe we're having this conversation," she muttered.

Destiny looked past both of them. "There you are, dammit," she said to an empty space. "Ronnie, what are you doing here this time of night? I've been searching all over for you."

Jamie and Max glanced around the room. "Where is he?" Jamie asked.

"Sitting next to your dog." Destiny walked over to Fleas, once again staring at an empty space. She put her hands on her hips. "It's time to go home, Ronnie," she said. "If you don't go to the light, you'll keep wandering around lost. I know you're not anxious to see your dead mother, but you've got to face her sooner or later." Destiny paused and looked at Max and Jamie. "Ronnie knows his mother is going to read him the riot act for getting drunk and falling out of that pickup truck."

Max and Jamie exchanged glances.

Finally, Destiny sighed. "Okay, I'll let you hang around my place for a while longer, but you can't go running off like this because I'll worry."

Jamie was intrigued. "How come you can see Ronnie, but we can't?"

Destiny shrugged. "Everyone has some psychic ability," she said, "but they don't use it."

"What does he look like?" Jamie asked.

"He's short and bald with a beer gut." Destiny gave a grunt. "Yes, Ronnie, you do have a beer gut. Now are you coming with me or not?" She glanced at Max and Jamie. "Ronnie can be stubborn at times."

"Well, I'm sure the two of you will work things out," Max said. He walked into the bedroom for the rest of his clothes.

Jamie couldn't hide her irritation. "Destiny, you're going to have to keep up with your dead spirit. I can't have him showing up here at all hours of the night." She suddenly remembered what Max had said about dead spirits attaching themselves to other people. "Ronnie isn't, um, an evil spirit, is he?" she asked, and then realized how strange her question sounded.

"Oh, no, he's quite friendly," Destiny said, "even if he is a real pain in the ass." She paused. "Yes, Ronnie, you *are* a pain in the ass, and I don't know why I put up with you. Now let's go home and let these people get some sleep." She crossed her arms and tapped her foot impatiently. "I'm waiting."

Max reentered the room, still buttoning his shirt. "You haven't come up with any more information, have you?"

Destiny shook her head. "Sorry. I think I'm still blocked."

"Max said you didn't think the dentist looked suspicious."

Destiny shrugged. "He seemed harmless to me, but he did have golf clubs in his office, and I suppose one of them could have been used to kill that poor woman. Maybe something will come to me soon. In the meantime, I'll be in the office early Monday morning to pick up my mail."

"Your mail?"

"I assume I'll have responses to the new column you mentioned to your readers."

Jamie doubted it, but she didn't want to hurt Destiny's feelings. She had almost been too embarrassed to run the announcement and couldn't imagine anyone in Beaumont writing in for advice from the Divine Love Goddess Advisor, but for some insane reason she had posted it anyway.

Max stepped forward. "By the way, I was hoping you could follow one of the suspects around for a couple of days."

Destiny shrugged. "Sure."

"I don't want you to get too close, but he needs to be watched."

"How will I know what the guy looks like?"

Max described him. "Do you have a pair of binoculars?" he asked.

"They're easy enough to buy."

"His name is Larry Johnson, and he owns a local car dealership. It would be best if you parked across from his place of business. He'll probably be at the car lot all day tomorrow. He'll be easy to spot since he's the only salesman on the lot. He also hangs out in the lounge at the Holiday Inn at night. Like I said, I don't want you to get too close."

"What am I looking for?"

"I'd just like to know who he's spending his evenings with."

"Okay." Destiny suddenly glanced sideways. "No, Ronnie, I don't think that's a polite question to ask."

"What does Ronnie want to know?" Jamie said.

"I'm almost too embarrassed to say, but he is asking what happened to your dog's hair."

"Coon attack," Jamie said, irritated that people were always finding flaws with her pet. "Um, it's getting late, Destiny, and I don't mean to be rude, but do you think you could take your dead spirit home now?"

Max looked amused.

"Okay, I'm out of here," Destiny said. "Come on, Ronnie." She turned for the door, and then glanced over her shoulder. "We need to figure out who the murderer is right away because I have to have oral surgery next week. The dentist said my wisdom teeth have to come out"

Jamie watched Destiny pull away in her Mercedes. Max came up beside her and put his hands on her shoulders. "That woman needs help," Jamie said. When Max chuckled, she went on. "And you're only encouraging her."

"I'm just trying to find a killer. Any way I can," he added.

"You don't think it's strange for a woman to show up at my door at midnight looking for a ghost?"

He grinned.

"It's not funny, Max," she said. "If you want to play ball with her and her imaginary playmate, go for it, but I'm out." He removed his hands from her shoulders, and Jamie wished she hadn't been so brusque with him.

"If you don't want her around, tell her," he said. He glanced at his wristwatch. "Look, I need to be going. I've got to make a few phone calls."

"At this hour?"

"I'm calling countries in a different time zone. Besides, we're both tired. How about I catch up with you tomorrow?"

Jamie felt her jaw drop. He was leaving? Just like that? She didn't want him to go.

Or maybe they needed a little distance. If Max stayed, they would finish making love, and if that happened, she was a goner. Once she made love with Max Holt she would fall hopelessly in love with him. She didn't have time to fall in love, not with a murderer on the loose.

"Maybe that's best," she said at last.

Max climbed into his car and started the engine. Muffin came on. "Boy, that was quick. I figured the two of you would go at it all night."

"Very funny."

"Uh-oh," Muffin said. "I can tell by the sound of your voice it didn't go well. Did you guys have an argument?"

"No."

"I'm confused," Muffin said. "What's the problem? Why this constant tug-of-war? It's obvious the two of you are hot for each other."

"Okay, Muffin, I'll level with you. I'm beginning to worry that Jamie might want more out of this relationship than I can give her."

"So is this the part where you tell the woman in question that you can't possibly make a commitment and you try to soften the blow with flowers?"

Max didn't answer.

"Because if it is I'm telling you right now it's not going to work," Muffin went on. "You're not willing to let Jamie go. Face it, Max. You've got it bad."

Max didn't respond at first. "Do me a favor, Muffin," he said, changing the subject. "I want you to check out a Destiny Moultrie for me. I want to know everything you can find on her."

"So we're not going to talk about it, is that it?"

He didn't try to keep the irritation from his voice when he spoke. "I don't want to talk about Jamie right now if it's all the same to you."

A few minutes later, Max pulled into the parking lot of his hotel and parked. He sat there for a moment before getting out of the car and making his way to his room. He gazed at the empty bed. "Shit."

Jamie awoke to the smell of Fleas's breath on her face. "Oh God!" she cried, shoving him away. "I hope you haven't been licking yourself again."

He simply stood there, watching and waiting.

"You need to go out, is that it?" She dragged herself from the bed and headed for the back door with him on her heels. She paused to unlock the door, and he bumped into her. Dog and master exchanged looks. "You do that every time," Jamie said. "You know I'm going to have to stop and unlock the door, but you insist on running into me. Why is that?"

He thumped his tail once.

"And why am I in such a sour mood this morning?" Suddenly she remembered. She frowned as she opened the door so Fleas could go out. Max had just walked out on her the night before. Just walked out. She wished it didn't bother her so much. She wished she knew where she stood with him.

"Stop kidding yourself," she said aloud. "You know exactly where you stand." That's what hurt. It didn't matter that they were just itching to climb into bed together; the fact was Max didn't want anything permanent, and she was just going to have to accept it.

It was time she faced facts.

Fleas made straight for Jamie's one rosebush. Worse, he glanced back at her as if to say, "So what're you gonna do about it?" He hiked his leg and whizzed right on it. Jamie gave a sigh, went inside, and turned on her automatic coffee maker. It gurgled to life.

Her stomach growled. She wondered if Max was going to show up with doughnuts. She wasn't counting on it; it was already seven o'clock, and he would have been there by now. He was probably sitting in his hotel room practicing his great rejection speech. Well, he could shove it, as far as she was concerned. She didn't need him any more than he needed her. She had her pride.

Still, it hurt. They had been through so much together. How could a man look at her the way Max did and not feel something? How could he touch her and kiss her and remain so casual about it? Well, she wasn't made that way.

Fleas scratched at the door, and Jamie let him in, then she went into the bathroom. Fleas followed. Jamie stared at her reflection. Her hair was a mess, her mascara smudged. Her sleep shirt bore more wrinkles than Fleas's face. She glanced down at the dog.

"Would you just look at me?" she said. "I've let myself go."

Fleas cocked his head to the side as though trying to understand.

"We can't continue living on junk food," Jamie went on. "We're both at the age where we need to start taking better care of ourselves or our arteries are going to need Drano to get them unclogged. You know what that means? No more doughnuts and ice cream."

Fleas sank to the floor and put a paw over one eye. Jamie knew he didn't understand a word she said—he mainly reacted to her tone of voice—but one would have thought he was capable of taking in her every word.

"Yep, this means I need to start eating more vegetables, and you need to eat that expensive dog food I buy you. I'm serious, pal," she said, trying to convince herself as much as him. "I'm going to turn over a new leaf today, and I'm going to get Max Holt out of my system if it kills me. I'm going to stop eating those brownies."

Jamie went into her bedroom and changed into a pair of sweats, an old T-shirt, and running shoes. Fleas watched her, as if he expected something big was about to happen. Jamie tried to remember when she had last done anything that resembled jogging. Jeez, she would probably have a heart attack before she cleared the driveway.

Fleas followed her outside. It was already muggy, the air thick with humidity. She could literally feel it on her face and arms. If only the weather would break. Jamie regarded Fleas. "You can't go jogging because you just got neutered," she told him. "Besides, it requires physical activity, and we both know that's not your strong suit."

As if he understood, Fleas walked over to the nearest tree and plopped down in the shade. Jamie began doing a few stretches to prepare her poor body for what she was about to put it through.

She did not see the French poodle dash across the yard, but the next thing she knew Fleas was howling in protest, and a poodle was trying to mount him. Fleas darted behind Jamie as if hoping she could protect him.

"Oh, good grief!" a woman cried. "Precious, you stop that this instant!"

Jamie glanced in the direction of the voice. The woman wore a tight polka-dot dress and spike heels, had big blond hair, and she was doing her best to walk through the high grass in Jamie's yard. "Dammit, Precious, I said stop!"

Jamie stared in disbelief as the poodle chased Fleas around a large oleander bush. Finally, Fleas skirted around the back of the house with the poodle right behind him.

"Miss, I am so embarrassed," the woman said. "Precious tries to mount everything in sight. It's like he has just gone off the deep end. It's so embarrassing."

"Your dog is a male?" Jamie asked. "So is mine."

"Yes, he's a male, but that wouldn't stop him. It's humiliating." She sighed heavily.

"I'd better check on my dog," Jamie said, worried that Fleas would pull his stitches out running from the poodle. The last thing she needed was another vet bill. She hurried around the back of the house with the woman behind her. Fleas had found refuge in the old truck Jamie had parked in her backyard. The poodle was jumping up and down like a yo-yo trying to reach the tailgate.

"I think it'll be okay now," Jamie said. "Your dog doesn't seem to be able to reach the bed of the truck." She took another look at the blonde, who seemed to be in her early forties. "I don't recall seeing you before. Are you new in the neighborhood?"

"Oh, yes, I'm renting the house next door. My name is Barbara Fender."

"Jamie Swift." Jamie saw the woman's eyes suddenly widen, and she turned. Max had arrived with coffee and doughnuts.

"Who is that hunk?" Barbara whispered.

"His name is Max."

"Is he your boyfriend?"

"Well, um, it's complicated."

"All relationships are complicated," the woman said sourly. "You ask me, they're not worth it."

Jamie found herself nodding in agreement.

"Sorry I'm late," Max called out. "I had to make a lot of calls this morning." His eyes combed her in her baggy sweats. "Nice outfit."

Jamie felt like crawling beneath the truck, but she

was afraid the poodle would start humping her. "I was about to go for a run."

"Why? Is your car on the blink?" Max looked at the woman beside Jamie. "Hi. I'm Max."

"Barbara."

All at once, the poodle raced toward Max and started humping his leg. "Nice to meet you, Barbara," he said, trying to shake the poodle off. "Is this your dog? I have to admit I've always had a fondness for poodles. My grandmother raised them. I just can't remember any of them liking *me* this well."

Barbara tried to get her dog under control. Finally, she grabbed him and picked him up. "Precious is going through a difficult time right now. I'm so sorry."

"No need to apologize," Max said.

"Barbara is moving in next door," Jamie explained. Max nodded, and they were all silent, each of them obviously at a loss for words. "Would you like to join us for a cup of coffee?" Jamie asked, although she knew she didn't sound sincere. She was eager for the woman to take her dog home.

As if sensing Jamie was only trying to be polite, Barbara shook her head. "I think I need to get Precious home," she said, "but thanks just the same."

Max and Jamie waited until she'd disappeared inside her house before trying to convince Fleas to get down from the bed of the truck. Finally, Max pulled out a doughnut, and the hound climbed down, took the doughnut and almost swallowed it whole before racing toward the house.

"Wow, I've never seen Fleas run like that," Jamie said.

"How come you didn't want your neighbor to have coffee with us?" Max asked.

Jamie looked at him. "What makes you think I didn't?"

"You're usually friendlier. Even to people you've just met."

"I think it had a lot to do with her kooky dog."

"You don't like her."

Jamie didn't respond because he was right. It could have been her imagination, but she hadn't appreciated the way Barbara had looked at Max. But then, he always drew stares from the opposite sex.

Oh, jeez, she had been jealous. She had all the symptoms of being in love. She could try to convince herself otherwise, but she knew better.

Problem was, Max probably knew, as well. That was the worst part.

ELEVEN

Max followed Jamie inside the house with the bag of doughnuts. "About last night," he began.

"I'd rather not discuss last night," Jamie said, avoiding eye contact. "We've got a murder to solve."

"I'll grant you that, but we probably need to discuss what's going on between us."

Jamie looked at him. "And what *is* going on between us, Max?"

"It's complicated."

"Funny, that's the same word I'd use."

"I have very strong feelings for you, Jamie. The last thing I want to do is hurt you."

"Save it, Max. I think I know where this is going."

He stepped closer. "I don't think you do."

"Then tell me."

He hesitated. "I don't want to lose you. But I'm not sure what our future holds. I spent most of the night thinking about you. I need time."

Jamie knew better. Time would not change anything. "I really have a lot on my mind right now," she said, wanting to change the subject. Max did not have to spell it out for her.

"I know," he said softly. He was quiet for a moment. "So, you were going jogging, huh? You look like you're in pretty good shape to me."

She shrugged.

"I have doughnuts," he said.

Damn the man. He knew doughnuts were her weakness.

"Would you rather I leave?"

That was the last thing she wanted. "No."

Max offered Fleas another doughnut. The dog inhaled it. So much for her plan for the two of them to start eating healthy, Jamie thought.

The doorbell rang, and Jamie stood. Max looked at her. "What is this, Grand Central Station? Don't you ever have time to yourself?"

"Vera's test-driving another car," Jamie said. "She called earlier, wants me to have a look." Jamie opened the door before Vera had time to ring the bell a second time. The woman was dressed in a purple pantsuit and hot-pink scarf. It was obvious she'd taken a lot of time with her hair and makeup.

"What do you think?" she asked Jamie, turning around so Jamie could get a better look at her outfit. "My preacher's going to have a hissy fit when he sees me coming down the aisle for communion this morning."

"You look great," Jamie said.

"I feel great. I figure age is just a state of mind, know what I mean?" She didn't wait for a response. "Quick, come check out the cool wheels I'm test-driving. I don't have much time because I'm going to the early church service, then a bunch of us girls are attending the singles breakfast. Let the guys get a load of me in this outfit. 'Course, they're too old to do anything about it if you get my drift."

Jamie glanced past Vera and found herself looking at a white Jaguar. "Oh, jeez."

"It's eight years old," Vera said, "but you'd never know it. Isn't it beautiful? The dealer said he can give me a really good deal on it."

Jamie looked at her. "Why can't you buy something sensible?"

"Because I don't want to ruin my new image," Vera said. "Besides, I can afford a car like this as long as it's not brand-new."

"I think you'd better have Max look at it," Jamie said. She turned, almost bumping into an amused Max.

"A Jag, huh?" he said to Vera.

"Yeah. Would you mind taking a look at it?"

Max followed her outside where he spent a few minutes checking it over before Vera pulled away.

"I shouldn't have lent her the red Mustang," Jamie said. "I've created a monster."

"She's just having fun," Max said. "Speaking of which, why don't you and I spend the day investigating a few of the guys, then have dinner tonight."

Jamie wrestled with the thought. It was tempting.

"Say yes, Jamie."

She wanted to go in the worst way. "What should I wear?"

"Something a little dressy," he said. "And wear that black thing underneath it."

Jamie's stomach fluttered. She was playing with fire, and she was likely to get burned.

Destiny arrived at Jamie's house an hour later.

"I'm sorry if I sounded rude last night," Jamie said. "I still don't believe in all this otherworldly stuff, but we do need your help."

Destiny shrugged. "Like I said, I'm used to it." She looked at Max. "I drove by Larry's car lot on the way over and saw the new Corvette you mentioned parked beside the building so he's obviously working. I also picked up a pair of binoculars."

Max handed her a photo of Johnson. "This should help."

Jamie arched a brow. "How'd you come up with such a good picture in so little time?"

"Holt Technology, Swifty."

"Why aren't you going to the police with your suspicions?" Destiny asked.

"And tell them what?" Max said. "We don't have anything on him. Yet," he added.

"He's very angry," Destiny said. "I sense that about him even though I haven't seen him."

"You've got that right," Jamie said, then realized it was the first time she had agreed with anything Destiny said.

"Oh, by the way," Max said, "I'd like for you to try and meet with the chef today if you have time."

"What excuse is she going to use?" Jamie asked.

Destiny smiled. "I'll come up with something. I don't have trouble meeting men."

"Dumb question," Jamie said.

Max grinned. "I'm going to have Jamie pretend to have car trouble so we can get a look at the mechanic, then we'll try to set up a meeting with John Price, the accountant."

"What about the other guy? Mr. 'Deeper Than the Night'?"

"Don't worry, I've been saving him for you," Max said. "Why don't you call him today and see what you can work out?"

"Tell me this," Destiny said. "If he's rich and good-looking, why would he run an ad in a personals section?"

"He just moved back to town and is obviously looking for a way to meet women. He appears clean, but the fact that Luanne Ritter died only a week after he moved back to Beaumont makes him a suspect. *If* the murder had anything to do with the personals section. Plus, I have his cell phone record proving he and Luanne talked. She must've written to him the minute his ad hit the paper. I suspect she contacted everyone who ran an ad."

"She must've been very lonely," Destiny said.

Jamie spoke. "They could have met for drinks or dinner, but Sam decided she wasn't his type."

"Not a very good reason to kill her," Destiny said. She suddenly looked annoyed.

"What is it?" Jamie asked.

"Oh, it's just Ronnie being a pain in the ass as usual. Like I told you, he doesn't like the fact that I might actually meet a man and find him attractive. It's like I'm supposed to be content hanging out with spooks all the time. This Sam Hunter sounds like a real catch to me."

"If he's not a killer," Max reminded.

Destiny nodded. "Yes, well, a woman has to draw the line somewhere."

"We have to work out a plan so that I'll be available at all times for each of you," Max said. "The rules remain the same. You each carry cell phones, and you avoid being alone with these men at all costs." He looked at Jamie. "Understood?"

She nodded.

Max checked his wristwatch. "Jamie, I'm going to need the keys to your car. I'm going to pull it out of the garage and make a few adjustments under the hood so you'll have a reason to call the mechanic."

"I'm confused," Destiny said. "Why can't Jamie just call him, like I did the dentist?"

"This guy didn't list his telephone number in the ad," Max said, "so my, um, assistant had to find him through other sources."

"John Price didn't list his phone number in his ad," Jamie pointed out.

"We're going to use a different angle. You'll tell him you own the newspaper and that you were intrigued by his ad."

"Is that what you told Larry Johnson?" Destiny asked.

"No. He thought we were looking for a car."

Jamie went for her car keys while Destiny called the chef and made a date for later that day. When Jamie returned, she called the mechanic, who promised to be there in an hour, mentioning there would be an extra fee for coming out on his day off.

Jamie then called John Price, explained she owned the *Gazette* and had gotten the information from his ad. At first he was cool toward her, but he finally agreed to meet for coffee later in the day. "I don't think Mr. Price appreciated me contacting him the way I did," she said after she hung up. "Perhaps I should have written him via our post office box."

"That would have taken too long," Max said. "What other impressions did you get?"

"He sounded very cautious. I have a funny feeling he's hiding something."

By the time Jamie walked into the Downtown Café for her meeting with John Price, the mechanic, a good old boy by the name of Carl Edwards, had made the necessary repairs to her car and had asked her out. She'd taken his phone number and promised to get back to him. "Edwards might be a flirt," she'd told Max once the man left, "but he didn't come off as a murderer."

Max had shrugged. "Since when do murderers wear signs?"

John Price was in his mid to late fifties, a tall man with salt-and-pepper hair, dressed in neat slacks and a golf shirt. He looked embarrassed when Jamie approached the table.

"I was afraid of this," he said, standing until she was seated.

"I beg your pardon?"

"I thought you sounded a little young on the telephone. I probably should have asked your age."

"Is age an issue with you?"

"It is when the woman you're meeting for coffee is the same age as your daughter."

"I doubt that," Jamie said. "I'm thirty years old, not exactly a kid."

The waitress appeared and took their order for pie and coffee. "So, you own the local newspaper," Price said.

"Yes. It has been in my family for years."

"I'm sorry if I sounded rude to you on the telephone, but I was very surprised to get your call since I hadn't listed my number in the newspaper."

"I took it off the information you sent with your ad," Jamie said. "I didn't mean to infringe on your privacy," she added, "but I was intrigued. Your ad said you were open to new experiences. What exactly does that mean?"

He chuckled. "My doctor has accused me of showing signs of a midlife crisis," he said. "First thing I did when I turned fifty was buy a brand-new Harley and start dating younger women. My second wife was fifteen years my junior. Bad move on my part; we've since parted ways." He quickly changed the subject. "Now, I'm thinking of taking flying lessons."

Jamie noticed he had an easy smile. "Sounds interesting," she said.

The waitress appeared with their order.

They talked for an hour. Finally, John picked up the check. "Jamie, I had a delightful time, but I suggest you try meeting someone your own age. With your looks, you shouldn't have any trouble."

She glanced up in surprise. "Am I being rejected?"

He laughed. "No, but I would feel silly dating a woman twenty-five years younger than me. Please don't take it personally."

They said goodbye with a handshake. Max waited just down the street at Maynard's Sandwich Shop. "Mr. Price dumped me after the first date."

Max shrugged. "That's okay, you still have me."

Jamie didn't respond.

Destiny showed up later that afternoon. "The chef is about a hundred pounds overweight. Naturally, he's looking for a long-term relationship. I think he's already found one in food. I spent the rest of the day watching Larry Johnson. He didn't leave his car lot. He was the only one working today. I'm not surprised, since it's Sunday."

The three sat around the table discussing their findings and brainstorming. Finally, Destiny left.

Max stood to leave a few minutes later. "I need to go back to my hotel and make some calls," he said. "How about I pick you up around six?"

"Sounds good," Jamie said. "Where are we going?"

"It's a surprise."

Jamie walked him to the front door. He paused and looked down at her and for a moment she thought he might kiss her. Instead, he turned and headed for his car.

She sighed and leaned against the doorjamb. Now, why, when the timing had been perfect, hadn't he kissed her? She looked at Fleas. "See what I mean? I never know where I stand with that man."

Fleas responded by walking over to the refrigerator and glancing up at the freezer. "You're right," Jamie said. "When the going gets tough, the tough eat ice cream."

Muffin was waiting when Max climbed into the car. "I've taken care of everything you requested for your date tonight," she said. "Your plane will be here within the hour, and I made reservations at your favorite restaurant in New York City. Once you get off the plane, a limo will be waiting to take you there."

"Thanks," Max said. "You think Jamie will be impressed?"

"I think Jamie would be happy eating a barbecue sandwich at a local restaurant," Muffin said, "but if this is the way you want to play it, go for it."

Max was quiet. "You think I'm going overboard?"

"Hey, what do I know? She'll either think you're showing off or she'll be flattered. And since when do you worry what a woman thinks?"

"This is different."

"If I know Jamie, she'll be touched by your efforts."

"Were you able to get anything else on Sam Hunter?"

"I found nothing to indicate the man is not who he seems to be. No police record." She paused. "I'm beginning to wonder if Luanne's murder had something to do with her business. She had a lot of enemies."

"Lamar Tevis is checking into it."

"Which means we could be looking in the wrong place."

"I hope you're right, Muffin, but if you're not, there's a good chance we're going to have another murder on our hands before long."

TWELVE

Jamie was ready and waiting for Max by quarter of six. She wore a simple black dress with spaghetti straps, matching heels, and carried a small purse. The see-through body suit beneath it, her purchase from Sinful Delights, was strapless and hugged her tightly. After her talk with Max she wondered why she was wearing it.

She was taking a big chance, and she knew it. She was risking a broken heart. Max Holt had made it plain he didn't know what their future held; he had not promised her happily-ever-after. But he had a hold on her heart, and there wasn't a damn thing she could do about it.

"How do I look?" she asked Fleas, who was napping in front of a kid's TV show since she did not allow him to watch anything with sex or violence. He didn't budge, didn't bat an eye. Jamie knew he was pouting because she was going out. It didn't take a genius of a dog to realize she didn't wear her best black dress every day.

And Fleas was no genius.

"Okay, be that way," she said, "but I deserve a night out once in a while. It's not like I don't try to take you with me everywhere I go. Lord, you even go to work with me."

Still Fleas made no movement.

"And I was going to give you another bowl of ice cream before I left. That's two in one day for you, pal."

Fleas suddenly raised his head. He might not be a genius, but he had learned to recognize the words *ice cream* and *doughnuts*.

"I knew that would get your attention," she said.

He thumped his tail and pulled himself into a standing position. Jamie watched him make his way into the kitchen where he sat down in front of the refrigerator and waited.

The doorbell rang. Jamie had been so busy trying to get a response from her dog that she hadn't heard Max pull up. Her stomach did a series of tiny flip-flops as she opened the door. Max stood on the other side looking like something off a magazine cover in a dove-gray suit and blue shirt and tie.

Several seconds passed before either of them said anything.

Finally, Max spoke. "Are you wearing anything under that dress?"

Of all the questions he might have asked, Jamie had not expected that one. "Um, not much."

"You know, Swifty," he said, stepping inside, "we could always stay in and order takeout."

"You look pretty good yourself, Holt."

"If we don't leave soon—"

"I just need a couple of minutes," she said. "I promised Fleas he could have ice cream."

"Of course."

Max followed her into the kitchen where Jamie dipped out a healthy serving of butter pecan ice cream into Fleas's bowl. The dog never took his eyes off her. Finally, she set it down before him. "There now. He's had his dinner, and I let him out, so he should be okay until I get back." Jamie grabbed her purse, and they started for the door.

"Aren't you going to turn off the TV?" Max asked.

"No, he likes having it on while I'm gone. It helps

with his separation anxiety." Max shook his head sadly as they stepped outside. He took the keys from her and locked her door while Jamie waited, then he walked her to his car. She was nervous. This seriously smacked of a date, and she and Max weren't in the habit of dating. What did it mean? Was she reading more into it than she should? Max was right. She did too much thinking. Couldn't she for once allow herself the luxury of enjoying herself without all the what-ifs? Just for once?

Max helped her into the car and closed the door. He climbed in beside her.

Lord but he smelled good, she thought.

They were on their way in minutes. "It's quiet in here," Jamie said. "Where's Muffin?"

"She's not feeling well so I gave her the night off."

"What do you mean she's not feeling well? She's a computer."

He shook his head. "She's been researching all this pregnancy stuff for Dee Dee so she's suffering the same symptoms."

"Tell me you're kidding." Not that Jamie should have been surprised. Muffin had gone through menopause when it seemed as if Dee Dee were suffering the symptoms and Muffin had researched it. "That is the craziest thing I've ever heard," she added.

He smiled. "So is feeding your dog ice cream in front of the TV set. It's a strange world in which we live, Swifty."

Max reached over and took her hand. He raised it to his lips, and his gaze met hers. "Have I told you lately that you're beautiful?"

Jamie felt her heart in her throat. Was it her imagination or did he seem different tonight? His eyes searched her face. What was he looking for? Did he suspect the depth of her feelings? She was the first to look away. "Thank you, Max," she said at last.

It was almost as if they'd unconsciously agreed not to discuss Luanne Ritter's murder and their investigation as Max drove through town. Instead, he filled her in on what was happening at Holt Industries. Jamie was amazed at what she heard. Not only was Max on the cutting edge of technological research, he was involved in biomedical research and pharmaceuticals, among other things. He had offices all over the world. She listened as he described where some of his research could actually lead. It seemed there was nothing the man wasn't interested in exploring.

Jamie arched one brow when he took the road that led to the small airport.

"Where are we going?" she asked.

"I told you, it's a surprise."

Jamie's jaw dropped clear to her collarbone when Max pulled up near the runway where a medium-size jet waited with the words "Holt Industries" emblazoned on the sides. Lights were flashing, and airport personnel hurried about. Two pilots stood near the steps of the plane, each dressed in khaki slacks and navy blazers.

"Good evening, Mr. Holt," one of them said as soon as Max pulled to a stop and stepped from the car.

Jamie's door was immediately opened, and the other pilot helped her out. "It's a beautiful night for flying," he told her with a smile.

Max held out his elbow as Jamie, still gaping, took it and walked with him toward the jet. "We've filed the flight plan," the older pilot said. "We're ready to go. Our ETA at LaGuardia is eight-thirty."

"LaGuardia?" Jamie asked as Max prodded her up the steps leading inside the luxury cabin. He nodded. "But that's in New York City," she said.

"I told you I wanted to take you someplace nice."

Jamie stepped inside the cabin and found herself enveloped in luxury. The sizable sitting area was done in a rich tan, but there were touches of navy blue that set it off.

She turned and looked at Max as the pilots disappeared through a curtain in the cockpit. "I've never been on a jet like this."

"It's perfectly safe if that's what you're worried about. I'll show you around if you like."

They took a tour of the front area first, the lavatory, a small galley, and a built-in cabinet that held a stereo, DVD player, satellite phone, and whatever else Max might need in order to relax or conduct business during his flight. Finally, he led her to the back of the plane where a small but more than adequate bedroom was situated, complete with a lavatory that included a small tub.

"Holy mackerel," Jamie said. "It's got everything."

"I specifically designed it so I could rest during international flights." He studied the look on her face. "How about a glass of champagne?" he said. "I usually have a flight attendant on board when I travel on business, but I wanted us to be alone tonight."

Jamie smiled. She felt like Cinderella. Someone had even thought to put out a plate of hors d'oeuvres. "Except for the pilots, of course," she said.

Max nodded. "Yes, I'm afraid there was no getting around that, but they won't bother us. Please—" He motioned toward one of the sofas. "Sit down and relax, and I'll open the champagne."

Jamie did as he asked, but it was all she could do to keep from gawking. The jet should come as no surprise, she reminded herself. Any man who drove a two-million-dollar car was bound to have a nice jet.

Lord, if Vera could see her now.

She jumped when she heard the champagne cork pop. A moment later, Max carried in an ice bucket holding a bottle; in his other hand were two flute glasses. He poured them each a glass and toasted her, just as one of the pilots told them to fasten their seat belts for takeoff.

"To you, Swifty. For bringing so many good things into my life."

She didn't want to think what that meant. "From the looks of it, you already have a lot of good stuff." The plane started moving.

"A man can have all the material things he needs and still be lacking. You fill up that empty space."

Jamie couldn't have been more surprised. What did it mean? "That's the nicest thing you've ever said to me, Max." They touched glasses and took sips of their champagne.

"Maybe I should start saying more nice things," Max said. "Seems we spend all our time chasing bad guys."

"You may have something there, Holt. Feels like we're always knee-deep in trouble."

"Yeah, but you'll have to admit we make a great team. The bad guys don't stand a chance."

She laughed. "Yeah, but we've had our share of close calls."

"I like that you're adventurous."

"I haven't had much of a choice since you came into my life."

"True. But you'll have to admit I'm not boring."

"I'd settle for boring once in a while. I'm allergic to bullets."

"I guess I like a challenge now and then."

"Now and then, Max? You would never be happy living a normal life."

"What do you consider normal?"

A house surrounded by a picket fence came to mind, but Jamie suspected the thought would scare him to death. It would smack of settling down, and she doubted

Max would ever be satisfied with such an existence. "Maybe there's no such thing as normal after all," she said after a moment.

"You know what I think?" Max said. "I think you need to be challenged, too. And you know what else? I want to kiss you." He took her glass and set it on the coffee table in front of the sofa.

She didn't protest as he placed his hand beneath her chin and lifted her head slightly before gently touching his lips to hers. Jamie found herself leaning into the kiss, and she welcomed it when he took her in his arms and held her close. He kissed her temple and her eyelids and pressed his lips against the hollow of her throat before capturing her lips once more.

Jamie clung to him, loving the taste and smell and feel of the man who held her. She reached up and curled her hands around his neck. The kiss deepened, and Max slipped his tongue past her lips, exploring the inside of her mouth, tasting her thoroughly. Jamie boldly met his tongue with hers. She felt him draw a quick breath of excitement.

Max gathered her up in his arms and stood, tugging off her heels as he went. Jamie knew where they were headed, knew she wanted Max Holt as much as he wanted her.

It had been that way from the beginning. Their gazes locked as Max carried her into the bedroom. He dipped his head forward and kissed her again. Just like in the movies, she thought. Once again, lips parted, tongues mingled. Jamie could feel her insides growing as soft as warm butter. For once she didn't think about what tomorrow or the next day might bring.

She was willing to take a chance.

She felt the bed sink beneath her as Max gently laid her on the mattress. He turned long enough to close the door and lock it, and then he began removing his clothes. He draped them over a chair. He never once took his eyes off her face.

He was naked and already aroused when he joined her. He raised her up slightly, just long enough to unzip her dress, which he draped over his own clothes. "Oh, Jesus," he said, staring at the filmy black body suit. "I'm going to buy stock in the company that makes those things."

Once again, he was beside her, kissing her, running his hands over her body. Using his tongue, he teased her nipples through the fabric of the body suit.

"Oh, Swifty." He smoothed one hand over her hip, her belly, then slid one finger along the lace edge of the body suit, slowly, leisurely.

Jamie moaned and arched against him. She reached for him, but he smiled. "We're in no hurry, sweetheart. Just lie back and enjoy."

Jamie closed her eyes as he pulled the wispy fabric from her body and kissed his way down, pausing only briefly between her thighs before touching her with his tongue. She cried out softly. He flicked his tongue lightly over her before parting her with his fingers and tasting her fully. Jamie's breath caught at the back of her throat.

When she could no longer stand it, Max entered her, and it was all she could do to keep from crying out.

Max paused for a moment as if he needed time to get himself under control. "Damn" was all he could say in a shaky voice.

They began to move together, slowly at first, but each thrust from Max's body brought them closer to the edge. Jamie could feel the intensity building with sweet anticipation, even as Max's brow beaded with sweat, and he gritted his teeth in an obvious attempt to restrain himself.

Jamie was the first to feel the burst of pleasure, a

pleasure so intense that she called out to Max who immediately joined her in the last frenzied moments.

They clung to each other long afterward, waiting for their heartbeats to slow, waiting for the fog of passion to lift. Jamie snuggled against Max, knowing as long as she lived she would never want another man the way she did the one beside her.

"Max?"

He pulled her close. "Yeah?"

She wanted to tell him how she felt, confess her love, but fear alone prevented it. "I've never felt this way before," she said instead. There, she'd said it.

He kissed her forehead. "I knew we'd be good together, Swifty. I knew it the first time I saw you."

It was probably the closest she was going to get to what she'd wanted; an admission of love, but Jamie said nothing. Instead, she made to get up.

Max tightened his grip on her. "Where do you think you're going?"

"I saw a small tub in the bathroom. I thought—"

He interrupted her with a kiss. "There's plenty of time for that." He pulled her face close to his for another kiss.

Lord, she was a goner.

Jamie was touching up her makeup when Max reentered the bedroom and told her they needed to prepare for landing. She followed him into the sitting room, fastened her seat belt, and waited until the plane touched down and came to a halt, and the captain gave them the okay to move about the cabin.

Max checked his wristwatch and ushered her off the jet into a waiting limo. Jamie had never felt so pampered. The driver immediately whisked them away.

"I've never been to New York City," she said.

"You live in one of the prettiest towns I've ever seen,"

he said. "Why would you want to leave it?" Max hit a button, and a window slid up, separating them from the driver. He grinned and pulled Jamie onto his lap. "It's only half an hour from here to the restaurant," he whispered. "I'm putting you in charge."

Jamie shivered when his tongue made contact with her ear. "In charge of what?" she asked.

"Not letting us get carried away back here."

"You're talking to the wrong person, pal," she whispered as she snuggled against him and raised her lips to his for a kiss.

Emilie's was an intimate French restaurant with tiny white lights attached to a dark ceiling that gave one the feeling of dining beneath the stars. After sharing an appetizer of pâté de foie gras and wafers, Max and Jamie ordered filet mignon with a béarnaise sauce that Jamie claimed was to die for. Max teased her unmercifully as Jamie ordered chocolate pecan pie for dessert, but it was obvious he enjoyed watching her while he sipped his coffee.

"You remind me of a little girl sometimes," he said, when she caught him staring. "I don't think you ever had the chance to be a little girl when you were growing up."

A slight shadow crossed Jamie's face. "It often feels like I grew up too fast, but my dad and I had some pretty good times together."

Max smiled. "Tell me."

Jamie looked wistful. "He took me to Charleston from time to time, and we would eat at nice restaurants and visit the art gallery or the museum. I would wear my prettiest dress. My dad was the best. I don't remember a time he scolded me, except when I wanted to leave college and work full-time at the newspaper. He wouldn't hear of it."

"I'm glad you have so many good memories of him," Max said.

"Vera said he spoiled me shamelessly, and I guess he did."

"Why do you suppose he never remarried?"

Jamie's eyes clouded. "I don't think he ever got over my mother leaving him. He kept her clothes for the longest time. Vera finally made him give them to the Salvation Army."

"He never dated?"

"No. And it wasn't because he didn't have the opportunity. My father was a handsome man. Would you like to see a picture?" Jamie didn't wait for a response; she was already reaching into her purse for her wallet. She flipped it open to the image of a dark-haired man and handed it to Max.

"I can see the resemblance," Max said. He returned the picture. "You must've loved him very much."

Jamie nodded. "I was devastated when he died."

"Why do you suppose Vera never married?" Max asked, changing the subject.

"Vera was in love with my father, Max," she said simply.

"I guess I've always assumed as much," he said.

"She's never admitted it to me, but I knew."

"I wonder why she never told him."

"Vera's a proud woman. She would never have made her feelings known because he spent his life grieving the loss of my mother."

"Do you miss her?" Max asked.

"How can you miss someone you never knew?" Jamie pondered the question. "There were times, of course, when I wanted a mother. I envied the girls at school whose moms helped with parties or participated in school outings. Not that Vera didn't help out," she added quickly, "but it wasn't the same."

"I'm sorry, Jamie."

"Don't be. I had all the love and attention a kid could have possibly wanted. I just hope—" She paused and blushed.

Max waited. "What do you hope?"

Jamie met his gaze. "I just hope, if and when I have children, that I'm a better mother."

He smiled. "You'll be a fantastic mother, Jamie."

"I don't know," she said. "I've already spoiled Fleas something awful, and he's a dog."

Max laughed, and the two continued conversing for more than an hour before he signaled for the bill. Once he'd paid, he looked at Jamie. "Now, tell me. Is there anything in particular you'd like to see while we're in New York?"

It didn't take long for her to answer. "Times Square."

"You got it, Swifty."

The limo was waiting when they left the restaurant. Jamie stared out the window, awed by the skyscrapers that disappeared into the night sky. "I can't believe all the people," she said, noting the crowded sidewalks. When Times Square came into view, Max had the driver open the sunroof of the limo so Jamie could peer out.

"It looks just like it does on TV," she said, feeling a surge of excitement as she gazed in delight, much like a child on Christmas morning. They spent an hour riding through the streets before Max told the limo driver to stop at Sardi's where they had coffee.

When it was time to head back to the airport, Jamie turned to Max. "Thank you," she said.

Max smiled at her enthusiasm. "It was my pleasure. I'd like to bring you back during the day so you can see Central Park. I would love to take you to other places, say, Paris and Rome and Hong Kong, just to see them through your eyes."

"Don't you enjoy them?"

"Most of my travel is business related."

"Max, this is me you're talking to. I'm sure you've had your share of lovely companions."

"Does that bother you?"

It did, but she wouldn't admit it. "It's none of my business." Still, she wondered how many women he'd taken with him on his private jet.

"There are different types of relationships, Jamie. Some are more meaningful than others."

She paused and met his gaze. Her heart thumped wildly in her chest. "Yeah?"

"Some are nothing more than two people providing, as you say, companionship. Both people are mature enough to know up front that it isn't likely to last. Then there are those worth hanging on to."

Jamie stared back at him for so long she was sure her eyes had crossed. What the devil was the man trying to say? "You know what your problem is, Max?"

"Uh-oh."

"You don't know what you want."

"Or maybe it's that I want something so badly, and I don't know where it will lead," he said ruefully. "Ever thought of that?"

Was he referring to them? she wondered. "Are you scared? That's hard to believe."

"I'm human."

Jamie saw the vulnerability in his eyes. "People take risks when they fall in love," she said softly.

"Do you love me, Jamie?"

Her heart turned over in her chest. He had just asked her the million-dollar question. "I don't know," she hedged. "I keep telling myself it would be a mistake."

"Why?"

The look in his eyes was sincere. He wanted to know. "I don't think we're looking for the same thing, Max."

"Would it matter if I told you I'm looking for a way to spend more time in Beaumont? Frankie and I are discussing the possibility of bringing much-needed industry to the area."

"How come nobody told me?"

"It's still in the planning stages."

"What would you manufacture?"

"The same material my car is made of. It's a newly identified polymer that is lightweight but has the durability of the strongest steel. Think if that same material could be used on other automobiles. It could save a lot of lives. I just need to find a way to make it more affordable to the consumer."

"And you'd lower the unemployment rate in Beaumont," she said, thrilled at the prospect. "Oh, Max, this is exciting news."

"It's confidential for now," he said. "I don't want it announced until we know it's a sure thing." He paused. "The main reason I'm telling you is because I want you to know I'm hoping to be around more. If that means anything," he added.

Jamie's stomach turned somersaults at the thought. "I could probably adapt," she said.

"Yeah?"

"Yeah."

They arrived at the airport and boarded the plane. Once they'd taken off and were able to move about the cabin, Max and Jamie found themselves back in his bedroom where they made love until the captain announced they would be landing soon. They dressed hurriedly and took their seats in the front cabin. Jamie couldn't stop grinning.

"Why are you smiling?" Max said.

"Why do you think I'm smiling? I've been flown to New York on a private jet, eaten at a fancy restaurant, seen Times Square, and I've been laid three times."

Max laughed out loud. "The things you say. That's what I like best about you."

As Max drove Jamie home shortly after three A.M., she leaned her head back in the seat and sighed happily. "Thank you, Max, for a wonderful evening."

"We should do it more often," he said.

They arrived back at Jamie's house, only to find Destiny's car sitting in the driveway. Jamie frowned. "I don't believe this," she said. "What is *she* doing here at this hour? I'm beginning to think she's following me."

"I'm beginning to think the same thing," Max said in annoyance, surprising Jamie.

Jamie suddenly felt afraid. "I hope it's not what I think it is." She rushed from the car as soon as Max parked.

"Oh, thank goodness you're finally home," Destiny said.

"What on earth are you doing here at this hour?" Jamie demanded.

"I've had several visions." She suddenly sneezed. "They were awful."

"We're listening," Max said, still sounding irritated.

"It's about the next victim," Destiny said, looking directly at Jamie. "She's going to be somebody you know."

THIRTEEN

Jamie felt as though her breath had been knocked out of her. "Oh my God!" she cried. "Who is it?"

"I can't get a fix on the person," Destiny said.

"Come inside," Jamie said, noting that the woman was trembling badly. There was fear in her eyes.

"Ronnie is with me."

"He can come in."

Jamie handed a silent Max the keys to her front door, and he started ahead of them as Jamie and Destiny waited. Once inside, Max, maintaining his silence, put on coffee.

"Now, tell me what you saw," Jamie said.

Once again, Destiny sneezed. "Like I told you, the victim is going to put up a fight, and she'll leave scratches on the murderer's arms. I can't get an image of a face or name. But I'm positive you know her." Destiny began to wring her hands. "Do you have any friends who might answer a personal ad?"

"No one I can think of."

They moved to the kitchen as soon as Max had the coffee ready. "Max, I think we should go ahead and notify the police," Jamie said.

"Lamar can't find out the kind of information I can. Muffin is working around the clock doing background checks."

"Muffin is out of whack right now," Jamie said, "since

she talked to Dee Dee. She thinks she's pregnant, remember?"

"She's still able to do her job."

"Your secretary is pregnant?" Destiny asked Max.

Max shifted in his seat. "She just thinks she is."

"Has she seen a doctor?" Destiny asked.

"It's a long story," he said, "but she's good at background checks. As a matter of fact, she did one on you."

Jamie turned to the woman. "Max does background checks on everyone. He even did one on me."

"So you think you know all about me, do you?" she said, anger having replaced the scared look in her eyes. "If you're so smart, tell me what you've learned."

Max didn't hesitate. "I know that before you married into money you made your living as a fortune-teller in one carnival show after another. I know you were arrested more than once for operating illegally out of your home. You've changed your name several times."

"My real name is Betty Sue Jenkins," Destiny said. "Of course I changed it. Who's going to take a psychic seriously with a name like that?"

Max looked at Jamie. "She's been married five times, and the authorities exhumed the body of one of her husbands because his children suspected poisoning."

Destiny hitched her chin high. "They found nothing. His kids were a bunch of spoiled brats who resented the fact I was awarded the bulk of their father's estate. And do you know *why* I was awarded it? Because I was a damn good wife to him, and I was the one who cared for him when he was sick. His children couldn't be bothered."

Jamie realized she was staring and rubbing Fleas's head frantically. The dog seemed as agitated as she was. She stood. "I don't care about Destiny's past, Max. All I care about is finding a killer. You're the one who said we should use every means possible."

"I don't need you to defend me, Jamie," Destiny said. "I've lived with this sort of thing all my life. I'm going home now and get some rest." She paused to sneeze. "I'm sorry I bothered you."

She was gone. Jamie sank into her chair and looked at Max. "What's going on?"

"I'm beginning to have my doubts about her. She hasn't given us anything we could go on. I wasn't going to tell you what I found out at first, but I don't appreciate her barging in at this hour and scaring you. And think about this. Suppose she did get away with poisoning her husband. That would make her a murderer. Luanne Ritter's murder didn't occur until after Destiny Moultrie hit town, right?"

Jamie gaped at him. "You're not insinuating that Destiny killed Luanne? What would be her motive? She didn't even know Luanne Ritter."

"We don't know that. She could have done business with Luanne."

"She doesn't need money; her husbands left her well off."

"I just think it's possible that Destiny might have ulterior motives. I'm not certain what they are, but her past speaks for itself."

"My instincts are pretty good, and I believe Destiny has a good heart. Her only motive for contacting me was to write a column for the newspaper, but she got dragged into this situation when she had a vision about Luanne Ritter's murder. Maybe it's all been just one big coincidence after another, but I believe she saw something tonight. You saw how upset she was. The woman was terrified."

Jamie got up and let Fleas out, then went about picking up dirty coffee cups. All at once she heard Fleas yelp. She and Max raced to the door.

The poodle next door was chasing Fleas across the

backyard. "Oh, it's that damn poodle again," Jamie said, racing out the door, just as her neighbor, Barbara Fender, hurried over.

"Precious, come here this instant!" the woman cried, although the dog paid no heed. She and Jamie reached the dogs at the same instant. Barbara pulled her dog free, and Fleas took off for the pickup truck parked close by.

"Jamie, I am so sorry," the woman said. "Precious woke up having to go to the bathroom."

Jamie noticed the woman had changed her big hair. It had been cut into a flattering style and colored, giving her a softer look. Jamie felt bad that she hadn't tried to get to know her better; the woman probably didn't know a soul in town. Then Jamie reminded herself she'd been too busy trying to catch a killer.

As though realizing Jamie was staring at her hair, Barbara touched it self-consciously. "What do you think?" she said. "I figured it was time for a change. New town, new people, new hairstyle."

"I think it looks nice," Jamie said. She smiled. "Tell you what. I'll call you first chance I get. We'll get together, and I'll tell you about my dog's emotional problems. Then you won't feel so bad."

"I'd like that," Barbara said.

Max joined them. "Come on, Fleas," he said, trying to coax the hound from the back of the pickup.

"He's not going to get down," Jamie said.

Max finally picked up Fleas and carried him into the house. Jamie and Barbara said good night, and Jamie headed for her house. She found Max inside feeding the dog cheese curls. "There you go, spoiling my dog."

"He deserves it after what he's been through. That's the ugliest poodle I've ever laid eyes on."

"Are you okay, boy?" Jamie asked her pet. But he was more interested in the cheese curls. Finally, Max poured the rest of the bag into Fleas's bowl.

Max checked his wristwatch. "Wow, it's almost four A.M. I'm beat, how about you?"

"Exhausted," Jamie said.

"You need to get to bed."

"I was thinking the same thing."

He slipped his arms around her waist and kissed her lightly on the lips.

"I'm just so confused, Max. I don't know what to think anymore. If Destiny is right—" She paused and shuddered. "I don't even want to think what might happen."

"I should get going," Max said, although he looked reluctant. "You need your rest."

"Yeah, like I'm going to be able to sleep. I'm afraid, Max."

His look softened. As if to ease the tension, he suddenly smiled. "If I stay, your neighbors will think you're a floozy."

She knew he was trying to lighten the mood. "Everyone already thinks I'm a floozy, not to mention the town drunk."

"Frankly, I liked seeing that side of you. I hope to see more of it." He released her.

The last thing she wanted him to do was leave. "Um, Max?"

"Yeah?"

She made a poor attempt at trying to return his smile. "If I let you stay, will you still get the doughnuts after we wake up?"

When Jamie awoke it was after ten o'clock. She bolted upright on the bed, just as Max came into the room with a tray of doughnuts and coffee.

"Don't panic," he said. "I called Vera and told her you would be late coming into the office." He set the tray on the bed. "Breakfast is served."

Jamie suddenly realized she was naked. Then she recalled that, despite both of them being tired when they'd gone to bed at four A.M., they had made love again. She had needed him desperately, had needed to feel his lips on her body, feel him inside her. Only Max could chase away the fear in her heart and give her something good to cling to. Exhaustion had forced her eyes closed afterward, but at dawn she had jerked awake in the throes of a nightmare. Max had gathered her close, coaxing her to sleep once more with his steady voice at her ear.

Now with the sun up, she felt less afraid. What she did feel was self-conscious at being stark raving naked. She pulled the sheet higher over her breasts.

"No need for that," Max said. "I've already seen every square inch of you, and I like it."

Jamie blushed and reached for her cup of coffee. "How do my eyes look?" They felt gritty from lack of sleep.

"They look very blue and beautiful, as always."

She noted Max was dressed in casual clothes. "You've been up a while."

"Yeah, I drove over to my hotel and showered. I needed to change clothes."

Jamie quickly ate two doughnuts and polished off her coffee. "I've got to grab a shower," she said. She glanced around. "What happened to my sleep shirt?"

"I have no idea."

"Max?" Her voice was stern. He'd probably tossed it in the trash. "Oh, what the hell." She climbed from the bed and turned for the door leading toward the bathroom. She could feel Max's eyes on her. "Take a picture, Holt," she called back over her shoulder.

"Don't need to. I've already burned your image in my brain."

Jamie was thankful when she reached the privacy of

her bathroom. She turned on the shower, waited for the water to heat up, and climbed in. She thought of Destiny's visit the night before and experienced the same sense of dread. She tried to push it from her mind. Maybe Destiny was wrong. Hadn't she admitted that her predictions weren't one hundred percent accurate? Maybe this was one of those times. Jamie prayed that was the case, but she still remembered the look of fear in the woman's eyes.

She shook her head, trying to clear it. Since when did she believe in Destiny's visions anyway? Anybody who claimed to have a dead spirit following them everywhere they went had to be a little kooky, didn't they? Didn't they?

She was too wrapped up in the case, Jamie told herself. She and Max had done nothing but work on it since he'd hit town. She needed a break. She needed to check her schedule so she could have lunch with Maxine Chambers. Or maybe she could get together with her new neighbor. Barbara was probably anxious to start making friends; and she most likely needed a break from all her unpacking.

Jamie did not hear the door open, but the shower curtain suddenly parted and Max stepped in as naked as the day he was born.

"What the—"

He smiled. "I've often wondered what it would be like to take a shower with you."

"Isn't this your second for the day?"

"Yeah, but who's counting? Give me your soap and washcloth."

"I can do this myself, you know."

"Come on, Swifty, give a guy a break."

Jamie did as she was told. Max lathered the washcloth and started at the nape of her neck, working his way down to the heels of her feet. The feel of his hands on her body did wonderful things to her insides, made her forget things.

"Okay, turn around," he said.

She turned. Max busied himself washing her breasts, leaning forward to tongue each nipple once he rinsed them of soap. Jamie was suddenly enveloped in a world of sensations and tingling nerve endings. "I usually shower in half this time," she managed.

"Yeah, but think how dull it is to shower alone." He worked his way down her abdomen, her flat tummy, and finally between her thighs where he explored her with deft fingers. Jamie moaned; all logical thinking ceased, worries dissipated like smoke in a breeze. She grasped his shoulders for support as he brought her to the height of pleasure.

She was trembling by the time she climbed from the tub and toweled herself. She caught the glint of desire in Max's eyes, the slight tilt of his mouth. He knew damn well what he did to her. She glanced down at him.

"As you can see, the feeling is mutual," he said, drying himself. He smacked her behind lightly and chased her into the bedroom.

Jamie giggled like a schoolgirl. It felt good to laugh. "I have to go to work," she protested.

"It'll wait," he said. "Besides, I'll be there to help you."

They fell onto the bed together. Jamie suddenly felt less shy with him. She ran her fingers over his chest, and nipped one of his nipples playfully.

He shivered.

"You're asking for trouble, Swifty," he said.

"You ain't seen nuthin' yet, bubba." She toyed with his chest for a moment before lightly running her fingers down his stomach where the hair thinned slightly, and then she moved lower. She stroked him. Finally, using the very tip of her tongue, she tasted him.

"Oh God, I'm a dead man," he said.

Jamie smiled and put him in her mouth. Max gazed down at her with a look of dazed passion. The husky moan he gave prodded her onward.

Jamie swirled her tongue around him. It was exhilarating to know she could wield so much power over a man who was accustomed to calling all the shots.

Finally, he pulled away, eased her gently onto her back, and using his own tongue, brought her to the edge of orgasm. She moaned and reached for him, and he entered her. Their sighs of pleasure rose like music.

Max moved against her slowly at first, but soon they were caught up in an erotic dance, and Jamie's cries were stifled by Max's kisses.

Afterward, Max gathered her in his arms, where Jamie snuggled against him like a soft kitten. She felt safe and secure.

"A man could get used to this, Swifty," he said.

She nodded, reveling in the fact that she had Max Holt spent and naked beside her. Her hand on his chest measured each heartbeat, and she remained quiet until his breathing slowed. She could smell the heady scent of their lovemaking mixed with Max's soap and aftershave.

Jamie rose up on one elbow and gazed down at him, a self-satisfied look on her face. His own expression was lazy and contented. "A woman could get used to this, too, Holt."

"Yeah?"

"Yeah." She knew she was grinning too broadly for any sane woman; that Max would take one look at her goofy expression and guess the truth. Just as she had expected, she had fallen head over heels in love with him, and there wasn't a damn thing she could do about it.

It was almost noon by the time Max and Jamie arrived at the newspaper office, with Fleas in tow. Vera was dressed in a fire-engine-red pantsuit and tall heels that she seemed to have trouble maneuvering. She handed Jamie a large stack of mail.

"I have to leave for a while," Vera said, "because a bunch of women from my church are picketing Maxine Chambers's lingerie store this morning. I want to be there to take pictures."

"Why don't people leave the poor woman alone?" Jamie said.

"Because she's displaying unmentionables in her front window," Vera said. "And wouldn't you know it; Agnes Aimsley's grandson is the ringleader. Most folks don't like Maxine anyway 'cause she was such a snooty librarian."

Jamie gave an enormous sigh. "I don't believe this. I'm going with you, but I'll be the opposition. The woman has a right to run her business without a bunch of old church ladies interfering."

"I'm with you." When Jamie looked surprised, she went on. "After all, this is a free country. Besides, I've been thinking I might buy one of those push-up bras she has in her window. I might just give Destiny Moultrie a run for her money." She grabbed her camera. "This could be good headline material, you know."

"I need to make a few calls," Jamie said before Vera hurried out the door. "Maxine is going to need support." Dee Dee was first on her list. She was outraged and promised to call her friends. Jamie then called several old high school buddies, all of whom promised to meet her outside Maxine's store and rally their support. She even phoned Destiny.

"I've got to run," she told Max, who'd walked in on the tail end of one of Jamie's calls. "A bunch of old church biddies are going to picket our new lingerie store, and I'm going to try to put a stop to it."

"I thought we had a paper to get out."

"This won't take long," Jamie promised. "But I can't just sit back and do nothing while an army of angry women descends on Maxine Chambers's place of business." She hurried out the door.

By the time Jamie arrived at Maxine's shop there were at least fifty women gathered out front, many of them chanting, "Close this store!" Agnes Aimsley and her grandson were right in front. A nervous Maxine peered out the window. Jamie gave her the thumbs-up, and the woman looked relieved to see her.

Jamie spotted Dee Dee, Beenie, and Destiny and hurried over. "How many do we have on our side?" she asked.

"We just arrived," Dee Dee said, "but I don't think we have more than ten or twelve. Those church ladies look pretty vicious if you ask me."

Beenie appeared anxious. "I wish I had stayed home. I'm afraid they'll kick my butt."

Jamie spied Vera on the sidelines, snapping pictures as fast as she could. "I need something to stand on," Jamie said. She hurried two doors down to Lowery's Hardware and returned with a ladder. She didn't see Max pull up across the street and get out as she climbed the ladder.

"Ladies, please hear me out," Jamie said, trying to talk above the roaring crowd of female voices. "At least give me a chance to have my say."

Brent Walker looked annoyed. "The town has spoken," he said. "We want Maxine Chambers to pack her slut-wear and close shop."

Obviously feeling braver now that Jamie had arrived, Maxine Chambers stood at the front door of her shop, arms folded across her breasts, a defiant look on her face. "I have as much right to run my business as any other person," she shouted.

The crowd booed their disapproval. Jamie finally

quieted them. "Maxine is right," she yelled. "As long as she pays rent she has just as much right to operate her shop as the next merchant. And without being harassed," she added.

"I can't believe you're taking her side, Jamie," Lyle Betts's wife, Lorna, said.

Jamie regarded the woman. "You don't have the right to judge Maxine," she replied. "Your husband is selling aphrodisiac-laced brownies and cakes with naked people on them."

All eyes turned to Mrs. Betts.

She squared her shoulders. "That's a lie. Lyle would never do something like that."

"Then I suggest you march right up to his bakery and demand to see his new 'Adults Only' catalog."

Brent Walker frowned. "I can't believe you're supporting this woman," he said, pointing at Maxine. "But that should come as no surprise what with your new personals ads. Men and women need to meet in church."

Jamie ignored him and turned to another woman. "And what about you, Mrs. Frazier?" she called out. "Are you going to tell me that you and Mr. Frazier don't have adult videos in your store? I know you do because I've seen them."

Mrs. Frazier looked embarrassed. "Some people enjoy watching that sort of thing. We have to keep up with our competition."

"And some people enjoy wearing pretty lingerie," Jamie said, "myself included."

The women gasped.

"There's a difference," Edna Wilburn said. "I love pretty nightgowns, but I wouldn't think of displaying that trash in my front store window. It's not fair that the rest of us are forced to see it every time we walk by."

Jamie hitched her chin high as she regarded the

woman who was married to the owner of Wilburn's Garage. "You want to talk about what's fair, Edna?" she said. "Is it fair your husband charges a fortune for his work? Is it fair that he preys on women because he knows they have no idea what it costs for parts and labor to repair their cars?"

"Well, I never," Edna said in a huff.

"Jamie's right," Vera called out. "How do you think you got that new swimming pool?"

Edna looked shocked. "Why, Vera Bankhead, I never knew you felt that way about my George."

Agnes Aimsley stepped forward. "Maybe we can solve this like good Christians," she said in her fruity-textured voice.

Everyone glanced her way. "What do you suggest, Mrs. Aimsley?" Jamie asked.

Agnes didn't hesitate. "Why don't we all agree to stop bothering Maxine if she agrees to use a little more, um, decorum in her window display."

Brent looked at her in astonishment. "What are you saying, Gram?" He pointed to Maxine. "Why are you defending this, this—"

"Watch what you say, Brent," Jamie said. "You know what the Good Book says about judging people."

His face reddened. "I feel it's my Christian duty to clean up this town."

"Is that why you visited Luanne Ritter the night of her murder?" Jamie realized she'd gone too far the minute the words left her mouth.

The women went silent and fixed their gaze on the man. Brent shot Jamie a menacing look. "So you're the one," he said. "For your information the police have already visited me, and I've been cleared of any wrongdoing. Perhaps you should concentrate on running your newspaper, Miss Swift, and leave innocent people alone."

"Oh, why do we have to have all this bickering?" Agnes said. "Why can't we all get along?"

Jamie nodded. "Sounds like a good idea to me, Mrs. Aimsley."

The woman faced her grandson. "I like pretty nightgowns. I think Miss Chambers should be able to run her store as she sees fit. I don't know why everybody insists on making trouble for her. If people don't like what they see, they should just stay away."

Finally, Maxine spoke up. "If you people will agree to leave me alone, I'll take some of the more, um, offensive items out of my window."

"That sounds fair," Agnes replied.

Brent gaped at his grandmother. "Well, I for one refuse to give in to the devil's work." He looked at Maxine. "You'll pay for your actions. Mark my words." He stalked away.

Dee Dee stepped up. "I haven't been in your store before, Maxine, but Jamie has told me all about it. I plan to have a look before I leave here today."

"Me, too," Beenie said. "I love women's lingerie."

Jamie's high school friends promised to visit the store, as well.

All at once, a police car skidded to a stop and Lamar Tevis and one of his deputies stepped out. They were in uniform, but instead of wearing slacks, they wore shorts.

"What in the world?" Vera said to Jamie the minute she saw them. "Would you look at how Lamar and his deputy are dressed?"

"Oh my," Beenie said, fanning himself. "Would you look at that deputy? I'd like some of that."

Even Jamie had to admit the shorts bordered on indecent. "I guess they changed to shorts because of the heat," she said.

"Okay, ladies," Lamar said. "What's going on here?"

He was tugging at his shorts as if he found them uncomfortable.

Jamie opened her mouth to speak, but was cut off by Lamar's deputy. "Lamar, these women are obviously picketing, and they don't have a permit. They're breaking the law. We'll have to arrest them."

This brought another gasp from the crowd. Jamie didn't know if they feared jail or were afraid the men would bust out of their shorts.

"I'm guilty," Beenie shouted, waving both hands in the air. "I insist that your deputy take me away immediately."

Lamar looked bewildered as he gazed at the crowd of women. "Are you sure about that, Joe?" he asked the deputy.

"Yes, sir."

Jamie stepped forward. "Lamar, you don't have a jail large enough to hold all these women." She tried to ignore Beenie tugging on her blouse.

"Well, that's true. But like Joe says, you're breaking the law, and I can't just stand by and do nothing."

Vera shot Lamar a dark look. "You wouldn't dare arrest us. Besides, nobody is picketing anyone. Maxine Chambers is holding a big sale, and we're standing in line to get into her store."

"I'm confused," Lamar said.

"That's obvious," Vera said, "or you wouldn't be dressed like that."

"Huh? Oh, you mean the shorts. I think the measurements were off because they're kinda snug."

Beenie moaned and bit his hand.

Jamie called out from her place on the ladder. "Ladies, Chief Tevis has the mistaken impression that we're picketing Maxine's store without a permit, which is against the law. We could all be arrested. But Vera just assured him that we're here for Maxine's grand opening sale, so what do you say? Who wants to buy a new nightgown today?"

Everyone in the crowd raised their hand.

Max looked pleased with Jamie when she crossed the street to his car. "Why are you grinning?" she asked.

"I'm proud of you, Swifty. You stood up for what you believed in. And from the looks of it, the lady who owns that store is going to make a hell of a lot of sales today."

Max and Jamie spent most of the day working to get the newspaper out on time and pondering what information Muffin had for them. By the time they sent the newspaper to press, both were tired. They dropped Fleas off at Jamie's house, and drove to a nearby Chinese restaurant for dinner.

Jamie noticed Max was quiet. "What's wrong?" she asked.

He shrugged. "I'm disappointed that we don't seem to be any closer to solving Luanne Ritter's murder than we were in the beginning."

Jamie nodded. "I'm worried, too, Max. Especially since Destiny said there was going to be another murder, and it would be someone I know." Max remained quiet. "I know I didn't take Destiny seriously at first, and I'm probably crazy for saying this, but what if, just what if she's right? What if the killer is still out there looking for his next victim?" When Max didn't respond, she went on. "Are you listening to me?"

"Yeah. You just don't want to know what I'm thinking."

She leaned back in her seat, noting the serious look on his face. "What is it?"

Max met her gaze. "We've never discussed this, but it's been in the back of my mind all along. If Luanne

Ritter's murder had something to do with her business dealings, that's one thing. If her murder involved the personals section, that's a different story. But if he strikes again, it's a whole new ballgame, you know that, don't you?"

"What do you mean?"

"It means we're dealing with a serial killer."

Vera was oddly quiet when Max and Jamie arrived at the office the next morning with Fleas on their heels. Jamie spoke to her and grabbed the morning mail. When Vera didn't respond, Jamie looked up. The woman looked pale, the lines around her mouth drawn. "Is something wrong?" Jamie asked.

Vera glanced from Jamie to Max and finally to Jamie again. "You haven't heard, have you?"

Max and Jamie exchanged looks. "Heard what?" Jamie asked.

"Maxine Chambers was found dead in the back of her store last night."

FOURTEEN

Jamie dropped the mail and it scattered across the floor. She felt her stomach take a dive. All at once, her lips became numb, her knees rubbery, and she felt a blackness descending. Max noted it right away and reached for her. "Are you okay?" he asked.

"I—I need to sit."

He helped her into her office as Vera followed. "I'm sorry I just blurted it out," the older woman said, "but I haven't been myself since I heard the news."

"I think I'm going to be sick," Jamie said, sitting on the sofa.

Max immediately shoved her head between her legs. "Get some wet paper towels," he told Vera.

Fleas came to Jamie's side as though he sensed a problem. Jamie kept her head down until the nausea passed. Vera returned with the wet paper towels and handed them to her.

"What happened?" Jamie managed.

"One of Lamar's deputies saw the lights on when he drove by late last night and decided to check it out," Vera said. "The back door was open."

"How did she—" Jamie couldn't say the word.

"Same as Luanne Ritter. A fatal blow to the head."

Jamie felt sick again, mopped her face with the wet towels.

"Take deep breaths," Max said.

She gulped in air.

"I feel so bad for her," Vera said. "Especially after everybody gave her such a hard time yesterday. I tell you, something isn't right in this town. I'm wondering if the two murders are connected in some way."

Max and Jamie exchanged looks.

Vera checked her wristwatch. "Oh, darn, I'm supposed to be at the doctor's office in fifteen minutes."

"Are you ill?" Jamie asked.

"No, it's just my yearly checkup, but if I cancel there's no telling how long I'll have to wait for my next appointment. Not that I'm in much of a mind to go," she added. She studied Jamie, as if unsure what to do.

Jamie continued to breathe deeply. "You need to go," she said between breaths. "I'll be okay."

"Are you sure?" Vera said.

"I'll stay with her," Max said.

Vera left a few minutes later. Max touched Jamie's shoulder. "How are you feeling?"

"The nausea has finally passed." She felt the sting of tears, blinked them back. "It's just such a shock."

Max retrieved the mail and placed it on the coffee table before her. "Is there anything I can do?"

"Yeah, we need to find the killer." Jamie glanced at the stack of mail and shuffled through it if for no other reason than to have something to do. There were five new ads for her personals section, but more than a dozen addressed to the Divine Love Goddess Advisor. She was surprised to find they'd written in so soon. She put the mail aside and looked at Max.

"Destiny was right. Not only do we have a new murder on our hands, I knew the victim personally."

"It's a small town, Jamie. You know a lot of people."

She wasn't listening. "Brent Walker," she said suddenly. "He threatened Maxine yesterday." She jumped as someone knocked on the door. Destiny peeked in.

"I heard the news on the radio and came straight over. Are you okay?"

Jamie shrugged.

"We'll find the person responsible."

"Yeah, but how many people have to die in the meantime?" Jamie's eyes glistened. "Poor Maxine. She had so many dreams for her store."

Destiny seemed at a loss for words. The three of them were quiet for a moment. Destiny glanced at the mail. "Is any of that for me?"

Jamie swiped at her eyes. "Most of it's for you."

They were interrupted by another knock on the door. Jamie wasn't surprised to find Police Chief Lamar Tevis standing there.

He glanced at Destiny, studied her a moment, then moved to Jamie. "From the looks on your faces I take it you've heard."

Jamie nodded. "We all feel awful about it."

Lamar glanced at Destiny again. "Jamie, I need to speak to you and Max. In private," he added.

Jamie feared the worst was to come. "Lamar, this is Destiny Moultrie. She has been helping Max and me study the case. You can speak freely in front of her. But please, won't you sit down? Would you like coffee?"

Lamar shook his head as he sat on the sofa. "I've been up all night, had my quota of caffeine." He hesitated. "I'm afraid I have some more bad news for you. We searched Maxine's store and her house, and we found a clipping of the personals section from your newspaper on her kitchen table. We don't know if she actually called anyone, because none of the ads had been circled, but—" He paused and reached into his shirt pocket. He pulled out a sheet of paper and unfolded it.

Just what Jamie had been dreading.

"I have a court order here," he said, handing Jamie an official document, "for you to hand over any information you have on those who've placed or answered ads in your column. In the meantime, I'm going to request that you stop running the column. At least until we get to the bottom of this."

"I'll need to make copies for you," Max said, reaching into his briefcase for the file they'd started.

Jamie stood. Her knees still trembled. "I'll make them," she said, needing to do something. She hurried out to the reception area, thankful that Vera was not around to ask questions. When she returned with the copies, she handed them to Lamar.

He glanced through them. "Larry Johnson. Now there's a name I recognize. We've already had a few run-ins with him, a domestic-violence charge being one of them. Unfortunately, his wife dropped the charges."

"He has a serious alcohol and anger problem," Jamie said.

Max nodded. "When he's not working, he hangs out at the lounge at the Holiday Inn."

"I see you've made notes on the rest of these guys," Lamar said. "That will be real helpful for us since me and my men have been focusing on Luanne's business dealings instead of the personals section."

"Destiny and I set up dates with these men," Jamie said. "At first blush they seemed harmless. Except for Larry Johnson."

Destiny spoke. "Don't forget he keeps a crowbar handy," she reminded Jamie.

Jamie looked at Lamar. "One in his car and one just inside his front door."

"You should probably check them for trace evidence," Max told Lamar.

"And let's not forget about Brent Walker," Jamie said. "He publicly threatened Maxine yesterday. I could be wrong, but I think the man has a few loose screws."

"He's been preaching on street corners, scaring folks

half to death with talk of doom and gloom," Lamar said. "One of my deputies threatened to haul him in if he didn't stop. 'Course, Walker started yapping about freedom of speech and all that.

"We suspect he visited Luanne Ritter the night of her murder," he went on, "but we have no proof. He claims he was home reading Scripture. It's not exactly an air-tight alibi; Agnes wasn't feeling well that night and went to bed early. I mean, who else would have left all that religious material in her mailbox?"

"There is one other person who could have put that religious literature in Luanne's mailbox," Max said. He told him about the Reverend Heyward. "He ran an ad. He's strange."

"Do you know if Luanne contacted him?" Lamar asked.

Max shook his head. "I managed to get my hands on Luanne's cell phone records, did a cross-check on the phone numbers, but I got nothing. She obviously made the calls from her home or office phone."

"Any return addresses on the envelopes of those who responded to the ads?" Lamar asked Jamie.

She shook her head. "Like I told Max, they would have wanted it confidential."

Lamar shuffled through the ads. "You've met with all these men?"

"Except for Sam Hunter," Max said.

"I've left several messages on his answering machine," Destiny said. "He must be playing hard to get."

Lamar looked at her. "If you don't mind my asking, what is your involvement in this case?"

"She's psychic," Max said.

"Oh, Lord, not one of *those*," Lamar said with a sigh.

"Actually, she has visions," Jamie told him. "She knew there would be another victim, but since we had nothing specific—"

"The scratches," Destiny interrupted. She looked at Lamar. "Maxine Chambers put up a fight before she died. She left deep scratches on the killer's arms."

Lamar looked from Jamie to Max. "Several of her fingernails were broken. I had my men bag her hands for nail scrapings. I'd like to have a look at Larry Johnson's and Brent Walker's arms. Would ya'll excuse me just a minute?" He got on his radio while Jamie and Destiny headed to the small kitchen for coffee.

"Maybe I could help you, Chief Tevis," Destiny said, once she and Jamie had returned with their coffee. "If I could take a look at the murder scene, you know, I might get a feel for something. I can't make any promises."

Lamar seemed to struggle with the idea. "The guys would laugh me right out of my job."

"But what if it works?" Max said. "What if it saves another woman's life? You won't know until you try."

Lamar finally relented. "Oh, okay, you can come with me, but don't tell the guys why you're really there. I'll think of something on the way over." They started for the door.

"I'll have to bring Ronnie."

"Who's Ronnie?" Lamar asked.

Jamie cleared her throat.

"Never mind," Destiny said.

Agnes Aimsley awoke in her easy chair with a start. She felt tired and haggard after a fitful night. She had awakened when Brent had come in after midnight, only to toss and turn for hours. She had finally given up on sleep and had risen at four A.M. She glanced at the clock, reached for her remote control, and turned on the midday news where the top story of the day brought a gasp from her lips.

Brent found her there when he came through the front door several hours later. The TV was off. Agnes hadn't moved from the chair except to answer the door once and make a cup of tea.

"What's wrong, Gram?" he asked.

She didn't answer.

"Gram?"

"The police came by earlier."

He gave an exasperated sigh. "What do they want this time?"

"They didn't say. Brent, the most awful thing has happened. Mrs. Chambers was murdered last night."

"Who?"

"Maxine Chambers from the lingerie store."

"Oh, great, the police probably want to pin that on me, too."

Agnes looked at him. "What are you talking about?"

He sank onto the sofa and raked his hands through his hair. "They questioned me about that Ritter woman. I left some spiritual literature in her mailbox so they naturally assume I killed her."

"I don't understand. What was your business with Mrs. Ritter?"

Brent gaped at her. "Surely you know that she was hounding several members of the church, Gram. They had taken out loans with her and were having a hard time making payments. Ritter sent a couple of her goons out to scare them. These guys scared one of the members pretty bad. I'm surprised you haven't heard."

"I thought they were just rumors."

"Somebody had to take the woman to task," Brent said. "I felt it was my Christian duty."

"You visited her?"

Brent nodded.

"Do the police know this?"

He hesitated. "I don't want to involve you, Gram. The less you know the better."

"You've always been able to talk to me."

Brent clasped his hands together and stared down at the floor. "I had to lie to the police, Gram. I told them I never set foot inside Ritter's house. That's not true."

Agnes went deathly still. "What happened?"

"She let me in, said she'd give me five minutes to have my say. It turned into a yelling match. I was so mad." He raked his hands across his face. "I don't want to talk about it."

"You should have told the police the truth, Brent. It's not like you to lie."

"I had no choice. They're desperate to pin this thing on someone. And now they're going to come after me over that Chambers woman. I lost my temper yesterday, said some things I probably shouldn't have. My guess is somebody reported it. Probably that newspaperwoman."

Agnes suddenly looked afraid. "The police asked me if you went out last night. I told them yes, that you didn't come home until late."

Brent paled. "I was out driving around," he said. "Driving and thinking. I might as well tell you things aren't going well at school."

"Then I suggest you return immediately and straighten them out, young man," Agnes said sharply.

Their gazes locked. "Yes, of course," he said. "I can be packed and out of here in less than an hour."

Vera was not happy. "I can't believe you're going to pull the personals section to give that crazy woman more space for her Divine Love Goddess Advisor column."

"It's just temporary," Jamie said. "Did you see the stack of mail Destiny received?"

"Yes. It just goes to show you people aren't thinking straight if they're seeking information from somebody like her. They must be spending too much time in the sun. Or maybe they're eating too many of Lyle Betts's brownies."

Dee Dee and Beenie came through the front door. It was obvious Dee Dee had been crying. "We heard the news about Maxine, and we just stopped by to make sure you were okay. I know you liked her."

"Thank you," Jamie said. "It came as a real shock."

"And we wanted to invite you to lunch," Beenie said.

Dee Dee nodded. "That's right. We haven't had lunch together in ages. We used to do it all the time when I first moved here."

It was obvious they were trying to cheer her up. "I wish I could join you," Jamie said, "but I've been so upset over Maxine that I haven't been able to concentrate on my work, and it's going to be difficult enough meeting today's deadline. I need to stay here."

"Do you know if the police have any suspects?" Dee Dee asked nervously. "Do you know if Luanne Ritter's death was connected?" she added, without waiting for an answer. "I shudder to think we have a killer walking the streets. I mean, what if he strikes again?" She had to pause to catch her breath.

"Dee Dee didn't take the news well," Beenie said, meeting Jamie's gaze. "She's really trying to be brave about the whole thing."

"I'm afraid the police don't know much at this time," Jamie replied, not wanting to give out too much information. But she was just as worried as Dee Dee about the possibility of another murder.

"Well, I for one am going to make sure my doors are locked at all times," Vera said.

Dee Dee took Jamie's hand in hers, squeezed it reassuringly, but it was obvious the woman was equally distressed. "Perhaps we'll have lunch soon?" Her bottom lip quivered.

Jamie offered the closest thing she had to a smile. "Of

course we will. And try not to worry. It's not good for the baby."

Dee Dee nodded. "I promise." She and Beenie left a few minutes later.

I need to talk to Max," Vera told Jamie, later that afternoon.

Max stepped out of Jamie's office. "Did I hear someone mention my name?"

Vera nodded. "You're just the person I'm looking for. I've decided I like Jamie's Mustang so well that I want you to find me one."

He shrugged. "That shouldn't be a problem. Any specific color?"

"Pink."

"Then pink it is. I'll get right on it."

"Just like that?"

"Just like that."

The rest of the day passed quickly for Jamie as she and Max worked together on the newspaper. By the time they sent it to press, Jamie was dog tired. Worry had etched lines on either side of her mouth, and when Mike Henderson had handed in his piece on Maxine Chambers, she'd asked Max to look at it.

Destiny came in for her mail as Max and Jamie prepared to leave the office. "I'm afraid I wasn't much help to Lamar. Ronnie was yakking in my ear the whole time so it sort of blew my concentration. He doesn't particularly like policemen since he had a few run-ins with the law when he was alive."

Jamie nodded as though it made complete sense.

"Oh, and guess what I did? I applied for a job as bartender at the Holiday Inn and they asked me if I could start tonight since they're short of help. I figured, what better way to watch Larry Johnson."

"Good idea," Max said.

"Do you know anything about making cocktails?" Jamie asked.

"No, but I suppose I can pick it up in no time. And here's the best news. Sam Hunter finally returned my call. He's going to come by for a drink tonight so we can meet."

"Just as long as you remember to stay in a public place with him," Max said. "Two women have died. We're not taking any chances."

Mike Henderson peeked in, and his eyes widened at the sight of Destiny. "Well, hello again. Have you thought any more about my offer to take you to dinner?"

Destiny stepped just outside the door with him. "I appreciate the offer," she said, "but I work nights."

"Oh, yeah? Well, that's no problem for me. I can pick you up after you get off."

Destiny smiled. "Look, Mike, I'm really flattered, but I'm sort of interested in someone."

He looked disappointed. "Oh, well, I guess that changes things," he said. "But, hey, if it doesn't work out you can always give me a call."

"How about we make it an early night?" Max told Jamie as they climbed into his car. "I'll call out for pizza. Besides, I need to be available for Destiny, even though I don't expect her to run into problems."

"Sounds good to me," Jamie said, although she didn't have much of an appetite. All she could do was think about Maxine and hope the woman hadn't suffered.

Muffin came on, and Max filled her in.

"Did anyone check Larry Johnson's or Brent Walker's whereabouts last night?" Muffin asked.

"Lamar said he'd put his deputies on it," Max said.

Once home, Jamie checked to make sure her neighbor's dog was nowhere in sight, then let Fleas out of the car. After they had decided what topping they wanted on their pizza, Max placed a takeout order and started a bath for Jamie.

Jamie headed for the bathroom. She stripped off her clothes, climbed into the hot bath, and sank deep into the water.

Once again, she thought of Maxine. Maxine, who'd been so proud of her new shop, had finally taken a chance in life and gone after her dreams. Jamie had admired her for it and was sure they would have eventually become good friends.

Now Maxine was dead, and it was probably related to Jamie's new personals section. That was the toughest part.

Max returned some twenty minutes later with the pizza. Having dressed in shorts and a T-shirt, Jamie grabbed plates and silverware and set the table. She placed a slice of pizza on each plate, only to sit there and stare at her piece.

"Are you okay?" Max asked.

She looked at him. Tears pooled in her eyes. "I'll be fine."

Max pushed his chair from the table and reached for her. Jamie immediately went to him, and he pulled her onto his lap. She let her head rest against his chest.

"I feel responsible for all of this," she said.

Max pressed his lips against her hair. "Jamie, we don't know if the newspaper is involved, and even if it is, I've already told you, you can't control the actions of a cold-blooded killer." He paused. "You know, I've been thinking. Maybe we should leave Lamar to his investigative work and go away for a few days."

She gaped at him. "I can't leave while there's a killer on the loose." She didn't realize she'd raised her voice. "I can't believe you'd even suggest it. We have to find out who's behind this, Max."

"You're taking it pretty hard," he said. "I've never seen you like this."

Jamie opened her mouth to respond, but the doorbell rang. "Oh, damn, who could that be?" she said. She got up and made her way to the front door.

Beenie and Dee Dee stood on the other side.

"Oh, Jamie, I am so glad to see you," Dee Dee said, in her little-girl voice. "When you're in trouble, the first person you want to see is your best friend." She walked into the living room with Beenie on her heels. He held Dee Dee's Maltese, Choo-Choo. Behind them stood a bevy of servants carrying luggage.

"What's wrong?" Jamie asked, noting Dee Dee's eyes were swollen. She'd obviously been crying again. "Did something happen?"

"It's Frankie and all his wrestling buddies," she said. "They're driving me crazy."

"Dee Dee needs peace and quiet in her, um, fragile condition," Beenie said. "She's not getting it at home, not with all those wrestlers around. They can be loud and obnoxious."

"So I've left Frankie," Dee Dee said. "I was hoping it would be okay if Beenie and I stayed with you until we found a place of our own. It is okay, isn't it?" Her staff began stacking expensive suitcases in the living room as Dee Dee spoke.

Jamie blinked back her astonishment. Of all times for Dee Dee to show up. "I, um, of course it's okay, honey. Come on in." She was only vaguely aware that Max had entered the room.

"What's wrong, Dee Dee?" he asked.

Beenie answered for her. "Frankie has totally lost interest in Dee Dee," he said. "All he does is hang out with his wrestling buddies."

Dee Dee burst into tears. "Beenie's right. Frankie doesn't seem to know I exist."

Fleas walked into the room and sniffed her dress. "Eeyeuuw! Is that your new dog? The one that came with the truck?" she added as she backed away.

"Yes," Jamie said, hoping Dee Dee wouldn't ask about the missing hair on his back. "I'm very attached to him. In fact, he sleeps with me."

"Eeyeuuw!" Dee Dee's jaw dropped clear to her collarbone. "What happened to his hair?"

Jamie sighed. "It's a long story, honey, but if you plan to stay, you'll have to get used to him. He's really very sweet."

Dee Dee attempted a smile. "What's his name?"

"Fleas."

"Eeyeuuw!" Both Dee Dee and Beenie huddled together. Even one of the staff carrying in the luggage paused.

"You're joking, right?" Beenie said.

"I didn't name him that, and he doesn't really have fleas." Jamie paused. "You'll have to sleep with me," she told Dee Dee. Beenie can use the other bedroom."

"I thought you had three bedrooms," Dee Dee said.

"I converted one of them into an office a long time ago."

"I still think we should go to a nice hotel," Beenie said, staring at the dog with disdain.

Dee Dee almost snapped at him. "I can't go to a hotel. How would it look if the mayor's wife just up and left her husband? Especially after we've announced my pregnancy to half the town."

Max stepped forward. "Dee Dee, I'm sure you and Frankie can work this out. It's not often he and his wrestling buddies get together."

"Yes, but they've decided to stay a month. I can't take it. All they do is talk about the good old days and eat Vienna sausage, potted meat, and sardines right out of the can. They claim that's what they lived on before they became famous wrestlers." She shuddered. "And that's not the worst of it. Snakeman and Big John have tons of girlie magazines lying about. That's the last thing Frankie needs to be looking at since I'm going to blow up to the size of a watermelon soon." She suddenly burst into fresh tears.

Beenie patted her shoulder. "There, there," he said. "You'll only ruin your makeup, and tomorrow your eyes will be twice as puffy. You're going to have to be brave for the baby's sake."

Max tried to calm her, but it was obvious he was accustomed to her dramatics. "Beenie's right," he said. "You need to calm down. For the baby's sake."

"How will I support myself?" she cried. "The only thing I've ever done is jump out of cakes at bachelor parties."

"Oh, that *is* going to be a problem," Beenie said. "You certainly won't be able to pay my salary on that." He suddenly brightened. "Oh, pooh, your husband will still take care of you. It's his child you're carrying."

"Excuse me, but where am I supposed to put these suitcases?" one of Dee Dee's staff asked.

Jamie pointed toward her bedroom. "How many bags do you have?"

"Only seven or eight."

Only seven or eight. Jamie realized she should be grateful there weren't more.

"Does Frankie know you've left?" Max asked.

Dee Dee shook her head. "He and his buddies went bowling. They'll probably go to Charlie's Sports Bar after that. No telling when they'll get in."

"He's going to call here looking for you the minute he finds out you're gone," Jamie told her.

"We won't answer the door," Dee Dee said.

"If he wants to see you badly enough, he might break it down."

"You really think so?" Dee Dee looked hopeful.

"That sounds so romantic," Beenie said.

Max put his hand on Jamie's shoulder. "Listen, I hate to break up the party, but I think I'll just go back to my hotel. I have a lot of work to do. Besides, I know you're anxious to get your guests settled." Then he kissed his sister on her forehead and left.

"Well, now," Dee Dee said. "I suppose we should order something to eat."

"There's pizza in the kitchen that hasn't been touched," Jamie said, perturbed that Max had left her to deal with his histrionic sister. As if she didn't have enough on her mind.

"Pizza!" Dee Dee cried. "Eeyeuuw, that is so fattening. Do you have any lettuce?"

"You can't just eat lettuce," Beenie said. "You're pregnant. One slice of pizza isn't going to hurt you."

Jamie nodded. "Come on in, and I'll fix you a plate."

"Would you mind if I turned in early tonight?" Dee Dee asked. "Having all those wrestlers in my house has been exhausting, and I've been thinking about poor Maxine all day. I just want to rest."

"I second that motion," Beenie said on a sigh. "If she rests, then I can finally get some rest."

Jamie nodded. "You can turn in any time you like." She figured the sooner she got them to bed the better. At least it would give her time to think about how she could arrange a quick reconciliation between Dee Dee and Frankie.

Jamie was awakened at midnight by the ringing of the doorbell. It didn't take a rocket scientist to figure out who it was.

Dee Dee opened her eyes. "It's Frankie," she said. "Would you please tell him I'm never coming home?"

"Never is an awfully long time for a woman who is

deeply in love with her husband and carrying his child," Jamie said. "As I see it we have two problems here."

"Oh, yeah?" Dee Dee looked at her.

"We have a woman going through hormonal changes which are perfectly normal, and we have a houseful of wrestlers who have overstayed their welcome."

"I'm too tired to go anywhere right now," Dee Dee said.

Jamie climbed from the bed and searched her closet for a bathrobe as Frankie began pounding on the door. The best she could come up with was a raincoat. She slipped it on and hurried into the living room. She spotted Frankie's worried expression through the peephole of her door.

"Jamie, I'm sorry to wake you," he said once she opened the door, "but I need to talk to Dee Dee."

He looked distraught. Jamie smiled and touched his shoulder. "Everything is okay, Frankie, so stop looking so concerned. Dee Dee is just very tired and needs a break from your wrestling buddies."

"She left me. She's never left me, not in twenty years of marriage."

"She's never been pregnant, either."

"It's because I haven't been giving her enough attention," he said mournfully, "but all that is about to change. My buddies are going home tomorrow, and everything will be back to normal." He took in her attire. "Is it supposed to rain?"

"I couldn't find my bathrobe. Listen, why don't you let Dee Dee sleep here tonight, and you can come over tomorrow and talk to her."

"Do you think she'll come back home?"

"Perhaps you should send roses before your visit. You know how Dee Dee loves roses."

It was as if a lightbulb had gone off in his head. "Yeah, that's what I'll do. And I'll start reading those baby books with her. I've been so busy with my friends I haven't had time for my own wife. Thank you, Jamie, for helping us out."

"Good night, Frankie."

Jamie closed the door and went back into her room. She shucked off her raincoat, draped it on a chair, and lay down. Dee Dee had already drifted off to sleep once more, her Maltese snuggled beside her. Sprawled across the foot of the bed, Fleas raised his head. He glanced at Dee Dee's dog, and gave a disgruntled sigh. "It's okay, boy," Jamie said. "Go back to sleep."

The dog needed no further prodding.

Jamie was pacing the floor, and Dee Dee was sleeping soundly when the first of the roses began arriving. Beenie stumbled into the room in a satin Ralph Lauren dressing gown. He took one look at the roses and shrugged as though it were an everyday occurrence to find a living room half-filled with long-stemmed red roses.

"Coffee?" he whispered, sounding desperate.

"In the kitchen," Jamie said. "You'll find everything you need beside the automatic coffee maker."

Max arrived shortly after the second load of roses was delivered. He whistled under his breath. "Well, there goes the Rose Bowl parade this year. Have you heard from Frankie?"

Jamie told him about Frankie's visit the night before.

"Eeyeuuw!" Dee Dee cried from Jamie's bedroom. She appeared in the doorway a moment later in a lavish Christian Dior nightgown and robe. "Your dog is taking up half the bed." She paused at the sight of the flowers. "Are those for me?"

"Yep," Jamie said. "Compliments of Frankie. I don't know where or how he was able to find so many red roses, but it must've cost a king's ransom. Personally, I think you got his attention."

The doorbell rang. Max opened it, and Frankie stepped in looking handsome in a dark gray suit. His eyes immediately sought out his wife, and he hurried to her. "Dee Dee, I just dropped the guys off at the airport. Things will be back to normal now. Please come home."

"Things will never be completely normal again, Frankie," she said in her Betty Boop voice. "Don't you understand? We have a baby on the way." Her bottom lip quivered. "I'm not ready to come home. Please have the rest of my luggage delivered."

Jamie sighed inwardly. This was not going the way she'd hoped.

"Dee Dee, are you crazy?" Beenie said. "Frankie has put his friends on an airplane. He's willing to jump through hoops to get you back. This place is too small for three people, two dogs, *and* your luggage."

"I'll come back home when I'm darn good and ready," Dee Dee announced to Frankie, "and not a moment sooner."

A crestfallen Frankie left several minutes later, and Dee Dee disappeared into the bathroom for what she termed a well-deserved bubble bath.

Beenie shook his head sadly. "I'm going to have another cup of coffee," he said and made his way toward the kitchen, leaving a baffled Max and Jamie in the living room.

"Of all times for this to happen," Jamie said. "We've got a murderer to catch, and your sister and companion decide to move in. Are there any normal people in your family?"

"Yeah, a whole bunch of them. But they're up in Virginia. Remind me to introduce them to you someday."

Lamar Tevis showed up at the newspaper office shortly after Jamie and Max arrived. "Okay, here's what we've got so far. I have an eyewitness who claims he saw Maxine Chambers leave her shop with a man night before last. Unfortunately, it was dark so the witness couldn't give me a description of him. He recognized Maxine when she stepped beneath a streetlight, but the guy obviously kept to the shadows."

"Did the witness notice what kind of car the man was driving?" Max asked.

Lamar shook his head. "He didn't look since he saw nothing out of the ordinary. What we think happened is Maxine had a date with this man, and he took her back to the shop afterward, probably so she could pick up her car. Maxine went back inside her shop, I believe, to pick up her deposit bag since it was her habit to make her deposits at the bank first thing each morning. Also, we found the deposit bag next to the body."

"Any sign of forced entry?" Max asked.

"Nope. She probably just ran inside to pick up the bag, not bothering to lock the door. She entered through the back. The killer had to have entered only seconds after she went in. Either her date followed her in or somebody was there waiting for her and slipped in right behind her."

"Anything taken from the bag?" Jamie asked.

"No. Which means robbery was not the motive."

"What kind of weapon was used?" Max asked.

"We found a baseball bat in a nearby Dumpster with blood and hair on it. We checked it out in the crime lab, and it's definitely the murder weapon. Unfortunately, there were no fingerprints."

"I don't know if this is going to help," Jamie said, "but Destiny Moultrie started working in the lounge at the Holiday Inn last night. Both Larry Johnson and Sam Hunter had a couple of drinks, but they left right after happy hour."

"Yeah, one of my deputies followed Johnson home.

He was alone, and he didn't go back out. Could be he suspected he was being watched and decided to lay low." Lamar sighed. "I shouldn't have wasted so much time looking into Luanne Ritter's business dealings. This latest murder sheds a whole new light on things. Two murders in a week. We don't know if and when this person is going to strike again."

Jamie felt a chill race up her spine.

FIFTEEN

Vera's pink Mustang arrived later that day, looking as though it had just come off the showroom floor. The woman was ecstatic.

"I don't believe it," Jamie said to Max. "She only asked you yesterday, and you've already found one. How did you manage to find one so quickly?"

Max smiled as he watched Vera circle the car in delight. It was obvious he was enjoying her excitement. "Muffin and I had already made a lot of contacts when I was picking out the red one for you. It was just a matter of getting it here overnight." Max had already sent the driver to the airport in a taxi; the man would be flown home courtesy of Holt Industries.

Vera couldn't stop grinning. "It's perfect," she told Max, "and it fits the new me to a T. Wait till my friends see me driving it." She paused and suddenly looked worried. "Can I afford it?"

Max suddenly looked ill at ease. "I was hoping you would accept it as a gift. For all you've done for Jamie."

It was the first time in Jamie's life that she could remember Vera being speechless. Finally, the woman hitched her chin high. "I can't do that. It would feel as though I were accepting charity, and I've always worked for what I wanted."

"It's a gift plain and simple," Max said. "If you don't want it, then I'll have to go to the expense of sending it back. Now, why don't you take a spin in it and see how it runs?"

Vera thought long and hard. "I don't know what to say," she said, looking genuinely touched.

"Just say thank you," Jamie told her.

"Thank you doesn't seem to come close," Vera replied, eyes suddenly tearing, "but thanks just the same." She hugged Max. "I can't wait to get behind the wheel."

Jamie was glad they had something to smile about after the past week. Luanne's and Maxine's murders had left a dark cloud hanging over everyone's head. But Vera, more than anyone, deserved to be happy.

Jamie raised her eyes and met Max's gaze. His look seemed to reach right out and touch her. She offered him a silent thank-you, and was rewarded with a tender look.

That's what love is, she thought.

They were still standing in the parking lot of the newspaper office when Lamar Tevis pulled up. Vera showed him her new car, and although he tried to look excited about it, Jamie could tell his thoughts were elsewhere. She hoped it wasn't more bad news as she ushered him inside her office a few minutes later.

"You were right about Larry Johnson," he said. "I visited his ex-wife, and she told me he could be rather heavy-handed with his fist at times. The only reason she didn't file for a divorce on the grounds of physical cruelty was because Larry agreed to all the terms of the divorce, which means he walked away with the clothes on his back. Guess he didn't want folks to know he was a wife beater."

"I knew he was scum from the beginning," Jamie said.

"Yeah, he's real tough where the ladies are concerned," Lamar said, "but he didn't act so tough when we questioned him. He and Maxine Chambers had drinks together the night of her murder."

"So that's who the witness saw lurking in the shadows," Jamie said. "Maybe there was a reason Larry didn't want to be seen."

"Of course, Larry claims he never went inside her place of business," Lamar went on. "Said he met her at the door and drove her to the Holiday Inn. They had a couple of drinks and left. Said they didn't hit it off. Not a very good reason to kill someone if he's the one," Lamar added.

"Does he have an alibi for later that night?" Max asked.

Lamar shook his head. "Nope. But he offered to let us have a look at his apartment and car, so my deputies are combing them now."

Vera glanced at herself in the rearview mirror and tried to smooth the frown lines on her forehead. She was clearly irritated as she followed the highway that led to Moseley, the next town, and the restaurant where she was to meet her date.

She sighed aloud. "This is ridiculous driving almost twenty-five miles for dinner," she told her reflection. "Whoever heard of such?"

Still a bit peeved, Vera turned off the highway a half hour later and located the restaurant. She checked her lipstick and stepped from the car. The air hung thick with humidity, but she didn't seem to notice as she smiled at her new Mustang. She stepped inside the cool restaurant a moment later and made her way toward the lounge where her date had suggested they meet. It was not yet six o'clock. John Price had agreed to meet for an early dinner so Vera wouldn't have to drive home in the dark.

The lounge was empty except for a couple at one

end of the bar, and a man with broad shoulders and salt-and-pepper hair. He was neatly dressed in a navy blazer and white slacks. He stood and hurried over.

He smiled warmly. "You must be Vera. I'm glad you could make it."

She offered her hand. "I just want you to know I don't usually do this sort of thing, and I've most certainly never been in a bar, but your ad sounded so interesting I felt I should respond."

"I promise you won't regret it," he said.

"So what I'm thinking, once we find the killer—and we will find him, Jamie—we need to get away," Max told her once they left the newspaper office shortly after seven. It had been a long day, trying to deal with a murderer on the loose and meet deadlines, as well. They'd been late finishing up, but the production manager, who normally would have complained about it, had taken one look at Jamie's face and kept quiet.

Now, Jamie was exhausted.

"We could fly up to my place in Virginia," Max said. "You need the rest and a little pampering. It'll take your mind off things."

Jamie didn't respond to his suggestion; she had more pressing matters on her mind. "Do you think Dee Dee had a change of heart and went back to Frankie today?" she asked.

"Oh, man, I'd forgotten about her," Max said. "Who knows?" Five minutes later, they had their answer when they found a catering truck in the driveway. The grass had been cut, the flower beds weeded and filled with pansies.

"Wow, would you look at that?" Jamie said, glancing at her house to make sure they were at the right one. "Are you responsible for this?"

He shook his head. "No, but it's pretty impressive.

Looks like my big sister has been busy. Probably trying to keep her mind off her troubles." He parked and they went inside.

"Surprise!" Dee Dee said.

Jamie glanced around. "Dee Dee, what have you done?" Jamie asked, going from room to room. Most of the furniture had been replaced, and new window treatments put up.

"I called my decorator as soon as you left for the office this morning, and I told her you needed all new stuff. You'll have to admit yours was old and worn. I described your house, and she immediately sent a truckload of furniture in from Charleston. She's been here all day, just finished putting up the new curtains before you arrived. She left not five minutes ago. Isn't it to die for?" Dee Dee said.

Jamie shook her head, trying to take it all in. How Dee Dee had managed to get it all accomplished in one day was beyond her. Of course, she'd probably had a dozen people working as hard as they could. "I don't know what to say."

Beenie spoke. "I told Dee Dee you wouldn't appreciate her barging in and changing everything." He had his hand on one hip. "I just want you to know I had nothing to do with it. Oh, I did insist that Dee Dee not get rid of a couple of pieces that looked like antiques."

"This must've cost you a fortune," Jamie told her friend. She and Max went into the kitchen where they found two men filling cabinets and her refrigerator with various food items.

Dee Dee waved off the remark as she followed them. "I'm rich so I can afford it. You were out of groceries. Don't you ever buy food?"

"Fleas and I eat out a lot."

"Well, from now on you can eat healthy food. My chef is coming over soon to cook. We're having salmon with cream sauce, new potatoes, and Caesar salad. I've decided to go off my diet for the baby's sake."

Jamie looked at Max. "May I have a word with you?"

"Sure."

"Don't let us stop you," Dee Dee said. "We've got plenty left to do." She went back to supervising the men.

Max and Jamie stepped outside. "Has your sister lost her mind?"

"Probably," he said, "but you'll have to admit it was a nice gesture, and everything looks great."

"But I liked my place the way it was. I mean, I don't want to sound ungrateful, but it's going to take some getting used to. I'll be afraid to sit on the sofa."

"Do you like what the decorator chose?" he asked.

"It's beautiful."

"Then let Dee Dee do this for you," he said. "I'm sure it means a lot to her. When you've been given a lot in life, it feels good to give something back."

"Is that why you gave Vera the Mustang?"

"I wanted her to have the Mustang and not worry about paying for it," he said. "But I was truthful when I told her the main reason. She's been like a mother to you. I can't help but appreciate that kindness."

"I guess I owe Dee Dee a genuine thank-you," Jamie said. "But that still doesn't solve the immediate problem. My place isn't large enough to accommodate three people and two dogs."

"So tell her."

"I can't tell her."

"Then I'll tell her."

"No, you can't tell her, either," Jamie said quickly. "It'll hurt her feelings. Plus, I'd feel like a real jerk after all she's done."

"Okay, Jamie, what do you want me to do?"

"I want you to think of a way to get her and Frankie back together right away. I can understand that Dee Dee is going through all these hormonal changes, but why hasn't Frankie been a little more insistent about her coming home?"

"His pride has probably been hurt, plus he could be embarrassed. I'll drive over and see if there's something I can do. Frankly, I'm getting tired of worrying about everyone else. It leaves us little time to worry about what's really important here, namely us. And I want more time alone with you."

"I'm beginning to think that'll never happen."

"We have to make it happen."

"Things should settle down once all this is behind us," she said.

"I'm going to drive over and talk to Frankie now," he told her, a resigned look on his face.

Max headed for his car and Jamie turned toward her house. Beenie met her at the door. "Oh, darn, I wanted to ask Max if he'd stop by the store for me."

"Do you need something?" Jamie asked.

"Yes. Dee Dee made me pack in such a hurry that I didn't get a chance to bring all my toiletry items, and I really need to exfoliate."

"Can't you borrow what you need from Dee Dee?"

"I'm allergic to the products she uses." He tapped his lips with his index finger. "Oops, I almost forgot. Lamar Tevis called only minutes before you arrived. Wants you to call him right back. I hope he solves those two murders soon because I'm afraid to go out at night and Dee Dee is beside herself with worry."

Dee Dee came up behind him. "Beenie, why would you even bring up those poor women at a time like this? You know how upsetting it's been for me. I'll never get to sleep tonight thinking about it."

Jamie reached into her purse for her cell phone. She didn't want to make the call where she could be overheard, but the phone wasn't in her pocketbook, and she couldn't remember using it that day. Must've left it in her car, she thought.

"I have to run out to the garage," she told them. "I'll be right back."

Jamie hurried through the laundry room that led to her garage. Since Max had arrived, she'd spent most of her time riding with him and using his cell phone, which probably meant hers was dead. She opened the door to her car and found the phone lying on her console. She reached for it.

All at once, she felt the hairs on the back of her neck prickle. She jumped and turned and found herself staring into Larry Johnson's face. A rush of adrenaline hit her.

"Hello, Jamie," he said.

She blinked several times. "What are you doing here?"

"I want to know what you told the cops. They've been on my ass ever since our date."

Jamie could smell the alcohol on his breath. "I don't know what you're talking about," she said, knowing it was best to lie.

"They questioned me about those two women who were murdered, and then they proceeded to search my car and apartment. They took both crowbars." He stepped closer. "Don't you think that's a coincidence?"

"What I think is that you have no right hiding in my garage," she said, knowing he'd had to pick the lock on the door that led from the garage to the backyard. "You're trespassing."

"You're not only a tease, you're a bitch. Just like my ex-wife." He flexed both hands. "Somebody needs to teach you a lesson."

Jamie stiffened. "Are you threatening me? Because if you are, I'm going to scream this house down over our heads. My guests will come running. Now, get out of here and stay off my property or I'll have you arrested." Jamie punched the automatic garage door opener, and the door swung open. "Now," she ordered.

Larry's look turned menacing. "I'm not done with you yet, lady. You cause me any more trouble, and I promise you'll regret it." Jamie waited until he'd cleared the door before closing it. She suddenly realized she was trembling. She reached for the phone and called Lamar.

"I just wanted to let you know we didn't find anything on Larry Johnson," he said.

Jamie's voice quavered as she spoke. "He just paid me a visit." She told Lamar what had happened.

"Do you want me to pick him up?" Tevis asked.

"No, I think it would be better if your men just kept a close eye on him."

"Try not to go anywhere alone if you can help it," he said. "I think Johnson's dangerous, but I can't pin anything on him. I promise we'll keep trying."

That was a wonderful dinner, John," Vera said to the man sitting across the table from her. The hostess had seated them in the dining room where all the tables were draped in crisp white tablecloths and napkins were folded fanlike at each place setting. "Thank you for inviting me."

"You only took a few bites of your prime rib."

"I guess I'm a little nervous," Vera confessed, her gaze falling on the small glass-enclosed candle between them.

John reached across the table and touched her hand. "I feel very fortunate to have met you."

Vera shifted in her seat. "John, may I ask you a question?"

"Of course."

"In your ad, you said you wanted to meet a woman for a discreet relationship. Why are you so concerned about discretion?"

He didn't answer right away. "I'm a very private person, Vera, and the last thing I want people to know is that I ran an advertisement in the newspaper to meet a woman. I know it's silly, but that's how I feel."

"Yes, well, my minister would certainly frown on that sort of thing."

"I've dated a couple of women in town, and I could tell up front that nothing would come of it, but I must say, you and I seem to have a lot in common." He grinned. "Anybody who drives a pink Mustang is definitely my kind of woman."

Vera smiled. "It's a new acquisition."

"Plus, if I might say so, you're very attractive."

Vera patted her hair. "Why, thank you, John."

The waiter brought their check. John Price pulled out a credit card and handed it to him, and the man hurried away. "I hope we can get together again soon," John said.

"I'd like that, too."

"Is tomorrow night too soon?"

Vera laughed. "Well, gee, I guess tomorrow is okay." She paused in thought. "You know, I wouldn't normally do this, and I don't wish to sound forward, but how would you like to come to my house for pot roast tomorrow evening? Everybody always brags about my pot roast."

"Wow, a home-cooked meal. It sounds great to me since I eat out so much. I'm afraid I'm not much of a cook."

Vera pulled a small notebook from her purse on which she wrote out her address. "I'll expect you around seven."

John walked Vera to her car and waited until she climbed in. "I'll see you tomorrow night," he said.

She started her engine and pulled away. She was humming a tune under her breath as she turned onto the highway leading home. She did not notice that she was being followed.

"I can't believe Dee Dee just up and left me," Frankie told Max. "We've never had a serious argument in our life."

"Your wife is pregnant," Max said. "She's going to be moody once in a while. She needs you right now more than she's ever needed you before."

"What can I do when she refuses to come home?" Frankie asked.

"Jewelry might help."

Frankie seemed to ponder it. "I'll take care of it first thing in the morning. I need to run by the bank as soon as it opens. I've got something in my safe-deposit box that just might do the trick."

Max, Jamie, Dee Dee, and Beenie shared a gourmet dinner in Jamie's small kitchen that evening. Once the chef and his assistant finished up, Max suggested he and Jamie take a walk. It wasn't until they had cleared Jamie's yard that Max spoke. "You've been awfully quiet this evening," he said. "I can tell something is wrong."

Jamie told Max about Larry Johnson's visit. She sensed his anger before he even responded.

"I'd like to get my hands on Johnson and show him what it's like to fight a man," he said, "but I have a feeling I wouldn't stop until it was too late."

"Too late for what?" Jamie asked.

"Never mind." He stopped walking. "Look, Jamie, I want you to come back to the hotel with me tonight."

"And leave Beenie and Dee Dee?"

"Larry Johnson isn't interested in hurting them. I'll ask Tevis to keep an eye on the place. Besides, Frankie is coming over in the morning, and I think he'll be able to convince Dee Dee to come home this time."

Jamie smiled. "Meaning diamonds will exchange hands."

"Something like that," Max said, but he didn't look amused. "Either way, I'm not leaving you alone tonight. You'll have to stay with me or I'm camping out on your sofa."

"I'll go to your place," she told him, "as long as you don't mind having Fleas along. I don't think he likes sharing our place with Choo-Choo."

"But I'd feel guilty running you out of your own house," Dee Dee said when Jamie broached the subject of staying with Max at his hotel. "It's bad enough that we just showed up on your doorstep without warning."

"Not to mention completely redecorating her house without her permission," Beenie said.

"Which was very sweet of you," Jamie told her. Even though it would take her time to adjust to her new surroundings, Jamie knew her friend had had good intentions. "You're my best friend," Jamie told her. "Of course I would expect you to come here."

Dee Dee suddenly looked sad. "Frankie hasn't even called me."

Jamie could see that her friend was truly in pain, but she was sure Dee Dee's pride would not let her call him. "I think Frankie's feelings are just hurt," she said. "I wouldn't be surprised if he showed up on my doorstep tomorrow. In the meantime you need to rest."

Dee Dee nodded. "I think it's great that you and Max will have a chance to spend some private time together. Will you be taking Fleas?" she asked hopefully.

"Yes. I'll make sure you and Choo-Choo have the bedroom all to yourselves tonight."

Jamie packed a small bag and climbed into Max's car

a few minutes later. Fleas sat in the back seat. "They're not going to allow us to have a dog in the room," Jamie said when she saw that Max had booked a room in one of the nicer hotels.

"See, that's where being rich comes in handy," Max said. They went inside the hotel with Fleas on his leash, and although they were awarded several stares from the staff, nobody said anything.

"How much did you have to pay to get permission to bring my dog in?" Jamie asked Max.

Max looked at her. "Don't worry about it."

"Not everything comes with a price tag," she said as they waited at the elevator.

"You're right," he said. "You can't pay for what's really important. I did what I had to do because I wanted you with me tonight. I was afraid for you."

Max's cell phone rang as soon as they stepped inside his room. From the conversation, Jamie could tell it was Destiny calling. Max hung up a few minutes later. "Destiny said Larry hasn't been in tonight. I'm calling Lamar to make sure they've got someone on his tail." Max placed the call. Once he was finished, he hung up and faced Jamie. "Brent Walker left town today. Agnes Aimsley told Lamar he had to return to school."

"I don't know whether to be worried or relieved," Jamie said.

"Lamar has already informed the police in Atlanta. Walker will be questioned." He paused. "You look exhausted." He pulled her into his arms and kissed her softly on the lips. Finally, he raised his head and smiled. "I'm crazy about you, Swifty," he said. "What do you think of that?"

SIXTEEN

Jamie stared back at him. She didn't know what to make of it. *Crazy* was not the word she hoped for. "It's the sex," she said, trying to sound flippant so he would not read the disappointment in her eyes.

"The sex is fantastic, but that's not why I like you so much. I like your spunk, and the fact you've never been a quitter. I like that you stand up for what you believe in, like when you rallied to keep Maxine's store open."

"I suppose you know the feeling is mutual," she said, determined to keep it light.

"Like I said, you're going to be seeing a whole lot more of me in the future. No more three-week intervals." He kissed her again. "So what do you think? Think you'd like to see more of me?"

She nodded. It was a start.

Frankie arrived at Jamie's house before eight a.m. the following morning. "Dee Dee, I can't live without you," he said to his wife, who was still in her nightgown. They both looked tired from lack of sleep. "I promise to get more involved with the preparations for the baby, but I need for you to come home. It's where you belong."

Dee Dee gazed lovingly into his eyes. "I feel the same way. I've been miserable without you."

He reached into his pocket and pulled out a small velvet box. "I brought you a gift."

"Oh, Frankie, you didn't have to do that. I would have come home anyway." Dee Dee opened the box. "Oh my, it's the ring I saw in Tiffany's."

"I've had it for some time," he said. "I was saving it for a Christmas gift, but this seems the perfect time. After all, we're celebrating a baby on the way."

Dee Dee looked genuinely touched. "I have a lot of luggage with me."

"I brought some of the staff," Frankie said. "They're waiting outside."

"You're mighty sure of yourself," she teased.

"Oh, I was planning to convince you to come home no matter what," he told her. "Even if I had to pick you up and carry you out."

"Oh, Frankie, that's so romantic."

He pulled her into his arms for a kiss.

Beenie came into the room, still wearing his silk pajamas. "Oh, thank God you've made up. I'm ready to go home. I can't sleep on cotton sheets. They irritate my skin."

Max and Jamie had awakened early and made love, only to spend the next hour cuddling and talking. As Jamie showered, Max ordered room service, and they took their time enjoying breakfast together. It was almost nine by the time they climbed into Max's car and started for the office. Muffin came on right away.

"I've done some more digging on John Price, and I think I may have hit on something."

"I'm listening," Max said.

"Price was questioned by the Atlanta PD six months ago about a murder that took place in his neighborhood. The woman lived two doors down from him. The reason it didn't show up when I checked to see if he had a police record is because he was one of about ten who lived in the area that were questioned. I would never have found it had I not thought to look for murders in Atlanta over the last couple of years. And get this. Same MO. Somebody bashed in her head."

Max looked at Jamie. "Very interesting."

"Not only that, I found the service provider he uses for his cell phone. The reason it took so long is because the company is brand-new. It's called In Touch Communications. They weren't in the telephone book; the Better Business Bureau doesn't even have them listed yet."

"Oh, crap," Jamie said. "I completely forgot about them. They ran an ad with me a couple of weeks ago offering free phones for those who signed up. Muffin's right, they just opened for business. As a matter of fact, they've got salesmen going door to door."

"They obviously convinced Price to try their service because that's who he's using," Muffin said. "But I've been saving the best for last. Price was in touch with Luanne Ritter only three days after his personal ad hit the newspaper. She must've written to him immediately, probably the same day his ad came out."

"Bingo," Max said. "What about Maxine Chambers?"

"No record of a call placed to her number, but he could have called from another phone. I haven't found her name listed with any service provider in the area. As hard as it is to believe in this day and age, she must not have had a cell phone."

"Anything else?"

"I followed up on the dentist, the chef, and the mechanic. The dentist and chef checked out fine, but the mechanic, Carl Edwards, had had a run-in with the police. Seems he and another guy got into a fist-fight outside a bar a couple of years ago. Nothing serious; just a couple of good old boys who had too much to drink and one of them accused the other of cheating in a pool game."

"How come it didn't show up on his record?" Max asked.

"I suspect the cops just talked to them and sent them on their way because neither of them was officially charged. I found the information by checking on calls made to the dispatcher in the last three years. They list complaints in the computer, even if there are no arrests made."

"Good work, Muffin," Max said. "From here on out I want you to make Price your top priority. Find out why he left Atlanta so soon after the murder in his neighborhood."

"Will do."

"By the way, did you happen to get anything else on Sam Hunter?"

"Nothing looks suspicious. No police record, not even a parking ticket. He kept the same job for ten years. His cell phone records indicate that he was somewhat of a ladies' man, but all his ex-girlfriends are alive and well and working in New York City. Max?"

"Yeah?"

"After we figure out who committed these murders, I'm taking some time off. I don't feel so good."

"Muffin, you are *not* pregnant," Max said. "You're just having the symptoms because Dee Dee fed you the information."

"Then why are my hormones acting up?"

Max sighed. "You don't have hormones, you're a computer."

"Yeah, and you programmed me to have emotions. I do too have hormones. Just ask my friend at MIT. He's accused me more than once of having PMS. Just this morning, as a matter of fact."

"I thought the two of you broke up."

"You know how it is, on again, off again. I can't get him to make a commitment. I think I intimidate him, but what can I say? Besides, he's just a laptop, and he's not being fed information from experts around the clock like I am. He needs an upgrade; somebody needs to install more memory in him."

"Let's just try to concentrate on the case, okay?"

Muffin sounded testy when she spoke. "I've never once let my personal feelings get in the way of my work, but I do need a life." With that she was gone.

Max looked thoughtful. "I'll inform Lamar about Price, but I think it would be a good idea to drive by his house tonight and see if there's any activity."

"Only if you promise not to break in again," Jamie said. "I don't think my nerves can take it."

"Deal," Max said.

"Well, Destiny will be relieved that Sam looks clean," Jamie said, changing the subject. "I think she has a crush on him."

"Don't get her hopes up," Max said. "Until we find the murderer, everybody is a suspect."

Max and Jamie worked throughout the day, breaking only for lunch, which consisted of sandwiches at Maynard's.

"Is it me or does Vera seem to be in a really good mood today?" Jamie asked as they left the sandwich shop and walked back to the office.

Max grinned. "Maybe she's getting laid."

"Max!"

"Well, you asked."

They left the office at six p.m., only to find that the night had not cooled.

"This has been the hottest summer I can remember," Jamie said. "No wonder people are acting kooky in this town, Vera included. There's definitely a change in her." Jamie was almost certain the woman was wearing padded bras.

They arrived at Jamie's house and found a note from Dee Dee saying she had made up with Frankie and gone home. "Well, that's one less thing to worry about," Jamie said.

"Frankie must've taken my suggestion and bought something nice for her," Max said with a grin.

"I don't think Dee Dee is as materialistic as you think, Max," Jamie said. "She genuinely loves Frankie. Twenty years is a long time to stay married these days."

"Not if two people work at it," Max said. "Do you think you'd want to be with somebody that long or longer?"

Jamie couldn't have been more surprised with his response. Had Max Holt just made a favorable comment about marriage and commitment? She felt like pinching herself to make sure she wasn't dreaming, and then realized he was waiting for her answer. "I wouldn't get married unless I was prepared to do just that," she said.

There was plenty of food in Jamie's cabinets and refrigerator, thanks to Dee Dee. Once they'd eaten, Jamie took a shower and changed into shorts while Max made calls to Holt Industries. They waited until dark before getting into Max's car. "We're going by John Price's house," he told Muffin.

"Speaking of Price, I discovered a few more things you might find interesting," Muffin said. "His divorce a year ago was less than amicable."

"Most divorces aren't real friendly," Max said, although his had been, thanks to his generosity.

"Yeah, but listen to this. Price swore out a warrant shortly after the separation, claimed his ex was stalking him. The police checked into it but no charges were filed for lack of proof."

Max looked thoughtful. "How soon can you get me a complete file on her?"

"I'm about to send it through the printer now. She has an apartment in Atlanta, but her employment history is spotty. She obviously quit work after she married Price because I can't find anything after that."

Max was thoughtful. "If Price thought she was stalking him, that might explain the guard dogs and the expensive security system."

"I wonder if he's afraid she'll find him," Jamie said. After a moment, she changed the subject. "We should probably check in with Destiny." Max made the call. He was frowning when he hung up. "Larry Johnson is there with a woman."

Jamie felt a chill race up her spine. "I hope she's armed."

"Sam Hunter is sitting at the bar. Destiny says they've really hit it off."

"I wonder what Ronnie is making of Destiny's crush on Sam," Jamie said, if for no other reason than to lighten the mood. She could see that Max had a lot on his mind. "Maybe Ronnie will finally take the hint and be on his way. Toward the light," she added with a smile.

They drove by John Price's house twenty minutes later and found it dark. Max frowned.

"What's wrong?" Jamie asked.

"Something doesn't seem right here. I get the feeling we should be someplace else."

John Price arrived at Vera's house at precisely seven o'clock carrying a bouquet of flowers.

"Oh, John, how thoughtful," she said, as she put them into a vase with water. Vera had put the pot roast in a Crock-Pot that morning before leaving for work, then cut up new potatoes, carrots, and onions and placed them in the pot on high so they'd be ready in time. Although her house was kept neat, she'd dusted and vacuumed before freshening her makeup. It was obvious she'd wanted to make a good impression.

"May I offer you a glass of sweet tea?" she asked John.

"I would love something cold after coming in from that heat," he told her, wiping his brow. "I took a shower before I left the house, but I was perspiring before I got to my car."

"This has been the hottest summer we've had in years," Vera said, "and the humidity doesn't help. I dread seeing my power bill because I've used my air conditioner so much this season. Now, why don't you take a seat on the sofa, and I'll get us both something cold to drink. Dinner should be ready soon."

"I'm in no hurry," John said. "I'd much rather get to know you better."

"I'm afraid my life would sound boring to you," Vera said, returning with two tall glasses of iced tea with lemon. She took the chair opposite him. "I've lived in Beaumont all my life. Never traveled more than a couple of hundred miles away, and that was with my church friends. I'm sort of a homebody."

"I used to do a lot of traveling with my job," John said. "My ex-wife didn't like my being gone so I tried to cut back as much as I could."

"She obviously missed you while you were gone."

John shifted uncomfortably in his chair. "She was somewhat, um, possessive. She liked being able to put her finger on me at all times." He took a sip of tea. "I'm sorry; it's rude of me to discuss her with you."

"Oh, no, I don't mind. How long were you married?"

"A year."

Vera looked surprised. "That's all?"

"The marriage was doomed from the beginning, but

I fancied myself in love. She was quite a bit younger than me. Plus, it was a second marriage. I hadn't been divorced all that long before I met her. I was married to my first wife for twenty-seven years. I regret that we drifted apart." He sighed. "Anyway, I married Celia less than three months after I met her. I guess I was just lonely after the divorce and wasn't thinking straight."

"Do you have children?"

"Oh, yes, a beautiful daughter by my first wife. She studied business at college and graduated with honors, and then decided she wanted to go into nursing. She graduates in the fall." He glanced around. "Your place is very cozy. You have a real eye for decorating."

"Thank you. I study the latest magazines for ideas. Luckily, I sew," she added proudly. "I was able to make the slipcovers for the sofa and I made all the draperies, as well. But you're probably not interested in hearing all that."

He smiled. "On the contrary," he said. "You sew, you cook, you decorate, and you're a devoted employee. I'm beginning to think there's nothing you can't do."

Vera blushed. "Oh, I have my faults," she said. "I'm a very impatient woman. I want things done right away because I don't believe in wasting time. People at the office will tell you I can be quite demanding at times."

Price nodded. "You're obviously a hard worker." He paused. "Vera, I'd like to continue to keep our friendship discreet for a while longer."

She gave him a funny look. "Well, of course, if that's the way you want it."

"Maybe we could continue to meet privately for a while," he said.

"I suppose so." But Vera was frowning as she got up to check the vegetables. "Dinner is ready," she called out. "I hope you're hungry."

* * *

Business was slow in the lounge at the Holiday Inn, which didn't seem to bother Destiny at all since Sam Hunter was the only one at the bar.

Sam watched Destiny closely, as though trying to size her up. His eyes followed the way her short skirt lifted each time she reached high for the bottle of Johnny Walker Red which two men at a nearby table were drinking, to the way her oversize breasts bounced as she washed glasses. Finally, Destiny sashayed toward Sam, took one of his hands in hers, and turned it over so that she was looking at his palm. "I didn't tell you I was a palmist, did I?" she asked.

He smiled, showing off his good looks. His thick brown hair had not begun to gray at the temples like that of a lot of men his age. "You failed to mention it," he said.

"I'll be happy to give you a reading," she said. "No charge, of course."

He chuckled. "Of course."

"This is your lifeline," she said, tracing one of the lines that ran across his open palm. "It shows that you're going to live a long life."

"That's good to know."

"And this line—" She paused and gave him a coy smile. "It says you're going to meet a beautiful woman. You will quickly become smitten with her."

Sam smiled and captured her hands in his. "I think I already have. What time do you get off?"

Destiny didn't respond. If Sam noticed her staring across the room at the couple leaving, he didn't say anything. "Would you excuse me," she said. "I need to make a quick phone call."

Max's cell phone rang, and he picked it up. Destiny spoke from the other end. "Damn," he said. "How long ago?" He listened. "Okay, thanks."

"What is it?" Jamie asked.

"Larry Johnson just left the Holiday Inn with a woman. I hope Lamar is doing his job." He looked thoughtful. "Maybe we should drive over."

"And do what?" Jamie asked. "We can't exactly knock on his door."

Max looked thoughtful. "If he took her to his place, I think she's relatively safe. Johnson isn't dumb enough to try anything at his apartment. My concern is he'll take her home. That might put her in danger. We might be wasting our time, of course," he added. "I think Johnson suspects he's being watched. If that's the case, he's not going to take any chances."

"Unless he gets drunk enough and lets down his guard," Jamie said. "Then anything is possible."

"Vera, that was the best pot roast I've ever had," John said. "I can't believe you never married, what with your looks and cooking skills."

Vera waved off the remark. "Flattery will get you everywhere. Wait until you see what I've made for dessert."

"Dessert? I'm already busting out of my pants from that meal."

Vera got up and cleared their dishes away before cutting them each a slice of Key lime pie and filling two cups with coffee. She carried them to the table on a silver tray.

"You shouldn't have gone to so much trouble," John said.

"It wasn't any trouble. I love to cook."

John waited until she sat down before he spoke. "Tell me something," he said. "How come you never married?"

Vera shrugged. "I was in love once, but he wasn't able to make a commitment."

"I find that hard to believe."

Vera looked sad for a moment. "I wasted a lot of years hoping he'd change." Finally, she shrugged. "But I had a job with the newspaper that I loved, and I was always busy with church activities so it wasn't like I sat around moping about it."

John shifted in his chair. He suddenly looked nervous. "You didn't mention our date to anyone at the *Gazette*, did you?"

"Of course not."

He looked relieved as he took a sip of his coffee. He watched her closely from over the rim of his cup. He didn't make a move for his pie.

"Aren't you going to eat your dessert?" Vera asked.

"Could you make it to go?"

"Oh, are you leaving so soon?"

"I'm afraid my day has caught up with me," he said. "I was at the office before six, and what I need right now is a good night's sleep. I hope you don't mind."

"Well, of course not. Actually, I was thinking of turning in early myself."

John left a few minutes later after promising to call the next day. Vera locked up after him, and began cleaning the kitchen. The phone rang, and she answered.

There was no response.

"Is anyone there?" she said after a moment.

Finally, a click.

"Well, now, that was odd," she said to herself as she hung up.

She was in the process of preparing for bed when the telephone rang for the third time. She picked it up. Once again, no answer. "Listen, I can hear you breathing, what do you want?"

Nothing.

"I'm sick and tired of you calling this house. Don't call me again, do you hear?" She slammed the phone down. "Probably a bunch of kids playing pranks," she said.

"I have more news for you," Muffin said as Max and Jamie headed for Larry Johnson's apartment. "It concerns John Price. Do either of you know a Barbara Fender?"

"That's my new neighbor's name," Jamie said. "Why do you ask, Muffin?"

"Bad news," Muffin said. "Barbara Fender aka Celia Brown Price is John Price's ex-wife."

Max and Jamie exchanged looks. "Are you sure?" he asked.

"Am I ever wrong?" Muffin asked.

Jamie stared at Max in disbelief. "She followed John from Atlanta."

"I don't like what I'm thinking," Max said.

"Tell me anyway."

"John Price filed charges that his ex was stalking him, but there was no proof so they were dropped. And later, he was questioned about a woman murdered two houses down from him. I'm willing to bet he was involved with her." He sighed. "It never occurred to me that the killer could be a woman. What I don't understand is why she's doing it. Unless she's insanely jealous," he added.

Jamie felt the familiar sense of dread. "Or maybe she's trying to set him up for a murder rap. She must really hate him. This is scary, Max."

"We need to talk to Price right away."

"Problem is, he isn't home, and he could unknowingly be putting someone else at risk," Jamie said. She had begun to fidget with her hands. "Assuming he isn't the killer."

"First we need to find out if Barbara Fender is home." Max whipped his car around and headed back to Jamie's house, making the drive in record time. Barbara Fender's car was not in the carport.

"This isn't good," Jamie said.

"If she was really stalking Price, odds are she's somewhere watching him. Do you have his phone number handy?"

"Yes, it's in his file."

"Why don't you call and see if he's home yet?"

Barbara Fender drove slowly past Vera Bankhead's simple ranch-style house. Darkness had descended; lights burned bright in the windows. Barbara parked her car down the street, cut her headlights, and turned off the engine.

And waited.

Vera grabbed a quick shower, changed into her nightgown, and climbed into bed. "Oh, that feels good," she said, yawning wide as she slipped between the sheets. She didn't read her daily Scripture as was her custom; instead, she turned off her lamp and closed her eyes. She was asleep in minutes.

Jamie dialed John Price's number. He picked up on the third ring. "Mr. Price, this is Jamie Swift from the *Gazette*," she said quickly. "I'm terribly sorry to bother you, but it's important."

"How may I help you, Miss Swift?" he asked.

"My partner and I need to speak with you. Is it okay if we come over?"

"Actually, I was just getting ready for bed. Can this wait until tomorrow?"

"It's rather urgent or I wouldn't be calling. We only need a minute of your time."

Silence. "In that case, please come over."

*   *   *

Vera opened her eyes and stared into the darkness as the clanging of something metal sounded from the back of her house. "It's that stray dog in my garbage can again," she muttered. "I'll have a mess to clean up in the morning." She dozed off again.

SEVENTEEN

Jamie and Max arrived at John Price's house in half the time it would normally have taken. As they climbed from Max's car, they heard the dogs barking. John called out from the doorway.

"Don't worry about the dogs," he said. "I've got them penned."

Max and Jamie hurried up the front walk. John stepped back to permit them inside. "Mr. Price, I'd like you to meet my partner, Max Holt," Jamie said.

Price arched one brow. "Not the Max Holt I've read about in all the financial magazines."

"That's me," Max said.

Price looked impressed as he motioned them toward the living room. "Please come in and sit down. And call me John." Max and Jamie sat beside each other on his sofa. Price took the chair on the other side of the coffee table. "You said this was urgent. How can I help you?"

"We're here to discuss the ad you ran in the newspaper," Jamie said, "among other things."

Price glanced at Max, then back at Jamie. He looked embarrassed. "I was hoping that would be kept confidential."

"It would have been," Jamie said, "but a couple of women have been murdered, and we think it may be related to the personals section. I'm surprised the police haven't already questioned you. I was served with a court order to release the files."

Price looked annoyed at the news. "I read about the murders," he said after a moment.

"We know you were in contact with Luanne Ritter," Max said. "What about Maxine Chambers?"

Price hesitated. "I received replies from both ladies right after my ad came out. I took each of them to dinner, but that was the extent of it." He glanced from Max to Jamie. "I had nothing to do with their murders."

"You were questioned about the murder of a woman in Atlanta," Jamie said. "I believe she was a neighbor."

He looked surprised. "You've been checking on me. I wasn't the only one questioned in that incident."

"Were you involved with her?"

"We had coffee once or twice. We were both going through a divorce at the time; we sort of used each other as a sounding board. It was nothing more than friendship."

"The murder was never solved," Max said.

"I regret that. She was a nice woman."

"John, didn't you think it odd that both women you dated were murdered?" Jamie asked.

Once again, he hesitated. "Of course I did, but since I had nothing to do with it I felt no need to go to the police. I'm new in town, and I've recently started my own business. The last thing I need is to get entangled in a murder investigation."

"Why did you leave Atlanta?" Max asked.

"I had my reasons."

"Did they concern your ex-wife?" Jamie asked.

Once again, he looked annoyed. "Why all these questions?"

"It could be a matter of life or death," Max said.

Price's eyes widened. "My ex-wife was hounding me. She didn't want the divorce, and she did everything possible to make my life a living hell once I left her. My apartment was ransacked twice, and the tires slashed on my car. She even started calling my boss. I swore out a peace bond against her, but it didn't help. I couldn't prove she was behind any of it. So I decided to move away and start over."

"Does anyone know you're here?"

"Only my daughter and first wife. I still send money for our daughter's education."

"Where do you mail the checks?" Max asked.

"To my first wife's mailbox, of course. She lives in Marietta, Georgia, just north of the Atlanta area."

"Did your second wife know her address?"

"It was listed in our address book. She would have seen the address where I mailed the checks."

"That might be one way Barbara found him," Jamie told Max. "She could have gone through his first wife's mailbox."

"Who's Barbara?" Price asked, obviously confused.

"That's the name your ex-wife is using," Max said. "She's going by the name Barbara Fender."

Price instantly paled. "Oh God."

"What is it?" Max asked.

"That's the name of the neighbor in Atlanta who was murdered."

Price stood and shoved his hands in his pockets. "Her real name is Celia." He paused and regarded them. "Look, I knew Celia had problems, but I don't think she's capable of murder."

"We don't have proof of anything," Max said, "but there are a lot of coincidences."

"She's moved in next door to me," Jamie said.

John was quiet, as though trying to take it all in. "I don't know what to think. Celia was jealous of everyone I had anything to do with, my daughter, and my friends. She followed me when I left the house. I was always looking over my shoulder because I didn't know what to expect. I asked her to get help, but she refused. When I filed for divorce, she threatened to get even."

"Does she hate you enough to try and pin a murder rap on you?" Max asked.

John met his gaze. "She could be cruel. I didn't know about her problems before we married, but it didn't take long before she began showing her true colors, so to speak. I regretted the marriage almost from the beginning, but I thought I could help her."

"You went out earlier this evening," Max said, changing the subject.

"I had a dinner engagement."

"With a woman?"

"Yes. She answered my ad."

"Do you mind telling us who the woman was?"

"I would like to keep that confidential. For her sake," he added.

"John, she may be in danger," Jamie said.

He suddenly covered his face with his hands, and his voice trembled when he finally spoke. "I thought it was finally over. I thought I could start living a normal life again. If Celia was responsible for the death of those women, then it's because I asked them out."

"John, we have to know who you were with tonight," Max insisted.

He looked at Jamie. "She works for you," he said. "Vera Bankhead."

Jamie felt the blood rush to her ears.

The sound of breaking glass woke Vera a second time. She bolted upright and reached for her telephone to dial 911. The line was dead. Quietly, she climbed from her bed.

"My purse," she whispered to herself. "Where did I leave it?" She started down the hall, feeling her way. The house was bathed in shadows.

There was a click at the kitchen door, the sound of the lock being turned. A hand fumbled, found the chain, slid it free.

Vera reached the living room, her hands searching the sofa blindly for her purse.

The kitchen door creaked.

Vera found her purse and reached inside for her gun. She raised it, aimed it toward the dark kitchen. "I don't know who you are or what you want, but I'm holding a thirty-eight Smith and Wesson, and I know how to use it."

Suddenly, a bright light hit her face. Vera was blinded. She raised her free hand to cover her eyes, as a baseball bat came down hard on her arm. Vera cried out and dropped the gun. It hit the carpet with a dull thud. "Why are you doing this?" she cried, trying to see the face behind the light.

"It's a pity you won't live to find out," the woman said with gritted teeth. The bat came down a second time. Vera cried out again and sank to the floor.

Jamie was the first to spot Barbara's car parked a couple of houses down from Vera's. "There it is!" she cried. "Hurry, Max!"

Max whipped his car into the driveway. "Muffin, hit the siren, and call 911."

Barbara Fender raised the bat high, a determined look on her face as she aimed for Vera's head. She jerked around as a siren split the night, and then turned once more for Vera. She shone her flashlight on the floor as Vera reached beneath the sofa for her gun.

Jamie felt the adrenaline gush through her body as she raced toward Vera's back door with Max on her heels. "Vera!" she called out loudly.

Inside, Barbara ignored both the siren and the voice

and raised the bat once more. Vera rolled away, and the bat slammed against the sofa. She raised her gun and fired twice.

The woman staggered once and fell.

Jamie reached the dark kitchen and searched frantically for a light switch. She turned it on and gasped at the sight of Vera pulling herself up and Barbara Fender, with big blond hair, sprawled on the floor. A wig, Jamie thought.

"I think I hit her in the stomach," Vera said, dropping her gun as the woman writhed in pain.

Jamie saw that Barbara had been hit; her dress was already blood soaked. "Help is on the way," she said, although she found little reason to pity her. She reached down and checked her arms. Sure enough, she found several deep scratches.

Jamie paced the waiting area in the emergency room as she waited to see Vera. Celia Price had been rushed there by ambulance and was undergoing emergency surgery; Vera had ridden in another ambulance. Lamar Tevis had arrived on the scene only minutes after the injured women had been whisked away. He sat in the waiting room with Max, Jamie, and John Price, as he waited for a chance to question Vera, who had suffered a broken arm.

"I honestly had no idea Celia would resort to murder," Price told Lamar, "but it all adds up. I feel terrible about this." He'd already told Lamar about the murder in Atlanta, and his suspicions that his ex might have been responsible.

Jamie noted the man's face was a chalky white. He was obviously in shock. "It's not your fault," she said. "You can't control the actions of others." She said it as much for herself as for him.

Lamar nodded. "I'll notify the authorities in Atlanta

to reopen the case." He frowned. "Why do you suppose she did it?"

Price shook his head. "Revenge, maybe. I think part of me suspected she would find me one day." He looked at Max. "That's the reason for the dogs. Still, nothing could have prepared me for this."

A nurse stepped out. "Is there a Mr. Price here?"

"I'm John Price," he said, standing.

"Miss Bankhead is asking for you."

John followed the nurse through the metal doors leading into the ER. He stepped inside a small room where Vera wore a cast on one arm.

"Max told me everything as we were waiting for the ambulance," she said.

"Vera, I'm so sorry," he said. "I don't know how I will live with this."

"You're not responsible, John. You had no way of knowing."

"I should have put two and two together. I should have known Celia would stop at nothing to get back at me for leaving her. Those poor women." He raked his hands through his hair. The look on his face was bleak. "She could have killed you."

"But she didn't, and it's behind us now. Your ex-wife, if she survives the surgery, will never have the chance to kill again."

John stepped closer to Vera's bed and took one of her hands in his. "I'm almost afraid to ask, but where does this leave us?"

Vera hesitated. "I don't know, John. I need time."

He nodded. "I guess we both do. At least until we get through this."

"We can still be friends."

A look of vulnerability crossed his face. "Thank you. I'm going to need a friend."

* * *

Destiny and Sam rushed through the doors to the ER. "What's wrong?" Destiny demanded.

"What on earth are you doing here?" Jamie asked.

"I had this feeling that something was terribly wrong. I called the police. All they would tell me was that there had been a shooting. So I asked Sam to give me a ride over. Who's hurt?"

Jamie filled her in.

Sam regarded Destiny with a look of awe. "You were right. You *are* psychic."

"I tried to tell you," she said.

"Hello, Sam," Jamie said. "It's been a long time." They shook hands, and she introduced him to Max.

"What do you think of Destiny's friend, Ronnie?" Max asked Sam, as though to lighten the mood.

Sam offered him a blank look. "Who's Ronnie?"

Destiny shot Max a look, reached for Sam's hand and patted it. "We'll talk about it later, honey." She turned to Jamie. "This is probably a bad time to bring it up, but I answered most of the mail."

"More has come in since the last batch," Jamie said. "The responses have been overwhelming."

"I knew that. I'll pick them up and give you the other letters tomorrow. After it stops raining," she added. "I like to sleep late when it rains."

"That makes two of us," Sam said. They shared a private look.

"Rain?" Jamie said. "The weatherman isn't forecasting rain. In fact, the temperatures are going to be even worse than they have been."

"The weatherman is wrong," Destiny said with a shrug. "It's going to rain and finally cool things off. And not a moment too soon, if you ask me."

Destiny and Sam stayed and chatted a while until John Price joined them and told Jamie that Vera was asking for her. Jamie joined the woman a moment later.

"How are you?"

"How the heck do you think I am? I have a broken arm. But don't worry, I'll still be able to work."

"Maybe you should take a vacation," Jamie said. "You've certainly earned it after what you've been through."

"Oh, fiddlesticks, a broken arm isn't going to stop me. Besides, who will run the newspaper if I'm not there?"

"True."

"I called you back here because I want first dibs on this story."

Jamie arched one brow. "I should have known."

"I'll give you editorial control, but I think it's high time you let me write some of the articles. I *am* the assistant editor, after all, and I'm tired of watching Mike get all the glory."

"Okay, Vera, whatever it takes to make you happy."

"So, what do you think of John?"

"He's a very nice man, but he's having a hard time dealing with all this. So am I."

Vera took her hand and squeezed it. "I know, honey. But we've gotten through tough times before, and we'll get through this." She brightened. "So, you think I should let John sleep over tonight?"

"Vera!"

"Just kidding. But if I start dating him, I'm going to need a few pointers."

Jamie was glad Vera could be so upbeat after what she'd been through. "It's always a good idea to follow your instincts. Don't do anything until you know you're ready."

Vera sat up in the bed. "I've got to get out of this place. If I stay here any longer, I'm going to catch something. Would you please find my doctor and tell him I said to get his fanny in here? He's the young one who looks like Andy Garcia. If I were forty years younger, I'd jump his bones."

"Vera?"

"Yes, dear?"

"Lay off the brownies."

Jamie awoke the next morning to the sound of rain. "Holy cow!" she said to Max. "Destiny was right."

Max smiled beside her. "You know what this means."

"Um, we're going to need an umbrella?"

"Nope. It means you're going to be late for work." He reached for her.

"I can't be late for work. Vera's got a broken arm."

"That's not going to stop her, and that's why I'm not worried about taking you back to Virginia with me for a few days. We'll take the small six-passenger plane so Muffin can have some time off."

Jamie did a bit of eye rolling. "Max, do you know how that sounds? I've never been involved with a man who owned a fleet of airplanes and a two-million-dollar car. I'm going to have to get used to your being so rich."

"It has certain advantages."

Jamie suspected it wasn't a bad idea. She needed to get away. Somehow, she had to put the bad stuff behind her and go on, and she found solace in Max's arms. She smiled. "So you're taking me to Virginia, huh?"

"I want you to meet my family, Jamie."

"Jeez, Max, that sounds serious."

He gazed back at her. "I guess it does. Maybe it's time I let down my guard and went with my feelings."

Jamie waited for him to say more. "What does that mean exactly?" she asked when he didn't elaborate.

"You're asking me to go out on a limb here." His look grew serious. "Jamie, do you love me?"

She was surprised he hadn't figured it out for himself. "Men are so dumb."

"Is that a yes?"

Jamie glanced away, afraid he would see it in her eyes.

"I haven't used that word in a long time, Jamie," he said, "and I ended up being wrong."

"So take a chance, Holt."

"I asked you first."

"Come on, Max, give it up."

"It certainly feels like love. The fact that I don't want to be without you, and I can't stop thinking about you when you're not with me is a good indication that something serious is going on between us." He grinned. "Your turn."

"You didn't say the words, Max."

His look turned tender. "I love you, Swifty."

Jamie felt her heart turn over in her chest. "See, that wasn't so hard. I love you, too, Max. I have for some time."

He looked relieved. "This smacks of commitment, you know. I usually run as fast as I can when a woman mentions that word."

"And now?"

"I'm tired of running. I love you," he repeated. He suddenly grinned. "It gets easier every time I say it."

Jamie studied him. He was sincere; she could see the love in his eyes. "You know what else I love?"

"What?"

"Rainy days."

"It's still early. I know how we could fill the time." He kissed her deeply. Before long they were aching for each other. Max began to unbutton her gown.

"Uh-oh," Jamie said. "Something tells me I'm going to be really late for work. I'll miss out on the fresh doughnuts."

He laughed. "Those doughnuts are going to be very stale by the time you show up."

Epilogue

Dear Divine Love Goddess Advisor:

I'm a single gay male, and I have a crush on a policeman. Every time I see him in his shorts I get hot all over—he's got a behind to die for. I've watched him closely, and I suspect he's gay as well, but he doesn't seem to know I exist. I've tried jaywalking, not putting change into parking meters, and parking more than eighteen inches from the curb. He writes me tickets but he's all business. What I want to know is whether or not I should confess my feelings to him and risk rejection, or take a chance.

> Signed,
> Flaming Hot in Beaumont

Dear Flaming:

The Divine Love Goddess strongly suspects this man feels the same about you, but he is trying to come to terms with his sexuality. My advice to you is to confront him, and see where it leads before you go broke paying fines. Who knows, maybe he'll handcuff you, take you home, and show you his nightstick. You might just end up on his "Most Wanted" list.

See you at the policemen's ball!

> Signed,
> The Divine Love Goddess
> Advisor

Dear Divine Love Goddess Advisor:

I have been married for a long time to a wonderful man. I recently found out I was pregnant. I am concerned my husband won't be attracted to me once I begin to gain weight because I have always taken very good care of myself, maintaining a perfect size-six figure. How can I be certain he will love me when I'm big as a house?

> Signed,
> Growing Day by Day

Dear Growing:

The Divine Love Goddess knows that your concerns are unwarranted. Your husband loves you very much and looks forward to sharing this special time with you. Many men find pregnant women very sexy, and I suspect your husband will, as well. I suggest you not worry so much about your figure and concentrate on the miracle growing inside of you, because your husband is going to love you even when your feet swell to twice their size, you blimp out, and start waddling like a duck.

> Signed,
> The Divine Love Goddess
> Advisor

Dear Divine Love Goddess Advisor:

I am a gay policeman who recently became attracted to another man. I think the feeling is mutual because he follows me everywhere. I think he might be trying to get my attention because he's racking up fines for parking violations. Should I come clean with this man and give him the frisking of his life?

Signed,
Uncertain

Dear Uncertain:

I am positive this man has strong feelings for you. (Read "Flaming Hot in Beaumont.") Don't wait until he becomes so desperate he has to call 911 to get your attention.

Signed,
The Divine Love Goddess
Advisor

Dear Divine Love Goddess Advisor:

I am in love with a wonderful man who recently confessed his love for me. I feel insecure at times because he's gorgeous and filthy rich and has dated his share of celebrities. Can you tell me what the future holds for us?

Signed,
Head over Heels

Dear Head over Heels:

One word: Fireworks.

Signed,
The Divine Love Goddess
Advisor